HE STOPPED AND STARED ACROSS THE HALL, TRANSFIXED THROUGH THE HEART BY A VISION.

She stood in a shaft of sunlight that fired her braids beneath the simple white veil to the precise colour of autumn oak leaves. The russet wool overgown was laced to the full, undulating curves of a nevertheless slender body, and as she approached the hearth the delicate gold embroidery at throat and hem glittered with trapped light ...

'Adam!' she cried joyfully, and with complete lack of self-consciousness flung her arms around his neck and drew his head down to kiss him full on the lips. The scent of honeysuckle engulfed him. Her eyes held all the colours of sunlit sea-shallows – azure and aquamarine, cobalt flecked with gold. His throat tightened ...

ELIZABETH CHADWICK

The RUNNING VIXEN

SIGNET

SIGNET

Published by the Penguin Group
Penguin Books Ltd, 27 Wrights Lane, London W8 5TZ, England
Penguin Books USA Inc., 375 Hudson Street, New York, New York 10014, USA
Penguin Books Australia Ltd, Ringwood, Victoria, Australia
Penguin Books Canada Ltd, 10 Alcorn Avenue, Toronto, Ontario, Canada M4V 3B2
Penguin Books (NZ) Ltd, 182–190 Wairau Road, Auckland 10, New Zealand

Penguin Books Ltd, Registered Offices: Harmondsworth, Middlesex, England

First published by Michael Joseph 1991
Published in Signet 1993
1 3 5 7 9 10 8 6 4 2

Printed in England by Clays Ltd, St Ives plc

For Roger, Ian and Simon

ACKNOWLEDGEMENTS

I would like to acknowledge the assistance I have received from Mr R. Venner and the staff at West Bridgford County Library who have enthusiastically helped me to obtain the often obscure works that are vital to my research of the medieval period. I would also like to acknowledge the debt I owe to my wonderful literary agency Blake Friedmann, and to everyone at Michael Joseph for making my foray into the world of publishing an unalloyed pleasure

CHAPTER 1

THE WELSH MARCHES, AUTUMN 1126

ON THE DAY THAT Adam de Lacey came home to the borders after an absence of more than a year, the monthly market at Ravenstow was in full, noisy cry, and thus it was that numerous witnesses watched and whispered behind their hands as the small but disciplined entourage wound its way through their midst.

The young man at the head of the troop paid scant attention to their interest, to the bustling booths and mingling of scents and stenches, the cries and entreaties to look, to buy – not because it was beneath him to do so, but because he was both preoccupied and tired. He passed a woman selling fleeces and sheepskin winter shoes and jerkins. The lilting cadences of the Welsh tongue pleased his ears, causing him to emerge from his introspection and look around with a half-smile on his lips. In its place he had grown accustomed to heavy, guttural German, spoken by humourless men with a rigid, gilded sense of rank and order, their lifestyle the complete opposite of the carefree, robust Welsh, who owned few possessions and pretensions and set very little store by those who did.

The outward journey to the mourning court of the recently deceased German Emperor had been filled with the violence and hardship of long days on roads that were often hostile, and the route home even worse owing to the vicious temper of his charge. Adam was an accomplished soldier, well able to look after himself where the dangers of the open road were concerned. The lash of a haughty woman's tongue – and she the King's own daughter and Dowager Empress of Germany – was a different matter entirely. Her high estate had prevented him from defending himself in the manner he would have liked, and the obligation of feudal duty had made it impossible for him to abandon her on the road, forcing him to bear with gritted teeth what he could not change; but then he was used to that.

A crone cried out to him, offering to tell his fortune for a fourthing. The half-smile expanded and developed a bitter quality. He flung a coin towards her outstretched grimy fingers but declined to wait on her prophecy. He knew his future already – the parts that mattered, or had mattered until the pain of wanting denied had numbed them dead. Abruptly he heeled the dun stallion's flanks and clicked him to a rapid trot.

Ravenstow keep, the seat of his foster-father's earldom, shone with fresh limewash on the crag overlooking the busy town. It had been designed and built during the reign of William Rufus by Robert de Belleme, former Earl of Shrewsbury and King Henry's prisoner these past fourteen years, his evil power a fading but still potent memory; too potent for some who had lost their friends and family to the barbaric tortures he had practised in his fortress strongholds.

Adam's own father had been de Belleme's vassal and his name steeped in that same vile filth. Adam knew from servants' tales, whispered in corners of a dark winter's night and designed to frighten naughty children into good behaviour, the kind of man his father had been: a murdering paedophile who had enjoyed watching a tortured man writhe the way a glutton enjoys sitting down to a feast.

The drawbridge was down but the guards on duty were swift to challenge him, and only rested their spears when they had taken a close look at his gonfanon and the face revealed to them by the thumbed-back helmet and unfastened ventail. Then they let him pass with words of greeting and speculation rife in their eyes.

Eadric, the head groom, emerged from the stables to take

the dun and deployed his underlings among Adam's men. 'Welcome, my lord,' he said with a white half-moon grin. 'It has been a long time.'

Adam stared around the busy bailey which looked just as it always had. The smith's hammer rang out clear and sweet from the forge against the curtain wall; a soldier's woman was tending a cooking pot tripoded over an open fire, and the savoury steam drifted tantalizingly past his nostrils like an houri's veil, reminding him that he had not eaten since well before prime. Hens pecked and crooned underfoot, doves from Countess Judith's cote cooing and pirouetting among them. A curvaceous serving wench carried a tray of loaves across the ward and was whistled at by a group of off-duty soldiers playing dice and warming their backs against a sunny, storeshed wall.

'A long time, Eadric,' he agreed with a sigh and the wary smile that the head groom so well remembered. 'I haven't been home to Thorneyford yet. Is Lord Guyon here?'

'Out hunting, Lord Adam, and the Countess with him.' The servant shrugged, looked apologetic, and then brightened. 'Master Renard is here though, and Mistress Heulwen.'

The smile froze and then splintered. Adam's whole face changed. He set his hand upon his stallion's bridle as though he would mount up again, and twisted round to look at his men. He could hear their groans of relief and see the way they stretched stiff muscles and rubbed sore backs. They were tired, having ridden a bone-jarring distance, and it would be both stupid and grossly discourteous to ride out now that their presence was known. The smell from the cauldron suddenly made him feel sick.

A young man with a stork's length of leg came striding towards him from the direction of the mews, stripping a hawking gauntlet from his right hand as he advanced – a broad-shouldered young man with pitch-black hair and strong features just beginning to pare out of childhood's unformed roundness. It took Adam a moment to realize that this was

3

Renard, Earl Guyon's third son, for when last encountered the lad had been a lanky fourteen-year-old with less substance than a hoe-handle. Now, although still on the narrow side, his limbs were beginning to thicken out with pads of adult muscle and he moved like a young cat.

'We thought you'd gone for good!' Renard declared, greeting Adam with a boisterous clasp on the arm and a total lack of respect. His voice was husky and a trifle raw, for it had only broken in the spring.

'So did I, sometimes,' Adam answered wryly, and took a back step. 'Holy Christ, but you've grown!'

'So everyone keeps telling me – but not too old for a beating, Mama always adds!' He laughed merrily, displaying white, slightly uneven teeth. 'She's taken Papa hunting because it's the only way she can get him to relax his responsibilities for a day, short of spiking his wine – and she's done that before now! There's only myself and Heulwen here. She'll be right glad to see you.'

Adam dropped his lids, guarding his eyes, concealing what they held. 'Is her husband here too?'

They went up the forebuilding steps and through the curtained archway into the great hall. The deep, sweet-scented rushes crackled underfoot and sunlight from the high, narrow unshuttered windows slashed them with yellow streaks and sparkled on the thread-of-gold embroidery on the banners adorning the walls. Renard crooked his finger at a serving girl, then tilted his visitor a sidelong look from narrow, dark-grey eyes. 'Ralph was killed at midsummer by the Welsh.'

'God rest his soul,' Adam crossed himself, the customary words and gesture emerging independent of his racing mind.

Renard shook his head. 'It was a bad business. The Welsh have been biting at our borders like breeding fleas on a dog's back ever since it happened. Warrin de Mortimer it was who interrupted them at their work, drove them off and brought what was left of Ralph home. Heulwen took it badly. Appar-

4

ently she and Ralph had quarrelled before he rode out, and she blames herself.'

The maid approached them with a green-glaze pitcher and two cups, her eyes flickering circumspectly over Adam. He stared straight through her, a muscle bunching and hollowing in his cheek. Mechanically he tasted the wine she poured for him. It was a rich, smooth Rhenish and he almost retched, remembering Heulwen's wedding day and how he had drunk himself into such a stupor on this stuff that Lady Judith had forced him to be sick in order to save his life. Afterwards, the incident had faded into a memory recalled with wry chuckles by all saving himself. Sometimes he wished that they had been sufficiently charitable to let him die.

Renard sat down on a fur-covered stool before the hearth, dangled his cup between his knees and grimaced. 'De Mortimer's been buzzing around Heulwen like a frantic wasp at an open honey-jar. It's only a matter of time before he formally asks Papa for her.'

'And do you think your father will agree?'

Renard jerked his shoulders as if ridding them of something that chaffed. 'It's a useful bond, and being as Warrin was once one of Papa's body-squires, he'll probably get a generous hearing.'

Adam filled his cheeks with the wine and swallowed. He remembered the rasp of dust against his teeth, the feel of a spur-clad heel grinding on his spine, a mocking voice telling him to get up and present sword again. The bruises, the humiliation, the tears swelling painfully in his throat and choked down by fear of further scorn; the struggle to rise and face his adversary, knowing that he would be knocked down again. Training, it was called: at thirteen years old facing a man of twenty, whose sole concern was to display his superiority and put the most junior squire firmly in his place. Oh yes, he well knew Warrin de Mortimer.

'And Heulwen herself?' he asked with forced neutrality.

'Oh, you know Heulwen. Playing hard to get as only she

can, but I think she might have him in the end. Warrin offered for her before, you know, but was turned down in favour of Ralph.'

'And now Ralph's dead,' Adam said without inflection.

Renard cocked him a curious look, but something in Adam's manner caused him to bite his tongue on the remark that he had been about to make and ask instead, 'What's Maud like?'

Adam rubbed his stubble-grizzled jaw. 'She'd rather be known by her full title,' he said wryly. 'She's a haughty bitch, proud and hard as a chunk of Caen stone.'

'You don't like her,' Renard said with interest.

'I didn't get close enough to find out – she tried to turn me to stone too!'

The younger man grinned broadly over the rim of his goblet.

'It's no cause for laughter, Ren. Henry hasn't just summoned her home to comfort his dotage or her widowhood. She's to be our future queen, and when I see her behaving like a spoiled brat, it freezes my blood.'

'Just why did the King send you to fetch her?' Renard asked. 'You personally, I mean?'

Adam smiled darkly. 'I've served at court, so I suppose Henry knows that I'm discreet and stolid, unlikely to boil over in public at being called a mannerless oaf with mashed turnip where my brains should be.'

'She said that to you?' Renard's eyes rounded. He stifled his deepening grin within the depths of his cup.

'That was the least of her insults. Of course, most of them were in German, and I didn't ask to have them translated. Even a mannerless turnip-brained oaf has pride. Besides ... ' He stopped and stared across the hall, transfixed through the heart by a vision.

She stood in a shaft of sunlight that fired her braids beneath the simple white veil to the precise colour of autumn oak leaves. The russet wool overgown was laced to the full, undulating curves of a nevertheless slender body, and as she approached the hearth the delicate gold embroidery at throat and hem glittered with trapped light.

Adam closed his eyes to break the contact, swallowed, and prepared to endure. He would rather a hundred times over have faced the haughty scorn of the Empress Mathilda than face the woman who approached him now: Heulwen, Lord Guyon's natural daughter out of a Welsh woman whom his own father had murdered during the war of 1102.

He rose clumsily to his feet and some of the wine slopped down his surcoat, staining the blue velvet. He could feel his ears burning and knew that he had coloured up like a stumbling, gauche youth.

'Adam!' she cried joyfully, and with complete lack of self-consciousness flung her arms around his neck and drew his head down to kiss him full on the lips. The scent of honeysuckle engulfed him. Her eyes held all the colours of sunlit sea-shallows – azure and aquamarine, cobalt flecked with gold. His throat tightened. No words came, only the thought that Mathilda's remarks were perhaps not insults but the truth.

She released him to step back and admire the new style of surcoat he wore over his hauberk, and the heavy, ornate German swordbelt. 'My, my,' she teased, 'aren't you a sight for sore eyes? Mama will be furious to have missed greeting you. You should have sent word on ahead!'

'I was in half a mind to ride to Thorneyford first,' he said in a constricted voice, 'but I have a letter to your father from the King.'

'Churl!' she scolded, eyes dancing. 'It's fortunate that some of us are not so lacking in courtesy. There's a hot tub prepared above.'

Adam stared at her in congealing horror. It was not that he minded or was unaccustomed to bathing; indeed, he enjoyed the luxury and relaxation it provided. What did fill him with dread was the knowledge that Heulwen, as hostess, would be the one to unarm him and see to his comfort – and it was too long since he had last had a woman. 'I haven't finished my

7

wine,' he said woodenly, 'or my conversation.'

Renard spread his slender fingers and said unhelpfully, 'You'll only have to repeat it all later to my parents anyway, and there's no law against taking your wine above.'

'And being as I have gone to the trouble of preparing a tub, the least you can do is sit in it. You stink of the road!' It was hardly the way to speak to a welcome guest, and Heulwen could have bitten her tongue the moment the words left her mouth. Since Ralph's death that she had suddenly found herself spitting venom without cause or prudence, and people made allowances – those who knew her well. It had been a long time since she and Adam had shared the closeness of their childhood friendship.

Adam stared obdurately at the wall beyond her head, refusing to meet her eyes. 'Well that's because I've been on it for a long time, too long I sometimes think.'

She touched him again, eyes full of chagrin. 'Adam, I'm sorry. I don't know what made me say such a thing.'

'Because you have gone to the trouble and I am not suitably grateful?' he replied with a grimace that just about passed for a smile. 'Well if I am not, it is because I've had a crawful of being ordered around by a woman.'

'*A l'outrance!*' crowed Renard at his blushing half-sister.

'No insult intended in my turn.' Adam put down the cup which was still more than half full of wine, and went towards the curtain that screened off the tower stairs. 'Bear with me awhile until I've found the grace to mellow.'

'Jesu,' grimaced Renard, 'he hasn't changed, has he?'

Heulwen folded her arms thoughtfully. 'I don't know. When I mentioned the bath, I thought he was going to turn tail and flee.'

'Perhaps the Germans mutilated him below,' Renard offered flippantly, then shot her a shrewd glance. 'Or perhaps they didn't.'

Renard was like that. The unwary were lulled into seeing a likeable, somewhat shallow youth, wallowing through the

8

pitfalls of adolescence towards a far-distant maturity, and then Renard would suddenly shatter that assessment with a piercing remark or astute observation far beyond his years or seeming capabilities.

'Rubbish!' Heulwen snapped impatiently. 'I've bathed enough men in courtesy to know what sometimes happens if they've been continent for too long. I won't be embarrassed.'

'No,' Renard quirked his brow, 'but he might.'

She cocked her head to one side, her cheek dimpling mischievously. 'Do you really think so?'

'I think,' said Renard repressively, 'that those who play with fire get their fingers burned.' And draining his wine, he returned to the mews.

In the chamber above, Adam stood in blank contemplation of the steaming tub; around him the maids bustled, checking the temperature of the water, scattering in a handful of herbs, laying out towels of thick softened linen, setting more logs on the fire and fresh charcoal in the braziers to offset the seeping cold from the thick stone walls.

'I'm sorry if I made a mistake,' Heulwen said, lowering the curtain behind her. 'I thought that a bath would be a comfort after a long day on the road.'

His mouth smiled, but his eyes remained on a vacant distance beyond her. 'And so it is. As you said, I was just being a churl.'

She gave him a considering look. There had been no warmth or conviction in his voice; indeed, she might be speaking to a tilt yard dummy for all the response she was receiving, and her irritation flared.

'Is it just a matter of venting the heat?' she asked dulcetly. 'Shall I summon one of the soldiers' sluts?'

This elicited a gratifying widening of his eyes. 'What?' The pitch of his voice revealed that he had heard her perfectly well, but did not quite believe his ears.

'Well, what other reason could you have for refusing a bath? Surely you are not shy?' she scoffed.

'I didn't refuse.' The wideness narrowed. The muscles cording his throat were tense.

'Well, you tried.'

'Because I'm tired and I haven't the wit or patience to match bright talk with you!' he snapped, and through the anger and shock, it suddenly came to him that she was baiting him to see just how far his temper and credulity would stretch. As of old indeed.

'That's better,' she approved. 'I was beginning to think you had remained in Germany and sent a wax effigy home in your stead, and that you were afraid of it melting in the bath water.'

Adam swallowed, suppressing the urge to throttle her out of hand; and then his sense of humour fought its way to the surface and stepped carelessly upon the ruins of his pride. He snorted. 'The vixen's colouring is not just coincidence, is it? You did that deliberately.'

'I wanted to destroy that po-faced mask you were wearing, and I succeeded did I not?' Her generous mouth pursed, and with her head cocked, a mannerism of hers, she studied him. 'Was the Empress so awful, then?'

'I've experienced worse,' he said, smiling now.

'Churl!' she repeated, and laughed. 'All right, I'll stop pla-guing you for the nonce. Here, give me that surcoat!' Efficiently, she whisked the garment from him. It was made of the finest azure-blue Italian velvet, and she exclaimed with pleasure over the quality of the fabric, and with regret that it was badly marked with rust from his hauberk.

'It keeps the sun off your mail,' he said, laying aside the ornate swordbelt, glad at the change of direction. 'And it's a display of wealth and importance to passing peasants – essential to the escort of an empress.' His tone was ripe with neutral sarcasm.

Heulwen busied herself removing his stained link-mail hauberk. 'This'll need scouring before you can wear it again,' she murmured practically, 'I'll send one of the lads down to

10

the armoury with it. There have been several Welsh attacks this year, including the one that killed Ralph.'

Carefully she rolled the garment into a neat but bulky bundle, and before he could protest that he was not intending to stay and that there was no need, his hauberk had been spirited away for refurbishment.

He clenched his jaw and sat down on a low stool to remove his boots and hose. 'When I left, the Welsh situation was fairly quiet, otherwise I wouldn't have gone.'

'Well it's fluid now,' she said wryly. 'They have a new lord over the border and he's been cutting his teeth on your lands during your absence and on Ralph's since early summer. Papa hasn't had the time to engage him properly. Miles would have been of an age to take some of the burden, but Miles is dead — we can't even mourn his grave because he drowned.' She bit her lip before it could tremble and betray her. 'John's chosen the church because he's blind as a bat, so he's little use. Renard's shaping up well, but he's not old enough to bear any serious responsibilities yet, and Henry and William are still only children.' She gave him a tight, slightly challenging smile. 'Still, now you are home you can set the worst of it to rights, I am sure.'

'Oh, there's nothing I enjoy better than a good fight,' he said flippantly, and lowered his eyes to the unwinding of his cross-garters.

Heulwen's smile dropped, and faint vertical lines appeared between her strong red brows. Adam had always been the difficult one. Although not her brother by blood, she had always regarded him as such. She had romped with him in childhood — climbed trees and swung from a rope in the stables, stolen apples from the undercroft and honey cakes from beneath the cook's nose. They had both shared a passion for the fine blood-horses that her father and grandfather bred. A bareback race for a dare had resulted in a thrashing. She had been confined to the bower for a week and Adam had been sent in disgrace

11

to one of her father's other keeps to ponder the folly of his ways.

Adolescence had caught them both unawares. She had matured quickly, and at fifteen had married Ralph le Chevalier, a neighbour of theirs who was a tenant of the crown and past master in the art of training her father's great war stallions. It had been her admiration for his dextrous handling of all that power that had first brought them together.

As her love for Ralph had budded and then blossomed, Adam had retired into non-communicative brooding sulks, his natural reticence becoming a full-blown unwillingness to have ado with anything or anyone apart from the horses. She could still see him now, his expression surly, his face cursed by a red gruel of spots, and his body long-shanked and uncoordinated. His saving grace had been a pair of strong, capable hands, gently probing a destrier's leg for a swelling, his head pressed fearlessly into the stallion's muscle-contoured shoulder.

Taking his shirt now, she clucked her tongue over its thread-bare state. 'I see that the Empress was not so finicky about garments not on display,' she remarked. 'You must let me measure you and get the seamstresses to stitch you a couple of new ones.'

'Organizing my life for me?' he was driven to needle.

Heulwen laughed and handed his remaining garments to the maid. 'What else are sisters for?' As she looked teasingly over her shoulder at him, the laughter on her face froze to ice and her stomach turned over. Her mind had been talking to the lanky, spotty boy of her childhood years. Now the falsehood was stripped bare, as if shed with his garments, and she found herself confronting Adam the man, a stranger she did not know. Renard had warned her and she had taken it as a challenge and now, suddenly, it was too late.

The spots had been replaced by the ruddy glint of beard stubble prickling through his travel-burned skin. His hair was sun-streaked, the russet-brown bleached to bronze where it had been most exposed, and his eyes were the colour of honey or

12

dark citrines, thickly lashed, the edges tipped with gold; beneath them the points of his cheekbones jutted boldly. The line of his thin, fine nose was marred midway by a ridge of thickened bone where it had been broken and reset slightly askew, and a faint white scar from the same incident ran from beneath his nose into the lopsided long curve of his upper lip. There were scars on his body too that had not been there before, the scars of an active warrior. One of them, obviously recent and still pink, curved like a new moon over his hip and nudged the curling ruddy bush at his groin, and what dwelt there was magnificently naught of boyhood either.

She compressed her lips, her throat suddenly dry and her loins, in contrast, liquid. Never in her wildest dreams would she have thought to apply the term 'beautiful' to Adam de Lacey, but the cygnet had shed its down. 'You have seen some hard fighting recently,' she said weakly to cover her shock, and busied herself finding a dish of soap.

He stepped into the oval tub and sat down. The water was hot, making him gasp slightly and flinch, but at least if his half-thickened shaft did decide to burgeon all the way, it would be concealed from her view. 'We were attacked several times on the road by routiers and outlaws. They picked the wrong victim in me, but some of them took the devil of convincing. Am I supposed to use this?'

'What do you mean?' She took the soap dish back from his outstretched hand.

'I shall smell as sweet as a Turkish comfit!' he elaborated with a genuine laugh.

Irritated at her mistake, she clucked her tongue and replaced the rose and lavender concoction with something less scented.

Silence descended. Heulwen was too troubled to break it with small talk and Adam's was not a garrulous nature. She understood the reaction of her body to his. Once, in the early days, she had felt that way about Ralph, but the promise of their marriage had turned sour, tarnished by his infidelity. If she could not have the whole, then she did not want the part

13

that was tossed to her like a crust to a beggar outside a feast hall.

'Renard told me about Ralph,' Adam said into the thickening atmosphere. 'I'm sorry. He was a good man, and I know that you loved him.'

She blinked and refocused, drawing herself together. Yes, Ralph had been a good man: a fine warrior and superlative horseman, all that men would admire. But he had been a poor husband and a fickle lover, rutting after other women the way his war stallions rutted after mares on heat – and then there was the matter of all that unaccounted for silver in their strongbox.

'It's never safe to build on quicksand,' she said with a hint of bitterness, and fetched him a shirt and tunic of her father's, his own baggage still being below with his men.

'What about Ralph's stallions?'

Heulwen shrugged her shoulders. 'I thought I might sell them, but two of the three are only half-trained and could be worth much more if they were properly schooled.'

He returned to his ablutions. Women and horses. Le Chevalier had been expert in the art of both. Adam only had the latter, a skill learned out of a jealous need to prove that he was as good as the man Heulwen had chosen to love, a skill in which, as a mature man, he now took a deep and justifiable pride.

Always a stallion, a destrier was trained to a high degree of response so that it became not only a means of propulsion and a battering ram in battle, but an additional weapon, taught to turn on the minute space of a silver penny, and at a given command to leap, to stand still, to bite and kick, to come at a certain call, to lie down at another.

'I could finish Ralph's work,' he offered with a nonchalance that disguised how interested he really was.

Heulwen hesitated, then shook her head. 'Adam, I couldn't take advantage of you when you're so recently home.'

'You'd be doing me a favour. I haven't worked on a horse since leaving for Germany, and it will give me some space to

14

relax between curbing the Welsh and organizing my lands. It is I who would be beholden to you.'

She studied him. His eyes met hers and then averted. He was still very tense. 'Well then, thank you,' she capitulated with a nod. 'There are two half-trained stallions as I said, and one that Ralph was hoping to sell at Windsor this Christmas feast.'

Adam stepped from the tub and dried himself on the towels laid out, quickly donning the clothes she had found for him. Struggling with a sense of hopelessness, he felt like a fish caught by the gills in a net. *Oh Heulwen, Heulwen!*

'They're stabled in the bailey. Papa and Renard have been exercising them since Ralph died.' Her expression brightened. 'You can see them now if you like, if you're not too travel-worn. There's time before dinner.'

'No, I'm not too travel-worn,' he said, glad of an excuse to leave this chamber and the smell of her, of honeysuckle and woman, so distractingly close by. Although it was she who had made the initial suggestion, it was he who moved first towards the doorway. 'I'm never too tired to look at a good horse.'

Her mouth quirked oddly. 'That's what I thought you'd say.'

Hands on hips, Adam watched Eadric and two under-grooms lead the three destriers around the paddock at the side of the stables. There was a rangy dark bay, handsome and spirited, a showy piebald, eminently saleable but of less calibre than the bay, and a sorrel Andalusian with cream mane and tail and the high-stepping carriage of a prince. It was to the latter that Adam went, drawn by admiration to slap the satin hide and feel it rippling and firm beneath his palm.

'Lyard was Ralph's favourite too,' Heulwen murmured, watching him run his hand down the stallion's foreleg to pick up and examine a hoof. 'He was riding him when he died.'

Adam looked round at her and carefully set the hoof back down. 'And the Welsh didn't keep him?'

15

'I don't think they had time ...'

'I'd have made time.' He nodded to the groom, and with a practised leap was smoothly astride the stallion's broad, bare back. The destrier jibbed and yawed the bit, but Adam soothed and cajoled him, gripped with his thighs and knees, and urged with his heels.

Heulwen watched him take Lyard on a circuit of the paddock and felt her stomach jink as he went through the same routines as Ralph had done with the same assurance, his spine aligned to every movement the horse made. Even without a saddle, his seat was easy and graceful. Lyard high-stepped with arched crest. He rapidly changed leading forefeet. A command from Adam and he reared up and danced on his hindlegs. Another command dropped his forefeet to the ground and eased him into a relaxed trot and then a ground-consuming smooth canter. A quick touch on the rump and he back-kicked.

Adam brought him round before her and dismounted, pleasure flushing beneath his tan. 'I've never ridden better!' he declared with boyish enthusiasm. 'Heulwen, he's worth a king's ransom!'

'God send that you should ever look on a woman thus!' she laughed.

His face changed, as if a shutter had been slammed across an open window. 'What makes you think I haven't?' he said, giving all his attention to the horse.

Heulwen drew breath to ask the obvious question, but was forestalled by the noise of the hunting party clattering into the bailey, and turned instead to shade her eyes against the slant of the sun and watch their return.

Guyon, Earl of Ravenstow, sat his courser with the negligence of a born horseman. He was bareheaded, and the late summer breeze fingered his silver-scattered black hair and carried across to Adam the sound of his laughter as he responded to a remark made by the woman riding beside him.

A pack horse bearing the carcass of a roebuck was being led away towards the kitchen slaughtersheds. The houndkeeper and his lad were taking charge of the dogs that knee-deep enveloped the humans. A brindle Irish bitch clung jealously close to the Earl's side, nose thrusting at his hand.

'Yes, he's still got Gwen,' Heulwen murmured. 'It's the first time since her pups were born that she's left them to run with the hunt. If you ask Papa nicely, he might give you one once they're weaned.'

'Who says I want a dog?'

'Company for you at Thorneyford.'

He angled her a dubious look and started across the crowded bailey.

The Earl, alerted by a groom, lifted his head and before Adam had taken more than half-a-dozen paces, was striding to meet him, his wife gathering her skirts and hastening in his wake.

'We'd given you up for a ghost!' Guyon cried, clasping Adam in a brief, muscular bearhug.

'Yes, graceless whelp, why did you not write!' This reproach was from Countess Judith, who embraced him in her turn and kissed him warmly. Her severe expression was belied by the laughter lines around her hazel-grey eyes.

'It wasn't always easy to find parchment and quill and a quiet corner the places and predicaments I was in, and you know I have no talent like that.'

The Countess laughed in wry acknowledgement of the truth. Her foster-son was literate through sheer perseverance – hers and the priests – but he would never write a fluent hand. His characters had a disturbing tendency to arrive on the parchment either back to front or upside down. 'No excuses,' she said sternly, 'you could have found a scribe, I am sure.'

'I doubt it,' Guyon said dryly.

Adam tried without success to look crestfallen. '*Mea culpa.*'

'So,' said Judith with a hint of asperity that reminded Adam for a moment of her half-sister the Empress, 'what brings you to the sanctuary of home comfort when you could be preening yourself at Court?'

Adam spread his hands. 'My task was completed and the King gave me leave to attend my lands until Christmas.'

'He is back in England then?' Judith took his arm and began to walk with him to the keep. 'Last we heard he was in Rouen.'

'Yes, and in fine spirits. He gave me letters for you and your lord. I have them in my baggage.'

The Countess of Ravenstow sighed and looked ruefully over her shoulder at her husband. Letters from Henry were rarely social. Frequently they were commands or querulous complaints, and usually they elicited ripe epithets from her husband who had perforce to deal with them. 'Can they wait until after dinner?' she asked hopefully.

Guyon gave a caustic laugh. 'They'll either spoil my dinner or my digestion. What's the difference?'

Judith shot him a reproving scowl. 'The difference is that you can decently wait until Adam has settled himself. If the news was urgent, I am sure he would have given it to you immediately.'

'Scold!' Guyon complained, opening and shutting his hand in mimicry of his wife's jaw, but he was grinning.

Her eyes narrowed with amusement. 'Do you not deserve it?' Turning her attention from him, she looked around the hall. 'Where's Renard?'

'Training the falconer's daughter to the lure I very much suspect,' Heulwen said. 'That new hawk of his is past needing his full attention.'

'Jesu God!' Judith's eyes rolled heavenwards. 'I swear that boy has the morals of a tom cat!'

'Not even those,' Guyon said, unruffled. 'He'll settle down soon enough once the novelty of what he can do with it wears off, and the falconer's wench is no innocent chick to be devoured at a pounce. She'll peck him where it hurts if he dares beyond his welcome.' He nodded down the hall at the knot of men clustered at a trestle and smoothly changed the subject. 'I see that Sweyn and Aubrey are still with you, but I don't recognize the other two or the lad.'

Adam took the hint. 'I'll introduce you,' he said with a sidelong glance at the irritated Countess, and Heulwen who was smiling. 'Stephen took a German wife, and Saer the cross. I had to replace them. The boy's my squire, Derby's bastard. His father had him marked out for a career in the church, but he was thrown out of the noviciate for setting fire to the refectory and fornicating in the scriptorium with a guest's maidservant. No vocation whatsoever, and therefore no livelihood. Derby asked me to take him on and fit him for a life by the sword. He's shaping well so far. I might ask to keep him when he's knighted.'

Guyon, thirty years of winnowing wheat from chaff behind him, looked the men over with a critical eye. Sweyn, Adam's English bodyguard, was as dour and solid as ever, his mouth more like a weathered crack in a chunk of rough-hewn rock, his fists on the board as red and huge as hams. Aubrey FitzNigel had been with Adam for more than ten years now – a softly spoken Norman with light watery eyes, a sparse blond moustache, and the lankiness of a pale, sun-drawn seedling. His appearance was deceptive. In point of fact, he was as tough and sinewy as a strip of boiled leather.

Stephen and Saer's replacements were two Angevin mercenary cousins with dark eyes and white sharp smiles, and Guyon would not have trusted either of them further than he could lift one of the standing-stones from the circle upon Caermoel ridge. Ferrar's bastard was a compact, sturdy lad with greenish hazel eyes, a tumble of wood-shaving curls, and freckles spattering a snubbed nose that made him look younger than the seventeen years he actually owned, and a good deal more innocent than Adam's summary proved him.

The group also numbered a dozen hard-bitten men-at-arms, survivors of numerous skirmishes both on the Welsh borders and across the patchwork of duchies and principalities lying between England and the German empire. A chancey crew, but all wearing the cocky assurance of proven, honed fighters.

'They're good men to have at your back in a tight corner,'

Adam said, as they left the soldiers alone to arrange their belongings out of the way of the trestles that were being set out in anticipation of the evening meal.

'Were my doubts so plain?' Guyon looked rueful. 'I must be getting old.' And then, thoughtfully, glancing sideways at Adam, 'Will they not grow restless without battle?'

'Probably, but I don't foresee a problem. I'm not expecting to see much peace.'

The glance hardened. 'In that case, you had better let me see that letter now,' he said softly.

Adam shrugged, unperturbed. 'I can tell you and spare my squire's feet. I know what's in it because I was there when Henry dictated it to his scribe. You are summoned to attend the Christmas feast at Windsor, and your family with you.'

Guyon relaxed, and with a grunt led Adam to the small solar at the far end of the hall, which was screened from the main room by a rather fine, carved wooden partition and a curtained archway. 'Not just for the joy of seeing his grandsons, I'll warrant,' he said cynically, and picked up a child's abandoned wooden sword from a pelt-spread stool and sat there himself. 'Since the death of his heir, Henry's been so eaten up with bitter envy of my own brood that it hasn't even been safe to make mention of them, let alone set them beneath his nose, William in particular.'

Hardly surprising, thought Adam. King Henry had fathered over a score of bastards, Countess Judith among them, but his only legitimate son had drowned and his new young wife showed no signs of quickening. The White Ship had been a magnificent vessel, new and sleek when she was boarded in Barfleur on a cold November evening by the younger element of the court, intent on catching up with the other ships that had left for England earlier in the afternoon. The passengers were well into their cups, the crew as well, and the ship had foundered on a rock before she even cleared the harbour, with the loss of almost everyone on board. Guyon's firstborn son and heir had also been a victim of the White Ship, but there were four other boys to follow, the last one born only a month after the disaster. 'He's inviting everyone else too, for the purpose of binding their allegiance to Mathilda as his successor.'

Guyon rubbed at a bark stain on his chausses. 'Bound to come I suppose,' he sighed. 'She is, after all, his only direct heir, but it won't be a popular move. Is he expecting a rebellion?'

'Baulking yes. Rebellion no.'

The slight age-seams at the corners of Guyon's mouth deepened. 'Some will come very near to it,' he said, frowning. 'It's going to stick in the craw to have to render homage to a woman – a foreign woman at that – and from what I hear of her, Mathilda won't offer them a sweetener to help them swallow their bleeding pride. She'd rather see them choke on it.' He cast Adam a speculative look. 'What about William le Clito? He's the King's nephew by his older brother, and certainly has prior right to Normandy, if not to the throne?'

Adam stared at him. 'Are you one of le Clito's supporters?'

'God's balls, no!' Guyon gave a short bark of laughter. 'What do you take me for? The lad's no more set up to rule than a blinkered hawk's capable of flying! He's done nothing all his life but dance like a puppet on the French King's scheming strings! Good Christ, if I favoured anyone, it would be Henry's other nephew Stephen of Blois, and even then I'm not so sure. He's too good-natured and simple to be strong like Henry.'

Adam nudged a sprig of dried lavender among the rushes with the tip of his boot. 'What about Robert of Gloucester?' he asked. 'He's Henry's son, and he's got the stamina that the house of Blois lacks.'

Guyon dismissed Adam's candidate with a wave of the wooden sword. 'Peasant stamina. He's base-born, Adam. If we allowed ourselves to think of him as our future king, we'd have to consider all the other royal by-blows, and they number as many as the years Henry's been on the throne. Besides, Rob's not like that, and I know him well enough to trust my second-youngest in squirehood to him. He's not the kind to enjoy the weight of a crown on his head, and he used to worship the ground Mathilda trod on when they were children.'

Adam inclined his head, 'Point taken,' he smiled.

Guyon cut the air with the toy weapon, then rested it across his knees and looked shrewdly at Adam. 'But, if we swear for Mathilda, then we also swear for her future husband, whoever he might be – or do we have a say in that? Knowing Henry for the slippery creature he is, I think not.'

Adam mentally took a wary backstep, realizing from whom Renard had inherited his sudden thrusts of perception that were so capable of throwing an opponent off balance.

'Do you know who he might be? No clues on your long tramp from Germany?'

Adam felt his ears burning. 'No, my lord,' he said, watching his toe crush the strand of lavender and all the little dried balls fall off into the rushes. The smell drifted astringently to his nostrils.

'Fair enough.'

'It's not that ...'

Guyon exhaled sharply. 'Oh forget it. Doubtless I'll learn soon enough. Suffice it that you are keeping your fighting men. I know what to expect.'

'I'm not keeping them so much for that purpose as for the Welsh.' Adam uttered the half-truth, half-lie with what he hoped was plausible sincerity. After all, it was only what he had inadvertently overheard between the King and the Bishop of Salisbury, whose tentative discussion had been more an examination of possibilities than anything solid. 'Heulwen said that there is a new lord across the dyke causing trouble?'

'Davydd ap Tewdr.' Guyon grimaced as he spoke the name. 'And trouble is not the word. Either that or I'm slowing down. He's been running rings around me and the patrols; claims that my tenants and Ralph's have been encroaching on his traditional lands, and that we're pushing the border inwards. Well, you can't stop the farmers grazing their beasts where they see good pasture, and the animals can't tell the difference between Welsh grass and English grass – it all tastes the same.

22

There's bound to be some encroachment, and I'd be a naive fool if I believed it was all one-sided.

'I suppose I should take some men across the border and hunt him down, but he's skilled in woodcraft, and I'd probably come off the worst. I've even toyed with the thought of offering him a marriage alliance now that Heulwen's a widow. She's Welsh on her mother's side and on part of mine through her namesake my grandmother, but I've as good as committed myself to de Mortimer's offer when it officially comes.'

'Jesu – you surely don't mean to accept!'

Guyon shrugged. 'Warrin's father, Hugh, is a personal friend of mine. He mooted the idea of a match between the two of them more than ten years ago, but Heulwen had already drawn her bow at Ralph and I turned the offer down. Since then, Hugh's been trying to pair off his infant daughter with Renard, but I'm in no hurry. This will either ease the pressure, or remove it completely. Besides, with the Welsh being so troublesome, we need authority like Warrin's along the border. Widows don't stay widows long in the marches. It is too dangerous, and Heulwen accepts the fact of an early remarriage.'

'You are willing to sacrifice her in the name of policy?' Adam demanded, swallowing.

Guyon looked irritated. 'Grow up, Adam. How often are matches made without a practical reason behind them? Besides, it's hardly a sacrifice. Ask her yourself if you doubt. She likes him well enough, and Warrin's grown up since those early days. Still likes his own way and has the will to get it, but that happens to be an advantage when it comes to dealing with my daughter. She'd walk all over a man of less character. You know what she's like.'

'Not the kind to live in amity with a man of de Mortimer's ilk for long,' Adam said thickly. 'What will you do if he thrashes her? As I remember, it was his every remedy for those who baulked his will or answered him back.'

'I don't know. Hold my peace I hope. God knows, she has always been able to twist me round her little finger – the only girl in a brood of boys and precious for the memory of her mother as well as for herself. I have never been as strict with her as I should have been.'

'So you will permit Warrin de Mortimer that liberty in your stead?' Adam's brows rose incredulously to meet the wayward flop of his hair.

Guyon's face darkened and his lips thinned. 'I realize that you and Warrin hate the sight of each other, that it runs gut-deep, and I know that you are tired from your journey, otherwise I'd be justified in telling you to get out. The final choice is my daughter's. I won't constrain her to anything she does not desire of her own free will, and she knows it.'

Adam pinched the bridge of his nose. Gut-deep, so Earl Guyon had said. Yes, it affected him thus: a quivering tension in the belly, but it was more than that. It ran bone-deep, soul-deep, and was not something he would ever be able to discuss with dispassionate detachment. Better to change the subject before there was too serious a rift.

'How fares Lord Miles? Is he still hale?'

'Spry as an elf, considering his years!' Guyon laughed, an edge of relief in his voice, equally anxious not to quarrel. 'The damp plagues his bones and he tires far more quickly than he used to, particularly since Alicia's death. She was a full ten years younger than he, and he always thought he would go the first. He's taken William up to Caermoel for a few days. The boy wants to learn to track like a Welshman, and my father's obliging, although I don't believe the lad's capable of keeping still for longer than the time it takes to blink. They're due home tomorrow or the next day.'

Adam said ruefully, 'I keep thinking of William as a babe in arms, it hardly seems a day since his christening.'

'Three months after the White Ship went down and all our future security with it.' Guyon tossed and caught his youngest son's small wooden sword and set it gently down, his expression suddenly old and harsh. 'God grant William a warrior's arm and a lawyer's cunning when he comes to manhood. He's going to need both.'

CHAPTER 2

ADAM SNAPPED OPEN his eyes and listened to the darkness with pounding heart and straining ears. The air in the small wall-chamber was as thick as black wool and as difficult to breathe. The sweat crawled over his body like an army of spiders. He wrestled with himself, torn between seeking to remember the blood-filled horror of his dream and thrusting it away in relieved revulsion, and chose the latter, bending his forearm across his eyes and groaning.

At the foot of his pallet the straw rustled. 'My lord?' queried the disembodied voice of his squire. The straw rustled again as the lad fumbled about for tinder and flint, and felt his way over to the solid iron stand upon which the night candle was staked. Light flickered weak and dim amid a jumble of huge, fuzzy shadows.

'Lord Adam?'

He took his arm away and saw the frightened, dark glitter of his squire's eyes. 'I'm all right, Austin, a bad dream, nothing more.' Sitting up, he motioned to the wine jug.

The youth splashed a half measure into the cup beside it and anxiously handed it across. His lord had been groaning and twisting in the throes of his dream like a man stretched on the rack.

Adam drank thirstily, then looked over the cup's rim at the youth. 'Oh in God's name, stop looking at me like that, I'm all right. With the sort of life we've led recently, the wonder would be if I did not ride the nightmares!'

Austin chewed his lip. 'Sorry, lord. It is just that I thought you were somewhat troubled earlier before we retired.'

Adam snorted – troubled was not the word. He shook his head mutely at the youth and thought of Heulwen in her tawny gown, his gaze drawn to the full, smooth swell of her breasts by the double loops of crystal and topaz fastened at her white throat. He had been hard-pressed to keep his eyes on his meal and his thoughts upon what people were saying to him.

Perhaps she had been right, perhaps he did need a woman. He thought about that, dismissed it as a fanciful indulgence and lay down again, hands laced behind his head and, closing his lids, saw the necklace once more in his mind's eye. It had been Ralph's bride-gift. Ralph, whose taste in jewels, horses and women had never been less than impeccable.

Sleep had flown. His mind tossed restlessly like a bird on a storm wind. The linen covers scratched his skin. The boy's anxiety reached out, stifling, and he began to wish that he had made him sleep below with the other men of the escort. He was well aware of the adulation, and the heroic qualities with which the lad had imbued him as his saviour from the cloister, and was both amused and irritated by it. He was only human, and the sooner Austin grew out of this phase of treating him like a god and grew up, the more comfortable they both would be.

Adam sat up again and reached for his clothes. 'Go back to sleep lad,' he murmured, beginning to dress with swift economy of movement. 'It's still the dead of night. I'm going up on the wall walk for a breath of clean air.'

Solemn-eyed on his pallet, Austin watched his lord fasten the clasp on his cloak and slip quietly out onto the torchlit stair. He knew that something was badly wrong, something that had a connection with the bold, flame-haired widow who called Lord Adam 'brother'. She was very beautiful, and he was sure that Lord Adam had groaned her outlandish name as he threshed, a captive of his dream. It was not something he could ask about, nor did he have the scope to understand, for as yet, women were no more to him than a passing carnal interest. In the end, puzzling and anxious, he lay back down and shut his eyes, but it was a long time before he slept.

The night was clear and cold, more than a hint of autumn on the fresh breeze rising from the river Dee. Adam paced the wall walk and inhaled the scent of distant white starlight and glinting dark water. In the stables a horse neighed and the sound carried up to him as did the laughter of the men on watch as they warmed their hands at a fire in an open part of the bailey.

Adam remembered the numerous nights he had spent as a squire, taking his turn on the watch, eyes skinned upon empty moonlight. Henry's reign had been mostly peaceful and Ravenstow was impregnable to Welsh assault, but the guard duty was taken seriously. It was a practice for the warfare which might be visited upon them if the King's robust health should fail, or if strife should arise from this swearing of allegiance to his daughter, Mathilda.

He thought about his own lands. His father's possessions had been confiscated by the crown during the rebellion of 1102, but Thorneyford and its dependent manors were his, and there was another small keep near Shrewsbury. He was by rank of land a small fish in a wide ocean, but his connections nonetheless made him an important one. He was the Earl of Ravenstow's foster-son, had spent his late adolescence as a squire in the royal household, and had made influential friends and contacts while in attendance there. Henry trusted him – as far as Henry trusted anyone – and had promised him reward for his loyalty and service. Adam was wise enough not to anticipate the event too eagerly: promises were one matter, their fulfilling, where the King was concerned, quite another.

A guard ascended the wall walk, a huge brindle alaunt padding leashed beside him, and saluted Adam. The latter acknowledged, admired the dog's snaggled armoury of teeth from a wary distance, and turned to pace the battlements, the desire for sleep still eluding him. He so seldom slept in the privacy of a personal bedchamber that to do so unsettled him Usually in nomad style, he bedded down among his men, either in some great lord's hall, a monastic guest house, or rolled in his cloak beneath the stars, a camp fire glimmering at his feet.

Another guard in a cowled cloak was leaning against one of the merlons, his face in shadow. When he failed to salute, Adam paused in surprise and backstepped. Ravenstow's constable took the keep's discipline seriously and would lean hard on a man neglecting his duty.

'Look sharp, soldier!' he snapped, realizing too late as the figure turned with the gasp of a startled dreamer, that it was not a guard at all. 'What are you doing here?' he demanded, more than half in anger that even up here on the wall walk in the dead of night there was no escape. Heulwen stared up at him, eyes round with surprise. He could see the starlit gleam of their whites. 'I came here to think,' she said a little breathlessly 'It's open here, your thoughts are not squashed by walls.' She considered him, head cocked on one side. 'And you?'

'I came for solitude,' he said harshly, then swore beneath his breath. 'Sorry, I'm being a churl again aren't I?'

He sensed the deepening of her smile. 'Yes, you are.'

'I – I had a nightmare, and my squire was making a fuss.' He looked down. 'I don't remember what happened, and I don't believe I want to.' He shivered, the hairs on his spine prickling against the thought.

'At least yours was only a dream.' She turned, putting down the hood of her cloak so that her face emerged, framed in the weak silvery glow of the sickle moon.

Adam swallowed. Her hair was loose, brushed down as he had not seen it since her wedding day. She was very beautiful. His mind and body blended into one dull ache. 'I know that you grieve deeply for Ralph,' he said unsteadily.

One side of her mouth turned up. 'Ralph!' she exhaled mockingly. 'Jesu God, I've been grieving for years, but not for him.' She glanced at him quickly. 'I had to have him, Adam,

29

whatever the cost. Do you know what it is to burn? I don't suppose you do. Well, I burned, and was burned, and if I have taken it badly, it is because he left me nothing but cold ashes.' She rubbed her arms within her warm, coney-lined mantle.

Adam, who knew precisely what it was to burn, could only stare at her, burning still, unable to touch. 'Heulwen, I . . .'

'No, don't commiserate.' She laughed bitterly. 'I don't think I could bear it, and besides, it doesn't suit you.' She laid her hand on his sleeve and drew a sudden, impulsive breath. 'Look Adam, I know it's late, and I know you came here for solitude, but there is a matter sorely troubling me, and I need to talk to someone.'

Adam gnawed his lip, desiring to deny her and bolt for the safety of the restless bed he had so recently absconded, but was powerless to do so. Her eyes were soft and suddenly pleading, her hand gripping his sleeve felt like a manacle. He looked down at it. It was slender and long-fingered, the feminine image of her father's and adorned on the wedding finger by two rings of braided gold.

'How could I refuse?' he asked with the faintest twist of a grim smile, and wished that he knew the answer.

The wine made a musical sound as she poured it into two trellised glass goblets. The candles lit from the main night sconce reflected on the bronze flagon, which had a handle shaped like a dragon's head, the eyes inlaid with winking red garnets, the tongue curling between sharply incised fangs and over the fierce snout. An embroidery frame was set up near the brazier and he went to peruse the boldly-worked pattern. It was the hem of a man's tunic, sewn with couchant leopards in thread of gold on a dark velvet background. Lady Judith's work he thought, recognizing the style. Heulwen had never owned the patience for more than the most rudimentary needle-craft.

'It's a new court robe for Papa.' She handed him the wine. 'He'll be needing it if what I heard is true?'

30

'That all the tenants-in-chief are summoned to swear for Mathilda you mean? Yes, it's true.'

'Ralph said something about it before he was killed,' she murmured, 'about Mathilda being our future queen.'

Adam swallowed a mouthful of his wine as a matter of form and put the cup down. 'Well, it was fairly obvious once Henry summoned her from Germany.'

Heulwen toyed with the patterning on her goblet and looked at him through her lashes, but assessingly now, without a hint of coquetry. 'No. There was more to it than that. He knew something, and it was setting him on edge. I asked him to tell me, but he laughed, said that it was nothing, patted me on the head like a dog, and rode away to his death.' She gnawed her lip for a moment as if debating whether or not to take the final step, then drew a sudden swift breath. 'When the funeral was being arranged, Adam, I had cause to check our strongbox. Ralph always kept the keys himself; he wouldn't let me near it, so I never knew until he was dead how rich we actually were — too rich for our standing. I know that he made a good profit from the horses, but not to the tune of what was in that chest.'

Adam looked at her sharply. 'You mean it was ill come by? Heulwen, how much?'

She told him, and he whistled. 'Christ, that's nearly as much as an inheritance relief on a major barony.'

'A great amount for a "nothing",' she said savagely.

Adam's lips remained pursed. 'But,' he mused, 'was he being paid to keep it a "nothing", or was he being paid to reveal it in all its glory? Or perhaps both?'

Her voice was alarmed. 'Adam, what do you mean?'

'Ralph travelled far and wide. He was renowned for his skill and valued for it by men of much greater estate than himself. I know for a fact that on more than one occasion he carried messages between Henry and Fulke of Anjou ...' He paused. Her eyes had gone wide with shock. 'You didn't know?'

The wine shook in one hand, while the other was clenched

31

in the folds of her gown. 'I was ever the last one to know,' she said bitterly. 'I suppose that it has been common knowledge for the past ten years or whatever.'

'Not common knowledge,' he said gently, 'except to those of us involved in that kind of game.'

'Adam?'

He gave her a quick, vinegary smile. 'It's a night for surprises isn't it?'

'You are saying that you and Ralph were — are spies for Henry?'

He snorted, almost laughed. 'Not quite, I wouldn't say that. We have occasionally carried messages, verbal ones that could not be entrusted to parchment.' His look became thoughtful. 'But the payment for such was never a tenth so high.'

'Then betrayal . . .' she whispered, appalled.

Adam shrugged. 'I'd certainly say that he was dabbling his fingers in a murky broth, but how deep I don't know.' He rubbed his chin. 'Have you spoken to anyone else about this?'

'No, I've kept it to myself, half the reason my temper has been so foul. Papa has too much on his trencher already, and I was so confused in my own mind that I tried to pretend it didn't exist.' She shivered. 'But it does, and I'm frightened.'

It was the lost, forlorn note in her voice that finally undid him. Until then he had succeeded in maintaining a neutral front, but the sight of her so close to tears, trembling with fear, her spirit subdued, was too much for him to bear, and before he could rationalize the move, think better of it and step away, he had put an arm round her shoulders and drawn her against him. 'It's all right, Heulwen,' he murmured with a mingling of tenderness and flooding desire, 'I won't let any harm come to you.'

A sob was wrenched from her throat, followed by another. She pressed her face into his chest, stifling her grief into the dark wool of his tunic. Adam murmured reassurances and stroked her hair. It was thick and silky under his fingers and smelled faintly of herbs. His body became aware of the pressure

32

of hers, breast and hip and thigh, and the arm that held her against him, slipped of its own volition down to her waist. 'Heulwen . . .' he muttered against her hair, and lowered his head, seeking sideways beyond the thick sweep of her tresses, finding and kissing her cheek and temple, and then, as she raised her head in surprise, her mouth.

It opened beneath his, pliant and warm, dewy as the heart of a flower. His hand tightened on her waist and slipped down over the curve of her buttocks, moulding her closer. For less than the space of a heartbeat her body undulated and yielded to his, and then her mind took horrified command of her wayward flesh. She jerked like a skittish horse fighting a saddle, tore her mouth from his, and levered herself violently out of his embrace.

'Adam no!' she panted, stricken by disturbing sensations that she had thought were dead and buried, and certainly did not require resurrecting here and now. She dragged her sleeve across her mouth as if to rid herself of the taste of him. Her legs had gone to water. 'Dear God, no!'

'Heulwen . . .' He took a step towards her, hand outstretched in entreaty. 'It's not . . .'

Quivering, she backed away from him. 'Don't touch me.' She grabbed her cloak off the stool where she had flung it, panic in her eyes. 'I – I mean it. One step closer and I'll scream down the guards on your head! I'm not some slack-thighed kitchen wench to be tumbled at your whim. If you want that sort of pleasure, you know where the guardroom is!'

Adam's eyes darkened. Torn between fury that she should bring it down to this base level, and shame at his own loss of control, he could only stare at her, bereft of words. Heulwen stared back. The air between them trembled. With a little cry, she turned from him and fled.

'Oh blood of Christ!' he snarled and plunged after her, taking his chance with the possibility of being arrested for rape. But in the darkness he stumbled over someone's pallet and came down hard among the rushes, the disturbed sleeper cursing him in English. Adam snapped a scalding reply in gutter French, and struggled up again. In the dim light from the banked fire he could see the snoring servants and men-at-arms, the polished brown highlights of the lord's oak chair set on the dais, a couple moving together beneath a blanket, a dreaming dog twitching its paws. Of Heulwen there was no sign.

Adam swore again, this time at his own stupidity, and dug his fingers through his hair. He had meant only to comfort, had not realized until he held her how precarious was the line between the need to comfort and the need itself, and his lack of judgement had just cost him dearly. The thought of her frightened anger made his flesh crawl upon his bones. The thought of her body flowing against his filled him with a heat he was powerless to command.

He returned to the solar, found the garnet-eyed flagon and his cup, and set about seeking oblivion in lieu of the sleep that he knew would never come.

CHAPTER 3

ILES, LORD OF the holdings of Milnham and Ashdyke, watched his youngest grandson leap and turn and, with his wooden sword, cut beneath the defences of an imaginary foe. The old man sighed deeply and propped his aching legs on the footstool that Heulwen attentively fetched for him.

'It's a long time since I was even half so agile,' he told her wistfully. 'He moves faster than a flea.' In his eyes there was pride, for there was much of himself in the slight, elfin boy, or at least as he remembered himself in the unfettered days of a long-distant childhood.

Heulwen watched her half-brother too, wincing as he clipped the laver and almost sent it crashing over. 'I suppose you let him wear you out, Grandpa,' she scolded gently, and brought him a cup of wine.

'Nay,' Miles grinned, 'it was a pleasure to have him with me. He managed to snare a coney all by himself you know, and clean it too. Your stepmother's promised to make him a fur-edged tunic from the skin for the Christmas feast, and in return, he's giving her one of the feet on a silver mount to hang from her girdle.'

Heulwen smiled dutifully, the expression not quite reaching her eyes which were full of care. Miles sought her fingers and squeezed them. She looked down at his hand. It was brown and darkly mottled with a twisting blue rootwork of knotty veins, but it was hard and steady and it was her own young unblemished one that trembled. She bit her lip, darting him a look which he returned with the serenity of ancient years. 'We

35

had a visitor while you were away with William, Grandpa.'

Miles slowly nodded and smiled. 'I know. Young de Lacey. Eadric told me as I lit down in the ward. I daresay when I've rested these old bones enough to want to sit a saddle again, I'll ride over to Thorneyford and welcome him home.' He looked at her shrewdly. 'Are you going to tell me what's wrong?'

'Grandpa, I've quarrelled with Adam,' she said in a small voice and swallowed, thinking of the incident of two nights since. She had asked him to the solar, forced her dilemma onto him, and then, when his sympathy had begun to turn into something far more dangerous, she had reacted like a wild animal striving to break free of a trap. Even worse, she had accused him as though it had all been his fault, when she knew to her shame that it was not. Her own body had quickened readily to desire, and when she had run from him, she had been running from herself. All the following day she had pleaded a megrim as an excuse not to come down to the hall and Adam, without personal invitation, could not go above. He had asked to speak to her and she had sent her maid Elswith to tell him that she was not well. He had taken the hint, gathered his men and ridden out, and the silence left behind weighed so heavily on her conscience that she could not bear it.

'There's nothing new in that, as I recall from your childhood,' Miles said wryly.

William danced up to them. Heulwen opened her mouth and then shut it again tightly. Panting, the child paused to regain his breath, and bestowed upon her a dazzling, mischievous smile. The youngest of her father's sons, he had a profusion of bouncy black curls, green-blue eyes like her own and her grandfather's and a bone structure that would advantage him for the rest of his life.

'Heulwen, can I go and see Gwen's pups?' He put on his pleading face, managing to look almost as soulful as Gwen herself, so that she was forced to laugh. 'Papa's gone into the town to talk to the merchants and Mama's busy in the dairy. Eric said I had to ask you.'

She tousled his hair. 'Go on then but be careful, and don't get too close. She's still very protective.'

'I won't, I promise. Mama says I can have one for my very own when they're old enough to leave Gwen. I've seen the one I want – the brindle dog with the white paws. I'm going to call him Brith.'

Heulwen felt a pang for childhood's earnest enthusiasms, the passionate joy in small things, the blissful ignorance of wider concerns, and the tragedies forgotten in as long as it took to wipe away the tears. William smiled up at her again, offering his face to be kissed, gave her a brief, tight hug and, sword still in hand, ran off down the hall.

'And Judith worries about Renard and women!' Miles laughed. 'William is going to outstrip him a hundred-fold when the time comes! I can only be glad that I won't be here to wince as the sparks fly!'

'Don't say that!' Her tone was sharp.

'It's the truth, girl, and we both know it. I'm borrowing time hand over fist these days, and when I do go, I daresay I'll be glad.' He leaned back against the carved oak chair and steepled his fingers against his lips. His eyes were still keen, his voice steady without the quaver that so often affected the elderly, and his face betrayed to Heulwen none of the fatigue that was inwardly sapping him. He could not however sustain bursts of energy for long periods of time these days, and had to husband his strength like a housewife coddling a contrary tallow flame. He was four score and one, an age very seldom attained and, slowly but inexorably, his body was beginning to fail his will.

'Now then,' he said comfortably, 'what about this quarrel of yours. Can it not be mended?'

Hesitantly at first, but gaining impetus, Heulwen told him the tale, omitting the details about the suspect silver in Ralph's strongbox. 'I know I should have been more tactful Grandpa, but I was frightened. One moment he was comforting my grief, the next he was kissing me ...'

37

Miles closed his eyes and conjured up the image of Adam de Lacey as he remembered him: a quiet young man of serious countenance and direct, dark-gold eyes set beneath a sleek, thick mop of bronze-brown hair. A superlative horseman, good with a sword, even better with a lance, and not given to the kinds of folly just described to him. He looked thoughtfully at his grandaughter, well aware that she had not told him the whole tale, and that she knew that he had guessed this, for she had lowered her eyes and her cheeks had turned pink.

'Foolish,' he snorted, 'but not to be wondered at. In part you brought it on yourself. You do not need a gazing glass to know that you are attractive to men. Their eyes have always told you.'

'I didn't bring that on myself!' she objected indignantly.

'You interrupted me,' Miles said with a patient smile. 'I was going to say that any young man who found himself alone with you, at your invitation, in the darkest hours of the night might well be pushed over a brink he never even knew was there. His first intention probably was to offer comfort. As far as I know, Adam de Lacey is no womanizer. Your father never had trouble with him the way he did with young Miles and his wenching.'

'Do you think I owe him an apology?' she asked woodenly.

'Not necessarily, but I think perhaps you were a little harsh with him. You have created a mountain out of a molehill.'

Heulwen looked down and fiddled with the enamelled links of the girdle at her waist. Her grandfather's great age had in no way incapacitated his wits, and his shrewd scrutiny was making her uncomfortable. She said quickly, 'Grandpa, I think you're right. I'll make amends as best I can.'

The light caught the silver tips of stubble on his throat as he swallowed. 'You could do worse than consider Adam de Lacey for a husband,' he said, watching her. 'Obviously the lad's attracted to you, and he's very well thought of in marcher and royal circles.'

She dropped to kneel in the rushes at his propped feet, her

knees having weakened at the very prospect of such a fate. Her mind scurried, necessity making it nimble, finding an excuse out of what had once been the truth but was now the truth no longer. 'Grandpa, I couldn't, it would be like marrying one of my own brothers,' then added defensively, 'anyway, I'm as good as spoken for already.'

'I see,' he nodded wisely. 'So you are still set on accepting de Mortimer's offer?'

'Yes, Grandpa.' She looked at him from beneath her soot-darkened lashes. 'After Ralph, I'll be grateful for a man whose absences are not going to send me into a jealous frenzy.'

Yes, he thought, she had known passion and been burned by its heat, but there had been no healing balm of love to temper its destructive force, only lies, deceit and self-delusion, and she had been too young to understand. A marriage that was more of a business arrangement than anything else would suit her very well for the present, but what of the future? Her braids were the colour of liquid fire and they reflected her spirit. No good would come of trying to squash herself into a niche for which she was not made – but how to explain it to her when for the nonce she could not see the wood of the future for the trees of the past.

'Heulwen . . .' he began and then subsided as a great seeping weariness overcame him. He felt as if all the marrow was trickling slowly from his bones and soaking into the rushes.

'Grandpa, are you all right?' She leaped to her feet, frightened by the spreading patches of grey beneath his eyes. 'Here, drink some more wine.'

Miles watched her fumble for the flagon and then closed his eyes. When she pressed the cup back into his hands, he opened them again, lids feeling as though the death pennies already weighted them down.

'Grandpa, I'm sorry, I shouldn't have bothered you.' Her voice trembled.

He put out his free hand and lightly touched her face as she bent over him. Her cheeks were wet. 'Nay love, don't fret,' he said, summoning the travesty of a smile. 'I'm all right, just very tired. We'll talk again when I've had a chance to rest.'

'It doesn't matter, Grandpa. I'll make my peace with Adam, and as soon as Warrin returns from Normandy I'll accept his offer, and that's the end of it. I'll go and get Mama.'

'Child, what about telling me from the beginning?' he whispered huskily, but to thin air, for she had gathered her skirts and was running down the hall.

CHAPTER 4

SWEATING, ADAM CLOSED his eyes against the glare of the sun and, throat rippling, gulped the wine straight from the skin. Opposite him, Aubrey FitzNigel rested his swordpoint in the dust and wiped his forehead upon the back of his hand.

Red juice ran down Adam's chin and throat and diversified into sparkling rivulets tracking through his sparse golden chest hair. Finished, he handed the skin to the knight, and bending over, hands on knees, blew out hard through puffed cheeks.

'You're out of practice,' grinned FitzNigel, who drank heartily, and gasping with satisfaction added, 'I'd have killed you then if we'd been using sharpened blades instead of these whalebone pretences.'

'You wouldn't,' Adam grinned back with the surety of self-knowledge. Practice was practice, a repetition of various moves in a shifting dance of aggression and avoidance until perfection was accomplished – necessary, but devoid of the deadly competition that gave true battle its sparkle. There was a certain gut-piercing exhilaration in pitting your skill against that of another man and knowing that the stake was either your life or his. Being as he had no intention of murdering his captain, Adam's edge was as dull as the rebated sword he was using.

Aubrey finished drinking, stoppered the skin and tossed it over to Austin, for whose edification this bout was partly taking place. 'Care to wager?' he challenged Adam and, spitting on his palms, raised his shield and dropped behind it to a battle crouch.

Adam wiped his right hand down his chausses and applied

41

it once more to his swordgrip. 'I'd not part you from your hard-earned coin,' he retorted, shifting his stance on Thorneyford's gritty tilt yard floor. As Aubrey attacked, he leaped over the low swing of the blade and beneath the knight's guard, feinting at the shield and sweeping under it. Aubrey sprang backwards like a startled hare and a breath came hard between his teeth. Laughing, Adam pressed his attack.

Horses clattered through the main gateway and into the bailey. Grooms went out and a servant came running in and spoke to the squire.

'Lord Adam,' Austin called, 'Miles le Gallois is here. He's brought you some horses and craves a moment of your time.'

Adam misjudged his stroke, lost his balance, and found himself once more looking down the fuller of Aubrey's sword and into Aubrey's dagger-bright rheumy eyes. He shoved the knight's weapon disgustedly aside.

'Sorry, lord,' said Austin, biting his lip.

'My own fault lad, I'm not concentrating.' He thrust the blunted sword at the boy. 'Here, take my place and see if you can improve on my performance.'

'Shouldn't be too difficult,' Aubrey mocked.

Adam stuck two fingers up at him in an eloquent English gesture, dropped his shield to pick up his shirt and draping it over one shoulder, walked between two storesheds and into the main bailey.

An old man was dismounting carefully from Ralph's bay destrier. Behind him, an expression of wistful pleasure on his face, Renard was loosening the sorrel stallion's girth, while beyond on a leading rein, the piebald sidled friskily.

'Lord Miles!' Adam strode forward with genuine pleasure and held out a calloused palm. 'This is indeed a surprise!'

Miles clasped the proffered hand. 'And so it is,' he answered warmly, gaze quizzical upon Adam's state of undress and the dusty shirt draped over his shoulder.

'I've been practising my swordplay in the tilt yard, and not with any great success. It's a relief to leave it.' He used his free hand to push his sweat-darkened hair off his forehead.

'Grandpa has brought you these on his way home, being as you forgot them in your haste to leave us,' Renard gestured towards the horses, his mouth curving mischievously. 'My sister doesn't usually have that effect on men, rather the opposite.'

Adam eyed Renard coolly. 'Perhaps I know her too well,' he retorted.

Renard shrugged. 'Or not well enough.' He fondled Lyard's whiskery muzzle and glanced towards his grey crossbreed remount. 'It's like riding silk. Old Starlight's going to seem as rough as sackcloth by comparison.'

Miles smiled at him sidelong. 'You're developing expensive tastes, boy.'

'Why not, I'm the heir aren't I?' It was spoken flippantly, but Renard's eyes, before he guarded them with his thick-lashed lids, were grim, almost bitter. The sound of weaponplay drifted towards them from the direction of the tilt yard. Renard left the horses and sauntered towards it.

'Too sharp for his own good sometimes, that one,' Miles said, as the grooms set about unsaddling the destriers and leading them and the remounts to the stone water trough. It had once been a coffin so the priest said, undoubtedly Roman, for there was a vague weather-beaten inscription in Latin just visible on its side. 'With a tongue like that in his head, he's got to learn when to keep it sheathed.'

'He's not yet sixteen, and most lads of that age are indiscreet to some degree,' Adam said, thinking of his own squire's recent misdemeanours.

'Or that's what you tell yourself in lieu of throttling him.' Miles eased himself down on the mounting block with a sigh, and spread his palms upon his knees.

Adam laughed and, nodding wry acknowledgement, signalled to a servant. 'You'll stay to eat meat?'

Miles inclined his head and added judiciously, 'Nay, he's a good boy really. They've sent him to see me home. Partly it's

43

to be rid of him for a few days, and he needs the responsibility and experience of commanding men. Partly it is because I wasn't well a few days ago.'

Adam looked concerned. Miles waved the air and a disgusted expression crossed his face. 'It was nothing, my own fault. I exhausted myself trying to keep up with a child of six. They say the old return to their infancy. Well by God, I paid for my foray. Judith and Heulwen had me posseted up in bed for two days and wouldn't let anyone near me.' A mischievous sparkle lit within the wrinkle-crenellated depths of his eyes. 'I told them I'd have more company laid out dead in the chapel, and made myself so difficult a patient that in the end they saw sense and just about pushed me out of the keep!' He looked across at the horses snuffling around the trough, their shadows mingling in the mellow dust, then sobered and flicked a shrewd glance at Adam.

'Heulwen told me why you quarrelled.' he said quietly.

Adam tossed his shirt on to the ground and sat down beside it, his back to Miles so that the latter did not see his frown. 'Did she?' he said indifferently, and twisting his fingers around a clump of grass growing near his feet, uprooted it from the dry soil.

Adam's back might be turned, but Miles could see the tension cording the muscular shoulders, could feel it in the quality of the atmosphere, and thanked Christ that Renard had gone to investigate the tilt yard. He nodded towards the three stallions and said, 'She sent them by way of an apology. She's ashamed, knows that she has treated you unfairly.' The wrinkles deepened around mouth and eyes. 'She's also very stubborn.'

'Did she tell you everything?' Adam looked round at Miles. The sunlight was in his eyes, narrowing them, concentrating their colour to a fierce, clear amber.

Miles spread his hands. 'As much as any woman. A carefully adjusted version of the truth, I hazard. She did not explain what the two of you were doing in the solar at midnight in the first place.'

Adam stared a moment longer, then lowered his gaze to the grass clod dangling between his fingers. 'We spoke of another matter too, concerned with Ralph and what may be an affair of treason. Heulwen was worried, and so was I when she told me – and one thing led to another.'

'Do you want to tell me? About Ralph, I mean?'

Adam threw away the grass and stood up in one lithe movement that filled Miles with envy. 'No.' He rotated his left arm to ease a muscular ache and eyed the horses. 'Not yet.'

Miles shrugged and eased far more circumspectly to his own feet, the fire of dry joint pain knifing through his knees.

Adam went to the three stallions and began looking them over again with a knowing hand and an admiring eye. He stroked Lyard's muzzle. The stallion butted him and musically mouthed the bit. He took the bridle and started to lead him towards the tilt yard, a deep frown knitting his brows. He had his truce. Now all he had to do was find the grace to accept it and forget.

'It's a pity,' Miles added, limping beside him, 'if only you hadn't grown up with her, she wouldn't be thrusting the caltrop of "brother" under your nose, and in my opinion, you're far more suited to her needs than the strutting cockerel she's determined to wed.'

They passed between the shadows cast by the corridor of the two storesheds and Adam did not see the quick, calculating glance that was cast his way. All he knew was that there were goosepimples rising on his flesh that were not caused by the shadow. He wanted to crash his fist into the wooden wall and cry denial. He was not her brother and never would be.

They emerged again into the open sunlight. Miles regarded him with concealed satisfaction, his suspicions confirmed. Adam had not spoken, but had it not been for the tan of a summer spent in the saddle, his face would have been ashen. Gently he touched the young man's arm. 'Are you all right?'

Adam flinched. 'Yes,' he said through stiff lips, and gathering the reins, mounted up and trotted Lyard across the tilt yard to a bundle of jousting lances that were stacked against the wall.

The men paused in their sword practice and turned to watch him. Aubrey took another swig of wine from the skin and passed it to Renard, who was now stripped to the waist and in possession of a whalebone sword and a large triangular shield.

Adam leaned over the saddle and took up one of the lances, then trotted the sorrel over to the quintain course on the far side of the tilt yard.

Smiling slightly, Miles strolled over to the knot of expectant men and paused beside his grandson.

'He's using the French style,' Renard said with interest and more than a little envy, as Adam couched the lance under his arm and fretted Lyard back on his hocks.

'Well that's because it's a French sport,' said Aubrey. 'Besides, underarm's better than over. More thrust behind it when it's positioned like that.'

Renard shook his head. 'I've tried, but God's life, it's difficult.'

'Watch,' said Aubrey, giving him a silencing look. 'Hold your tongue, and learn.'

The quintain was a crossbar set on a pivot, with a shield nailed to one edge and a sack of sand to the other, the object being to strike the shield cleanly in the centre and thus avoid being struck from the saddle or severely bruised by a knock from the bag of sand. A recent sport, it was less than ten years old, and was used mainly as a practice for battle, training the eye and arm to coordinated precision; those who could master the art were at an immediate advantage on the battle-field.

Adam crouched behind the shield and positioned the lance across his mount's neck at an angle of forty-five degrees. He tightened the reins and Lyard's forefeet danced left-right on the ground. 'Hah!' he cried, and drove in his heels. Lyard arrowed down the tilt run, dust spurting from beneath his hooves, sunlight flashing on the bit chains, stirrup irons and bright sorrel hide. He moved effortlessly, eating the ground, and each stride that he took hammered the word *brother* into

Adam's skull like the four nail-heads hammered deep into the limewood, denoting the centre of the shield they were approaching with such fluid, inevitable rapidity.

The tip of the lance wavered and readjusted. Adam hit the target precisely where he intended and cried out in defiant rage that sounded to the onlookers like triumph as he ducked over the pommel, his face buried in the pennants of flying blond mane. The sandbag kicked violently on the post and grazed the air over his bent, naked back.

Lyard galloped on down to the end of the tilt. Adam sat up and reined him round, set heels to his flanks again and repeated the manoeuvre, swirled in the dust at the far end, and charged back down the tilt. The lance cracked the shield and the sandbag hurtled round. Adam ducked, drew on the bridle, and hurled the lance point-down into the dust. There was no sense in foundering a good horse just to take the edge off his frustration and fury. No sense in anything. He looked at the quivering ashwood shaft, wrenched the tip free of the ground and walked Lyard over to his audience.

'Christ!' declared Renard, eyes round with admiration. 'I'd hate to face you across a battleground!'

Aubrey FitzNigel was watching his lord with a peculiar look in his pale eyes. He knew Adam playing and Adam for real, and just now they had been permitted to witness a rare, deadly glimpse of the latter.

Miles kept his own eyes lowered and his thoughts to himself, but when Renard began to demand enthusiastically to be shown how it was done, he cut him brusquely short as was an elder's prerogative.

'It's all right.' Adam attempted and succeeded a smile as he slid down from Lyard's back. 'We all have to learn some time – don't we?'

CHAPTER 5

FRANCE,
LATE AUTUMN 1126

WILLIAM LE CLITO, claimant to the Duchy of Normandy and the English crown, both currently held most firmly by his uncle Henry, shoved the girl impatiently off his lap and scowled across the room at the immaculately dressed man drinking wine on the Saracen couch.

'You said it would be simple,' he accused, and pitched his voice in sing-song mimicry, 'An arrow from the rocks above, or a sudden ambush in the forest, or even a second White Ship – but there she is, safe at her father's court in London without so much as a scratch to show for your efforts, and all the barons and bishops preparing to do her homage!'

Warrin de Mortimer stroked his close-cropped flaxen beard and regarded the petulant man opposite with an irritation that did not show on his heavy, handsome features. Le Clito – The Prince. Prince of nothing. King Henry had robbed his own brother, le Clito's father, of England, Normandy, and his freedom in that order; but stung by conscience and the protests of his nobility, had left his son at liberty. The boy, now grown to manhood, had a genuine claim to the English crown. His bloodline was as strong or stronger than that of Mathilda, for his father was William the Conqueror's eldest son, as Henry was the youngest. The King's new young wife, praise God, was proving unable to give him a replacement, and Mathilda was the only serious impediment remaining.

'Yes,' he said to the glowering, stocky young man. 'And it would have been simple if she hadn't had so professional an

escort and you had provided me with more than fools.
We made several attempts, but de Lacey was ready for each
one.'

'He knew?'

Warrin twitched his shoulders irritably. 'Some of the information got back to him, but I put a stop to that. For the most
part he was too experienced in that sort of warfare to be caught
out. You don't grow up with men like Miles le Gallois and
Guyon of Ravenstow for tutors and emerge a simpleton in the
art of skirmish. Mathilda's escort did take wounds, but none
of them fatal.'

The girl sat down on a rug before the hearth and, piqued at
being ignored, hitched one side of her gown up high. Unfasten-
ing a garter, she began to roll the hose down – slowly and
provocatively – from a slender white thigh. Le Clito's eyes
faltered and swivelled to his mistress. She curved a smile of
malicious satisfaction at de Mortimer.

'So much for all the money paid out to get the information,'
le Clito grunted. 'We might as well have saved ourselves the
time and expense.'

King Louis' time and expense, Warrin thought cynically.
William le Clito had no serious funds of his own, but relied on
Henry's enemies to provide them for him so that he could
continue to be a thorn in his uncle's side.

'I intend recouping some of it before next Candlemas,' he
said with a smile, and contemplated le Clito's mistress. Her hair
was as brown and glossy as a palfrey's hide, her face daintily
shaped with huge, clear eyes. A tasty morsel, but not the
remotest challenge to the feast awaiting him at home.

Le Clito raised his brows. 'How?'

Warrin looked at his nails and admired a ring on his little
finger. 'I'm taking the next galley to England, where I shall
marry our informant's widow.'

Le Clito started to laugh, realized that his companion was
not jesting, and leaned forward, his mouth hanging open.
'You're what?' The girl extended her toes and wiggled them

at the fire, then reclined on her elbows, back arched, breasts outthrust, loose hair sweeping the sable rug.

'That way I can legally lay my hands on the silver and whatever else is bestowed in his strongboxes. I'll get a keep and three manor houses, and a blood-bond with the Earl of Ravenstow whose daughter the widow happens to be – and a very beautiful widow at that. She makes yonder wench look like a crone.'

Le Clito stared at him with glazed eyes, then he refocused. 'You sly bastard!' he chuckled.

'God helps those who help themselves.' Warrin polished the ring on his expensive fur-trimmed tunic and looked nonchalant.

'And is the lady in question agreeable?' Le Clito picked up his wine and grinned at him over the rim of the goblet, beckoning the girl from her sulky pose on the rug.

'I don't foresee any difficulties.' He rose, extending his tall, powerful frame in a luxurious stretch. 'I've trodden very softly around her these last few months and spoken her father fair. My own father's a personal friend of his and anxious for the match, so there's been some persuasion from that side too. All there is left to do now is obtain your uncle Henry's permission, being as le Chevalier's lands are in his gift. I have no reason to think he will refuse me.' He gave le Clito an acid grin.

The girl snuggled herself down beside le Clito and rubbed her hand over the v-shape of dark chest hair exposed by his loosened shirtlaces. 'All well and good for you,' he grumbled. 'A fat purse and a warm bed, but what of the future? I'm the heir in direct male tail to my grandsire the Conqueror, the eldest son of the eldest son. Are you going to abandon me and bow to my uncle's will, accept that high-handed bitch to rule you – and whatever cur he drags from the gutter to be her husband?'

Warrin grimaced. 'My father will give his fealty for our lands, not I. You know I'd rather sit in the stink of a blast of air from the devil's arse than put my hands between hers in homage. I'll be at Windsor for the swearing because I've got to be. I'll let you know what happens; find out who we can depend upon to renege at the first opportunity. Bigod for certain.' He shrugged philosophically. 'I had to get rid of le Chevalier, he was playing both sides of the coin, but I've still got some contacts at court.'

The girl's expert hand wandered lower and le Clito shifted on the settle to accommodate her ministrations.

'You ought to get married again,' Warrin advised as he lifted the curtain to leave. 'No good begetting bastards. Ask your uncle. He's got twenty-two of them, and not one of them can inherit his crown.'

THE BRINDLE BITCH yawned and scratched vigorously at a tender spot behind her ear. Her collar jinked. Four pups, bright-eyed, fat-bellied and inquisitive, tumbled and played beside her. Sunlight shafted down from an unshuttered window and bathed their fuzzy infant fur, picking out the elegant red and grey barring on their dam's adult wiry back.

Judith pushed the shears through the crimson velvet marked out on her sewing-trestle, the tip of her tongue protruding between her lips as she concentrated. It was to be a court robe for Renard and there was precious little time left to sew it, for they were well into November now, the slaughter month. The boy kept on growing; his best tunic, stitched only this midsummer, now revealed his wristbones and barely touched his knees when it had been made to hang below them. Flanders cloth it had been, of an expensive, bright deep blue, lavishly embroidered with thread of silver and scarlet. It would do for Henry later on, so all was not lost, but the new garment had still to be stitched, and prayers said with the sewing that Renard would not grow again for a while at least.

The curtain clacked on its rings. Heulwen exclaimed as she tripped over a curious pup, then swore as it dug its sharp little milk teeth into the hem of her gown and tried to play a growling tug-of-war. With some difficulty, she persuaded it to let go, and toed it gently sideways towards its dozing dam.

'Have you finished?' Judith deftly turned a corner. Crunch, crunch went the shears in the velvet. She looked a brief enquiry across the richly-coloured cloth.

'For the nonce.' Heulwen picked up a small pot of scented goose-grease salve from the coffer, took a dollop and began to work it into her dry, cold-reddened hands. Three pigs had been slaughtered for salting, and the supervising had involved a certain degree of demonstration. Washing excrement from pigs' intestines, scraping them and then packing them down in dry salt for later use as sausage skins was a form of purgatory, but then so was needlecraft, and on balance, Heulwen thought that she would rather wash sausage skins.

'I've left Mary filling the bladders with lard and Githa and Edith making a brine solution. I'll go down and check it in a while, but they've done it a hundred times before and should be all right. Thomas is dealing with the hams. We'll need more salt before Christmas.'

'I know.' Judith worked her way to the end and laid down the shears. 'You can help me pin this now you're here.'

Heulwen screwed up her face. Judith began to smile. 'You need the practice,' she teased gently, 'soon you will have a man of your own to sew for again.'

Heulwen felt the colour burn her cheeks and brow. She picked up a pin-cushion. 'Nothing is settled yet,' she muttered defensively. 'I know Papa's had Warrin's letter formally asking for me, but the King has yet to approve — and for that matter, so have I. Besides, Warrin's still in Normandy.'

'But due home any day now?' Judith started methodically to pin the cut edges together. Her fingers worked nimbly for a moment, then she paused and looked thoughtfully at her stepdaughter. 'In some ways the sooner the better for you, I think.'

'And you too, Mama.'

Judith's scrutiny sharpened, but she took no offence, indeed smiled a little. Several weeks of each other's company had begun to rub the amity a little threadbare, for much as the Countess was fond of her stepdaughter, she did not possess the calm, maternal patience that would have served in her best interests. Instead she was wont to snap, or say something tart, and Heulwen would bristle, bite her tongue, or occasionally retort in kind. It was hardly surprising that there should be frictions, Judith thought. Heulwen had married Ralph at the age of fifteen, and been a chatelaine in her own right for more than ten years. Adjusting to the codes of her former life for no matter how temporary a time must have been very difficult, especially when faced with an older woman who smiled, but resented the intrusion.

'Yes,' she laughed. 'For me too. I will relish the peace and quiet!' And then she became serious. 'But daughter, you must be sure that this match with Warrin is what you truly want for yourself. You know that your father and I would never push you against your wishes.'

Heulwen drew breath to say that yes, it was what she truly wanted, her mind made up, but what came out of her mouth was not of her conscious choosing. 'Mama, do you think that Warrin is a suitable match?'

Judith pursed her lips and pondered the matter while she set half-a-dozen more pins into the velvet. 'Suitable, yes,' she said at length. 'But whether he is right for you only time will tell. You've known him since childhood. He's ambitious, self-opinionated, and about as sensitive to the feelings of others as this keep wall. He'll expect you to decorate his bed and board as befits a man of his standing.' She straightened up and glanced at Heulwen's anxious face, seeking something to say that would even the balance.

'You certainly won't lack for anything. Warrin's always been generous. I daresay you'll even have maids enough to do all your sewing.' She smiled briefly, then sobered as she added, 'But if you have a need to go beyond the gilded trappings, then I would advise you to think again. To Warrin de Mortimer you will be a trophy, cherished for how highly others will envy him, rather than cherished for your own sake.'

'I realize that Mama, and it does not bother me,' Heulwen said with conviction. 'In fact I . . .'

'Heulwen, you've got a visitor,' Renard announced, lounging into the bower. He was eating a cinnamon and apple pasty filched from beneath the cook's indignant nose, and his narrow grey eyes were alight with mischief.

'Warrin?' She abandoned the pin-cushion and raised her hands to check the set of her veil and the tidiness of her braids.

'Wrong,' he said cheerfully, coming further into the room, and having crammed the rest of the pasty into his mouth, stooped at the hearth to pick up one of the hound pups. It wriggled and sought to lick him with an ecstatic pink tongue. 'Adam de Lacey.'

Heulwen had duskily blushed at the thought of Warrin de Mortimer. Now her colour faded, leaving her ice-white. Her hands fell nervelessly from her braids. 'Adam?' she repeated weakly. 'Why does he want to see me?'

Renard gave her a mocking grin, head held awry to avoid the strivings of the pup. 'Perhaps he wants to arrange another midnight tryst in the solar,' he suggested.

'Renard!' snapped his mother, glaring round at him with extreme disfavour. 'If you spent as much time exercising your brain as you did your tongue, you would have a wit to be feared indeed!'

'Sorry,' he said with the graceless joy of one who is not sorry in the least, and knows that he can cozen his way back into favour by way of his formidable charm. 'He's brought you your horses. You did say that you were going to sell them in Windsor didn't you? And you'll have to face him sooner or later.' He held the pup in the crook of his arm like a baby, tickled its pink tummy, and wandered over to the sewing trestle to look with idle interest upon his mother's endeavours.

She frowned up at him, dwarfed by his height. Childhood was still stamped on the face of the emerging man. There were crumbs on his upper lip amidst the dark smudge of a shaved moustache line. The crimson velvet would suit him very well. He was tall like Guyon and dark, with the grey, smoky eyes of his grandfather the King. He also possessed his grandfather's sleight of tongue, married to a lethal adolescent lack of tact.

The future Earl of Ravenstow and the responsibility, God help her, lay at her feet.

Renard kissed her cheek and looked across at his half-sister, eyes dancing. 'Do you want to send me back down with a message, tell him you're too busy sewing?'

The thought of what Renard might say galvanized Heulwen out of one kind of panic into another. She put the pins carefully aside, resisting the temptation to stick them in her brother instead of his new tunic. 'No Renard, that would be a lie, and anyway, I'd be pleased to see him. One misunderstanding does not make for a lifetime's enmity.' She widened her eyes sarcastically. 'What do you imagine happened in the solar? Or perhaps, knowing your mind, I shouldn't ask. The pup's just wet on you.'

'What?' Renard looked, swore, dumped the dog down, and began hauling off his tunic to his mother's stern reprimand about his language. Heulwen made her escape.

It was stupid to be so afraid, she thought as she twisted her way down the turret stairs and entered the great hall. Stupid to feel so nervously sick. 'He is my brother,' she said to herself, wishing that it were true, but that part of her past was gone forever, banished by the sight of a lean-muscled warrior in a bathtub. No, she amended, it was not stupid to fear danger or to panic when forced to greet it face to face.

Adam was in the courtyard talking to Eadric, his furred cloak thrown back from his shoulders, the cold sunlight reflecting off his hauberk and the ornate buckle and studs on his swordbelt. The groom had custody of Sorcerer and Jester. Lyard's reins were held by Adam himself, and as he spoke to the servant, his free hand caressed the bright sorrel neck, thick now in its full-grown winter fell.

Heulwen took a deep breath, gathered her courage in both hands, and walked across the ward to greet him.

'You wanted to see me, Adam?'

He turned to her, a blank, stiff smile on his face. His hand left Lyard's neck and dropped to his side. 'Yes, I did.'

'Will you come within to the hall?'

He hesitated. She saw reluctance warring with courtesy. His eyes were wary, his face the mask of his first arrival, guarding all emotion. Ralph had been the same, only his mask had been one of mobile laughter. Men laughed with him – women too, and never penetrated beyond that first vital layer. She shivered, and not just because the wind was cutting through her garments.

Adam gave Lyard's bridle to Eadric, inclined his head in resignation, and followed her back across the ward. A woman came up to her and asked a question about the pigs they were dissecting. Adam stopped and stared round; a serjeant was drilling his men, pikes scraping on gravel and clacking in forested symmetry, responding to bellowed commands. The maidservant departed with her instructions. Against the fore-building entrance, two small boys were playing marbles. One of them raised his head and flashed a brilliant blue-green glance at his sister and the visitor.

'Why aren't you at your lessons?' Heulwen demanded sharply. 'Where's Brother Alred?'

'Gone into town with Papa.' William pulled a face. 'We've to do our lessons this afternoon.' His look flicked again over Adam and stopped covetously on the ornate gilded scabbard and the contrastingly austere swordhilt protruding from it.

Heulwen looked at Adam. 'William wasn't here last time you visited,' she remarked, and then to the child, 'William, this is Adam de Lacey, my foster-brother. I don't think that you'll remember him.'

Adam crouched down and picked up one of the round, smooth stones, his expression carefully impassive, aware that she had said this deliberately.

'Can I look at your sword?' William asked forthrightly, eyes avid with longing. Belatedly he remembered to add 'please.'

Adam shot the marble at a larger one near the wall. He heard the crack of stone upon stone and briefly closed his eyes, fists clenched upon his knees. Then he stood up and, smiling down at the boy, drew the weapon from its fleece-lined scabbard.

'William, you shouldn't be so . . .'

'He's all right,' Adam interrupted in a relaxed voice, concealing the tension that was gripping him. 'I was the same at his age about your father's blade — about any blade come to that, because they were real and mine was made of whalebone.'

William took it reverently. His small fist closed around the leather-bound grip and he held it up to the light so that the iron gleamed bluishly. Inlaid down the blade in latten was the Latin inscription *O Sancta*, repeated several times to make a decorative pattern. The pommel was an irregular semi-circle of inlaid polished beechwood. 'Papa says I can have a proper sword of my own next year day,' William said eagerly.

'With a proper rebated blade,' Heulwen added. 'You do enough damage with the plain wooden one you've got now!'

Adam chuckled. 'I can imagine!' Gently, with more than a hint of poignant understanding, he took the sword back from the child, slotted it home, tousled the tumbled black curls, and continued with Heulwen into the keep.

She sent a servant to fetch him hot wine and offered him a chair on the dais set close to a brazier. He unfastened his cloak and draped it across the trestle, and unlatching his scabbard, placed it on top.

'Do you want to unarm?' Heulwen indicated his hauberk as he stretched out his legs to the warmth.

He shook his head. 'Thank you, but no, it's only a passing visit. I won't keep you long.'

Heulwen bit her lip and looked down, wanting to apologize for the way that their last encounter had ended, but unsure that a reconciliation was in her own best interests. White-hot physical attraction frightened her. She had sat at its blaze before, watched it go out, and shivered over the ashes of its corpse.

The maid brought them wine and a platter of the cinnamon apple pasties, and returned to her duties. Across the hall at another trestle, Adam's men sat around several substantial rye loaves, a dish of salted curd–cheese, and flagons of cider. Watching them Adam said, 'I've returned you Ralph's stallions so that you can decide whether you want to sell them at Windsor.'

Heulwen poured wine for them both, keeping her eyes lowered from his – not that he was looking at her. 'What are they worth? Have you had time to find out?' She spoke quickly, feeling flustered.

'The bay is almost fully trained and sufficiently well-bred to fetch you between seventy and eighty marks,' he said, his tone brisk and coldly professional. 'The piebald's not of the same calibre, but because of his markings you should get at least fifty marks for him. If I continue to school him over the winter, he should fetch a top price of around sixty.'

'And Lyard?' she matched his tone.

'That's really why I came.' He transferred his gaze from contemplation of his men and fixed hers instead. 'I want to buy him from you, Heulwen. I'll give you a hundred marks.'

She forgot her circumspection and openly gaped at him, stunned. 'How much?' she gasped faintly.

'It is what he is worth.'

His eyes were suddenly bright and intense, like those of Renard's new falcon, and he was leaning forward in the chair, obviously filled with the determination to convince her if she baulked. 'Adam no, I cannot accept such a sum from you!'

'But you would accept it from a complete stranger at Windsor,' he pointed out.

'I wouldn't feel guilty about taking a stranger's coin.'

He set his jaw, picked up the goblet, rotated it, then riveted his eyes on hers across the wine. 'Heulwen, I'm asking you as a boon, as a favour to me. Let me have him. You've slapped me in the face once. In Christ's name, leave me some small shred of self-esteem. Do you know what it cost me to come here today?'

She inhaled, mouth open, changed her mind and reached instead to drink her wine. 'Yes, I do know,' she said after a

59

swallow. 'The same that it cost me to come down from the bower to face you.'

Adam considered her from beneath his brows. His mouth curved into its familiar dark smile. '*Pax?*' he said gravely.

'*Vobiscum.*' She returned the smile, feeling as though a great dark cloud had been lifted from her horizon. 'All right Adam, for the sake of our mutual self-esteem, you can have Lyard, but I won't accept the full price – and before you start arguing, let me remind you that I owe you for the training and stabling of the other two horses. Eighty marks I'll take for him, not a penny more.'

'And if Warrin thinks that you have considerably undersold a part of his future property?' he asked with an edge to his voice.

'Then Warrin can just go whistle ... Oh Christ's wounds, no!' She went white.

'What's wr ...' He followed her horrified gaze down the hall and saw, as if conjured from thought, Warrin de Mortimer advancing up it in the all too solid flesh, cloak bannering behind him with the vigour of his stride, brows slanted down over his rich blue eyes at the sight meeting him on the dais.

'Adam, I will kill you myself if you start anything,' Heulwen hissed from the side of her mouth, as she rose and prepared to greet her husband designate.

'Me?' he said sarcastically. 'And why should I want to start anything? Do you think I want to be on your conscience for the rest of your life?'

Heulwen's knees went to jelly as the double-edged barb hit home, and Adam had perforce to lunge and grab her elbow before she fell headlong down the dais steps. At their foot, Warrin de Mortimer set his hands on his swordbelt and regarded Adam with a mingling of irritation and strong dislike. Heulwen freed herself from Adam's grasp and went to take Warrin's cloak with a warm smile of greeting. As she reached for his pin, he circled her waist with his hands and bent to claim her lips. The kiss did not linger, but it signalled possession.

'Home and unscathed from your jaunt with the Empress, I see,' he said to Adam.

'So it would seem.' Adam leaned across the table for his scabbard, and without haste began to belt it on.

De Mortimer gave him a look of contemptuous amusement, as though he were watching a truculent child over whom he had a clear and confident advantage. 'You know,' he mused, 'it doesn't seem a moment since we were sparring in that tilt yard out there.' The amusement showed itself in a nasty grin. 'I hear that you have learned from the drubbings I gave you.'

'A great deal more than you, Warrin,' Adam answered evenly, and turned to Heulwen as if the other man did not exist. 'The money is in my saddlebags. I'll have Austin bring it in to you. What about Jester?'

'I – I don't know,' she stammered, floundering in the currents of hostility she could feel emanating from the two men. 'I haven't had time to think.'

Adam flickered a jaundiced glance at de Mortimer. 'I'll leave him then. If I'm any judge of character, you'll not be selling him at Windsor either. As to the other matter, leave it in my hands. If I hear anything, I'll let you know.'

She nodded and swallowed. 'Thank you, Adam.'

'Think nothing of it.' His mouth was wry as he swept on his cloak and leaving his untasted wine, brushed past her and de Mortimer to summon his men.

'Aren't you going to congratulate us?' needled de Mortimer. 'I'll almost be your brother-by-marriage, won't I?'

Adam did not turn round. It was beyond him to do so, and he had to swallow his gorge to answer. 'Congratulations,' he said through stiff lips, and strode down the hall away from the temptation to do something utterly stupid.

Once outside in the cold, clean air of the bailey, he let go, crashing his fist into the solid forebuilding wall in lieu of Warrin de Mortimer's handsome, contemptuous face. His skin split and peeped away in small grated strips from the force. He looked at the blood, his chest heaving, welcoming the physical pain that blotted out thought.

'He affects me like that too,' Renard said strolling down the stairs to join him. 'He's so damned patronizing, treats me as if I were no older than William.'

'You act that way sometimes.'

'Are you going back to Thorneyford now?'

Adam examined his raw, bunched knuckles, the price of holding onto control for too long, then flickered a dark glance at Renard. 'Why?'

'Oh, no reason.' Renard shrugged nonchalantly. 'I thought I'd ride with you. Starlight needs the exercise and I'd rather not stay here while Warrin crows and struts before Heulwen like a dunghill cock longing to tread a hen. Did you see all the rings he had on his fingers?'

Adam looked at his ally and found a brief smile. 'Yes.'

'And he's wearing spikenard. I could smell it on him a mile away!' Renard wrinkled his nose. 'Jesu God, there's not going to be much room for Heulwen in his heart. He's madly in love with himself!'

Without comment, Adam went to Lyard, unlatched a saddlebag, and withdrawing a leather money pouch, handed it to his hovering squire. 'Go within, Austin, and deliver it to Lady Heulwen. Tell her that the other twenty are her wedding present. She will know what you mean.'

'Yes, lord.'

Adam watched him lope off, then turned back to the horse, and unslinging his helmet from the pommel, put it on. 'You'll need armour,' he said to Renard. 'But I suppose you know that. Do you have a hauberk?'

'I have the one that was my brother's before he drowned. It fits me better than it used to fit him. Will you wait for me?'

Adam nodded at the dun stallion resting slack-hipped beside Lyard. 'You can use my remount instead of your own horse if you like. I noticed you were outgrowing that grey when you came to Thorneyford.'

Renard's dark eyes kindled. 'Thanks Adam, you're a friend!' He thumped the latter's back with such enthusiasm that Adam staggered and wheezed.

'What do you do to your enemies?' he asked weakly.

'What's this for?' Warrin de Mortimer lifted the bag of silver just delivered to Heulwen by the snub-nosed squire, and jinked it back down on the trestle.

Despite the offhand tone of his asking, Heulwen could tell that he was irritated. Two deep, half-moon curves imprinted the flesh between the thin mouth and strong, straight nose, and the nostrils were slightly pinched. 'I sold him Lyard.'

Warrin flicked his forefinger against the side of the bag. 'For a goodly sum by the weight of it.'

'He insisted on giving me more than was due.' Her voice shook, betraying her. 'He's very stubborn. I didn't want it.'

'So stiff-necked that one day someone is going to snap it for him,' Warrin muttered.

'You?'

He laughed and shrugged his brows. 'Is it so obvious?'

'You were like a pair of dogs circling each other, waiting for the right moment to leap at one another's throat.'

'I don't like the bastard, I'll admit that outright.' He extended his hands to the brazier. 'Never knew his place as a junior squire, and I doubt he does yet.'

Heulwen watched him, her stomach a churning mass of tiny butterflies. His hands were steady over the heat. Broad and powerful, they did not suit the various rings with which he had bedecked them. Her father very seldom wore jewellery and neither did Adam. She thought of him and chewed her lip.

'What was the other matter of which he spoke?' he asked into her silence.

She shook her head, knowing a grievous mistake when she saw one. 'It was trifling,' she dissembled. 'Ralph sold a horse and I want to buy him back.'

'You could have asked me to do that,' he looked at her reproachfully. 'There was no need to involve Adam de Lacey.'

'You were in Normandy, and besides, Adam knows the owner.' His jaw tightened, but so did hers in determined response. 'Warrin, don't scowl at me like that. I am not your property yet and unlikely to be so if you're going to make a jealous pother out of nothing. Adam has been my foster-brother since I was two years old. If you cannot tolerate his occasional presence on mutual ground like Ravenstow, then you might as well tear up that letter you wrote to Papa and seek another wife!'

Immediately he was contrite, turning from the brazier to take her hands in his, eyes searching her face. 'Heulwen, I'm sorry. It's just that I arrived here eager to greet you, and I did not expect to find Adam de Lacey sprawled in your father's chair . . . '

'And you are accustomed to having your own way in all things,' she agreed sarcastically.

'Yes I am!' And before she could rebel, his hands had slipped around her waist again and his breath was warm on her cheek as his lips slanted down to claim hers and imprint them with that very same will. His arms tightened and his tongue probed. Heulwen stood passively within the embrace, neither welcoming nor rejecting it, but it was sufficient for him that she was warm and pliant in his arms, and he persisted, driven by the anxiety to possess, and a more basic, instinctual need.

The smell of spikenard was too powerful to be pleasant. It irritated her nose, made her want to sneeze. He was wearing his hauberk and the links began to bruise her arms where they were trapped by his. A small, inner voice asked her if she would have noticed such discomforts if Adam had been holding her. She tried to ignore it and respond to Warrin, but the pain and the heaviness of his jaw grinding on hers made it impossible. She broke the kiss. 'Warrin, you're crushing me.'

He was breathing hard and his eyes were a bright, opaque sky colour. He licked his lips, came to his senses sufficiently to realize where he was and what was at stake and, taking a grip on himself, released her to fold his long body into the chair that Adam had previously been occupying.

'In Christ's name Heulwen, let us soon be wed,' he said, his voice rough. 'I know you're still mourning Ralph, but time doesn't stand still — well, not unless you're abroad talking cheeses with some stuff-witted steward on your father's Norman lands, counting the hours until you can come home and gladden your heart with a sight such as you.'

'Flatterer,' she said lightly, and sat down beside him.

'It's true though. Heulwen, you're driving me mad.' He shook his head as though bemused at his own declaration.

She lowered her eyes. His arm rested on the trestle close to her dropped gaze. She rubbed her index finger upon his wrist, stroking the wiry golden hairs the wrong way. 'Once you and Papa have formally agreed the terms and you have asked the King for Ralph's lands, we can be married without further delay,' she said softly.

'It cannot come quickly enough for me.' He flicked her a glance and spread his legs slightly to ease the pressure across his congested loins, thinking of her full, but slender body beneath his in the marriage bed, and moreover of a chest full of recently minted silver — he smiled.

'Nor me,' she said, her own tone more grim than eager, her mind upon Adam and the lessons learned from her time with Ralph.

'No chance of a hot bathtub?' he asked hopefully, the glance narrowing, decidedly lustful.

Heulwen stopped stroking his wrist and stood up. 'A cold one might suit your need better,' she laughed. 'I'll see what the maids can do.'

It was only when she reached the haven of the tower stairs and stood there in the cold, musty silence that she realized how badly she was shaking.

CHAPTER 7

'SNOW,' GRUMBLED SWEYN, twitching his powerful shoulders and glowering at the amassing banks of greyish-yellow cloud piling in fast from the direction of the Welsh mountain ranges, driven by a bitter wind.

Adam's troop had emerged from the forest and onto the drovers' road that would lead them in a few miles to the Thorneyford fork. Behind them the trees clacked their branches and swayed like grey dancers striving to shake off the last vestments of parchment-dry leaves. The grass at the edge of the road was rank and limp, the road itself a muddy ploughed morass of hoofprints and the gouged out tracks of iron wain-wheels. Come full winter, it would qualify for the title of bog.

Lyard snorted and swung his head low to explore the unap-petizing fare at his hooves. Adam let the reins slide and turned in the saddle to look at Renard. 'Do you still want to come with us?'

Renard contemplated the threatening clouds with wind-stung eyes. He was wearing undergarments and a thick tunic, topped by a heavily padded gambeson and mail hauberk, all overlaid by a fur-lined cloak, and was thus, despite the wind, warm enough. The stallion beneath him was a pure joy to ride after the shortcomings of poor Starlight.

'I'd rather be snowed in with you than Warrin de Mortimer,' he smiled, and shaking the bridle, urged the dun onto the road.

'It's only November. It won't come to that.'

The smile became a mocking grin. 'Why take that chance? I notice that you didn't linger.'

The helm with its broad nasal bar concealed much of his

youth, and with the extra padding lent by his armour, he could have been a man grown. 'If you're coming, shut up,' Adam said frostily.

Renard shrugged, but the white glint of his teeth disappeared as he rode forwards.

'He's still a boy,' murmured Aubrey, joining his lord as they began heading into the sharp wind.

'For which I'm making allowances, or hadn't you noticed?'

'Oh I'd noticed,' Aubrey murmured, 'but then he's like his half-sister isn't he? Likes to season a stew for the pure mischief of seeing others grimace when they taste it. I know how you were, and still are over that red-haired Circe. And it's no use giving me one of your looks. It's the truth and you know it. I was there at her wedding remember? Who do you think it was fetched Lady Judith when you sank all that wine? Who do you think sat by your pallet while you recovered your senses, or what was left of them? And now she's free to wed and she's done it again. How far will you go when it's Warrin de Mortimer who takes her to bed?'

Adam's fingers jerked on the reins. 'Aubrey, let me be, you're worse than the boy,' he said through his teeth, and beneath him Lyard danced and tossed his head, rolling his eyes to show their whites.

'Sweyn and I were only saying to each other last night that what you need is to take a wife. There are bound to be barons in surplus this Christmastide with daughters for sale, and it's time you thought about settling to the yoke and breeding up heirs instead of living on dreams.'

Adam's temper snapped. He rounded on the knight to snarl his displeasure but got no further than 'When I want your opinion I'll ...' And then the breath locked in his throat and his eyes widened in horrified astonishment as an arrow sang through the narrow triangle of space between his hand on Lyard's reins and Lyard's neck, burying itself in the horse-hair pad of Aubrey's saddle flap. The heavy sky began to precipitate not snow, but death-tipped arrows, and Welshmen, either afoot and armed with bows or astride their small, tough mountain ponies, were pounding after them, mouths agape to yell outlandish war cries, their short swords glinting.

'God's fucking eyes!' Aubrey blasphemed through clenched teeth and, trying to control his plunging stallion, groped for his sword.

Adam wrestled his shield down onto his left arm. 'Close formation!' he bellowed, 'and don't give them any chance to hamstring the horses! Sweyn, get to Renard and guard him with your life!' It was all he had time to say, for the battle then closed its gaping jaws and swallowed them whole.

The first Renard knew of the rapid Welsh assault was the arrow that ripped a hole in his cloak and slammed into his stallion's belly. The animal screamed and went up on its hindlegs, forehooves tearing at the clouds, then came down stiff-legged and bucked. The high saddle and Renard's own swift reflexes kept him astride, but that was all that could be said. Of controlling a gut-shot horse there was not a hope in hell. If the dun went down, he would be crushed to death; and if it threw him in its frenzy he faced being trampled or broken by the force of the fall.

There was no time to think, only to act on instinct. He released the reins, kicked his feet free of the stirrups, and as the dun came down on all fours between twisting bucks, he used the high pommel to vault down from its back. He stumbled and felt his ankle wrench, but was able to duck away from the destrier's pain-filled madness and draw his sword. His shield still hung from the saddle and there was not the remotest possibility of him reaching it without being brained by the plunging shod hooves.

Battle clashed around him. A burly, black-eyed Welshman who looked as though he ate horseshoes for breakfast came at him with an iron-studded oak mace. Renard dodged the first vicious swing of the weapon. His enemy was laughing. Battle took some men that way, and obviously this one saw his opponent as a mockery of opposition. '*Cenau!*' he said contemptuously. A whelp indeed Renard might be, but of a warrior breed, trained from the cradle to fight. As the Welshman swung his mace for the kill, Renard ran under the blow and slashed at his enemy's bare thighs. Blood sprayed, spattering Renard's face as the honed edge sliced muscle, tendon and artery. The mace caught him glancingly on the shoulder, but it was the off-balanced blow of a mortally wounded man going down.

'*Yr cenau gan dant!*' Renard gasped, breathing hard as he finished it.

'Renard, ware behind!' roared Sweyn.

He spun quickly, but not quickly enough to avoid the thrust of a spear. Frantically he twisted as he felt his hauberk rings give and splay, and a vicious iron point tear his gambeson and score his ribs. He was caught like a fish on a spit, and in a moment he was going to die, the last thing he saw the snow-bound sky and the frightened, triumphant young face of his killer.

The thrust home was never executed because Sweyn reached him, and cursing, rose in his stirrups to bring the full weight of his axe down upon the young Welshman's skull which was only protected by a cap of *cuir-bouilli*, and thus split open like a carelessly dropped egg. Violently jerking, the body fell, tearing the lancehead free as it went.

'You bloody young fool, where's your shield?' Sweyn howled.

'On my saddle,' Renard said hoarsely.

The Saxon glared round and saw the foundered, threshing dun with Renard's shield now rolled to splintered remains beneath him. 'Here, take Fury,' he said gruffly and swung down from the saddle.

'I couldn't ...'

'Hell's death, boy, do as you're told. We're not in a damned tilt yard today! You're a liability on foot, one we can't afford!'

Colour flared up across Renard's cheekbones. He opened his mouth to say something, but thought better of it and jammed it shut, instead taking the black's bridle and hiking himself aloft. The pain in his side burned like fire, but he set his jaw and refused to show it; indeed, within the space of ten heartbeats did not even have the time to think of it as the fighting redoubled in fierceness, and the lessons learned by rote in the safety of a courtyard, and the grimly determined Saxon swinging an English axe at his stirrup, became all that stood between himself and certain death.

It was over. Adam slid down from Lyard's back, wiped his sword on the cloven corpse at his feet and stared into the spectral November silence that the retreating Welsh had left in their stead. The road was strewn with bodies, most of them Welsh, but among them were two of his own men, and another who had taken an arrow in the belly and would not last out the night. Bare sword in his hand, he studied the corpses and brushed at a persistent thread of blood running from a bone-deep nick in his jaw. There had been no time to secure his ventail.

'This one's still alive. Shall I kill him lord?' One of his Angevins was kneeling over a Welshman, hand grasping the cropped black curls to jerk back the unconscious head and

Adam walked over to look. It was a young man whose life hung in the balance, barely twenty years old, he would have said. His tunic was a plainly woven homespun and his short leggings were bound with crude leather thongs, but his boots had faded gilding around the top and his sword-belt was set with carnelians. 'How badly is he wounded, Thierry?'

'Bad enough. This lump on his head's bigger than a gull's egg, and he's taken a deep slash to the thigh.'

Adam dabbed again at his bloody jaw and made a swift assessment of the youth's chances. 'Bring him with us. He may be of some value if he doesn't die of wound fever or stiffening sickness.' He looked round. 'Sweyn, where's Renard?'

The Saxon jerked his head to the side of the road. 'Sick,' he growled. 'First taste o' hard battle, but he came through well in the thick of it. You all right, my lord?'

'I'll do.' He glanced up and blinked as a snowflake landed on his lashes. He sheathed his sword. The Welsh youth was draped unceremoniously over the back of a hill pony someone had captured. Adam took Lyard's bridle and walked him over to Renard. The lad was wiping his reddened dagger upon the bleached grass, but when he saw Adam approaching he stood up, and with trembling hands sheathed the weapon. His face was tear-streaked and ghastly-white, his teeth chattering uncontrollably, and not because it was cold. Death had breathed on him – his own and other men's, and even after the Welsh retreat he had been forced to kill again.

'I'm sorry, Adam,' he swallowed. 'Your dun. He was gut-shot, I had to do it.'

Adam followed Renard's gaze to the dun. A Welsh arrow protruded from its flank and the blood ran in rivulets from its slit throat. A faithful, sturdy companion, that particular stallion had carried him in safety to the German court and back again, had stood him in good stead for the past six years. 'Nothing else you could have done,' he said steadily. 'Just thank Christ it was his gut and not yours.' He glanced briefly over his shoulder to where Aubrey and another knight were gently lifting the dying man onto his horse. Mercifully, he was unconscious.

Renard wiped his hands together. There was blood on them and it was darkly crusted beneath his fingernails. 'I've never killed a man before,' he said, throat working. 'In a tilt yard it doesn't matter. The swords are blunt, and if they are not, then your opponent is made of straw. He doesn't cry out and bleed and die at your feet with his eyes on you ...' His voice shook.

Adam set one arm compassionately across Renard's shoulders. 'I felt like that the first time too, and the second, and the third. Everyone does, but it is a lesson you have to learn for yourself. No one can tell you.'

Renard's dark grey eyes went blank. 'It gets easier then?' he said through stiff lips.

'You learn to shut it out,' Adam gave a wry shrug, 'you have to. If you had not killed him, then he would have killed you.'

'I suppose so,' Renard said bleakly.

'I know so,' Adam tightened his grip and shook him slightly, imparting reassurance. Renard winced and drew a hiss of pain through his teeth, and his hand went up to clutch at his side. Adam released him, eyes sharpening. 'You idiot, why didn't you say you were hurt?'

'It's not serious – well at least I don't think so. Sweyn killed the man before he could put any weight behind his thrust.' Renard closed his eyes and fought the urge to retch as he saw again the axe cleaving down and the head splicing apart beneath it, life scattering into the wind.

'Are you fit to climb into a saddle?' Adam indicated Lyard. 'You'll have to sit pillion like a wench, but the way this snow's starting to come down I'd rather reach Thorneyford before dusk, and the Welsh may well have reinforcements close by. We couldn't withstand another brawl like this one.' He mounted up himself and extended his hand. Renard grimaced through clenched teeth, but hauled himself competently astride, and only when secure did he hang his head and let out his breath in a gasp of pain.

One of the men-at-arms stripped the dun stallion of its harness and loaded it onto the horse bearing the two dead men. The Welsh bodies they left where they had fallen and where they would presently be taken up and borne away by their own people. The snow floated down, covering the land in a soft, white healing blanket, curtaining the horsemen as they rode away, muffling the beat of hooves to silence so that the only sound was the keening of the wind.

CHAPTER 8

'DO YOU BELIEVE that I should have approved the match between Heulwen and Warrin?' Guyon asked his wife.

Judith looked at her reflection in the polished Saracen mirror, put down her comb and wondered why it should be her trial to have such soul-searching questions pushed at her all the time. She turned to face him. He was sitting before the hearth, looking indolently at ease with a cup of wine in his hand and his feet stretched out resting comfortably against Gwen's firelit rump, but she had been married to him for too long now to be deceived.

'What reason could you have had to refuse?' She went to him and laid her hand on his shoulder, felt the tension there, and began to work firmly on the knotted muscles. 'Both of them seem eager to have the marriage made. She's not a child any more Guy, she's long been a woman grown.'

He closed his eyes and gave a low-pitched sigh of pleasure at her ministrations, but his mind remained sharp. 'I know that, love, and I also know that it hasn't been easy for you having her here at Ravenstow.'

'And you wonder if you have given in too easily in the hopes of having a return to peace in your household?' she said astutely.

'Most assuredly that is part of it,' Guyon acknowledged with a laugh, then sobered. 'I just wonder why Warrin should be so fierce to wed her. Men of high estate do not marry for love. Well and good if love grows from a match, but it's not the foremost reason for tying a knot.'

'Heulwen married for love the first time,' Judith pointed out.

Guyon snorted. 'What she thought was love. Moonstruck lust in reality, and I was dotingly led by the nose to arrange a disaster.'

'It was a sound business arrangement,' she objected, stooping round to kiss the corner of his mouth. 'Ralph's skills, our horses. It wasn't just Heulwen's pleading that caused you to make the offer.'

'Perhaps,' he relented. 'But it has given me cause for doubt. Am I doing the right thing this time? Where Heulwen is concerned, I stand too close to see clearly.'

Judith continued kneading his shoulders in silence for a time. 'Might not the blood bond and her dowry coupled with what he feels for her be enough?' she suggested. 'He's known her for a long time, and he did offer for her before.'

'Mayhap,' Guyon said without conviction. 'Or mayhap he wants to wear her like one of his rings, showing her off to make others envious.'

'And who could blame him? She's very beautiful. After the way Ralph used to treat her, Warrin's pride will be like balm on an open wound.'

Guyon was silent. Judith eyed the back of his neck with exasperation, recognizing this mood of old. He would sit on his doubts like a broody hen on a clutch of eggs, and nothing would move him until either they hatched or went stale. How to send them stale? She pursed her lips: after twenty-eight years of marriage, she had several diversions in her armoury – short-term at least. She slid her hands down over his collarbone and chest, leaned round to kiss him again on throat and mouth, let her hair swing down around them, bit him gently . . .

'It was snowing on our wedding night, do you remember?'

Guyon's lids twitched but did not open. He caressed Judith's hair with a languid hand. 'Yes, I remember,' he said, with a slight smile. 'You were scared to death.'

74

She propped her chin on one hand and traced her index finger lightly over his chest. 'I was too young and badly used to know better,' she said softly. 'You gave me the time I needed and for that I'll always be grateful.'

'Just grateful?'

'What do you think?' She sought teasingly lower and giggled to hear him groan.

'Jesu, Judith, I'm not young enough to game all night any more!'

'What would you wager?'

'Doubtless my life if I made the attempt!' He laughed, and lazily half-lifted his lids to study her. The rich tawny hair was stranded with silver now, and fine lines webbed her eye-corners and spidered around her lips. But she was still attractive, her body trim despite the bearing of five sons and two miscarriages between. Theirs had been a political match, forced upon them both, and begun with mistrust and resentment on both sides; but out of the seeds of potential disaster had grown a deep and abiding love. His pleasure in her was still as keen as it had been in the early days, for Judith had an extensive store of devices and surprises to keep him interested, and he was essentially of a faithful nature, seeing no point in going out to dine on pottage when there was a feast at home.

'The trouble with Ralph was that he enjoyed pottage,' he murmured.

'What?' Justifiably bewildered, Judith stared at him.

'Nothing. Foolish thoughts aloud. I told you, you're flogging a dead horse.' Laughing, he pushed her hand away.

'Speaking of which, Renard will need another mount before we go to Windsor.' She kissed his jaw and laid her head on his shoulder. 'He bids fair to outstrip you in height and he's not sixteen until Candlemas.'

'So I'd noticed,' Guyon said with rueful pride. 'Starlight can go for use as a remount. There must be at least another five years left in him. He was only a youngster when Miles first had him.'

Judith felt the familiar pang strike her heart as he spoke the name of their eldest son; her firstborn, drowned with his cousin Prince William when the White Ship went down. How long ago was it? Six years, and still as if it were only yesterday she could see Guyon riding into Ravenstow's bailey with the disastrous news received in Southampton, and she eight months pregnant with William, the wind raw on her face, turning her cheeks as numb as her mind. No grave at which to mourn, just a wide expanse of grey, sullen water. There was an effigy in Ravenstow's chapel, but it did no justice to what had once been warm, living flesh.

She nuzzled her cheek against Guyon's bicep seeking to blot out the pain, and thought of her father the King, whose every hope and scheme had foundered in that vessel. Not only the loss of a son, but the loss of a dynasty in male tail. Miles could never be replaced, but at least she and Guyon had the grace of four surviving sons.

'I haven't seen Mathilda since she left to become an empress,' she remarked, thoughts of Henry leading her to thoughts of the small, truculent half-sister whom she had last seen at the age of seven, stamping her foot at Queen Edith and shrieking in a tantrum that she was not going to Germany, that no one could make her.

'Apparently you are fortunate,' Guyon said dryly. 'Adam was not impressed.'

'I feel sorry for her,' Judith defended. 'There cannot have been much pleasure in her life. A little girl adrift in a strange country, forced into different customs and language, and cut off from her family. I know that her husband was kind to her, but to a child of her age he must have seemed ancient.'

'A replacement for her father then,' Guyon said sleepily, and yawned.

'Probably,' Judith agreed. 'So when he died, and her real father started making demands on her to come home when it was he who had packed her off in the first place, is it any wonder that she should turn mulish and difficult? After all Guy, he hasn't recalled her out of loving concern has he? I'll wager he rubbed his hands with glee when her poor husband died! She knows very well that if Prince William were still alive, or if Queen Adeliza had proved a competent brood mare, she'd still be in Germany, the dowager empress and highly respected by people whom she knows and suits. As it is, all the barons are eyeing her with suspicion and grumbling into their beards, and a pound to a penny that there's another husband being marked out for her, strictly of her father's choosing.'

She paused to draw breath, realizing that her indignation on Mathilda's behalf had carried her too far. She clamped her mouth shut on further words, aware that, by association, they might lead back to the niggling treadmill of the match between Heulwen and Warrin de Mortimer, the very thing she had sought to distract Guyon from in the first place.

'Anyway,' she said, adroitly changing the subject, 'it will be a pleasure to see Harry and discover how he's progressing in Robert of Gloucester's charge, and it's a long time since I've had a good gossip with Rob's wife.' Her tone warmed with anticipation. 'That little booth's always there at Christmas, you know, the one that sells attar of roses and flower oils, and I need to buy some more thread-of-gold for that altar cloth in the chapel, and we've almost finished the saffron ...'

'Enough!' her husband groaned, laughing. 'You will clean me out of silver!'

'But in a good cause.' She nibbled his ear, and her tongue came out. Her hand strayed downwards again, teasing, knowledgeable.

'Wanton,' he murmured, shifting to accommodate her further.

'For a dead horse, you're remarkably lively,' she retorted, before he silenced her mouth beneath his own.

' ... a dead horse,' said the serjeant as Guyon gestured him to his feet. 'A dun stallion with an arrow in his belly and his throat slit wide. Our patrol came across him in the middle of the drovers' road; he was crusted in a night's fall of snow.'

'Any other signs of a skirmish?' asked Warrin de Mortimer, speaking around a mouthful of the best manchet bread and honey.

'I couldn't rightly tell, my lord. The snow had blown and drifted. At first we did not realize there was a horse there at all, until one of the dogs found him.'

'A dun.' Heulwen's cup wavered in her hand. She put it down, her colour fading. 'Adam had a dun with him yesterday, and it was the road he would have taken to Thorneyford, the quickest route.'

Warrin flicked her a sharp glance, a hint of irritation in his ice-blue eyes. Prudently he lowered his lids and took a gulp of cider to wash down his bread, hoping savagely to himself that the Welsh had done to Adam what they had done to Ralph. It would stop Heulwen agitating over the witless sod, and he could comfort her as only a husband could.

'And Renard went with him,' Judith said, one hand at her breast, the other clutching the trestle.

'He was riding a dun, I saw him leave,' said William. He had been sitting quietly at the end of the dais, a wooden soldier in one hand and heel of bread in the other, only half-understanding what was being said, but alerted enough by the fear in the adult voices to be frightened himself. 'It was Sir Adam's remount. He had a black mane and tail and a wide blaze.'

The serjeant swallowed and nodded.

'Holy Christ ... ' Judith closed her eyes.

'Mama, Renard's all right isn't he?'

She turned a blind, terrified gaze on her youngest son, changed it swiftly, but not swiftly enough, and gave him a meaningless smile. 'Yes, of course he is sweetheart ... ' After all, there were no bodies saving that of a slaughtered horse. William came to her and she drew him close, holding onto his small, warm body.

'Eric, get the men saddled up,' Guyon snapped at his grizzled constable. 'I want to see this for myself. We'll ride on to Thorneyford along the drovers' road.'

'I'll come with you,' offered Warrin, gulping down the last of his cider and standing up. 'You can use my men to swell the ranks of your own. Safety in numbers, I think.'

Guyon nodded brusquely and left the trestle to go and arm, beckoning the serjeant to come with him so that he could be further questioned as to what he had seen.

Judith bent over her youngest son, reassuring him, her heart clogged by a terrible dread. The November sacrifice, she thought: Two sons paid, three still to lose. She shuddered.

'Take care,' Heulwen said to Warrin, laying hold of his sleeve.

He looked at her. The light from the sconces turned her braids to fire and highlighted her strong, well-balanced bone structure and the generous curves of her body. 'Don't worry,' he answered with a slightly grim smile, 'I'm not going to be cheated out of what is rightfully mine.'

She bit her lip, frown lines marring the smoothness of her brow. 'Look,' he said with heavy patience, 'Adam de Lacey is too experienced a fighter to fall prey to a piddling band of Welsh – *more's the pity* – and if Renard's with him, then Renard will be all right. Trust me, sweeting.' He silenced her intention to speak with a hard kiss that took away her breath, released her, and went after Guyon, pausing only to squeeze Judith's shoulder reassuringly as he passed.

Heulwen watched him stride across the hall and from her sight, his pace assured and arrogant. A shard of ice lodged in her heart. She remembered a soft summer day and the dismayed cries of the servants as he rode into her bailey, Ralph's blood-soaked body hanging like a dead deer across Lyard's back. She remembered the black, sightless pupils, the brown iris almost obliterated, the wounds that had bled him white, and the expression that death had set on his face. Warrin telling her then not to worry; telling her again now, like a foretaste of doom. With a small cry she gathered her skirts and ran from the hall, ran until she came to the chapel and cast herself down on her knees before the altar, and there she wept for Renard, and for Adam . . . and for herself.

Adam paused, hands on hips, breath steaming into the clear, frosty air, and watched the men from Ravenstow ride into his bailey. A snort rippled from him when he saw the piebald stallion and the richly caparisoned Warrin de Mortimer astride. He glanced round at Aubrey. 'That's two marks you owe me. I said he'd be unable to resist him didn't I?'

The knight squinted against the cold glare of the sunlight and grimaced. 'That's two marks more than he's paid out over that horse,' he said acidly. 'But then what need when it's part of his future bride's dowry and you're fool enough to have trained him for love, not money?'

Adam gave his companion a hard stare. The watery-blue eyes returned it steadily. 'What need indeed?' he said tonelessly and crunched across the trodden snow to greet the horsemen.

'Adam, thank Christ!' Guyon exclaimed as he dismounted. 'What in hell's name happened?'

Adam shrugged his shoulders. 'What you would expect. The Welsh must have had their scouts out yesterday morning and seen me pass on the road to Ravenstow. We weren't laden with travelling baggage, so it wouldn't take a great intellect to deduce that we'd probably be returning soon that same way.' Gingerly he touched the clotted slash on his jaw. 'They bit off more than they could chew, but we didn't have it all our own way. I lost three good men and sixty marks worth of destrier, not to mention those wounded.'

'Where's Renard?' Guyon stared anxiously round the bailey for his son. 'Was he injured?'

'Minorly so,' Adam reassured him as they went towards the hall. 'He stopped a Welsh spear on his ribs, but Sweyn got to him in time. He's still abed, but only because I sent him there last night with a flagon of the strongest cider we had, and a wench from the village. I don't expect to see him this side of noon.'

'You did what?' De Mortimer looked at him with distaste.

'Oh don't go all mealy-mouthed and pious on me Warrin!' Adam snapped. 'The lad fought well, accounted for two of the bastards on his own and got himself clear of a gut-shot horse in the middle of a pitched battle – but it's a violent baptism for a fifteen-year-old raw from the tilt yard. He took green-sick afterwards. In the circumstances, I thought it best that he drown his dreams in drink and the comfort of a woman's body, and Christ alone knows why I am justifying myself to you!'

'Calm down, Adam.' Guyon touched his rigid arm. 'Probably I'd have done the same with him. Just thank God that you're both safe. When I saw that horse in the road ...'

'I was going to send to you this morning, but I've not long risen myself.'

'Did you take to drink and dalliance too?' needled de Mortimer.

Adam's jaw tightened, twinging his wound. He thought of several replies but decided that to utter them was to dance to de Mortimer's tune. 'We took a prisoner,' he said to Guyon, half-turning his shoulder upon the other's galling presence. 'He's got a nasty head wound and a slashed thigh, and he's still unconscious. Dame Agatha, the herb-wife from the village, has had a look at him and says he'll mend, but doesn't know how long it will be before he recovers his wits.'

'You had reason to make of him a prisoner then?' Guyon prowled forward to the hearth. The snow on his boots became transparent and slowly melted into the rushes. A dog came to sniff at the cold air on his cloak.

'He was wearing gilded boots and there were jewels in his swordhilt. Someone of note among his people I would say. If we had left him in the road he would have died.'

'What's one less Welshman except a blessing?' de Mortimer said moodily and kicked at the dog as it came to snuffle him.

'Not in this instance. It may be that we can barter him for peace.'

De Mortimer laughed as though Adam had said something extremely funny. 'And we all know a Welshman's notion of peace!' he sneered. 'If it had been me, I'd have left the whoreson to die!'

'I know,' Adam said tightly. 'Either that, or helped him on his way. You're good at that.'

It had been an insult flung like a wild blow in battle, but it certainly hit its mark as the colour drained from de Mortimer's face. For a moment he looked stunned, almost afraid, but he rallied rapidly and writhed his lips back to snarl, 'You stand need to speak so when your own father . . .'

'Christ on the cross let be!' Guyon said sharply. 'You're like a pair of brangling infants. For all the heed you've taken of the manners drilled into you at Ravenstow, I might as well have saved my breath!'

The blond man opened his mouth to argue, changed his mind and clamped it shut again, gaze fulminating on Adam.

There was a difficult silence. Adam cleared his throat. 'Do you want to see my Welshman?' he asked. 'It may be that you will know him.'

Guyon inclined his head, noting wearily that neither man was prepared to make an apology.

He lay on a pallet in one of the upper wall-chambers, a maid-servant tending him and a footsoldier posted outside the curtained doorway. 'Although God knows, with that leg, he's not going far,' Adam said as the woman curtsied and withdrew a little. A brazier had taken the chill from the room and was positioned near the pallet to afford the stricken man the best of the warmth. The room had no access to daylight, and the constant use of rush dips and candles had streaked the white-washed walls with soot. Their myriad flickering flames made the chamber look almost like a shrine, although the man they had come to view was worthy only of speculation, not reverence.

Guyon stared down at the bruised, blue-hollowed face. The black curls had been cropped away from a nasty bluish-red contusion the size of a gull's egg high on the forehead. Below it, the lids were lax and closed, thick black lashes fanning cheeks that were oily with the bloom of late adolescence. 'He's only a youngster,' he said, surprised into compassion, for lying there, the youth looked not much older than Renard. 'No, I don't know him. What about you, Warrin?'

Warrin shrugged indifferently. 'They all look the same to me. I haven't been much on the borders these last three years, and by the looks of him, three years ago he would still have been taking suck!'

'Someone's bound to claim him,' Guyon said. 'The Welsh blood-bond is sacred, and he's well-bred you say, perhaps even the leader of this escapade?'

'Could well be,' Adam nodded, 'the Welsh blood their young men early.'

'How bad is the leg wound?'

'He's stitched up like a piece of Bishop Odo's tapestry and likely to take the wound fever, but Dame Agatha is doing her best for him.'

Guyon started to turn away. Warrin made to follow him, but his cloak pin had worked loose and the brooch dropped onto the floor with a soft clink. Muttering an irritated oath, he stooped to retrieve it, and at that moment, the patient stirred and groaned, his eyelids rippling as his will struggled to raise them.

Immediately Guyon and Adam were bending over the supine form, but de Mortimer was the nearest, his square, strong bones illuminated by the golden rushlight, and it was upon these that the young Welshman first focused. An expression of sheer horror crossed his face and he shrank back into the pillows, crying out in Welsh.

'It's all right,' Guyon said quickly in that same language.

'No one is going to harm you. You are here to be healed and returned to your family.'

The youth shook his head, breath panting hard, eyes on de Mortimer.

'You say you do not know him, but he certainly seems to know you, and well enough to be afraid,' Adam said, plucking Warrin away from the bed while Guyon continued to soothe the patient.

'I've never seen the bastard before in my life!' Warrin growled. 'It's obvious. He's taken a blow to the head and his wits have gone wool-gathering. Anyone who looks even remotely Norman is fodder for his nightmares.'

'Perhaps,' Adam said noncommittally and flickered a tawny glance to the prisoner who had subsided against the pillows, his eyes closed, obviously exhausted and perhaps too frightened to raise his lids and look on Warrin de Mortimer again.

'What are you going to do about him?' Guyon asked as they spiralled down the steep staircase to the hall. 'You're due to leave for Windsor within the fortnight.'

Adam pursed his lips. 'I don't know. Perhaps ask your father to come up the march. He's acquainted with most of the Welsh clans and families of the region, related to half of them come to that. He's competent to deal with whatever arises, and I can leave Aubrey here with him. If the lad's family come to negotiate, then they can take the first steps without me, and I should be home by January's end to conclude them.'

Guyon rubbed his jaw and nodded agreement, eyes thoughtful.

'What on earth was all that gibberish he was babbling?' asked Warrin as they repaired to the hearth.

Guyon took his hand away from his chin. His voice was neutral. 'He said that he never meant to eavesdrop and that if you let him live, he would not tell a living soul.'

'Tell a living soul what?' Warrin looked blank. 'What does he mean?' A pulse throbbed hard in the base of his throat.

'I suppose we'll find out in good time,' Adam said, his voice calm and reasonable. His eyes however were full of threat, and he turned away to view the black-haired youth in shirt and chausses who had just collapsed onto a trestle bench on the high dais and now sat groaning and rumpled, his head clutched between his hands.

'Your heir,' Adam grinned to Guyon, 'safe and sound.'

Despite the sables lining her travelling cloak, Heulwen shivered as she stood beneath an overhang and waited for the grooms to lead her saddled palfrey out from the stables. The snow had become sleet, needling silver and white from a sky the colour of a dirty hauberk – and hauberks were in evidence everywhere as the final preparations were made for the journey to Windsor – and from the look of the weather, a wet, uncomfortable journey it was going to be.

Renard squelched across the bailey, furred cloak already mired at the hem, armour glinting beneath as he strode, a helmet dangling from his fingers. She was about to call out, but a slender, honey-haired girl came running out of one of the bailey buildings and accosted him. Renard glanced quickly round, set his free arm about the girl's willowy waist, and whisked her quickly into the darkness of a doorway, where Heulwen saw his cloak swirl around her to enclose, and his head bend to her offered lips. The falconer's daughter, she thought with the glimmer of a smile. Amazing what prowess in war did for a man's standing with women. Judith had scolded her son soundly, but behind the anger was pride, and behind the pride was fear. Renard's pretence at manhood was swift becoming reality.

Heulwen herself had been hysterical with relief at his safe return, but only a portion of it had been on Renard's account. The thought of Adam sprawled somewhere in a frozen puddle of his own blood, like Ralph a victim of the Welsh, had terrified her beyond all cohesive thought. Nothing had been the same since. She was still reeling and uncertain, balanced on a see-saw of want and denial.

She clenched her fingers into fists and fixed her gaze upon Warrin's broad, solid frame as he stepped out into the sleet, his face twisting into a grimace of discomfort. He was her betrothed in all but the pledge now that she had consented. All that prevented their union was the formality of the royal yeasay and there was no reason for that to be denied.

He came towards her, blowing on his hands, caught her gaze and smiled. She managed a wan response.

'Chin up doucette, you look as dismal as this Godforsaken weather!' He stooped and kissed her cold lips, standing away slightly to look at her.

'This journey is hardly going to be a jaunt to a fairing,' she responded, trying to draw some inner glow of feeling from his presence, but the only warmth that came was because he was shielding her slightly from the wind.

'I've brought you a present,' he said with that slightly patronizing smile that occasionally irritated her, and placed a small drawstring bag in her hand. 'It won't ease the misery of this weather, but it might lighten your heart, and it will certainly gladden mine to see you wear it. Call it your betrothal gift.'

She loosened the string with fumbling, frozen fingers and slid a circular cloak-pin out onto her hand. It was Celtic of execution, made of silver and inset with gold and silver filigree, punctuated by small, circular jewels of amber and rock crystal and, discordant at its centre, a huge purple amethyst.

'It's beautiful!' she cried, turning it over and thinking to herself that it was also ostentatious and predictable of her future husband's attitudes and tastes.

'Here, let me pin it on for you.' He reached eagerly to pluck loose the pin that already held her cloak; it was a simple thing by the standards of the gorgeous object she now held, worked by the Ravenstow bronzesmith in the shape of a snarling leopard with tiny ruby eyes. It was her father's device, given to her by him on her seventh year day. It made her feel uneasy to see it so summarily dismissed. Carefully, tenderly, she put it in the empty leather bag.

'Is it not a risk to display such wealth as this on a long journey?' she asked him doubtfully. 'Surely it would be more sensible for me to wear it when we reach Windsor, perhaps when you ask the King for me?'

Warrin snorted with patronizing indulgence, making her feel in truth no more than seven years old. 'You worry too much over trifles,' he said, as he forced the new pin through the thick Flemish cloth. 'We are armed to fight off any chance attacks on the road. We could even deal with a horde of Welsh if they came at us. No, beloved, it pleases me that men should see the high value I set upon my prize.'

'Your future prize,' she reminded him, nettled at his superior tone.

'All right, my future prize.' He finished securing the pin and lowered his hand, as if by accident brushing the curve of her breast. 'My future wife.' His voice thickened and his mouth fastened on hers, leech-like, demanding. Heulwen, feeling like a whore who has been paid in advance to show gratitude, responded with the unthinking expertise taught to her by Ralph, her heart as numb as the cold fingers she linked around Warrin's muscle-thickened neck.

CHAPTER 9

THE WELSH PRISONER opened his black-brown eyes to full consciousness and stared in weak, febrile bewilderment at the limned white walls that greeted him. Rushlight flickered. Beneath his fingers he could feel the grainy texture of a linen garment, and beneath that the rapid beat of his feverish body. His parched throat worked and his lips formed soundless words.

'He's awake,' Adam said softly, and touched his companion's knee.

Miles grunted. His chin jerked up from his chest and his drowsing lids lifted. He turned to the youth on the pallet, and saw that despite a slight, sweating fever, he was lucid and aware, and he reassured him gently in Welsh that he was meant no harm. The dark eyes remained puzzled and suspicious, but the boy drank greedily of the watered down mead that Adam brought to him. He listened in silence while Miles introduced himself in the proper Welsh fashion, naming all his antecedents and relatives before telling him of Adam's identity, where he was, and how seriously he had been wounded.

'It was foolish to attack Lord Adam's troop,' Miles added gently. 'He might not speak the *Cymraeg* beyond a smattering, but that does not mean he is an idiot in matters of border warfare.'

The youth's mouth twisted downwards in a sour smile. 'I don't need lecturing,' he said. His voice was hoarse, rusty from three days in the scabbard.

'No,' Miles nodded benignly, 'perhaps not from me, but

your kindred will be only too delighted to point out the error of your ways, I am sure.'

The smile vanished, but the mouth remained twisted down and was joined in direction by thick black brows.

Miles translated what had been said so far. Adam put the mead down. 'Ask him who they are.'

Miles opened his mouth, but the youth had heard and understood, and glancing up said in halting French, 'My brother won't be delighted, he'll be furious. You needn't have gone to the trouble of saving me. He'll murder me with his own hands when he finds out.'

'Your brother?'

'Davydd ap Tewdr.' He looked down again. 'I'm Rhodri, and younger than him by ten years. We're born of different mothers.'

A slow, beatific smile lit up Adam's face. 'Worth your weight in Welsh gold then,' he said softly.

'Or a peace treaty,' Miles said. 'He's ap Tewdr's heir as matters stand.'

'Go on,' said the youth miserably, 'gloat.' He shifted angrily in the bed and his body jerked taut, the breath locking in his canned throat, eyes squeezing shut.

'Aye lad, you've made a regular mess of that leg,' Miles pronounced. 'You're lucky it's not going putrid.'

'I'll send to your brother.' Adam offered him the mead again. 'There's a Welsh carrier plies his trade through here once a month. He's due next week and he'll know where to take word. And I'd be an innocent if I did not know that your brother has his own ways and means of discovering your whereabouts.'

The youth drank and said nothing, but colour crept up into his face.

Adam gently chewed the inside of his lip, eyeing his captive, and came to a decision. 'Tell me how you come to know Warrin de Mortimer?'

The colour vanished, leaving him clammy grey. 'He was

really here then?' he said hoarsely. 'I thought perhaps it was just part of a bad dream.'

Adam's mouth twitched. 'So did I,' he said half under his breath, and then, 'no, he was here, but he said that he did not know you.'

The lad shivered. 'It may be so.' He looked down at his fingers and interlaced them on the coverlet of mottled sheepskins.

'You said something about eavesdropping?' Adam pushed gently. 'That you promised not to tell a living soul?'

Rhodri dug his fingers into the springy fleece. 'He came to visit my brother under a flag of truce. They spoke together for some time ...'

'And you overheard?' Miles guessed.

'Yes.' A swallow and a look. 'Davydd never gives me any responsibility. He sends me out hunting or on petty scouting trips like a child.'

'Sometimes it is hard to know when a fledgeling is ready to fly,' Miles said mildly.

'And sometimes a fledgeling's wings are clipped!' the boy retorted. His mouth compressed to a single narrow line.

Adam folded his arms. 'So,' he prompted, 'what did you overhear?'

Rhodri worked his fingers through the thick, springy wool and kept his eyes on his actions. 'De Mortimer offered my brother silver to kill one of your barons – Ralph le Chevalier. He said that he had a loose tongue and had to be silenced. Davydd was agreeable. Le Chevalier was no friend of ours, and on more than one occasion he had trespassed with our women. I ... Is there any more mead?'

'Yes of course.' Adam exchanged glances with Miles as he poured a fresh measure into the cup and gave it to the lad.

Rhodri swallowed deeply and then leaned back against the pillows, his eyes closed, hair sweat-soaked. 'De Mortimer arranged the ambush and set le Chevalier up to be killed by us – but only Davydd knows that, and me. The rest of the men all thought it was sheer good fortune when we encountered them in the woods. De Mortimer was watching us, waiting until le Chevalier was down from his horse and bleeding his life into the ground before he made his move. He came down on us with his full force. If Davydd hadn't been expecting just that kind of treachery, we'd have been dead too. *Rhaid wirth lwy hir i fwyta gyda'r diafol.*'

'One needs a long spoon to sup with the devil,' Miles translated grimly.

'My brother was very angry about losing the chestnut stallion,' the young man added. He darted a sheepish look at Adam. 'I was going to gall him into a red rage by returning from this raid astride the very same horse he had missed, and instead he's got to ransom me and thank his enemies for saving my life.'

'Perhaps under the circumstances, he'd prefer to let you rot,' Miles said drily.

Rhodri gave him a weak smile. 'Brotherly love usually wins by a hair's breadth,' he said.

Adam paced across the solar until he reached the brazier, held his hands to the warmth and looked at Miles. 'You know what this means?'

Miles moved his shoulders. 'It could mean a lot of things,' he said thoughtfully. 'But the main one is that my granddaughter is about to pledge her life to her husband's murderer!'

'Miles, she cannot be allowed to do it.'

The hooded, wrinkled lids lifted to reveal the perceptions of a more than agile mind. 'Then stop her.'

'How?' Adam spread his hands. 'She knows I hate even the taste of de Mortimer's name on my tongue, and anything I try to tell her, she'll dismiss as raving or fantasy. What should I do? Abduct her over my saddle?'

'Worth a try if all else fails,' Miles said with a smile, and then grew serious. 'I'm past four score years, Adam. Do I have to spoonfeed it to you? Go to the King, put the matter in his hands, and while you are about it, ask of him a boon.'

Adam narrowed his eyes. 'What kind of boon?'

'Has he rewarded you for your tireless efforts to keep his delightful daughter alive? Knowing Henry, you've had a bagful of promises and a pocketful of nothing.'

'And he's unlikely to change!' Adam snorted brusquely. 'If it's going to hit his purse, then he'll refuse.'

'It is no concern of his purse,' Miles negated. 'Ask him for Heulwen to wife.'

Adam's citrine eyes widened. 'Ask him for Heulwen?' he repeated, voice rising and cracking as it had not done in ten years.

'You hold your tenure direct from him, as did Ralph, and I shouldn't think that after the first shock Guyon will object to your suit. In a way, he may be relieved.'

Adam shook his head and walked away from the old man to stare at a hanging on the wall. It had been worked by his mother long before his birth and the moths had begun to eat it bare. His thoughts raced to the erratic thudding of his heart.

'You need a wife,' Miles added, mischief lurking beyond his wrinkles. 'This place frequently bears resemblance to a midden.'

'I can't,' he said woodenly. 'I'm her foster-brother.'

Miles said something very rude in Welsh, then reverting to French asked, 'Is that how you feel?'

Adam swung round, sat down on a stool and placed his ringing head in his hands. 'No, it isn't,' he groaned. 'Once, yes, when I was small, I did love her like that, but it changed a long time ago, for me, anyway. Heulwen still thinks of me as a brother.'

Miles raised a sceptical brow. 'You know that for a fact?'

'It was rammed down my throat when I brought her the horses.'

'With more fear than conviction, I'll warrant.' Miles looked at him thoughtfully. 'I'd always suspected that you had a soft spot for the wench, but boys of that age can change their allegiance with the season and more often than not grow out

of their first lovesick longings. Girls are always more mature.'
Adam said nothing, remaining hunched and self-contained on
the stool. 'Of course,' Miles said gently, but with the precision
that had once made his sword arm so formidable, 'you don't
have to ask Henry at all, just tell him about Warrin and Ralph
and hope to God that he will act on it and that Heulwen finds
a better man in time. The choice is yours.'

Adam sat in silence. The candle fluttered in the sconce and
light rippled suddenly on the fittings of his belt, upon buckle,
latch and dagger grip, which flexed and flashed as he drew a
deep, shuddering breath and raised his head. 'What if she turns
on me with hatred?' he said, recoiling from the thought of
being rejected by her yet again.

'Then I would call it a disguise for other feelings. If by
mischance she should spit the word at you, have patience, it
will pass.'

Adam snorted and looked away, but within him the hopes
and terrors aroused by Miles' suggestion jousted with each
other for dominance. Heulwen. He could have Heulwen at his
board, living day to day with him, sharing his bed in the great
chamber above. The colour came up hard in his face. Heulwen
looking at him in disgust, fighting him, derision on her bladed
tongue, and unlike Warrin de Mortimer he did not think he
could find it in him to strike her silent if she baulked him, not
unless it was a matter of life and death. *Life and death.* He
thought of what the Welsh boy had told them, its implications.
Whatever the reasons, Warrin de Mortimer was undoubtedly
guilty of murder. He had probably known about the silver in
Ralph's strongbox, and had set out to gain it for himself by
the simple expedient of marrying his widow.

'I'll leave you to think about it,' Miles said, and pushed
himself out of the hard, high-backed chair. 'I'd like to see the
lass settled before I die, so you'd best make haste.'

'I don't know whether to kiss or kill you!' Adam ruefully
shook his head.

'Save the kiss for Heulwen and the killing for where it

93

belongs,' Miles advised him gravely, and legs stiff from having sat so long, limped carefully out of the room.

Adam stared at the archway through which he had disappeared, and slowly stood up himself, a bemused expression on his face, his thoughts withdrawn from his surroundings as they walked a mental tightrope. After a while, he began to realize that the rope was strung across a gorge that stretched into a distance he could not see, perhaps infinity, that behind and below snarled the demons and serpents of self-doubt and cowardice, and that the only possible way was forward. That decision having been taken, his burden suddenly seemed much lighter. He straightened and squared his shoulders as if preparing to take a blow and left the solar, calling for Austin and Sweyn.

CHAPTER 10

D OWN IN THE south, the snow had gentled to rain, if gentled was the correct word for the bitter, near-freezing drops that spattered and stung the eyes if they were not kept lowered to the mud-runnelled, garbage-strewn streets. Raised between squalls, they would have seen the banners and shields adorning the balconies of the wealthy, and the evergreen bunches outside every ale-house, welcoming the numerous members of Windsor's temporary population. The Court was here to keep Christmas, not merely the usual immediate Court, but almost every royal tenant-in-chief, a bevy of lesser but nevertheless important barons, the high clergy and David, King of Scotland, with his retinue, all present to swear allegiance to the dowager empress Mathilda, King Henry's daughter and designated heir.

Heulwen shivered and tried to huddle deeper into the folds of her cloak as the wind flurried her garments and blustered rain into her face. She struggled to display an interest she did not feel in the bolts of cloth laid out for her inspection upon the counter of the cloth-merchant's booth. Dutifully she rubbed the fine, bleached linen between her fingers and agreed that it would be perfect for making shirts and shifts, trying to smile as lengths were cut and folded to one side.

'Now,' Judith said with a note of satisfaction, her gaze discerning on the merchant's displayed bales of cloth, 'your wedding gown. What about that green velvet over there?'

Obligingly the merchant reached for the bolt indicated.

'I don't know, I had not thought.' Heulwen shivered, her face pinched and pale.

95

'Well in the name of the saints do so now!' Judith snapped with the exasperation that came of having trailed around the market place all morning with a limp rag in tow. 'Heulwen, you're to be betrothed tomorrow morning and married at Candlemas. You haven't time to dally like a drassock!'

'I'm sorry, Mama. It's just that I'm cold and out of sorts,' Heulwen excused, giving again that wan, forlorn smile that made Judith want to scream. 'The green will suit me very well.'

'God in heaven child, you haven't even looked at it!'

The merchant lowered his eyes from the irate older woman and the pretty, woebegone girl at her side, and busied himself unfolding the bolt and rippling the sea-green velvet across the counter.

Heulwen's lower lip trembled as she fought with tears. Fine sleet stung her face like flung shingle. Behind, two accompanying men-at-arms were stamping their feet to keep warm, and Helgund, her stepmother's elderly senior maid was grimacing at the pain from her chilblains.

'I trust in your judgement, Mama,' she said in a subdued voice and stared at the muddied hem of her cloak.

Judith closed her eyes and swallowed. A pack horse laden with brightly coloured belts was led past, and someone else's servant scurried by clutching a cloth-covered piedish, the savoury steam of which teased the nostrils and tortured the empty stomachs of those freezing at the draper's booth. 'Very well,' Judith said with commendable calm for one who was so sorely tried. 'Two ells of the green and an ell of that gold damask over there for an under-tunic. Have them brought to the Earl of Ravenstow's house and my steward will pay you.'

The merchant bowed, and sucking his teeth, started to refold the bolt of velvet, the swift upward dart of his eyes revealing his surreptitious curiosity as he worked.

As they left the booth, Judith's exasperation gave way to concern, for Heulwen was following her with the vapid docility of a mazed sheep. 'Perhaps this betrothal should be deferred until you are feeling better,' she murmured with a frown.

'No!' The response was sharp and swift and so at odds with Heulwen's current mood that Judith stopped in the act of setting her toe in her mare's stirrup, and just stared at her step-daughter with wide eyes.

'No,' said Heulwen in a more controlled voice. 'I'm not ill Mama. I need this betrothal to take place tomorrow. It is the waiting as much as anything else that is dragging me down. I cannot take an interest in my wedding gown when I have this dreadful fear that something will happen to prevent it.'

'Nonsense!' Judith said brusquely.

'I know, but it does not make the fear go away.'

Judith allowed the man-at-arms to boost her into the saddle. The frown remained on her face. Heulwen might be more than half-Welsh, but her nature was essentially practical, without the eerie sense of premonition with which so many of her race were gifted. If she was having brooding foresights, it was because she felt like a condemned prisoner who sees the moment of execution approaching, and is impatient for that moment to have come and gone and the peace of darkness to be upon him.

We might not have pushed her into this marriage, Judith thought grimly, but neither have we done anything to stop her, and if you let a boat drift with the tide, frequently it smashes to pieces on the rocks. Perhaps the betrothal should indeed be cancelled until Heulwen had had a full measure of time to recover from Ralph's mishandling of her, and the ultimate betrayal of his death.

'I was forced to marry your father,' she said gently as she shook the reins. 'I was unhappy and terrified and there was nothing I could do short of killing myself to prevent it from happening. It took a long time and a great deal of patience on your father's behalf before I began to learn trust, even longer before love grew out of it.' She looked across at her step-daughter. Heulwen's mouth was stubbornly set now, but whether to resist Judith or tears was not plain.

97

'It was different for you and Ralph,' she added. 'You wanted him from the beginning, but I do not believe that he was ever quite so sure about you. In the end, I think it was your dowry and the thought of a nubile fifteen-year-old in his bed whenever he chose to sleep there were the reasons that decided him, not love.'

'Mama, what are you trying to tell me?'

'Oh, I don't know. Perhaps that you should not let your experience with Ralph sour your future expectations.'

'It hasn't.' Heulwen moved her shoulders. 'Not soured, but lowered. I no longer think that the stars will fall down into my hands just because I reach for them. Was that how my mother felt about Papa?'

Judith reined back her mare to permit a loaded wain to splash past them. She had never concealed anything of the past from Heulwen, but it was seldom that she asked, and some parts were too painful for Judith to broach without direct demand. 'Yes,' she said thoughtfully. 'I suppose it was. Your mother knew it was impossible for them to wed – a Welsh merchant's daughter and a marcher lord – so she kept her heart guarded from him. I met her only the once, on the day before she was killed. She came to tell Guyon that she was severing the old ties and getting married; it was a business arrangement like your own.'

Momentarily diverted from her troubles, Heulwen cocked her head. 'Weren't you jealous of her? I know that when I found out about one of Ralph's women, I actually thought about taking a dagger to her throat and gelding him!'

Judith's lips twitched. 'Jealous?' She kneed the mare forwards again. 'Oh yes, so jealous that until I met her it gnawed at me like a poison, but I could not hate her. Besides, although your father had occasionally visited her, he did not lie with her after we were wed.' The twitch became an open, rueful smile. 'Oh, not for any reasons of moral nicety or to salve my feelings I am sure, but she was heavily pregnant with you, and by the time you were born, he was beginning to notice that he had a

98

wife for that kind of comfort.' The corners of her eyes crinkled. 'I did once take a knife to one of the women at Court though when she presumed too far on their old acquaintance – Alais de Clare. She's bound to be at court tonight. It's a long time since we met on that kind of battlefield – I wonder if she still remembers.' And her smile became a delightful, mischievous gurgle of laughter so that Heulwen's mood lightened enough for her to respond with the first genuine smile of the morning.

When they rode into the courtyard of their town house, the grooms were already occupied in tending several fine blood horses. A squire was fondling a strawberry roan trapped out in expensive gilded harness. The stallion's superb pinkish coat was as glossy as satin, revealing that its owner could afford to keep it stable-fed during the long winter months. The squire glanced round and a delighted grin flashed across his round face. Quickly giving the roan's bridle to another boy, he ran across the courtyard, first to help the Countess, and then Heulwen down from their mounts.

'Harry!' Judith kissed her fourth child joyfully. He squirmed away, concealing a grimace, and smoothed down the sandy hair she had just tousled, a red flush creeping up from his throat and mantling his freckled face. He was of his royal grandfather's build, stocky and compact, promising bull-like strength rather than the feline grace of his brothers, and he was the only one with her tawny-hazel colouring, the others all being dark like Guyon.

Heulwen, warned by his reaction to Judith's embrace, confined herself to a swift peck on the cheek and an admiring remark about the new dagger at his belt.

Smiling broadly, he showed it to her. 'Earl Robert gave it to me last night for serving so well at table,' he said proudly.

'You've learned something then,' said Judith dryly, and looked him over with brisk approval. Henry had been something of a tatterdemalion before leaving them to squire in Robert of Gloucester's household, but he had acquired a certain polish since then to judge from his spruce, outward appearance, and the smooth alacrity with which he had helped her down from the mare.

'He was dining with the Empress. She smiled at me. She's very pretty and not as . . . ' He left the rest of the sentence in mid-air and looked at Heulwen who was staring at a particularly handsome dark bay stallion tethered among the others.

'He's a beauty, isn't he?' Harry said enthusiastically.

'Harry, what's he doing here?'

The boy blinked at the sharpness of her tone. 'Lord Robert's just been over at the horse fair. He took a fancy to this one and being as it was Adam of Thorneyford selling and he's got a good reputation, he bought him. My lord said that the price was high, but probably fair for what he was getting.' Puzzled, he looked between his mother and half-sister. 'What's wrong? What have I said that's so funny?'

Heulwen shook her head, her underlip caught in her teeth. 'He was one of Ralph's stallions, Adam was selling him for me. What did Earl Robert pay?'

'Eighty-three marks in the end. What do you mean Adam was selling him for you?'

Heulwen touched his arm. 'I'll tell you all about it later,' she said, and still biting her lip, followed her stepmother into the house.

Before a smoky central hearth, Earl Robert of Gloucester, senior grape among the cluster of illegitimate offspring that King Henry had sired upon his vine, sat warming his feet at the fire, cup of hippocras in hand, high forehead ribbed with pleading sincerity as he addressed the dubious Earl of Raven-stow.

'Look, we need your support. I know you have your doubts about swearing for Mathilda, God knows, she'd tempt a saint to commit murder sometimes, but she's capable of ruling, I swear it.'

Guyon gave him a pained smile. 'I do not doubt her capabilities. I'm married to one of your clan myself.' His eyes darted with wry amusement to the threshold where his wife was handing her cloak to a maid. 'But men look to be ruled by a man, not a woman.'

'Do you?'

'By preference, yes – well in some ways anyway,' he added with another amused look at his wife, but then he sobered. 'What worries me, Rob, is that she will wed someone who is going to try the crown on for size and in consequence break us all.'

'My father is wiser than that. He will look and choose most carefully,' Gloucester objected, bristling slightly, 'and Maud's no meek maid to give up what is hers by right.'

Gnawing his lip, Guyon frowned, stared into the middle distance, and then back at the earnest face of his brother-by-marriage.

'It is not enough to say that your father will choose carefully. He will choose to his own dictates unless he is made to swear that he will not go about the purpose of arranging Mathilda's marriage without at least the yeasay of his tenants-in-chief.'

'You have been talking to Henry of Blois haven't you?'

'No I haven't. It is what any sensible man would say.' Guyon's nostrils flared with impatience. 'I've only seen Henry of Blois from a distance thus far. The only man to whom I have spoken is the Earl of Leicester, and that's because my son's a chaplain in his household – and Leicester is not in the least happy about swearing an oath to Mathilda, with or without a husband.'

Robert of Gloucester scraped his hands rapidly through his receding dark hair. Mustering support for his sister's cause was like ploughing a stony field; every few paces he met solid opposition, even from such reasonable loyalists as the Earl of Ravenstow whose own children were Maud's nieces and nephews, and it was grinding him down. 'Guy ...' he began again, but his brother-in-law spread his hands and, sighing deeply, said:

'All right, Robert. I'll swear to her, for her, and at her, but only if Henry promises not to tie her to some entirely unsuitable husband.'

'I am sure he can be brought to an agreement,' Robert said, with the smoothness of a diplomat, meeting the by now familiar response of a half-raised shoulder and a look of badly concealed disbelief. He judged the moment propitious to leave and let Ravenstow mull over what had been said, and if he made haste, there was still time to visit Bigod of Norfolk and sound him out before it was time to prepare for the evening's feast and make his report to Henry.

He stood up and turning, kissed his half-sister and then Heulwen in greeting and farewell.

'We were just admiring your new stallion,' Judith said. 'If Heulwen had known you were looking for another destrier, she'd not have trailed Sorcerer all the way to Windsor.'

'I beg your pardon?' He smiled and looked blank.

Laughing, Judith told him from whom he had actually purchased the horse. Robert laughed too, and as he set an elegant phrygian-style cap on his head, studied Heulwen. 'One of Ralph's stallions, no wonder! I did think it strange that young de Lacey should have a horse of that calibre to sell when he's only just home from the Empire. The sly fox, he never said anything!'

'Perhaps he wasn't sure that you'd offer the full price if you knew it was almost in the family,' Heulwen suggested, the insult negated by the dimple that appeared delightfully at the corner of her mouth.

Robert snorted. 'Very probably. He's as wary as an undercroft cat, that one. Doubtless since I paid him eighty-three marks for the beast, you'll be seeing him sooner rather than later.'

Heulwen fiddled with the ornate brooch pinned at her shoulder, heavy as a man's hand clasped in possession. She had not set eyes on Adam since the day of the Welsh attack and had managed in the interim to convince herself that what she felt was a passing lust, and that any male could as well be

102

substituted – but a substitute was not the genuine article. She thought of Adam's dark smile, that quizzical, brow-shadowed way he had of looking, the dryness of his humour retorting to hers, the gentle pressure of his hands on a horse's flank, or on her waist, gliding down over her buttocks ...

Robert of Gloucester, as proven by his current struggles, was far from insensitive to the moods of others and saw that somehow he had made a mistake. The girl's dimple had vanished and the sparkle had quenched in her aquamarine eyes. He cleared his throat and said with forced jocularity, 'I saw Warrin de Mortimer at the horse fair too. He and his father were trying the paces of a courser. I had a word with them about Maud and it came out that the young man's soon to be wed. He's very lucky, and I told him so.'

'I'm very fond of him,' Heulwen said colourlessly.

Guyon cocked a thoughtful brow at his daughter's response, and eased to his feet to see their guest out. 'I hope Warrin and Adam did not encounter each other,' he commented. 'Last time they were within rubbing distance I had to stop them going for their swords.'

Gloucester shook his head. 'No. They were at opposite ends of the field, and young de Lacey was making to leave even as I did.' He smiled secretively into his sable cloak collar.

Guyon looked a question.

Robert gazed across at Heulwen. 'Yours won't be the only betrothal we celebrate this feast-tide my dear. I have it on good authority that my father intends to offer Sir Adam a rich bride in reward for services rendered to the crown. There are one or two choice heiresses in his wardenship just now, and he is going to give young de Lacey first pick.'

After he had gone, Heulwen realized that she must have made the appropriate responses, for no one had remarked upon her behaviour, and they were all at ease, talking among themselves. They were her family, and yet she felt like a stranger, sneaking warmth from a hearth not her own.

The thought of Adam with a wife cut her to the quick. She

could mouth that it was what she wished for him, could say it with seeming sincerity, but the truth was different. For three months she had turned a blind eye in the same way that she had turned a blind eye to Ralph's infidelities – full knowing but refusing to acknowledge. But such blindness did not last forever, and the light when it returned was too dazzling to be borne.

She complained of a headache when at length Judith noticed her silent pallor, and allowed herself to be bundled up in warm furs and put to bed like a child, hot brick at her feet and a scalding honey posset between her cold fingers, permitting everyone to think that she had caught a chill from standing too long at the market stalls. When Warrin came calling, she told Judith to send him away and curled herself into a foetal ball of misery, wishing she were dead.

CHAPTER 11

Henry, by the Grace of God both King of England and Duke of Normandy, held up his hand to silence the scratching of the scribe's quill, and stared with shrewd, flint-grey eyes at the young man kneeling before him. 'You are quite sure of this?'

'The man had a fever sire, but he was still well within his wits,' Adam answered steadily. 'He knew what he was saying, and I judged it to be true.'

'But then your judgement may be coloured by the known fact that you and Warrin de Mortimer hate the sight of each other.'

'Miles le Gallois of Milnham-on-Wye was there too. He will bear out my story, and he has no particular axe to grind.'

Henry pursed his thin lips and continued to study Adam. The young man's father had been a rebel – violent, untrustworthy, ambitious and perverted, but a good warrior in the field, very good. To all outward appearances his son had inherited only the last trait, although it was never safe to take anyone for granted. It was a timely thought that like did not always breed like. Old Hugh de Mortimer was steadfast and bovine without an original thought in his skull. There was nothing bovine about Warrin, probably nothing steadfast either.

'Ralph le Chevalier acted the courier for me on several occasions last year,' he said, and rubbed his forefinger beneath his nose. 'You had several accidents between the empire and Normandy didn't you?'

Adam grimaced and recited, 'Two attacks by brigands, a sniper on the Rouen road, a fire at a priory where we stayed

105

overnight, and three barrels of pitch that mysteriously exploded on the galley we were to have taken from Barfleur had we not changed our plans at the very last moment. The last one was not on Ralph's slate, he was already dead by then, but I think you will find that Warrin de Mortimer was in Normandy at the time.'

Henry stared into the distance for a long time. The scribe stifled a yawn behind his hand and unnecessarily trimmed his quill. At length, the King leaned slightly forward in his chair. 'I understand he's been paying devoted court to le Chevalier's widow?'

Adam nailed his eyes to the cold, patterned flags that were paining his knees and stared at a red diamond-shape until his eyes blurred. 'Yes, sire.'

'On your feet. I cannot read your eyes when all I can see is the top of your head.'

Colour flooded Adam's face. He stood up. Henry regarded him without easing the cutting edge of his stare. 'And do the widow's family welcome the match?' he pursued in a stalking, soft voice.

'Earl Guyon's loyalty is without blemish,' Adam said quickly, seeing where this was leading and not liking it in the least.

'That is not what I asked.'

'Her family do not object, but neither do I think there would be any protest if the arrangement were broken. In point of fact sire, it is on that very subject that I would ask you to grant me a boon.'

The black, thick brows jerked towards the gem-stoned circlet of royalty in a moment of wary surprise. 'Yes?'

Adam clenched his fists and sucked a deep breath between his teeth. 'I want you to grant my plea to take Ralph le Chevalier's widow to wife.'

'Ah,' Henry said with satisfaction. 'Now we come to the meat of the matter.'

Adam's jaw tightened, but he held onto his composure

and continued doggedly, 'The formal ceremony of betrothal between her and de Mortimer still awaits your yeasay. There is no legal impediment to my request.'

The brows came down and levelled. 'Why this particular woman?' he asked.

'I want her,' Adam said bluntly, 'and I'd rather have her than Hawise FitzAllen or Olivia de Roche. I know her dowry is not as great, but there are compensations.'

Henry looked at him sharply. 'How did you know the girls I had in mind?'

'Your son the Earl of Gloucester bought a horse from me this morning. He thought as a favour to give me some extra space of time to decide, unbeknown that my mind was already made up.'

Henry snorted down his nose. 'A tender heart and a mule's brain,' he growled of his eldest son, but his eyes softened with a rare, genuine affection before his gaze pierced into Adam again. 'I ought to refuse. You are putting me in a very difficult position.' He drummed his fingers on the carved arms of the ornate, high-backed chair.

For what seemed an aeon, Adam returned his stare fearlessly but did not speak. It never did any good to remind Henry of the many debts and obligations that went unpaid on his part. To the King, a loyal man was a work-horse, and any toil performed merely his due.

'You want her,' Henry said incisively. 'Whim or conviction?'

Adam opened his mouth.

'Nay, I can see it in your face. You're beyond redemption.' He ran his tongue around the inside of his mouth. 'What does the wench say?'

'She will refuse me, but I can persuade her otherwise,' Adam said bleakly, wondering if it was true.

Henry grunted and bit his forefinger nail. 'Give me the silver in le Chevalier's strongbox, and you can have her,' he said. 'De Mortimer can be compensated by one of the other women I was going to offer you, if of course he doesn't lose his head for

107

treason. This needs investigating further.' He clicked his fingers at the scribe who wakened abruptly from his doze, fell off his elbow and began to write quickly as Henry dictated.

Dismissed, Adam breathed out a hard sigh that was not so much relief as the releasing of tension now that the first and simplest of his tasks was completed. All he had left to do now was convince Heulwen and her family to see matters his way, which was definitely more daunting than facing the small, stocky man before him who had over him the power of life and death.

Heulwen sat up in bed and, folding her arms around her raised knees, contemplated the hanging on the wall opposite without really seeing the hunting scene it so vibrantly portrayed. It had been stitched by the same group of women who had worked on Bishop Odo's tapestry and was worth a small fortune, or so Warrin said with his habit of setting a price on everything.

The shutters were closed against the bitter wind but she could hear it howling angrily against the cracks, javelining needles of sleet upon the slats. Below in the main room, only the servants were present. Her father had business elsewhere, her stepmother had gone to visit Mabel, Countess of Gloucester, with whom she had a friendship of several years' standing, and Renard and Harry were off watching a demonstration of French jousting over by the horse fair.

At last she stirred and put aside the covers in order to sit on the edge of her bed. A stoked brazier threw out heat. Judith said that a chill was best sweated out, but only Heulwen knew that she was not suffering from a chill unless it be of the soul.

Tonight she was to be presented at Court and tomorrow morning Warrin would formally ask Henry for his approval on their union in matrimony – strange how a haven could become a trap in so short a space of time. Her thoughts stifled her, like the pressure of Warrin's mouth on hers and the feel of his heavy hands on her body. The change was not in him, but in her, a gradual feeling, emerging from several weeks of unconscious thought and brought to its crisis by Lord Robert's news today.

Her mind went blank, baulking at the barriers it came up against. Ralph casually tossing her heart from hand to hand and tiring of it, permitting it to slip between his fingers and shatter at his feckless feet. She tried to swallow the knot of self-pity in her throat, and picking up her undergown and tunic from the end of the bed, fumbled with the laces of the former. Behind her the door opened and then gently closed. The latch rattled home. She tucked a loose swathe of hair behind her ear and turned, thinking to find her maid. 'Elswith, I want you to bring me – Holy Mother, what are you doing here!' The garments slipped from her nerveless fingers. 'Where's Elswith?'

'Below stairs ...' Adam's throat constricted his words into a croak, for the short shift was all that she wore, leaving very little to the imagination, and those the most tantalizing parts. 'I told her I needed a very important private word – I didn't realize that – Elswith said you were resting, I didn't think that ...' He shut his mouth, aware that he was stumbling badly.

'You never do!' She snatched up her bedrobe and hastened into it. 'What kind of manners do you have that you could not wait below?'

'It is not a matter of manners, Heulwen,' he said wearily.

'Then what is it?'

'A matter of murder – Ralph's.' He put down a leather money pouch on the coffer near the bed. 'Payment for your bay stallion.'

'What did you say?' She paused, the bedrobe half-tied, to stare at him, her eyes wide with shock and smudged black beneath from earlier weeping.

'Heulwen, sit down.' He gestured to the bed, and removing his cloak, draped it across the coffer beside the money.

She remained standing. 'The Welsh killed Ralph,' she whispered, 'do you tell me otherwise?' The candlelight made the red of her hair glow with a kindred flame and cast her skin with a false warmth. In point of fact she was icily pale.

'Yes, the Welsh killed him, so much is true, but they were paid to do it by Warrin de Mortimer.' It took an effort, but he managed to avoid appending an insult to his rival's name.

'I don't believe you,' she said flatly.

'I did not think that you would.'

'Adam, if this is a ruse to blacken Warrin's name to me it won't ... Oh!' She cried out as with sudden, frightening speed, he came round the edge of the bed towards her, grabbed her arm in a grip that was to leave bruises, and flung her down on it.

'Sit there!' he snarled, his breath ragged and hard. 'Stop running away and, God damn you, listen!'

She gasped at the force he had used, as if a tame dog had suddenly turned vicious, and stared up at him, shocked by the harshness of his expression. Brutally, without softening or compassion, he told her everything that his Welsh hostage had told him. 'Your grandfather was there, ask him if my word is not good enough,' he finished bitterly.

'I – no Adam, you must be mistaken ...' She bit her lip and looked at him desolately, like a woman he had once seen when her house burned down around her and she had lost everything. 'Why would Warrin do such a thing? Is he involved in this betrayal too? I cannot believe it ...!'

'You're deluding yourself if you don't,' he growled.

'You've always been quick to see wrong in Warrin!' she struck out, clutching at straws. 'Perhaps he had discovered that Ralph was betraying the King's trust. That would as easily explain things as your version.'

Adam swore and paced to the end of the room while he controlled himself, then turned back and sat jerkily down on the bed beside her. 'Warrin would not give a bucket of horseshit for the direction of Ralph's allegiance, not unless it jeopardized his own standing.'

'Don't shout at me,' she said miserably, and wiped the back of her hand across her eyes, smearing a trail of sooty tear streaks over her face. There were two small brown moles on her

110

forearm. Adam felt her vulnerability and a flood of guilt. It was just that she made him so angry with her deliberate blindness. He clamped his hands between his clenched knees to prevent himself from touching her.

'I'm sorry,' he said in a more controlled voice. 'It's just that I seem to be butting my head against a stone wall, and it's only natural to cry out at the pain.'

Heulwen bit the inside of her mouth and surveyed the ruins of her world: Warrin was Ralph's murderer by proxy, and the reasons for his courtship thus cast in a sinister light. There would be no betrothal, no marriage, nothing; the trap was sprung and she was free, but at what cost? She wiped her eyes again and looked at Adam through her wet lashes. He was gazing down at his clamped hands, his mouth bleak and thin. Impulsively she leaned and kissed his cheek. 'No Adam, the apology should be mine.'

Adam groaned softly and turned his head. Their lips met, and his hands burst free of their prison to seize her and crush her against him. He knew that he ought to tell her the rest of the tale, what he had requested of Henry and what Henry had demanded of him in return, but was afraid of breaking this moment and being brusquely rebuffed. The kiss momentarily broke as they surfaced for air. Gasping, Heulwen stared at him, but if her breathing was swift, it owed less to panic than it did to sheer physical desire. Having fought it since early autumn she had just been pulled over the brink, conceding defeat at last. Adam was to take a rich wife of Henry's offering and honour no longer bound her body to Warrin – least of all to Warrin. She joined her mouth to his again, leaning into his taut, quivering body, and they fell backwards together across the bed.

It was wild and desperate, frantic on both sides, so hot that it immolated all reason, leaving nothing but the white heat of skin on skin, of swollen flesh within flesh driving to a volcanic pinnacle that erupted molten, obliterating them both.

Adam slowly became aware of the rough sound of his own

breathing, tasted the salt of perspiration and felt beneath his lips the pulse that wildly thundered in Heulwen's throat. Her ribcage rose and fell rapidly against his own. He lifted himself a little to look tentatively into her face. Her eyes were closed, her lips parted. She licked them as if still seeking the taste of him in a gesture so sensual, that although he had peaked, he pushed forward into her warmth. She made a soft purring sound and rubbed a bent thigh along his hip-bone. He touched a coil of her hair, felt it slide like silk between his fingers, and was filled with an overwhelming mixture of tenderness and guilt. 'Heulwen,' he murmured tentatively. 'Heulwen, look at me.'

Her eyes opened. They were misty, still glazed with the ebbing aftermath of passion.

'I'm sorry,' he said. 'I didn't mean to go this far ...'

She covered his lips with the palm of her hand. 'It doesn't matter,' she whispered huskily. 'It was bound to happen, and I knew what I was doing.'

'Then you are not angry this time?' he asked, thinking back to the last occasion when he had kissed her and she had run from him.

Heulwen took her hand away and replaced it with her mouth in a slow, undulating kiss. 'Only at myself for driving you too fast. It was over too soon to be fully savoured.'

Adam stared down at her where she lay under him, becomingly flushed and tousled, and was startled by the sensual, frank regret he saw there.

'Does my boldness disturb you?' She tilted him a half-teasing, half-serious look.

'Disturb me?' He considered the thought for a moment, and then grinned. 'Well yes, it disturbs me a great deal, but in the sort of way I don't mind. You have my approval to be bold as often as you like!' And his own look was half-teasing, half-serious as he lifted himself off her. Instead of reaching for his clothes, however, he lay down at her side and wound the strand of hair he held around his fingers. The bed was warm from the

112

heat of their so recently fused bodies and the piled skins and feather mattress made it as soft and comfortable as a glimpse of heaven. The room was silent except for the sound of their breathing, the tick of the charcoal settling in the brazier, and the occasional sputter of the rush dips. Outside the world howled, tearing cold fingers at the shutters and striving to prise apart their encapsulated haven.

Adam turned his back on it to fill his eyes with the tumbled beauty of the woman lying beside him, and his hand moved involuntarily to stroke the full, milky-skinned swell of her breast. 'Heulwen, would you marry me if I asked?' His voice was mild and quiet, designed not to frighten her.

'I thought that Henry was going to offer you the pick of several wealthy heiresses? Robert of Gloucester told me so this morning.' Her eyes were clearer now, focusing on him as the pleasure faded to a background sensation.

'He did, and I refused them. I asked for you instead and he consented.'

'What do you mean?' The strand of hair was jerked from his fingers as she raised herself on one elbow to stare at him.

'What I said. I want you to wife. Listen Heulwen ...' He reached out to her as she sat up, her eyes furious and wild with fear.

'And did it not occur to you to ask me first!' she cried. The rough wool of his crumpled tunic prickled her thighs. She dragged it out from beneath her and pushed it at him.

'I am asking you now. You cannot deny that you want me as much as I want you.'

'That was lust, pure and simple,' she bit out. 'A mare will stand for any stallion if the time is right.'

Adam flung the tunic back down on the bed and grabbed her by the shoulders. She twisted in his grip. 'Let me go,' she spat, 'or I'll scream!'

'Scream, then – have the maids discover us like this. Peal the bells, let all of Windsor know!' But he released her and breathing hard, sat back.

113

'Adam, I won't marry you,' she said on a quieter but still determined note.

'Why?' It was not a plea, but one word spoken harshly, demanding the truth. 'And do not say it is because I'm your brother. I swallowed that one like a stewpond carp, but I've learned since then.'

She hid her face within her hands for a moment, then opened her palms and scooped back her tumbled hair, regarding him squarely. 'Because,' she said, 'I will not be bound by holy vows to that kind of hell ever again.'

'But you were willing to wed a turd like Warrin de Mortimer,' he objected. 'Perhaps I am being stupid, but I fail to see what recommends him above me?' He looked down at his bunched fists and with an effort relaxed them.

'Our arrangement was one of convenience,' Heulwen said, voice shaking. 'You would want more of me than I am prepared to give. Yes, my body answers yours, but such a need is fleeting. Ralph taught me that lesson too well for me ever to forget it.'

'I am not Ralph,' he leaned towards her, 'and it is far more than a fleeting lust. That, I could have slaked anywhere.'

'So you say now,' she retorted bitterly and picked up her shift. 'But what will you say in ten years' time?'

'If ten years past have not altered my heart, then I doubt ten years forward will have that ability.' He touched her shoulder, slid his hand down her arm until he reached her wrist, tugged her gently against him. His loins quickened, began to thicken and fill again. 'Heulwen, I love you,' he muttered against the hammer-beat of the pulse in her throat. 'Marry me?'

For an instant he felt her melt towards the gentle persuasion of his fingertips and stretched out his free hand to remove the shift that she held as a barrier between them. 'Marry me,' he said again, and sought her mouth with small, nibbling kisses.

Heulwen gasped, torn between the demands of her senses and sense itself. 'Adam, no.' Her voice was choked with tears, but her arms went around his neck of their own accord. 'Stop it, it's not fair . . .'

Outside a maid cried a warning, the sound rising to a scream and then cut off short. Heulwen and Adam sprang apart. Heavy footsteps pounded up the wooden outer stairs, coming at a run, and the door crashed open upon its hinges. Wind-spun snow swirled round the threshold, and over it strode Warrin de Mortimer, his face a blizzard of furious emotions as he surveyed the scene within.

'You misbegotten, hell-spawned son of a murdering pervert!' he roared, and the grating rasp of his sword clearing the scabbard cut the air like a launched blade-stroke.

'Warrin, put up that sword!' Heulwen cried, and swallowed. He was blocking the doorway, their only means of escape, and he was a murderer with murder in his eyes. Pale as ice they flickered briefly to where Heulwen stood naked and shivering, clothed only in her hair and the shield of her crossed arms. 'Hold your tongue, whore!' he growled contemptuously. 'Am I supposed to believe that this is one of your foster-brother's "occasional presences" that I must by necessity tolerate?'

Adam had been sidling nearer to the bed. 'I have the right,' he stated evenly. 'Heulwen has been vouchsafed to me this afternoon by the King himself.' He arched a sardonic brow. 'Dear me, you didn't know?'

Heulwen heard the baiting inflection in his voice. 'Adam, stop it!' she implored without much hope of being heeded, and took a step forward.

'Heulwen, get back!' Adam commanded, and on the same breath flung himself sideways as Warrin roared like an enraged bull and sprang forward. The sword slashed across the pillow which Adam managed to grab to protect himself; as the feathers snowed down, hampering Warrin's vision, Adam dived across the room and succeeded in grasping hold of Guyon's shield where it leaned against the wall. He jammed his left arm into the leather hand-holds and tried to reach the scabbarded sword standing further along the wall.

Warrin got there first, and it was only the speed of Adam's battle-trained reflexes that saved him from being skewered like

115

a coney prepared for the high table. A splinter of wood flew up from the surface of the shield and rebounded to stick like a porcupine quill in de Mortimer's cheek. He plucked it loose and dark blood marred his rage-whitened complexion.

'Do you enjoy murder?' Adam asked, ducking the scything swipe of the blade. 'A surfeit of Welsh hospitality for Ralph, and a sword through the belly for me. My Welsh hostage overheard a certain conversation between you and Davydd ap Tewdr, and was a witness to its result.'

Warrin's guard dropped for an instant and Adam lunged, buffeting the sharp shieldboss at his face, then made a dive for the sword. The tall night-candle stand crashed over, and Judith's expensive carved cedarwood box of tapestry silks went with it. A hinge splayed and snapped, and the bright silks spilled out to be ground underfoot.

Warrin recovered from his momentary recoil. 'I'll have your head for that foul slander!' he choked, and came on fast as Adam strove to free the blade from the scabbard.

Heulwen darted for the open door and screeched at the full pitch of her lungs for help. In the ward below Renard and Harry, just returned from their trip to see the jousting and already alerted from the squawking of the maids that there was something wrong, stared up the stairs in astonished consternation at the apparition shrieking at them.

'God in heaven!' Harry exclaimed, using one of Gloucester's favourite curses, hazel eyes huge with disbelief. Behind his naked half-sister, there came the sound of a muffled crash and a howl of fury.

'More like hell to pay by the looks of it,' Renard gave back grimly, and pausing only to gesture peremptorily at two gawking serjeants, pelted up the stairs.

'Renard, stop them, they'll kill each other!' Heulwen screamed at him, her eyes wild.

He pushed his cloak at her. 'Cover yourself,' he said brusquely, and thrusting her to one side, entered his parents' bedchamber. A hurled goblet crashed against the wall, nar-

116

rowly missing his head. The air was awhirl with goose feathers, some of which had drifted into the brazier – which was, remarkably, still standing – and there was a nasty stink of them burning. At the far side of the room, as mother-naked as Heulwen, Adam de Lacey was cornered behind a badly-scarred shield, and Warrin de Mortimer was swinging murderously at him. Breathing hard, Adam countered, the muscles jarring in his upper arm.

'In the name of Holy Christ, stop!' yelled Renard, his voice curving skywards as it sometimes still did when pressure was put upon it. He was ignored and his jaw, which was very much his royal grandfather's, tightened. He leaped onto the bed, took three paces ankle-deep in feathers and jumped down between the antagonists, ensuring that he faced de Mortimer rather than presenting him with the target of the space between his shoulder blades.

'Renard, keep out of this,' Adam said roughly to the youth's turned back.

'In my father's absence I have the authority here,' Renard said, voice once more on the level and controlled. 'Put up your swords.'

Adam shot a sidelong glance at the two hesitant but brawny serjeants standing to either side of the doorway, Heulwen shivering beside them, her face pinched and blue. He grounded the swordpoint in the rushes, but kept his fingers wrapped around the hilt, and did not lower the shield.

Warrin's lips writhed back from his teeth as he snarled at Renard. 'Don't get ideas above yourself, whelp! What kind of authority is it that allows your sister to play the heated bitch across the sheets with this forsworn cur!'

Colour slashed across Renard's cheekbones. 'Put up your sword,' he reiterated quietly, and nodded to the serjeants, who started forward. 'I think you should leave.'

Warrin de Mortimer stared into Renard's narrow, flint-dark eyes, then beyond them to where Adam stood poised, prepared still to defend, or attack. 'I'll have a reckoning for this,' he said thickly as he slotted his own blade back into the scabbard, 'on your body.'

'My pleasure,' Adam said with the faintest sarcasm of a bow. 'Better start praying, Warrin. I can see the flames of hell encircling your feet already.'

There was a moment's tense silence while their eyes met and held, will beating against will. Warrin pointed an index finger at Adam. An ostentatious gold ring trembled on his knuckle. 'You're dead,' he said hoarsely, and turning on his heel, stalked to the door. As he reached Heulwen, he struck her backhanded across the face, knocking her hard into the wall. 'Whore!' he repeated, spat on her, and slammed out into the bitter, snow-pocked wind.

Renard gestured the serjeants out after him. 'Make sure he leaves,' he said, tight-lipped, and went to pick up his sister from the floor. Adam shouldered him roughly aside, and dropping the shield, stooped to lift her himself. An ugly red blotch was fast marring the smooth skin of her cheek and closing one eye. Her breath came in great dry gasps.

Renard took a sheepskin from the devastated bed and threw it around her shoulders on top of his cloak. 'You've really set the fat into the fire this time.' He shook his head. 'Couldn't you have trysted somewhere less dangerous?'

'It wasn't intentional,' Adam said without looking round. 'It just happened. Put fat in a fire and you get a blaze you can't control.'

Renard arched a slightly sceptical brow, thinking of himself and the falconer's daughter, or that engaging little laundress at the palace with the pointed face of a kitten and claws to suit, neither of whom had ever fired him beyond the loss of all caution. He laid hold of the shield and set it carefully back against the wall.

'The trouble is,' he said, pursing his lips, 'you are likely to burn a lot of other people too.'

Adam flickered him a topaz glare in which there was more than a residue of recent anger. 'Renard, leave it alone,' he said with soft vehemence, and sat Heulwen down on the bed. 'Come, love, let me look at your face.'

She pushed him away. 'It's nothing, the least of my wounds,' she whispered and bent over, arms folded to her middle, her face screened in her coppery masses of hair, as she began to sob.

Adam stretched his arm around her shoulders, feeling helpless, and held her. 'Hush, Heulwen, it's all right,' he murmured over and over again like a litany, fingers smoothing and stroking.

Renard cleared his throat. 'I'll see if there's any usquebaugh below,' he said, and headed for the stairs, only to collide with his mother and her maid advancing up them. From the expression on his mother's face, it was obvious that the news was already on its way to scorching a path through the city.

Judith stared at the shambles of her bedchamber with a face that wore the calm expression of forewarned disbelief. She took in her work basket and the riot of spilled silks, the overturned candle-stand, the raw slashed wood showing its flesh through the leather skin of her husband's shield, the hacked pillows and the feathers that puffed gently into the air as she trod forwards, and finally, her gaze came to rest on the bed.

Adam de Lacey looked up at her. One powerfully muscled arm was across Heulwen's shoulder, his hand buried in her tangled hair. 'It's all my fault,' he said, meeting her eyes squarely, look for look. 'I'll make amends.'

Judith looked quickly around the wrecked room again and back to Adam. 'Don't worry,' she said severely, 'you will. I suppose you were caught in *flagrante delicto*?'

'Not quite,' Adam coloured. 'I'm sorry I ...'

'It's too late for apologies to be of much use,' Judith said waspishly, but having removed her cloak, she sat down at her stepdaughter's side. Her tongue clicked. 'Adam, put some clothes on before you freeze to death, and you'd better let me have a look at that wound on your arm. It needs salve.'

He looked blankly down at the oozing narrow cut running between wrist and elbow. 'I did it on the candle-stand,' he said vaguely, 'it wasn't de Mortimer's sword. You'd better look at Heulwen first. He struck her full force across the face as he was leaving.'

Judith contemplated her stepdaughter, or what could be seen of her through the screening swathes of tangled red hair. She was whimpering softly now, and Judith judged the pain of Warrin's blow to be the least of her agony.

'Adam, when you're dressed, I think it would be advisable if you went below to wait for Guyon,' she said in a gentler voice, and to Heulwen, 'Come child, calm yourself. No one yet died of shame.' She kissed her, and beneath the weight of her stare, Adam reluctantly relinquished his hold on Heulwen and began to seek out his clothes. Stony-faced, the maid picked up his crumpled shirt from the floor and handed it to him at arm's length. Awkward in the uneasy silence, he fumbled into it and struggled with chausses, hose and tunic.

'I suppose,' Judith said wearily, 'that I should have seen it coming.' And then on an angry, exasperated note, 'If you wanted each other this badly, why in God's sweet name did you not speak to me or Guyon!'

Adam stamped into one of his boots, then hunted around the room until he found its partner half-buried beneath a trailing length of creased sheet. 'I was going to if you had been here this afternoon, but ... well, the wain came before the ox.'

'Not just the wain but an entire load of caltrops!' Judith said tartly as he pulled on the other boot and began latching his belt.

Renard returned with the usquebaugh flask in his hand. 'Papa's just ridden in,' he announced cheerfully. 'Good luck, Adam. I don't know what he'll do to you when he sees the state of his shield.'

'Renard!' Judith's tone was peremptory. He gave the flask to Helgund and came to the bed, where he squatted lithely on his haunches to peer under and within Heulwen's curtaining hair. 'Come on, Heulwen,' he cozened. 'I'd have hated it to happen to me, but de Mortimer's been deserving a kick in his arrogance for so long now that it's a pleasure to see him get it. I'd rather have Adam for a brother-in-law any day than that self-conceited pea-brain ... All right Mama, I'm going.' Grinning, less than contrite, he sauntered out of the door.

'You'd better go down too,' Judith said, tight-lipped, to Adam.

He swallowed and nodded, but his feet drew him not to the door, but to stand and then crouch before Heulwen. He took her hands between his, saw again the two brown moles on her wrist. 'Heulwen, look at me,' he pleaded.

She shook her head. He released one of her hands and parted her hair to expose her face. For an instant her eyes met his, and they were full of a furious misery before she turned her head aside.

'Heulwen, please ...'

'Adam, go to,' Judith said sharply. 'Can't you see that she's in no fit state to deal with herself, let alone the burden you are trying to set on her?'

He bit his lip and stood straight, desiring somehow to set the thing to rights and knowing that what was right by his code was not necessarily right by Heulwen's.

The tightrope was blowing in a high and dangerous wind.

CHAPTER 12

GUYON LOOKED ACROSS the draughts board at the young man seated opposite, and suppressed with difficulty the urge to lay violent hands on him and throw him, bodily, out of the house. It was a gut reaction. Adam de Lacey sometimes looked so much like his father that Guyon would find himself forgetting that physical similarity was the only resemblance.

He dropped his gaze to the jet and ivory counters and nudged one gently across the squares, reminding himself that life, unlike draughts, was mostly marked out in subtle shades of grey. 'I do not know what to say to you,' he admitted, 'a part of me is so angry that I could kill you here and now without remorse, but only a part and that the lesser. I can see how it happened and how it unfortunately got drawn out of all proportion, but Christ alone knows how long it will take to unravel all the tangled threads and sew them into some semblance of order – and I'm not talking about my wife's tapestry silks.' He sighed heavily and followed the swirled pattern on top of the counter with a pensive finger. 'It goes pride-deep Adam, and you've done the equivalent of striking the de Mortimer family in the face with a rotten fish. Are you quite certain of your facts?'

'You saw the Welsh lad's reaction for yourself when he laid eyes on Warrin, and your father was with me when I received from him the full tale and will bear me out. The lad was not lying or mistaken, I would stake my life on it.'

'You will probably have to,' Guyon replied grimly, 'trial-by-combat is almost a certainty. Warrin's not going to admit to the crime, and he's got a very personal grudge now, hasn't he?' He flickered a glance briefly across the board to Adam and shook his head. 'Heulwen knows how to pick husbands,' he grimaced, 'all three of them.'

Adam felt the hostility emanating from the other man. His gut wrenched, but he was not really surprised. Guyon had shown remarkable calm thus far over what threatened to develop into a full-blown scandal and had caused a serious rift with the de Mortimer family, formerly close allies to Ravenstow. Now and then, like steam escaping from a lidded cauldron, a spurt of anger was bound to erupt.

'If I could undo it, believe me I would,' he said.

'Even down to retracting your request to the King?' Guyon asked with a raised, sarcastic brow.

Adam's eyes kindled with a harder, yellow light. 'No.' He clenched his jaw. 'I'm sorry if I went to him first, but I did not know how much time I had, and I had to stop her from pledging herself to de Mortimer.'

A small, uncomfortable silence fell. Into it Guyon said, 'It will break Hugh de Mortimer if Warrin is proven guilty.'

'Perhaps you would rather I retracted the accusation, gave up Heulwen and sailed on the first ship for Outremer!' Adam said, an edge to his voice as he heard Guyon's ambivalence.

'Perhaps I would,' Guyon snorted. 'But it wouldn't be justice would it?' And then he clenched his fist and crashed it down on the board, sending the counters leaping awry. 'Christ, Adam, why didn't you ask me for Heulwen before all this blew up in our faces like a barrel of boiling pitch!'

'Because I knew she wouldn't have me!' Adam gave back bitterly. 'She doesn't want a man who loves her or to love in return. She wants a cold-blooded contract of convenience!'

Guyon looked at him, and gradually his fierce expression softened as he sighed. 'It is not to be wondered at after the way Ralph treated her. She loved him so hard that it almost broke her when he took off in pursuit of other women.'

'I don't need other women,' Adam said intensely. 'I never have, except as a salve to soothe the wound of not having her.

123

I know that we have not had the best beginning, but God willing I'll spend the rest of my life making it up to her.'

Guyon made a rude sound. 'And a fine martyr you will make!' he scoffed. 'As I have heard the tale it was only half your fault. Granted, it was a serious breach of courtesy to go above uninvited, but I suppose that your news warranted it, and Heulwen didn't scream rape did she? If one of the maids did hear her cry out, it was certainly not for help.'

Adam cleared his throat and looked down at his hands as if their conformation was of great interest, and remembered her writhing beneath him, the sounds he had dammed against her mouth with his own as the last fragment of sanity was consumed in the conflagration. The stallion to the mare, she had said.

Guyon shook his head. 'Christ knows, Adam, for I do not. You escort that sharp-clawed termagant across Europe, rescue her from a handful of dangerous situations, weave your way with the skill of a diplomat through the courts of barons, princes and kings, only to bloody your nose on something as simple as this!'

'Perhaps because it's been too simple for too long,' Adam said wearily, and raised the hands he had been studying to dry-wash his face. 'I haven't the ability to fathom it any more.'

Heulwen watched her father remove his thick wolf-collared cloak and pace to the brazier to warm his hands. Two rings winked in the light: one was a seal ring bearing the authority of the earldom in the emblem of an engraved leopard snarling upon a castle motte; the other was a purely decorative piece of jewellery and were it not for court protocol, it would have remained buried at the bottom of a casket so seldom opened that spiders had been known to weave their webs across its lock before now. She put down her piece of sewing which was only a pretence anyway, something to keep her from wringing her hands uselessly together, and hastened to his side.

With a brief, tired smile, he gently tugged one of her braids. It was a gesture she remembered a hundred times from childhood – teasing, affectionate, conspiratorial, warning. It could mean a hundred things, but never anything less than love. Tears filled her eyes and she flung herself at him into the haven of his arms and wept against the breast of his emerald velvet court-robe. 'I'm sorry, Papa. If I'd known the trouble it was going to cause, I'd never have done it – I thought Adam was going to marry elsewhere – I thought that just once it wouldn't matter.'

'Hush, *cariadferch*, hush, you'll drench my robe and shrink it,' he said softly, lips at her temple. 'I thought you were supposed to be lying down. Judith said that she had given you poppy in wine and that you were best left to sleep.'

'I tipped it into the rushes when she wasn't looking,' she confessed, and sniffing, pushed herself out of his arms to look up into his face. 'I didn't want to sleep until you returned from Court, Papa. I had to know what happened.'

'You would have done better to drink the wine,' he said, and wandered from the brazier to his shield to examine its raw, splintered surface.

'Papa?' She swallowed, feeling frightened.

'What do you think happened?' he said dully. 'Warrin's fast, I'll give him that. He drew first blood: accused Adam of maligning his good name by a false claim of murder, and of deceiving and dishonouring you. It shifts the onus to prove the claim either way from his shoulders onto Adam's, and because Warrin brought it into the open of his own will, it diminishes the suspicion against him. Henry was quite content to agree to a trial-by-combat and I'm a cross-eyed leper if I don't know the reason why.'

'Why?' Heulwen was driven to ask, feeling sick.

'A fight to the death is going to make an excellent entertainment to follow up our swearing to Mathilda. It's going to take men's minds off their anger at having to swear to a woman. It's going to ease their frustration to see spilled blood, preferably Adam's, being as he was the man responsible for bringing Mathilda to us in the first place. Tomorrow's the swearing, and the trial's to take place the day after.'

'That's horrible,' Heulwen whispered, appalled.

'No, just expedient. You can't blame Henry for using it to his advantage. This reckoning between Adam and Warrin has been coming for more than ten years.' Guyon shrugged. 'It couldn't end any other way. It's not just over you, Heulwen, you're just the spark that ignited the dry tinder. Neither of them will withdraw so much as an inch.' He removed the decorative ring from his forefinger and tossed it down on top of the clothing chest.

Carefully she reseated herself, hands pressed to her mouth. Guyon looked at her with troubled eyes. He could see the imprint of himself stamped upon her features, and those of her mother. Her hair, although of a different colour, grew the same way as Rhosyn's, and the timbre of her voice was an exact, poignant reminder of the woman he had lost to the savagery of Walter de Lacey. And Adam de Lacey was Walter's son. Guyon cast that thought from his mind. Adam was no more like Walter de Lacey than a lump of flawed glass was like a polished jewel.

'Child . . .' he began softly, and crouched beside her.

'I'm all right, Papa.' Tear-tracks streaked her bruised face as she stared beyond him into some unpleasant distance. 'Only I think I'd like that poppy in wine now.'

CHAPTER 13

THE EMPRESS MATHILDA had cold, slender hands, and a coldly-held slender body which was encased this day in a clinging tunic and gown of frost-silver, trimmed with ermine tips at cuff and knotted hem. Adam set his own hands between hers and received an icy kiss of peace in return for his oath of loyalty to her and the future heirs of her body. Unsmiling, ungracious, she took it as her due, eyes remote and iconical, declining to acknowledge how many times over she owed him her life. Had she permitted her lips to curve, she would have been rather pretty. Beneath her silver gauze veil, her braids were a bright brown, and her eyes were of an extravagantly-lashed, sparkling lake-water blue, challenging every man who dared to look into them. On all sides of the great hall, the high barons and clergy of the land stood as witnesses to each other's swearing: Norfolk, Leicester, Derby, Gloucester, Ravenstow, Chester, Blois, Salisbury, Winchester, Canterbury. Adam stepped back to be engulfed by the throng and another baron took his place, kneeling to swear allegiance to Mathilda.

Henry was smiling in lieu of his daughter, not just a flimsy parchment smile to put a good grace on the proceedings, but one of genuine satisfaction. Adam supposed that it was indeed satisfying to him that all the barons had agreed to acknowledge Mathilda as his successor, which was in part due to the tireless persuasion of Robert of Gloucester. But if the barons had been brought to swear, then so had Henry — that he would not seek a foreign husband for his daughter without the baronial consent. But then what had oaths of that kind ever meant to the King, except the buying of time to break them later? Henry would marry his daughter to whomsoever he chose; that smile said so.

The celebration feast commenced with much pomp and ceremony as befitted so grand an occasion and the presence of so many important men. Adam, as a minor tenant-in-chief, was relegated to a place at the far end of the hall for which he was grateful. He had no particular fondness for these gatherings with their rife hypocrisy, everyone trying to outdo each other and glancing sidelong to see if they had succeeded. Then there was the back-stabbing and sly insults and, for him also, the hostile shoulder-nudges of men who wanted to see him lose the forthcoming trial-by-combat. Men who supported Warrin de Mortimer for the sake of his father, who was well thought of and respected at Court, and undeserving of the scandal now visited upon his house by a young man whose own family reputation was considerably more tarnished than that of de Mortimer. And then of course there was the gossip, the jests at his expense, the sniggers from behind palm-covered mouths, and the sly innuendoes. Adam bore them with a bovine endurance, but it did not mean that he was not inwardly goaded raw.

'I'm either going to marry you to Heulwen or officiate at your funeral, so you might as well speak to me!' complained a rich, basso voice at his hunched left shoulder.

Adam swivelled and stared at the grinning young priest who had just squeezed his way onto the trestle beside him, and found a sudden answering grin of his own. 'John! I hadn't thought to see you here!'

'The Earl of Leicester might feel in need of a confessor after swearing to an oath like that,' laughed Guyon's second son and namesake. To avoid confusion, he had early on been called for the saint on whose eve he had been born, and only on the most formal occasions ever went by his christened name.

'So might we all,' Adam said ruefully, 'the King in particular.' He stretched his arm and playfully patted the bald island of scalp ringed by a thick sea of reddish-black waves. 'You're ordained now?'

'Since last Martinmas.'

'So I've got to call you Father and treat you with a proper respect?'

John's dark, beautiful voice rumbled with laughter. 'Is that so much of a trial?' He folded his arms on the trestle. A serving girl dimpled at him as she leaned over to pour wine. He smiled back, but without noticing how pretty she was, not because he went unaffected by pretty women – indeed on occasion, celibacy had been a discipline he had failed – but because he simply could not see her clearly enough to know. Ever since early childhood when he had fallen over cradles, sewing baskets and hound puppies rather than walk around them, when he had been defeated in sword practice because he could not see the blows coming until it was too late, he had known that he was destined either for the priesthood or an early death. It was an obvious choice, and he had adapted himself excellently and already had a responsible post in the Earl of Leicester's household.

Adam glanced sidelong at the young man. 'Aren't you going to lecture me from your pulpit then?'

John narrowed his myopic eyes to focus them on a dish of eels stewed in herbs and wine, and answered with a question of his own. 'Do you know why my Lord Leicester chose me above several others to be his household chaplain?'

Adam shook his head.

'Because he knew that I wouldn't keep lecturing the soldiers about mere peccadilloes. Men will always gamble, take the Lord's name in vain, and fornicate where they shouldn't with someone else's woman, and then brawl about it. They're unlikely to take much notice of the bleatings of a mealy-mouthed priest young enough in some instances to be their grandson. I suppose I could hurl hellfire and damnation at them, but I prefer to keep that for the sins that really matter – like murder.'

Adam looked sharply at John. A soft, unseeing doe-brown his eyes might be, but they bore the clarity of knowledge. 'You believe me then?' He laughed bitterly. 'No one else does.'

'That is not true,' John contradicted. 'It is just that empty vessels make the most noise, and if you've noticed, it's all coming from de Mortimer's side. Don't worry Adam, we're not all out to knife you in the back. That's Warrin de Mortimer's own little particular vice.' He took a mouthful of the eel stew, swallowed, and added thoughtfully, 'I saw Warrin de Mortimer in the early spring when I was returning from my studies in Paris. He was a member of a hawking party that included William le Clito when they crossed our path.'

'He was what?' Adam grasped the dark wool of John's habit sleeve.

'There were a lot of other young men there, mostly from the French Court, I think. I do not suppose there is any harm in going hawking with William le Clito, it just depends what they were talking about, but I didn't hear any of that.' He reached for a piece of the fine white bread that had been baked especially for the feast. 'I saw Ralph, too.'

'What, with them?'

'No, the following day just outside Les Andelys. He was kicking his heels beside a water trough, obviously waiting for someone. I would not have recognized him, my eyesight being what it is, but my horse needed to drink and Ralph was too close for me to miss. He wasn't pleased at being discovered either, and not just because there was a woman clinging to his arm and me being Heulwen's half-brother.' He bit into the crust, moistened it with a sip of wine. 'He asked me not to say anything, told me that he was about the King's private business, and at the time I believed him. I had no reason to doubt then.'

He gave Adam's rigid intensity a reassuring smile. 'Don't worry, the King knows. I told my Lord Leicester last night as soon as I realized its significance and he took it straight to Henry, so even if this trial-by-combat doesn't favour your cause, it's not a lost one. Warrin de Mortimer is marked.'

'I thought that the victor's arm was aided by divine intervention?' Adam said dryly, as he attempted a morsel of the fish stew himself and grimaced. A favourite dish of Henry's it might be, but in his opinion, Henry was welcome to it.

'That is the theory,' John said with spurious gravity. 'But divine intervention is a fickle force to depend upon, and I should know, I'm a priest.' Then he sobered and fixed Adam with a troubled stare. 'Warrin used to be able to flatten you in the tilt yard when we were children,' he said softly.

'He's relying on that memory now,' Adam agreed, 'but I was only half-grown then, and he was almost at his full strength. We're much of a height now. I know that he is broader, but if so, then I have the edge on speed.' His smile was wry. 'Still, it won't do any harm to pray for me, and for Heulwen.' He reached for his cup and took a quick swallow of the wine. It was Rhenish, the kind he had lived on for several months of purgatory at the German court, the kind with which he had almost killed himself on the day of Heulwen's marriage to Ralph. 'I've loved her for a long time,' he murmured.

'The way she used to look at Ralph ought to have melted that ingrate's bones,' John reflected, shifting his shoulders uncomfortably, 'but he ran after other women instead.'

Adam put his drink down and tugged at a loose thread on the gold embroidery stiffening his tawny velvet sleeve. 'I think I would call him out too if he still lived,' he muttered, and snapping off the thread, sprinkled it from his fingers where it drifted, flickering with light, into a candle flame and was consumed in a brief, bright flaring. John knew when to offer glib platitudes and when to hold silent. He set his slender, long-fingered hand on Adam's shoulder and gave it a brief, hard squeeze.

The morning of the trial dawned knife-cold with a slicing wind from the east. Frost gleamed like crumbled loaf sugar on every rooftop and pinnacle, iced the keep a meringue-white, frilled the edge of the Thames in crackling silver praline and dredged

131

the beached boats like sugared marchpane confections. The air was grainy with minute frozen particles, sharp as crushed glass to breathe.

Adam rose as the first pale streaks of dawn sparkled on the thick swatches of frost tracing the shutters, broke the panel of ice in the bowl set on his travelling chest, washed his face, and went to first mass, his heart as heavy as lead within him but his mind impassively composed for the coming ordeal. He heard mass, he made confession, was absolved, and sat down to break his fast with Sweyn. Austin served them hot wine and bread and cheese, his manner at one and the same time both restless and subdued.

Sweyn rubbed one huge, calloused palm over the fierce thrust of his beard, loudly vibrated his larynx, and spat into the rushes. 'Watch his footwork,' he growled in his ashy voice. 'It was always his weakest point, and if you can fault him there, then you have him. Do not, whatever you do, try locking horns with him bull to bull. He'll kill you if you do.'

'I do have eyes in my head!' Adam snapped, and broke a hunk of bread from the loaf before him, took a bite, and without tasting it, washed it well down with a gulp of the acid, yeasty wine.

'What about brains?' Sweyn enquired, unimpressed. 'If you're not prepared to listen to some sound advice, then you're a witless fool.'

Adam inhaled to retort, saw the fear lurking behind the drawn-down bushy brows and half-lowered lids, and was silenced. 'I am listening,' he said instead. 'It's just my pre-battle nerves getting the better of me. You should know that by now.'

Sweyn's iron hatch of a mouth softened for a moment. 'Aye well,' he muttered, 'that's as may be, but you'll need them on an even keel before you step into that arena.'

'Have you ever known them not so when it has mattered?'

'Nay, but it has never touched you so closely before.' He corrected the set of his mouth to its customary thin slash, and

132

hands braced upon the board, shoved himself to his feet. 'I'll give you a workout to warm up when you've done eating – I'm going for a piss.'

Adam watched him to the door, then lowered his gaze to the bread between his hands. He did not really want it, but knew that he had to eat something. It might be unwise to go into a fight with a loaded stomach, but if the ordeal were to last any length of time, then an unsustained sword arm was liable to fail. He forced another piece down, took a gulp of wine, and became aware of the intent scrutiny of his squire.

'Austin, stop looking at me as though I were already corpsed in my coffin and go and fetch my sword,' he snapped irritably.

The youth rubbed his wrist across the dark down on his upper lip. 'They are laying bets in the alehouse down the road that you won't last more than ten minutes against Warrin de Mortimer,' he said, his young voice torn between indignation and doubt.

'Are they?' Adam arched one eyebrow. 'Because I am guilty of slander, or because my sword arm's supposedly weaker than his?'

'Both, my lord.'

Adam pushed the empty cup aside and swept his hand impatiently across the debris of bread on the trestle. 'Did you make a wager?'

The squire reddened. 'Yes, my lord,' he mumbled. 'They all laughed at me, but they were willing to take my coin. Their loss. They haven't seen you fight.'

Adam snorted. 'God knows what your father will think. He entrusted your training to me, and thus far I've set you a fine example haven't I? Drink, women and gambling.'

Austin's blush receded. He gave Adam one of his incorrigible looks. 'It was Papa who gave me the money for the bet and told me to put some on for him too while I was about it.'

'That's very encouraging,' Adam said with a pained smile, and then, 'Austin, I don't want you standing round catching your death of cold while I do battle. God knows, one fatality is enough without adding to it so carelessly. Get my sword lad, then I want you to go to your father's house and await my summons.'

Austin's throat rippled. 'My lord, I want to be there,' he said resolutely. 'It is my place as your squire.'

'It won't be pleasant whatever the outcome,' Adam warned, watching him with narrowed, thoughtful eyes, assessing the youth's degree of control and maturity. 'If I am killed, I expect all members of my household to behave with dignity. If you think your grief or rage are going to goad you into some act of folly, then I cannot permit you to come.'

'I promise to uphold your honour, my lord.' Austin stood straight, sudden tears glittering in his hazel-green eyes. 'Please do not send me to my father.'

Adam gave him a curt nod. 'So be it then.' He left the trestle and went to pick up and buckle on his swordbelt, giving the youth time to compose himself. Austin went to lift the scabbarded blade carefully from its leaning place against the wall. The gilded leather sheath resting across one palm, the pommel across the other, he suddenly straightened and stared at the woman standing in the doorway.

'My lady,' he mumbled, his face burning scarlet.

Adam swung round, his own complexion as dusky as his squire's before it slowly faded to match the hue of his bleached linen shirt. Without taking his eyes from Heulwen, as if fearing she would disappear if he did, he held out his hand for the sword and dismissed Austin with a brief gesture. The boy hesitated, then bowed, and with obvious reluctance went out of the room. Heulwen stood aside to let him pass, then closed the door and putting down the hood of her cloak, advanced towards Adam. He noticed that the ornate crystal and amber brooch no longer adorned her cloak but had been replaced by the leopard pin she had formerly worn.

'You should not be here.' His voice was level, betraying none of the conflicting emotions that the sight of her had aroused in him.

134

'I couldn't skulk behind my father's closed doors when I knew what you had to face today.'

'It might have been easier for us both.' He set his hand to the sword grip and gently eased the weapon from its sheath.

'But not the best or truest path.' She looked from his face to the gleaming steel and a visible shudder ran her length. 'Adam. I have to be present at this trial–by–combat, for Ralph's sake. It is my duty as his widow to be there whichever way it falls out.'

'Heulwen, if I fail, it won't be pleasant for you. You'll be branded a whore in full public view.'

Heulwen shrugged and forced a smile. 'I still have Papa and Judith and family friends between me and such disaster. I am not afraid on my own count.' And then her smile slipped to reveal the terror and tension beneath it. 'Adam, in God's name, put up that sword until you have need to draw it,' she whispered, 'it's making me feel sick.'

Carefully he resheathed the weapon and laid it down on the trestle, then crossed the three paces between them. One of her braids slipped and swung forward to brush against his hand. He touched it, using it as a rope for his fingers to climb until they reached her face. Tenderly he touched the purple and yellow swelling beneath her left eye. It was impossible to tell her that he had to draw the sword in order to sharpen it, for that would merely fix her mind more firmly and with new horrors on the fighting to come. Better to wait until she had gone.

'Am I then a matter of duty too?' he challenged softly.

'Adam, that's not fair!'

He stroked the other, unmarked side of her face. 'Am I more to you than a stallion to a mare?' he persisted, watching the desperate expressions fleet upon her face as she fought him.

'You know you are!' she cried with furious reluctance.

'Do I?' Her anger sent a pang through him. He wondered how long it would take to break through the resentful, wary

135

barrier that she had built so desperately around herself using the wreckage of her time with Ralph.

She made an impatient sound, at whom he did not know, and raised her hand to take his away from her face. 'When I saw you at Ravenstow in the autumn, I wanted you,' she said, her voice low and intense. 'Half my mind saw you as the boy I used to know, my foster-brother. The other half saw the man you had become, and between the two I did not know which way to turn. I still don't, and it's too late for choices now anyway. I'm trapped.' She turned his hand over so that it lay palm upwards in her own, the skin hard across the fleshy pads beneath each finger from the constant pressure of gripping a sword.

Ralph's hands had been fine-boned and tensile like the man. Adam's were those of an artisan – strong and square with spatulate, capable fingers that would have looked utterly ridiculous decorated with rings. A lightning jolt of terror shot through her at the thought of them gripping a sword in less than two candle-notches from now – or lying lax and lifeless – or mutilated. The loss of fingers was a not uncommon injury incurred during the throes of trial-by-combat. Her breath caught and her grip tightened.

'I've been trapped all my life,' he murmured, 'and it's not too late. After today, it is only the beginning.' He turned his hand in hers, linking their fingers, and drew her against him. For an instant she resisted, and then he felt her body flow and bend against his. He bent his mouth to hers, desire beginning to melt reason like a flame burning down the wick of a candle, stripping the wax.

In the doorway, alerted by Austin, Sweyn loudly cleared his throat. 'My lord, I've fetched the whetstone for your blade and you have yet to warm up for the fight.' He flickered a granite, impervious look at Heulwen and inclined his shaggy head. Adam sighed and fumbled for his grip on stark reality. The flame inside him steadied, receding to a flickering glow, but his eyes were intent as they memorized her face upturned to

136

his. And then he took a deep breath, controlling himself, and released her. 'Pray for me,' he said with a rueful smile. 'If all goes well, then we'll rejoice together later. If not,' he shrugged, 'at least we have had this opportunity to say our farewells. I'm glad you came.'

Heulwen swallowed, unable to speak for the tears crowding her throat. It was almost like being widowed again, worse in some ways. Ralph's death had struck her like a sudden bolt of summer lightning. This time she had the long, slow roll of thunder to warn her, oppressive and ominous. And if by God's mercy Adam lived, then Warrin would die, and even if he was guilty, she could feel no satisfaction at the thought of his death, only a weary sadness.

'God keep you safe,' she managed to whisper at last, and drawing up the hood of her cloak, hurried from the room before she broke down before him.

Hugh de Mortimer watched his tall, broad and only son stoop beneath the fenced-off arena in the tower's ward, and clenched his war-scarred knuckles into fists.

'He is innocent,' he said in a voice as harshly metallic as a sword-blade sliding over a dry grindstone.

Guyon stamped his feet to keep them warm and regarded the arena and the two young men now within it. Adam was moving restlessly, trying to keep his muscles from stiffening up in the raw, ice-spangled cold. 'I am afraid my foster-son does not share your belief, and although it pains me to say so Hugh, neither do I.' He looked along his shoulder at the older man standing beside him on the raised platform.

'You would take the word of a Welsh barbarian and a traitor's hell-begotten spawn above that of my own son?'

Guyon's jaw tightened. Several vicious replies burned on his tongue but he let them cool unspoken. What was the point in blistering an open wound? 'I don't wish to quarrel with you Hugh,' he said evenly, 'this goes hard with us both.'

'If wishes were horses then beggars would ride and whores

be restored their virginity!' his companion grated, inexcusably vituperant. 'Do you know how much store Warrin set by your wanton daughter?'

'I know how much store he set by his own vanity,' Guyon was driven to retort in Heulwen's defence. 'My daughter is not a wanton. Choose very carefully what you say to me.'

'Choose carefully? Blood of Christ, when I think what . . .'

'Peace, my lords,' said the King, stepping smoothly between them. 'It is grievous enough that these young men should be fighting at all, without the unseemliness of two of my senior barons turning the occasion into an open brawl.'

Guyon swallowed his anger and bowed to Henry. 'It was not my desire to cause insult or unseemliness,' he said, and held out his open palm to Hugh de Mortimer. The latter ignored it completely, but inclined himself stiffly to the King, his teeth snapping together within his full grey beard like a gin trap in long grass.

'A pity that you did not pursue such sentiments in the ordering of your own household, my lord,' said the cool silken voice of the Empress Mathilda who was now standing beside her father. She was wearing a velvet gown the precise colour of fresh blood, topped by an embroidered sable-lined cloak. Her glossy braids hung down from a gold tissue veil held in place by a circlet set with small dark gemstones that gleamed like preserved fruits.

Guyon regarded his wife's half-sister with a blank expression and no small disfavour, and his breath vapourized in a sudden hard cloud. 'I hazard we all have skeletons rattling to escape from the places where we have walled them up,' he said, his eyes seeking among the gathered nobility and resting for a pointed, benevolent moment upon Alain Fergant's bastard son Brien.

The Empress' face did not betray by so much as a flicker that she had understood what he meant, but he saw the twitch of her fingers within the fashionably long sleeves of her velvet gown, and knew without any satisfaction that his barb had hit the mark. Brien FitzCount was a handsome and intelligent young man with a forceful personality and all the finer attributes of a courtier married to the pragmatic approach of a common soldier. He was also the illegitimate son of a popular but only moderately important Breton count, and as such stood not a chance in the darkest pit of hell of becoming Mathilda's approved consort. What went on behind locked doors and closed shutters was another matter of course. Thou shalt not be caught was the eleventh commandment of the Court, and Mathilda had been fortunate enough not to violate it ... yet.

There was a brief flurry in the crowd that had gathered to witness the fight, followed by a burst of excitement. In the arena, the opponents turned their heads from hostile regard of each other and watched a group of men-at-arms approach the dais, escorting at their centre the Countess of Ravenstow and her by now infamous stepdaughter. The common folk craned to take a better look, murmuring between themselves, quoting the various superstitions connected with red-haired women and speculatively admiring the picture she made as she walked the path cleared for her by the Ravenstow serjeants. Her eyelids were modestly downcast on a skin so pale that it could have been moulded from ice, its pallor emphasized by the sombreness of her garb, unadorned except for the flash of agate rosary beads glimpsed briefly through the opening of her dark cloak as she walked.

From somewhere in the crowd the jeer of whore went up, but it was only echoed sporadically, for she did not look like a whore, and among the common people at least, there was more sympathy for a pair of lovers than there was among the nobility, where the protection of lineage was of singular importance. Counter-cries went out, good-humoured, egging Adam on, cheering Heulwen.

'It's a circus!' Hugh de Mortimer ground out through clenched teeth. 'Can you hear them? Thank Christ I didn't bring my little Eleanor to Windsor.'

'Why do you think they are here?' Guyon said, a hint of

disgust in his own voice. 'They want to be entertained.' He shouldered across the dais to his wife and daughter and helped them up the steps.

Hugh de Mortimer, who had smiled upon Heulwen and embraced her as his daughter on the last occasion they had met, now stared at her with loathing, the word harlot in his eyes if not physically on his tongue. Feeling as though she had been spat upon, Heulwen kept her gaze lowered as she curtseyed first to Henry and then the Empress. The latter gestured her to rise, subjected her to a thoughtful, thorough scrutiny, and then with a faint, acidic curve of her lips which hardly merited a smile, gave her the kiss of peace. 'Come, Lady Heulwen, sit by me if you will and warm yourself at the brazier. Wine?' She snapped her fingers at a servant.

It was a gesture both diplomatic and kind, but the swift, malicious glitter of Mathilda's eyes on first Hugh, and then Warrin de Mortimer, dispelled any illusion of Heulwen's that she was doing it for either of those reasons. Mathilda was playing; a cream-glutted cat patting a captive mouse between her velvet, dangerous paws.

Heulwen let herself be guided and sat down mechanically beside the gorgeously caparisoned Empress, feeling like a player in some monstrous mummer's show. She looked down at her bleached knuckles while the charges and counter-charges were read out and refuted, then raised her head to risk a glance at Adam as he made his denial and accusation. He was bare-headed, his hair curling and dark with icy water droplets, and like Warrin he wore no mail, only a quilted gambeson that ended wide-sleeved just below the elbows and beneath it an ordinary tunic. He had a shield, his sword and his skill, and Warrin possessed the same. Two living men had entered that arena, but only one would emerge.

Adam glanced once only and briefly at her, and half-raised his sword in salute; the edge shivered with blue light and cut her to the heart. Behind her, her father set his hand on her shoulder and gently squeezed. 'Courage *fy merch fach*,' he murmured in Welsh, the language of her birth and first few years. She bit back a sob and put her own hand up to grasp his, as Henry nodded at the steward beside him, and the man inflated his lungs.

'*Au nom de Dieu et le Roi, fait votre bataille. Laisser-aller!*' came the cry, and the silence of the crowd rolled in like a tide and beat against the barriers holding them back.

Adam crouched behind the shield and felt the ground delicately. Each blade of grass was a white, knobbled spear, slippery with potential death. Warrin sidled like a crab, sword and shield extended like pincers. On his cheek, there was a scabbed-over deep scratch, remnant and reminder of the brawl in the bedchamber.

He attacked. Adam parried the blow with a swift, economical move and twisted out of range. Someone jeered, but he was oblivious, his whole being taken up in the concentration of battle. This was no tilt yard session where their tutor would separate them before damage was done, no courtesy match where the victor would accept the yielding of the vanquished with smiling good humour. This was kill or be killed. Simple. Final. Adam was not about to risk himself until he had examined Warrin's strengths and weaknesses.

Warrin had a slight advantage of height – not much, for both men measured around the two yards mark, and Adam had the leg length whereas Warrin's was all in the body. The latter was more powerfully developed, but in consequence not quite so fast, and both men, trained in weapon play at Ravenstow, were no novices to sword, shield or footwork.

Warrin came on again and Adam parried. The blade bit his shield and rebounded with a dull, metallic thud. Adam struck his first blow and Warrin's shield was immediately there to catch it. The shock rippled along Adam's arm, jarring it to the shoulder socket. Warrin pushed and Adam leaped backwards, half-turned, and shield presented, swiped backhanded and low at Warrin's unguarded right knee. Warrin jumped and skidded on the frozen grass. The crowd roared and surged and were forced back by the Royal Guard. Adam followed through, but Warrin took the blow on his shield and behind its protection, regained his balance and attacked, driving Adam back towards the stakes in a savage flurry of hacking blows. The men fought each other forwards and back across the arena. Their swords crashed and thudded on scarred, abused limewood. Occasionally the grating ring of steel upon steel rang out as they parried blade to blade. Their breath began to come in harsh gasps of hard-expanded effort. First blood went to Warrin, and second too, both of them minor cuts, but witness that Adam was losing the edge of his speed.

Heulwen half-turned her head, her soul shrinking, her body constrained to remain and witness. Beside her, Mathilda was tense, a gleam in her lake-blue eyes. She looked like some ancient goddess presiding over a rite of sacrifice and was enjoying every moment.

'Ah,' she breathed softly and leaned forward a little. 'He has him now, I think.'

Heulwen swallowed and willed herself to look at what her incautious tongue and body had wrought. There was another wound bloodying Adam's gambeson, more serious she judged from the way he was holding himself, scarcely managing to parry the blows raining down on him, and the more enfeebled his defence, the more vigorous and confident grew Warrin's attack. His left arm dropped another degree, and without awareness, Heulwen cried out.

'God's death Adam, be careful,' Guyon muttered, his hand tightening on Heulwen's shoulder.

Warrin's sword flashed and bit down again. Adam gave ground, staggered, and slipped to one knee, his shield splaying wide in an invitation that the other man could not resist. The crowd roared.

Guyon's grip tightened like a vice upon his daughter's shoulder as she made to jerk to her feet. 'Be still,' he commanded against her ear, 'can't you see he did that apurpose?'

Warrin drew back his arm for the death blow, and in that

split second, Adam launched himself in a move so fast that Warrin had not time to recover and guard. His surprised grunt became a shriek of agony as Adam's sword took him across the ribs and abdomen and brought him down.

Gasping, bleeding, stance as unsteady as his sweat-stung vision, Adam laid the point of his blade at Warrin's throat, knowing that all he had to do was lean on it to cleanse away in blood the years of abuse he had suffered as a squire, the resentment, the insult to Heulwen. For Ralph's murder, or for himself? He squinted at the dais and through a blur saw Hugh de Mortimer gesticulating in agitation at the battleground and speaking rapidly to Henry. The King was listening, his expression impassive.

Adam forced himself beyond fatigue and pain to think with the speed of necessity. He had Warrin de Mortimer at his mercy, a single, short sword-thrust from death. Already his case was proven. To kill Warrin as he deserved was to gratify himself and end one small feud at the expense of beginning a far greater one that Heulwen's father could not afford.

Henry's eyes were inscrutable and flat as slate as the older man pleaded for his son's life, but his right hand started to move as if to make a command. Adam did not wait, for whatever it was would have to be obeyed. He stepped quickly away from his fallen, groaning opponent and moved unsteadily to the stand.

'My claim is proven,' he panted. 'Let him live with his dishonour.' He sheathed his sword.

Henry pursed his lips and gave Adam a narrow, calculating look before dipping his head the briefest fraction and turning to the man beside him. 'Lord Hugh, your son has seven days' grace to quit my lands. After that his life is forfeit.' He looked at Adam again and said in a tone as frosty as the weather, 'Adam de Lacey, your cause is upheld; God has found in your favour. You have leave to depart and seek attention for your wounds.'

Adam opened his mouth to give the formal, customary

143

reply, but his tongue refused to serve him as his vision darkened, and his last awareness was the elusive scent of honeysuckle and Heulwen's cry of consternation heard from a very long distance.

CHAPTER 14

'I**T ISN'T FAR NOW**.' Heulwen laid her hand on Adam's sleeve, her eyes anxious, for she could tell from the awkward way he sat in the saddle that his wounds were paining him.

'I'm all right.' He tossed her the pale semblance of a smile. 'Sore and tired. Nothing that Thorneyford's hospitality cannot cure.'

'You should not have set out so soon,' she remonstrated, not in the least reassured, for although his main injury was not mortal, it was too serious to be treated with the lack of respect he was affording it. The wind was bitter, stinging their faces, the sky the colour of a dusty mussel shell and full of fitful rain, and he had been forcing the pace. 'It was Warrin who was given seven days to leave the country, not us.'

'I have explained why it was necessary Heulwen, stop fussing.' He pressed his knees to Lyard's sides. She bit her tongue and threw a fulminating glance at his back. In her ignored opinion they should still be in London, allowing time for his flesh to knit properly and his strength to return. But Adam, as stubborn as ever, and a querulous patient as people of rude health so often were, had declared that he was surfeited with the city and the whole damned circus of the Court; that he had cauldrons simmering in the marches that he could not afford to let boil over – his Welsh hostage for one, his Welsh hostage's brother for another, his new wife's lands for a third – and nothing that his new wife in question had been able to say or do had shifted his resolve.

They forded the river and clopped through the village,

145

the dwellings cuddled together beneath the lowering sky. An urchin with a sling at his waist lifted a stone and contemplated folly until noticed and clipped around the ear by his horrified father, whose back was bent under a load of kindling for their croft fire. They passed the carrier with his train of pack ponies making for Shrewsbury via a night's lodging in Oswestry, and greeted the reeve astride his sturdy black cob descending from the keep. The news had gone ahead of them with their messenger, and they were congratulated upon their marriage.

Heulwen smiled and thanked the men whose eyes were frankly curious. Adam said nothing, but stiffly inclined his head, eyes guarded. They rode on up the low slope, her gaze still anxious on him as she thought back to their wedding four days ago on the morning that they had departed Windsor. As in all her dealings thus far with Adam, convention had been thrown to the four winds. They had made their vows at the convent of St Anne's-in-the-Field, the abbess of whom was her father's widowed half-sister Emma, and Heulwen's aunt. The ceremony, performed by John, was witnessed by immediate family and thirty nuns. Following a hastily organized, brief wedding-feast, they had left their guests to finish the celebration, if such it could be called, and set out at Adam's stubborn insistence on the road home.

It had taken them four nights, and their marriage had yet to be consummated. Adam was too sore and saddle-weary to take advantage of his altered state, and besides, there had been no privacy on their nightly stops. They had bedded down among his men in the great halls where they had been given hospitality, rolled in their cloaks around the hearth for warmth.

Heulwen had begun to notice an air of constraint in him, as if he had retreated once more behind the intractable barrier of adolescence. He scarcely addressed a word to her, and seldom met her eyes for more than the most fleeting of wary glances. If she had not been so concerned for his physical well-being, so unsure of her ground, then she would have rounded on him with the honed edge of her tongue. As it was, she kept that particular weapon in its sheath and tried her best to be meek and gentle, slavishly attentive, the perfect wife, not always succeeding, but striving close enough to distort her soul and tear Adam's.

Had Heulwen yielded to her first impulse and roundly cursed at him, she would have been spared much of her often-voiced anxiety. Adam, beset by the pain of his injuries and bodily weakness, was an easy prey to feelings of doubt. He reasoned to himself that Heulwen had not wanted this marriage, had been forced into capitulation by their circumstances, and the anxious, fussy concern that was all she seemed capable of displaying to him, smacking of guilt, was almost more than he could bear. The residue of volcanic heat had cooled into solid, enduring stone, and its weight was gradually crushing him.

He could feel her watching him now but knew that if he turned round, her eyes would drop to the wind-blown forelock between her mare's ears and not lift again until he was safely looking elsewhere. Giving vent to his frustration, he kicked Lyard with more force than was prudent as they reached the gatehouse and in consequence he received a jolt that sent the breath whistling between his clenched teeth.

The guards saluted him and a groom ran to catch Lyard's bridle. Adam gripped the pommel so hard that the oakleaf design carved upon it was imprinted on his palm. Before anyone had time to help her from her own saddle, Heulwen was down from it and hastening to her husband. The pain diminished to a narrow, bearable throbbing. He tasted the blood of a bitten lip and unclenched his lids to look down at Heulwen.

'I knew we should have rested up in Shrewsbury for another day!' she exclaimed with self-recrimination. 'Look, there's blood on your tunic!'

'Hush, Heulwen.' He glanced around the busy ward. 'Do you want my people to fear that I have brought a shrew to rule them?'

'Adam, it's no light matter!' she remonstrated, tears filling

147

her eyes. 'You have been very fortunate so far. You could still take the wound fever or stiffening sickness, or perhaps just die because you have pushed yourself too far! You deserve to be scolded.'

A little of the wary tension eased from him and some natural colour returned to warm his face. 'But rather in private than in public,' he qualified gently. 'I admit to folly, but there is no need to publish it abroad.' He touched her cheek and saw her own colour come up, giving her eyes a green luminosity in which he could have drowned. Abruptly he said, 'Your grandfather is waiting over there,' and removed his hand to command Austin to help him down.

She saw that his face had closed again, every plane taut and resisting, and with a feeling of helplessness she turned from him, lifted her skirts and cloak free of the bailey floor and almost ran to the old man who stood expectantly at the foot of the forebuilding steps. With a cry of relief, she cast herself into the haven of his embrace, her body riven by small tremors.

'How now, child,' he murmured softly, 'it is a smile that I thought to see on your face, not these floods of tears!' And then with a lightness that covered serious concern, 'Do not tell me, you and Adam have quarrelled again?'

'Worse than that, Grandpa,' she gulped. 'I've married him on the heels of disgrace, and it's been a terrible mistake. I know it has!'

'Wandering in the wood again looking for the trees,' he answered comfortably, patting her shoulder, and looked over the top of her head towards Adam who was advancing on them slowly and stiffly, his face wearing the guarded, defensive look that Miles knew of old. 'What's wrong with him?'

Heulwen dragged the trailing end of her sleeve across her wet lashes and turned in his arms. To her own eyes Adam was moving a little more easily now, only the taut muscles of his face betraying the pain. 'He took on Warrin in a trial-by-combat,' she said and felt his hand grip with surprise.

'Warrin's dead then?'

'No, but severely wounded and accounted the loser and banished from Henry's domains. It's been horrible Grandpa, and I don't really want to talk about it, not now. Can we go inside?'

He looked at her bruised face, seeing more than just the mark of bruises, and hugging her against him, turned to the forebuilding.

Adam eased himself carefully into the high-backed chair, closed his eyes while he mastered the pain, then opened them again upon Miles and the cup of usquebaugh-spiked wine he was holding out. He managed to give him the warped imitation of a smile. 'It's not as bad as it looks. I'm just stiff from the saddle, that's all.'

'How serious are your wounds?'

Adam drank and felt the usquebaugh hit his stomach like a swallowed hot coal. 'Not mortal, but sore. I'll wear a lifelong scar from hip-bone to lower ribs. I made a mess of things in Windsor, not just my body.'

'A trial-by-combat was always a possibility,' Miles said.

'Well yes, but you do not know the half of it.' Adam glanced at Heulwen. Her back was turned and she was talking in a low murmur to Elswith her maid as they unpacked the travelling chests.

Miles looked too. 'Like that is it?' he asked thoughtfully, remembering Heulwen's distress in the bailey.

'Worse.' Briefly, Adam gave him the flesh-pared bones of the tale.

Miles pursed his lips. 'No wonder you headed with such haste for the marches rather than make a prolonged feast for those vultures at Court.'

'I was an idiot.' Adam looked down at the cup between his hands. 'If I had not raced head-first into the thing I would not have come such a cropper, would I?

'Probably not,' Miles admitted, 'but at least Ralph's murder is avenged and you have your heart's desire.'

149

'Yes.'

Adam's tone of voice caused Miles to quirk his eyebrows and then, after a hesitation, to reach inside his tunic, 'I warned Heulwen against walking in the forest looking for trees, and if you are doing the same thing at the opposite end of the same forest, how are you ever going to meet?' he demanded gruffly, and held out on his shiny age-creased palm a piece of cunningly worked gold.

'What's this?' Adam reached, winced, and completed the movement to discover a circular cloak brooch of intricate Saxon craftsmanship – a wolf curved round, chasing its own tail, its eyes set with tiny red carnelians.

'It belonged to Heulwen's grandmother, my first wife Christen. She was Saxon and it had been in her family time without memory. I brought it to her out of the north, from her grandfather's deathbed and a bloody war. She treasured it the most of all her jewels, not for its beauty, but because it represented to us a new beginning. I was going to give it to Heulwen as a wedding gift, but perhaps it might be more appropriate coming from you when the time is right.'

Adam raised his head to meet the shrewd, age-caverned eyes. 'Is there anything you don't see?' he asked ruefully.

'Put it down to my ancient years,' Miles said with a like smile in reply. 'That, and knowing that you are both more stubborn than mules, and I do not have much time.'

Behind them the noise of two stalwart servants tipping buckets of hot water into a bathtub filled the small silence of words unspoken, and when all was quiet again, Miles changed the subject.

'It has been as peaceful here as a nest when the swallows have flown – neither sight nor sound of Davydd ap Tewdr in search of his fledgeling.'

'Does he know that we have the boy? Are you sure that the news has reached him?'

'The last two market days have been bustling with Welsh faces. He knows all right.'

150

Adam's brows twitched together. 'Then what is he waiting for? Why hasn't he come?'

Miles spread his hands. 'Perhaps Rhodri's expendable. Perhaps he wants to put the fear of God into the boy by making him sweat awhile. You could always organize to hang him in public one market day and find out.'

Adam flashed him a look. 'You are jesting of course!'

'Bluffing,' Miles said with a gentle smile. 'It is one way of testing brotherly affection.'

Adam snorted. 'And if my bluff is called? What should I do? Let him swing? Or prove my word is so much chaff and keep him neck-whole?'

'At least you would know whether to change the direction of your attack. If Rhodri ap Tewdr is no good as bait, he may yet make an excellent pawn.'

Adam narrowed his eyes at Miles. Their captive's attitude to his older brother had been ambivalent when he had spoken from his sick bed, and if Davydd ap Tewdr chose not to negotiate for Rhodri's life, it was hardly going to increase the love side of the balance. 'You mean replace Davydd ap Tewdr with someone a little more receptive to Norman ideas?' he murmured. 'Someone who has reason to be grateful that he was picked out of the road and restored to health rather than being left to die of cold among the corpses of his own folly?'

'Something like that. The lad's got a practical head on his shoulders, and while he might dislike us, he's not yet progressed into hard-bitten hatred. I estimate him redeemable.'

'So all I have to do is remove Davydd ap Tewdr and unleash Rhodri to replace him.' Adam drained his cup and sighed heavily. A dull ache pulsed behind his lids. 'I don't feel much like confrontation just now. I could sleep for a year.'

'At least a couple of days,' Miles amended cheerfully. 'Which is more than most newly married men ever get, you must admit.'

Adam looked down at the glittering brooch in the hand not holding the empty cup. 'Yes,' he said more wearily than ever.

'But then most men don't have to fight their way to the altar and take for their bride a woman who would rather run in the opposite direction.'

Through half-slitted lids, supine on the bed, his wound newly dressed, Adam watched Heulwen pick up his abandoned garments, consigning some to be taken by the maids for laundering and others to be folded away in his clothing-chest. His limbs were lethargic, but his mind moved restlessly like a confined animal. He was home, should have felt at ease and relieved, but perversely he was as tense and edgy as a horse smelling a change in the wind.

Heulwen set about removing her travel-stained gown, under-tunic and short shift, took off her veil and pinned up her braids, then waited beside the tub, shivering a little, while a maid heaved a fresh bucketful of hot water into it.

Adam perused the ripe swell of her breasts, the narrow waist curving into generous, but not overfull hips, and at the juncture of her thighs, almost like a target, a triangle of hair as red and bright as that on her head. He knew now how her body felt locked to his in the abandonment of passion. It was no longer a darkness of the imagination, but a tormenting, tantalizing memory of reality. His loins warmed and quickened, and he lowered his lids until all he saw was the blurred, distorted gleam of the night candle.

Heulwen dismissed the maid and stepped into the tub, which was shaped like a large barrel with a bench lodged across its width. She seated herself upon it and pensively contemplated the bed and its silent occupant. 'Adam, are you asleep?'

'No.'

'Do you want me to mix you something to ease the pain?'

'No thank you.'

She gnawed her lower lip, wondering how to cut through this hostile reserve of his when all her compliance and concern were rejected as though she had offered him an insult. She tried again. 'Adam, is there something wrong?'

152

'No. Should there be?'

'I do not know. I can't talk to you when you keep pushing me away like this.'

Suddenly he was no longer recumbent, but struggling to sit up, eyes wide and amber-bright with indignation. 'And is it any wonder?' he snapped. 'I haven't needed a nursemaid since I was a brat of six. I've been coddled and swaddled and scolded like some puling infant, and every time that I've baulked, you've either wrung your hands or gone into a sulk!'

The bath water swished as Heulwen grabbed the sides of the tub, her own eyes stormy. 'I am not the one who has been sulking!' she flashed in return. 'If you are going to act like a brat of six, then expect to be treated like one! You should be grateful for my care, not hurl it back in my face as though I had cursed you!'

'Grateful!' he choked. 'Grateful, when it makes me feel like a leper receiving charity from the hands of a guilty patroness!' Two spots of feverish colour limned his cheekbones.

Heulwen clenched her fingers on the side of the tub, throttling the wood in lieu of the man on the bed. 'Shall I then ignore your wounds?' she spat at him. 'Abet your stupidity by pretending they do not exist? Adam, you have been worrying me sick the way you drive yourself!'

The anger abruptly drained out of him. He slumped back against the pillows, pain etching two fine lines between his brows, and beneath them, his eyes were once more guarded. 'Perhaps I do it because I dare not stop,' he said wearily.

Heulwen finished washing and leaving the tub, dried herself on the linen towels that the maid had left to hand. Then she donned her bedrobe and as she tied it said in a voice as weary as his own, 'You should have taken one of those other girls that Henry was going to offer you. I will only make you unhappy.'

He conceded her words with a shrug of his brows. 'It's a risk I'll have to live with. Are you done? Stop standing there shivering and come to bed.' He shifted, making room for her.

She hesitated, unable to fathom his mood. His body was stiff, his tone unrevealing.

'Please.' He raised his lids.

'Oh Adam!' What she saw there brought her to the bed before she was aware of having moved. There was a lump in her throat. She leaned and kissed him on the mouth. It was meant to be a conciliatory gesture, contrition for hot words scattered abroad, but Adam's arm banded hard around her waist, pulling her down and the kiss deepened possessively before he broke it to investigate her throat, nudging aside the fabric of her bedrobe and seeking lower to the swell of her breasts.

Heulwen gasped, for the suddenness of this assault was not what she had bargained for in his tired, weakened state. She struggled to no avail as his weight came clumsily down on top of her, one knee wedging between her thighs. Her gasp became a cry of pain as he entered her. She was not ready and the hard driving thrusts hurt her more than a little. She closed her eyes and ceased to fight him, making herself go as limp as a piece of tide-rolled flotsam. Instinct moistened her body and the pain diminished, restoring to her the ability to think. Deliberately she arched and subsided to his rhythm, fanning her hands down over his narrow flanks. He was breathing in harsh, agonized gasps. Without fuss she increased her pace, urging him on, was touched by the edge of the maelstrom herself and felt pleasure burn along the driving pain inside her, but before it could intensify or culminate Adam cried out and gripped her, his body shuddering with the violent ripples of climax. She listened to his breath whistling past her ear, felt the sharpness of stubble scraping her throat and the rapid rise and fall of his ribcage inhibiting her own attempts to breathe. 'Adam, you're squashing me,' she told him in a calm, practical voice, and when he did not move, pushed at his broad shoulders, trying to lever herself out from beneath him.

Through the numbness of aftermath and the zig-zagging renewal of pain, Adam became aware of Heulwen's struggles,

154

and gathering himself withdrew from her. He rolled over on his back and with a groan bent one elbow across his eyes so that he would not have to look at her. Horrified images of his father blocked his mind from rational thought. He had just committed the act of rape upon his own wife, or as near as made no difference, and with such lack of control that it frightened him with its implications of what else lay hidden and capable within him.

'You're bleeding again and no wonder!' she reprimanded. 'Adam, you need not have been in such haste. If you bolted your food in the same way you'd have terrible indigestion, and serve you right!'

Cautiously he took his arm away from his eyes, drawn to look at her, but terrified of what he might see in her face. Her expression was cross, no, exasperated, and the look she returned him was speculative, assessing, as if an item taken for granted had suddenly sprung a hidden compartment. Nowhere did he read revulsion or disgust. She adjusted her bedrobe, left the bed, and fetched her bandages from the coffer near the brazier, then returned to him, tongue clicking. 'If only you'd taken the time to ask, I'd have shown you a way that would not have put pressure on that cut.'

Arrant surprise replaced the bleakness in his eyes. He pushed the sweat-damp hair off his forehead and stared at her. For a woman to admit to such superior knowledge of the bedroom arts was beyond his experience. Whores, or at least the high-paid ones he had occasionally bought were usually all soft, urgent compliance, begging and breathless in praise of his skill – and totally dishonest, he thought wryly – he had never owned a more permanent mistress to make him aware of anything different . . . until now.

Heulwen lifted her shoulders in a strange gesture, half defens-ive, half forced nonchalance. 'I was married to Ralph for ten years. He was the kind of man who grew bored without novelty. Once the freshness of my virginity had paled, he amused himself by teaching me all the other devious little paths to the centre of the maze, and once I was accomplished the boredom set in. I was his mare. I was saddle-broken. He moved on in search of a new mount. In the end, the times he came back to me I could not bear it, knowing that I was just a "good ride" among countless others.' Efficiently she rebound his wound with a roll of fresh bandage. Her hands were steady. It was her chin that wobbled.

'Your father was right,' he said gently after a moment. 'You do know how to choose your husbands. We've all been bastards.' He touched a tendril of her hair that had uncoiled from her pinned-up braids. 'If I behaved badly just now, forgive me. It was because I was afraid and overwrought. Starving men and feasts do not go very well together.'

She blinked hard and turned away to remove her bedrobe, surreptitiously wiping her face on it as she did so. She had cut through the protection of his indifference and seen what was layered beneath, but in doing so had revealed more of her own self than she wished to see. She felt soul-naked, vulnerable and frightened. Adam was watching her – she could feel his eyes boring into her spine. Quickly she pinched out the night candle so that abruptly there was darkness, but when he drew her against him, she went unresisting into his arms and rested her head upon his breast.

He felt her cheek cool and damp and, stroking her hair, wondered if he was in heaven or hell.

CHAPTER 15

MILES FELT THE GREY'S pace falter for the third time in as many minutes, and with a worried glance at the woolly-grey encroaching clouds, drew rein and stiffly dismounted, the pain in his joints a stiff, gnawing ache. He removed his gauntlets, to run his hand carefully down the stallion's suspect near fore and feeling the hot, swollen cannon, knew the worst.

'Trouble, my lord?'

He turned to face the knight in command of his escort who was himself dismounting, and spread his hands in a helpless gesture. 'It's an old strain. I thought he'd rested up enough after these weeks at Thorneyford, but obviously I've misjudged it. You'd best fetch the remount from the back of the wain and hitch him there instead. He'll not bear my weight for the distance we've to cover before dark.'

'Yes, my lord – are you all right?'

Miles smiled at the young face, so anxiously earnest behind the helmet's broad nasal. 'Naught that a warm fire and cup of hot wine won't cure, Gervase. My blood's running as sluggish today as the Dee in midwinter.' He struggled his gauntlets back on and clapped his hands together to try and revive the feeling. There was pain today, a thin knife wedging itself between his joints and grating them apart. The biting damp and cold shredded his lungs as he breathed it in, and sent an ague shuddering through his body. He wondered briefly if it was the homing instinct of a dying animal that had filled him with the urge to travel down the march to his mainholding, denying the weather and the exhortations of his granddaughter and her new husband that he remain with them at least until Candlemas. Perhaps. His body was a burden now, seldom a joy. He went slowly towards the wain where Gervase's squire was saddling up the brown remount.

'You could always sit within, my lord,' the young knight said, indicating the cart with its load of travelling chests and supplies for Milnham-on-Wye pressed on him by Adam and Heulwen.

'The day I cannot straddle a horse and take to one of those contraptions will be the day of my funeral,' Miles disparaged, suddenly grumpy. Yes, he was feeling his years, but was not yet prepared to admit dotage.

He set his foot in the long stirrup and allowed the squire to boost him into the saddle and, concealing his pain behind a tightened lower jaw, gathered up the reins. Face bright red, Gervase gave a command to the wain driver and turned to remount his own destrier, but paused half way into the saddle, his eyes widening in shock.

'Ware arms, the Welsh!' he cried, his voice whiplashing the cold air and finishing an entire octave higher.

Miles' escort closed around him. He fumbled with his shield-strap, swearing at the clumsiness of his gnarled, frozen fingers.

The Welsh wasted no time on the niceties of battle. Arrows were the means of destruction, arrows aimed at the Norman destriers to bring them down. A shaft struck one of the geldings harnessed to the wain, but obliquely in the rump, causing pain but little serious damage. The horse threw up its head and with a shrill whinney, tried to bolt. The driver cursed and strove to control its panic, but the horse was insensible to all save the instinct to escape from the danger and the pain. Another arrow hit the driver, pinning his arm to the structure of the wain. He shrieked, and the reins were torn from his grip by the jerking of the injured horse. It shied into its companion, which, terrified by the lack of a guiding hand and the stench of fear and blood, skittered sideways and attempted to bolt.

Miles saw it coming, but could do nothing about it. He was

aware from the corner of his eye of Gervase's squire leaping to try and grab the reins, a warning shout tearing hoarsely from his throat, his eyes wide and appalled. As if in slow-motion the baggage wain swayed and rocked like a drunkard caught out after curfew, and as the horses plunged and strained and kicked, it lurched and tipped over on its side, smashing its wooden-base frame into jagged, splintered spars, wantonly hurling its contents forth like tossed rags.

The horses threshed free and with harnesses trailing, bolted into the midst of the panic, adding to it. A flying sliver of wood shot into the eye of Miles' stallion, and with a scream of agony reared up, its forehooves pawing the sky. Miles tried to cling on to the reins and saddletree, but a lifetime separated his reflexes from Renard's and he was flung from the saddle, landing hard against the shattered carcass of the wain.

Ambushed, outnumbered and outmanoeuvred, it was quickly and bloodily over for the Normans. The Welsh leader, big and broad, with the legacy of the Irish Norse showing in his sturdy bones and bright blue eyes, nudged his horse around a mailed corpse and drew rein before the smashed ruins of the wain. A dead youth, his neck broken, sprawled close to the stallion's hooves. He pressed his knees and let the horse pick its way delicately around him, past the iron-shod huge wheels to the other side of the wain. For a moment he was filled with a sickening disappointment, thinking that his scheme had come to naught, but then the man on ground moved feebly and groaned.

Davydd ap Tewdr dismounted and bent beside the old man to examine him with the swift thoroughness of one accustomed to doing battle on the run and dealing with its casualties. 'Naught save cracked ribs and bruising,' he announced with relief in which excitement trembled, 'but he's bruised and badly shaken. Twm, get me a blanket. We've got to coddle him as tenderly as one of our own until we can exchange him for Rhodri.'

*

159

Adam couched the lance beneath his arm, held the shield well in to his left side leaving no gap, clapped his heels into the stallion's belly and shouted, 'Hah!'

Lyard leaped from his hocks like an arrow from an arbalester's wound bow and sped down the tilt yard. Adam's lance struck the quintain a solid blow. He ducked as the sandbag flung round and parted the air over his crouched frame. He turned Lyard in a compact swirl of hooves and repeated the move with an effortless liquidity that had the spectators all envying him his accomplished grace, and the young Welsh hostage viewing his own imminent attempt at the quintain with trepidation.

Adam lit down from the saddle with only the slightest hint of stiffness to mar his movement and suggest a recently healed wound. Walking Lyard over to the youth, he handed the lance up to him. 'Remember to keep your head down, your shield in tight, and don't sit up too soon afterwards or you'll get your skull well and truly rattled.'

'And I aim for that red triangle in the centre?' Rhodri sighted down the tilt, voice matter-of-fact, mouth nonchalant, eyes dubious in the extreme.

'That's right.' Adam's eye-corners crinkled for a moment before he schooled his expression to a teacher's benign neutrality. 'Not just the red triangle, but the dead centre of it, your enemy's heart. Good fortune.' He slapped the borrowed black destrier's glossy shoulder and stepped back.

Beside Adam, Heulwen paused on her way back from the somewhat neglected plesaunce where she had been planning some new herb beds, and linking her arm through his, felt the small, unseen ripple of amusement tremble his body.

'What's so funny, Adam?'

'Mmm?' The fact that she had spoken to him gave him the excuse he needed to break into an open grin. 'I know what's coming next.'

'What?' She watched the young man's throat move as he brought up the lance.

'It takes months and months of practice at the quintain to avoid that sandbag. The beginners can't divide their attention between aiming and ducking. They can't coordinate it all. He's in for a bruised back at the very least. Most likely he'll end up on the ground.'

'But I was watching you. It looked so easy!'

He chuckled. 'It is when you know how, but you learn the hard way, believe me.'

'As in all things,' she said with a small almost sad sigh, and then fell silent to watch Rhodri ap Tewdr gallop down the tilt to a rendezvous with his inevitable fate.

More by luck than judgement, he very nearly succeeded in being one of the elite few to cheat the sandbag on their first occasion – nearly, but not near enough. The spear tipped the target just slightly off centre, its impact unbalancing his seat in the saddle, and thus he was just a fraction too slow when he ducked and the sandbag fetched him a buffet across the back of the neck that swiped him out of the saddle and jarred him to the ground.

The black destrier jogged to a halt, and after one curious look over its shoulder, bent to nose at a tuft of grass. A grinning Austin ran out to catch the bridle.

'Not bad,' Adam admitted judiciously as he bent over the groaning, bruised young man. 'We'll have you jousting in Paris yet.' He took the reins from Austin and enquired with the faintest hint of challenge, 'Want to try again?'

The Welsh youth threw him a slitted glance, then turned aside to spit out a mouthful of bloody saliva. 'Go to hell!' he snarled, but struggled unsteadily to his feet, snatched the lance and the reins and pulled himself into the saddle again – teeth clenched and cut lip trickling blood – to attack the quintain once more.

'Bravo, lad,' Adam murmured, watching with calculating eyes the strike, the mistimed duck and the way he strove to stay in the saddle before finally conceding defeat and sprawling on the tilt yard floor, the last of the wind driven from his lungs.

161

Adam collected horse and spear and brought them back to him. Rhodri braced himself on his elbows, retching and fighting for air, wasted some of it regained on cursing Adam, but nevertheless got doggedly back on the horse as soon as his body was capable of obeying his will.

Rhodri turned the stallion in a quarter-circle and galloped not at the quintain, but straight at Adam, the lance levelled and deadly. Heulwen screamed. Adam's whole body tensed to move faster than he had ever done in his life if he had misjudged his man. At the last possible moment, the speartip changed direction and the horse swerved. A string of foam globbed Adam's gambeson. He smelled the strong odour of stallion sweat and was swept by the hot breath as the horse passed within a fraction of trampling him down.

'Jesu God!' Heulwen cried, rounding on him, her face as white as candle wax. 'Have you run mad, he might have killed you!'

'I don't think so,' he said in that thoughtful mild way of his that made her want to scream with frustration, and turned to where two of the watching knights had seized Rhodri's horse and were dragging him out of the high saddle, arms pinned and rammed behind his back.

'All right Alun, leave him be.' Adam gestured.

They let him go, but almost as roughly as they had seized him. The young man shook himself like a dog shaking off water, and rubbed one of his bruised arms. Blood smeared and stained his chin. His lower lip was swollen and dark. 'How did you know I would stop?' he demanded belligerently.

Adam's lopsided smile flashed briefly. 'A gamble on your nature and a guess that you wanted to live beyond a brief moment of glory.'

Rhodri spat blood at Adam's feet, then eyed him darkly. 'Rumour says that if my brother does not come, you are going to hang me from the highest tree on the demesne.'

'Does it?' Adam looked blandly at his nails, picked at a broken one, glanced obliquely back at the youth, and taking

Lyard's reins from Austin, swung smoothly back into the saddle.

'He won't swallow it, you know. He'd rather see me swing.'

'Then you'll have to hope the rumours aren't true, won't you?' Adam took up a lance and turned from his hostage to canter with negligent grace down the tilt and lightly rap the shield in the dead centre, avoiding the sandbag with mocking ease and swerving to an elegant halt at the end of the run. Rhodri scowled at him and touched his swollen, tender mouth.

'Adam, why did you bait him? I thought you were dead for sure.'

He threw down the balled-up wisp of hay he had been using to rub the horse down, wiped his hands on his tunic, and looked round at Heulwen. 'I wanted to test his mettle. I was curious to see if he would get up and try again after that first humbling in the dust.'

'Your life would have been a high price to pay for finding out!' she snapped. 'Did the King know how rash you truly were when he sent you to fetch his daughter?' Fear gave her voice a shrewish timbre, and hearing it in her own ears, she clamped her mouth shut and just glared at him.

Adam slapped Lyard's ruddy satin hide. 'Never buy a chestnut horse or have truck with a red-haired woman,' he quoted with a grin. 'They're both nags. I appear to have committed both crimes, don't I?'

'Adam ...'

He looked at the brimming temper in her eyes, their colour dazzling and sea-tinged against her flushed, furious face, and set his arm across her shoulders. 'Oh Heulwen, don't be such a scold for so small a crotchet.' He smiled and kissed her cheek.

She wrenched free of him. 'You're just as irresponsible as Ralph!' she threw at him. 'And when I complain, you make light of it, put me at fault!'

Adam sighed and pushed his hand through his hair. It was thick and straight and immediately flopped back onto his brow.

He opened his mouth to defend himself, saw how rigidly she was standing and realized that in a moment she was going to run from him and they would reach another impasse. Quickly, before she could bolt, he grabbed her resisting hand and drew her around the stallion and into the empty stall next door, where he dumped her down on the heaped dusty hay with its faded, evocative scent of summer and the memory of thundery sunshine.

'Look,' he said, throwing himself down beside her, 'I did not know for certain that he was going to ride at me. If I had turned and run, it would quite probably have tipped the balance and made him drive that lance straight between my shoulder blades.'

'You should not have goaded him into that state in the first place!' she snapped, anger unassuaged.

'I was testing his character. If he had remained down that first time, I'd have considered him short on guts, no staying power. The fact that he kept on getting up tells me that he's got courage and a stubborn streak,' and then wryly, 'and the fact that he rode at me is proof that he's foolhardy.'

Heulwen sniffed down her nose. 'That sounds like a pot calling a cauldron black!'

He conceded her a grin in acknowledgement. 'It was a calculated risk on my part. A man is always wise to study the temper of a weapon before he puts it to use.'

She frowned at him. 'What do you mean?'

A groom led another horse into the stables, peered over the partition and, clearing his throat, apologized and went out again.

'Miles and I had several discussions before he left — about replacing Davydd ap Tewdr with his younger brother.'

The straw crackled as he leaned back upon it and looked at her. In the dim light, her braids were almost as dark as beech leaves against the bleached linen veil, and her face was a pale oval with bold but feminine bones. He knew what he wanted to do, and also that it would be a mistake to suc-

164

cumb to that want. He had no wish to hear his name associated with Ralph's again, either to match up to or fail the comparison.

'What will you do, kill him when he comes to ransom the boy?' she enquired with distaste, feeling cold.

'It's a nice thought,' he admitted, 'but it wouldn't work. Rhodri would turn on us as you saw him turn just now, and he wouldn't stay his hand. Even if I killed him, that wouldn't be the end of it. We'd just have all the other big fish crowding the pool to feed on the small fry.

'No, if Davydd comes, I drive a hard bargain, as close to the bone as I can get. If he doesn't, I foster the doubts in Rhodri's mind and start needling my way into Davydd's territory.' He stopped speaking and studied her almost desolate expression. 'What's wrong, love? What have I said now?'

Heulwen shook her head. His tawny eyes had lost their calculating, ruthless gleam and were now open upon her, filled with nothing more dangerous than anxiety. She could not say that she had just seen his father's legacy in him – manipulating, cynical and cold – and that it had frightened her far more than his rashness to hear him plan so dispassionately, with his gaze as bright and impersonal as that of Renard's hawk. On herself now, it was still bright, but far from impersonal. Lowering her lids, she was aware of the rapid rise and fall of his chest and knew that it was not just an anxiety of the mind that awaited her response. Her body warmed as though he had physically touched her.

'Nothing,' she said. 'It is a side of you that I haven't seen before.' She cocked her head and gave him a guarded look. 'Although we grew up together, I don't really know you, do I?'

'You could learn,' he murmured huskily, and touched her cheek, then before it was too late, withdrew his hand and started to get up. That particular avenue was fraught with pitfalls and pain. They had made love several times since that first night of their homecoming, and while the experiences had not been disasters, neither had they spoken of overwhelming success.

Heulwen had been a willing enough partner – willing but not involved – happy to pleasure him, but reticent with her own responses. Part of it, he suspected, was that after Ralph she was wary of giving too much of herself away unless surprised into it. Certainly she seemed relieved rather than frustrated by his faster, more open response, but it did nothing for his ego. Give her time, Miles had said to him, but Adam did not know how long he could bear the burden of waiting.

As he reached Lyard's headstall, her arms suddenly came around his waist from behind, and he felt her cheek press hard against his back. 'I could try,' she murmured so quietly that he had to strain to hear, 'but Adam, I'm frightened.'

He turned around, reversing the embrace, and tipped up her face to study it. 'Frightened of what, Heulwen?' he asked, surprised. 'Surely not me.'

'I don't know.' A small shudder ran her length, as though tiny cold footprints had trodden up her spine. She could not say to him that with Ralph the learning had led her out of love and into trapped misery, and that she was terrified of it happening again. 'Adam, just hold me.' She tightened her grip on him and stood on tip-toe to reach his lips, moulding the soft points of her body to the lean strength of his. Adam felt the yielding resilience of her breasts, the pressure of flank and thigh, and tried to distance himself from the pleasure of the anticipatory, apprehensive heat already swelling his loins. As he tried to think of something else, all thought was then driven from his mind, all desire from his body, as Austin tore into the stables, his eyes so wide that the hazel iris was completely ringed by white.

'What is it Austin, what's wrong?'

'Lord Adam, come quickly. The carrier's just ridden in and he's brought a wounded man with him – sore wounded. I've got to fetch Father Thomas as soon as I've told you!' His ribs were heaving with exertion. Adam released Heulwen and set

166

his hand on the youth's wide but quivering shoulders, already seeing the portent of tragedy in the boy's demeanour. Austin swallowed, gulped in more air, and added, 'He's the driver of Lord Miles' wain. They were hit by the Welsh, so he says, stripped and massacred, saving Lord Miles whom they took away with them.'

'No!' cried Heulwen. 'No, oh no!'

'All right, Austin.' Adam's voice was reassuring and steady, the way it always was in times of crisis. 'Go and find Father Thomas, then tell Sweyn to get the men mounted up. Tell him also that we'll need pack ponies and ropes.'

'Yes, lord.' Austin ran. So did Adam, but in the direction of the gatehouse, not the keep, Heulwen struggling behind him and cursing the hampering drag of her skirts.

The injured man had been brought in slumped across one of the carrier's ponies like a half-filled sack of cabbages. Now he lay on an oxhide stretcher, his face bearing the clammy sheen of grey potter's clay, groaning spasms emitting from his throat.

'He's done for, poor bugger,' muttered the carrier from the side of his mouth, and spat copiously on the ground. 'Never seen anyone survive the blood poisoning and that wound in his arm's mortal nasty.'

Heulwen knelt beside the stretcher and gently raised the covering blanket, then winced. The man's right arm was bare to the shoulder, the sleeve ripped away and nothing to see of the muscle below it but a shredded, black clotted mess, inflamed and swollen. Torn between anger and sick pity, Heulwen bit her lip. 'Couldn't you have washed and bound it better than this?' she demanded, slanting an accusing look at the itinerant merchant.

He was a garrulous man, familiar by his trade with rank and beauty and not in the least set down by its ingratitude. He sucked the yellow stumps precariously rooted in his gums and shrugged. 'I did me best. I worn't going to hang around much in case any o'them Welsh bastards came back looking for som'at they'd missed, Poor sod were pinned straight through to the wood behind. It were the devil of a job to get him free, and if it worn't for me happenin' by, he'd still be there wi' only the dead for company.'

'Everyone was dead apart from him?' Adam asked, his voice composed in direct contrast to his wife's raggedly shaken one.

'As far as I know. I didn't stop to look too closely. Leastways nobody groaned, and the ones I saw had arrows and sword cuts that no man could survive. Proper mess. They must have ridden straight into an ambush.' He stopped to cough and wrap his tongue thirstily around his lips.

Adam snapped his fingers at a goggling servant. 'Where was this?'

'Heading down Ledworth way, close on Nant Bychan near that border stone that's always being disputed. Even going at full lick, you'll not make it there much before prime.'

The man on the stretcher groaned again, this time with more awareness, and stirred. Heulwen laid her hand on his brow. Beneath her cool palm, his lids fluttered open. 'Mistress Heulwen,' he croaked weakly, then coughed. Adam took the ale that the servant had been about to give to the carrier and handed it down instead to his wife. She took it, and carefully tilted up the injured man's head so that he could drink. He did so, after a fashion, the golden liquid spilling into his beard and staining his rough tunic.

'It was so sudden,' he said weakly, 'we could do nothing. They slaughtered us like spearing fish in a barrel. Lord Miles they took alive – it was him they wanted. The rest of us didn't really matter save as practice targets for their bows.'

Adam swore between his teeth. Heulwen looked up at him out of brimming eyes. 'What else do you do but find a bargaining counter of equal worth to barter?' he said flatly.

Surreptitiously the carrier reached down to the half-full cup of ale that Heulwen had put down beside the wain driver, then stepped back with it clutched triumphantly in his hand. Father Thomas waddled into the room, his five terraced chins wobbling, breath whistling in his throat as he knelt with some difficulty beside the stretcher and began wheezily to prepare the wounded man for confession.

Heulwen got unsteadily to her feet. The sound of the destriers being saddled up drifted across the ward from the stable enclosure and mingled with the intonations of the priest and the hesitant, weak replies of the wain driver. Adam swung towards the more distant noise, his face taut like a hound anticipating the hunt. Involuntarily, Heulwen put her hand on his sleeve as if she would leash him.

Adam looked down. 'Come and help me arm,' he said, turning her with him towards the keep, and took her restraining hand to clasp it in his. 'I want Rhodri ap Tewdr confined to the hall. No need to lock him up, but keep a close eye on him.'

'His brother is responsible for this isn't he?' she demanded, voice hard.

They had to separate to negotiate the twisting stairs to the upper floor and their bedchamber. 'I'd wager all the silver in Thorneyford's strongbox on it,' Adam nodded grimly. 'He's taken Miles for ransom.' He lifted his hauberk from the pole upon which it was resting.

'If you hadn't taken the boy prisoner in the first place ...' she began, then clamped her mouth savagely shut on the rest of the sentence.

Adam looked at her sharply, then lowered his eyes, but the anger at what she had almost said showed in the bunching and release of a muscle in his jaw.

'Adam, I'm sorry.' She touched his shoulder. 'Oh, curse me for being a shrew. I know it's not your fault. It's just that ...'

'You know I'll stand there and take it,' he finished for her, one eyebrow half-lifted. 'Just be careful how far you go. Do you think I do not care? Do you think that the thought has not crossed my own mind?'

Her chin wobbled. She struggled with tears and losing, began to weep. He swore and drew her down onto his lap and kissed her. 'Heulwen, don't.'

'He's not well!' she sobbed. 'He's old and sick. I've seen how he struggles to mount the stairs and climb on a horse. It will kill him!'

Adam did not seek to deny her fears. What she said was true. He had noticed the change in Miles himself, as if everything was going forward to meet the spring, leaving Heulwen's grandfather in a winter limbo. He pressed his lips to her temple and held her tightly until he felt the degree of her shuddering abate, then drew away to look at her. 'Come on love, help me arm up. I've got to go to the scene and see what has happened for myself.'

She sniffed, wiped her eyes and got off his knee. Ralph would have laughed at her and ruffled her hair, or else would have wanted to bed her for the novelty of watching her tears as he took her. Warrin would have blustered and fussed and flexed his muscles. Adam was full of a checked restlessness, eager to be gone, but for her sake containing it with admirable fortitude.

She lifted the hauberk from the bed and helped him to don it. Since its last wearing it had been scoured in a sack full of vinegar-dampened sand to remove all the dirt and rust, and had then been dried, carefully oiled, and hung on its pole to await further use.

The rivets made a whispering, silvery noise as the hauberk slid down over his body, and when he stood up in it, he looked twice as broad as he actually was. Next came the sleeveless surcoat of azure velvet and the gilded heavy swordbelt, and as he buckled on the latter she stepped back to look at the whole of him. A cold shiver ran down her spine. The man who had merely played at being the warrior was transformed into the warrior in truth.

'Adam, be careful,' she said unsteadily. 'I, I don't want to lose you too.'

He stooped to take his helmet where it lay at the foot of the hauberk pole and looked over his shoulder. 'I'll send word by messenger ahead of me,' he said with a glint of compassionate intuition. 'I know it is as hard to wait as to be doing.' Standing straight, he tucked his gauntlets into the helm, and curved his free, mail-clad arm around her waist, holding her carefully so that she would not be bruised upon the rivets. His kiss was fierce and hard, speaking all that his grip could not, and then he left her for the bailey and the men assembled there.

CHAPTER 16

MILES OPENED HIS eyes and stared with exhausted indifference at the black, blurred forest trunks. The pain in his chest and down his right arm was a dull, gnawing ache, but every breath drawn expanded his broken ribs and was pure agony. He was aware of the damp, cold air seeping into his very marrow – or perhaps it was just the creeping bony finger of death.

Welsh voices murmured among the trees – the language of his childhood, learned in the green forests of Powys at his Welsh grandfather's knee so long ago, and now suddenly so close that he could almost see the shadows of men, smell the damp woodsmoke of their fire and hear their bright laughter. But of course he could; he was their hostage and he was eighty-two years old, not eight, and his body was still earth-chained to pain. The laughter ceased and one of the shadows resolved itself into the tall, broad Welshman who had led the raid and was now holding out to him a stoppered bottle of mead and a heel of dark bread.

Miles shook his head, feeling neither appetite nor thirst, feeling nothing save perhaps a distant sadness that so many things familiar had not been permitted him the indulgence of a last look. 'You are being very foolish,' he said softly in Welsh.

Davydd ap Tewdr gave an ursine shrug. 'How so, old man? I bargain you for my brother. Where is the folly in that?'

'Corpses have little value.' Miles gave him the exhausted travesty of a smile. 'Oh not the lad ... yet. He's in fine fettle, but what happens when you put a failing candle in a draught? I haven't got long, and neither have you.'

The wind laboured through the bare January branches which snagged over their heads, striving westwards. Rain started to spatter down through the sparse canopy. The Welsh prince looked down at his frail means to an end, really looked, and saw that Miles le Gallois was not lying for his own sake. Part of it was the dull forest light emphasizing the grey-blue patches beneath the seamed eyes, but the rapid rise and fall of the old man's breast owed more to a struggle for air than to any fear or anxiety.

'God rot you in hell, you won't die on me, not until you've served your purpose!' he muttered.

'Do not wager on it,' Miles said, and closed his eyes, welcoming the darkness.

Heulwen, in the midst of a dutiful ave at the bier of the dead wain driver, was disturbed by FitzSimon, commander of the garrison in the absence of its other senior members.

'My lady, a group of Welsh are approaching the keep,' he said. 'They have a litter with them.'

Heulwen rose from her knees and beat at the two dusty patches on her skirts. 'There is no news from Lord Adam?'

'Not yet, my lady,' and added with ill-concealed irritation, 'it is too soon for that.'

Heulwen gave him a swift glance of similar irritation, but bit her tongue on her temper. 'All right, I'll come aloft,' was all she said, and having genuflected to the altar, left the small chapel and followed him out into the grey afternoon. The wind swirled disrespectfully around her woollen skirts and tugged at her veil; she held the former down with her right hand, the veil on her head with her left, and ascended to the gatehouse battlement.

Between twenty and thirty Welshmen had stopped just out of arrow range, all of them decently mounted, after their tenets, on shaggy mountain ponies. They wore the native garb of stitched fleeces and coarse linen, bows slung at their shoulders and the short swords they favoured at their hips. Narrowing

173

her eyes, Heulwen could make out a blanket-shrouded form on a litter to the forefront of their array.

One of their number detached from the group and rode forward immediately below the walls of the keep to request in accented, wind-drifted French to talk to Adam de Lacey. Heulwen peered down between the merlons. 'Ask him who wants to talk and why,' she told one of the keep soldiers who had been summoned aloft for the use of his deep, carrying voice. The question was relayed, there was a pause for consultation, and then the reply floated back to her; despite the fact that she had been half-prepared to hear it, it still hit her solidly in the gut. Davydd ap Tewdr, desiring to exchange her grandfather for Rhodri.

'Dear God,' she whispered, for there was now no doubting that the form on the litter was her grandfather – and on a litter meant that he was too weak to sit on a horse, the bastion of his stubborn will and pride.

'Baulk him until we can get a message to Lord Adam,' FitzSimon said and turned to command one of the men.

'No!'

His parted lips sagged and he swivelled to gape at Heulwen in disbelief. Accustomed to taking orders from men, and by his position in the keep hierarchy to giving them too, he was possessed of an arrogant certainty that women should defer to their male superiors, and was unpleasantly astounded by her denial.

'My lady, with all due respect, this is too serious a matter to be judged by us,' he said, recovering his dignity and twitching his shoulders within his cloak like a hawk settling ruffled feathers.

To be judged by a woman – a flighty, red-haired woman of more than half-Welsh blood. As if his head were transparent and the words written on his brain she could read his mind, and her chin came up a stubborn notch. 'It is also too serious a matter to leave until my husband's return!' she answered. 'That is my grandfather down there on that litter in their murdering

174

possession. Have Rhodri ap Tewdr brought up here to me now!'

He hesitated until he could hesitate no longer, then inclined his head in a stiff, scant formality and left her. Heulwen swallowed, bowed her head, and leaned it for a moment against the cold, gritty stone behind which she sheltered. 'Holy Christ, what do I do?' she murmured into the shadow created by her body. 'Adam, help me, what do I do?'

Rhodri, hands corded behind his back, was thrust into her presence, his eyes anxiously wide, his swollen mouth set in a thin, tight line. She straightened, adjusted her cloak, and faced him coldly.

'Your brother has come for you. I wish my husband had left you to die in the road.'

He returned her a measured gaze, for he had heard the news of his brother's raid and watched Thorneyford react to it like a disturbed anthill. 'My lady, I am sorry, believe me,' he said softly in Welsh. 'Even knowing that your lord intended using me for his own purposes, I could have wished myself free in different circumstances.'

'Spare me your condolences,' she snapped, 'you are wasting your breath.' She turned from him to the impassively waiting soldier. 'Tell him that Lord de Lacey is not here, and that in his absence Prince Davydd will have to deal with his wife, who is of Welsh blood herself and the granddaughter of Miles le Gallois.'

Heulwen collected the reins and thanked the man who helped her into the saddle. Her mare, sensing her tension, jibbed and sidled, and she had to put a gentling hand on the sweating grey neck and murmur soothing words.

'My lady, I still say that you are making a mistake in going out to treat with them,' FitzSimon muttered beside her and curbed his own restless stallion. 'It is much too dangerous. They might attack us.'

'I doubt it, but if they do, I trust in the might of your sword-

175

arm to deliver us.' Her voice managed to be both dulcet and corrosive at one and the same time. She set her heels into Gemini's sides and the mare moved anxiously forwards.

Feeling no taller than the span of his own hand beneath her scorn, FitzSimon glared at Heulwen's back knowing that if she had been his to beat, her body by now would have matched the slate-blue shade of the cloak pinned across his breast. Starting after her, he dragged viciously on the hostage's reins. Rhodri ap Tewdr sat his dun gelding in silence, his hands lashed to the pommel, his feet joined by a double loop of rope slung beneath the horse's belly and surrounding him, an escort of six serjeants.

As Gemini paced away from the safety of Thorneyford's outer bailey and comfortingly solid curtain wall, Heulwen felt apprehension and fear churning within her, threatening to make her sick. She swallowed valiantly, hoping that appearances and emotions were not one and the same. It was easier for the men, for their faces were half-concealed by their helms. Hers was open, vulnerable to Welsh eyes and whatever they might read into it – her fortune and her grandfather's. The responsibility was terrifying.

Davydd ap Tewdr watched warily as the group from the castle approached the prearranged meeting place, marked by a Welsh lance thrust point-down in the turf. 'All right,' he said over his shoulder. 'Bring him.'

The woman who drew rein and faced him across the wind-quivered shaft was strikingly beautiful – not classically so, her bones were too strong, but in an earthy, tempestuous way, appealing entirely to the senses.

'Lady Heulwen?' He gave her a charming, slightly wolfish smile and looked beyond her to Rhodri, who flushed duskily and averted his gaze.

'I hope we need not waste time on the formalities?' she responded frostily. 'Surely there is no more to be done than to make the exchange?'

Davydd ap Tewdr brushed his hand over his moustache and

refused to be frozen by the ice in her gaze. He noticed that not by so much as a flicker had she acknowledged the presence of her grandfather lying there on the pallet.

'He's still alive,' he said, and then, provocatively, 'and we have treated him with more courtesy than you appear to have extended towards my brother.'

'That was my own fault,' Rhodri said quickly, 'I fell off a horse this morning.'

Ap Tewdr gave his youngest brother a sharp glance. 'Last time you fell off a horse you were three years old!' he commented, but let it rest and turned smiling to Heulwen. 'My lady, by all means let us make this exchange. I have no desire to linger here, and I am sure you will want to take your grandfather within to warmth and comfort.'

Heulwen nodded stiffly, unable to speak, knowing that if she so much as looked at the litter, then like a piece of ice bearing too much weight, she would shatter apart. She raised her hand and gestured to FitzSimon.

Disgust evident in his every movement, the knight drew the sharp hunting dagger from his belt, and dismounting, stooped to slash the ropes that bound Rhodri to the dun, then pulled him down from the saddle.

Rhodri rubbed his wrists. FitzSimon pricked the dagger longingly through tunic and shirt. 'Don't try anything,' he growled.

'I'd have to be as mad as a *saeson* to do that with freedom so close,' Rhodri retorted, and the daggerpoint punctured his skin. The Welsh stiffened in their saddles, and hands went to swordhilts.

Heulwen flung herself down from her mare and rounded on FitzSimon. 'Give me that knife!' she cried, and held out her hand, her face and voice both white with fury. When he did not move — stunned that a woman, even one of rank would dare to command a weapon from the hand of a man — she wrenched it from him and pitched it as far away as her strength would allow. 'Don't you realize what is at stake?' she spat. 'Is your pride everything that you cannot take a childish jibe without responding like a similar child?' A look of disgust rippled the surface of her rage as she made a jerky gesture of dismissal. 'Return to the keep and wait for me there. I need you about as much as an arbalest bolt through the skull!'

FitzSimon recoiled as if from the venom of a striking snake. He was aware that the Welsh had subsided from their anger and were watching the scene with amused curiosity, and the pride she had spoken of with such scorn had either to be swallowed or choked upon. After a precarious moment, he chose the former, but with a very bad grace. Lord Adam was going to hear of this, by Christ on the cross he was! 'My lady,' he acknowledged, making the words sound like an insult. He went to his dagger, picked it out of the grass and wiped it meticulously before sheathing it, then mounted up and spurred his horse to a canter.

Heulwen watched him leave, her jaw set, then turned again to Davydd ap Tewdr. 'I apologize for him,' she said stiltedly, and swallowed. The rage had begun to drain from her. She felt very much like bursting into tears and knew that she dared not, for then they would see her as just another hysterical woman, rather than an authority with whom they must reckon.

'Don't,' said ap Tewdr with a laconic shrug, 'a Welsh arrow will put an end to him sooner or later.'

'I know all I wish to know about Welsh arrows,' she said frostily. 'Let us have this exchange over and done with.'

'By all means.' Ap Tewdr's tone was ripe with expansive mockery and Heulwen hated him for it. 'Give your lord my regards and regrets that we could not deal directly.'

'I will do so,' she said through her teeth, 'be assured of it,' and gestured the two serjeants forward to raise the litter. Still rubbing his wrists, waiting for a mount to be brought through the Welsh ranks to him, Rhodri looked down at the man lying there, and then quickly away, but it was too late. His eyes had already fixed the image in his brain.

'Be careful,' Heulwen cautioned the men, and as the Welsh

took charge of their leader's brother, slapping him on the shoulder, crowing over him and their success, she took her own first look at her grandfather.

He was awake and aware, watching her, and as the first sob was caught in her throat and choked down, he gave her the ghost of a smile, the merest contortion of his blue lips. 'You did well, *cariad*,' he whispered. 'Proud of you.' His hand twitched beneath the blanket, emerged after a brief struggle, and stretched towards her. She swooped down to take it, and the men stopped as she bent over him, her body wracked with shudders of grieving and relief.

'Come, *cariad*,' Miles husked, 'no tears, not now ...' He stroked her braid, then assailed by weakness, his hand dropped back onto the covers. He closed his eyes. Crying freely, distraught, but not to the point of being incapable, Heulwen tucked her grandfather's cold hand back within the covering of sheepskins, drew them up to his chin, and went to retrieve Gemini. Half-blinded by tears, she watched the Welsh ride away in the opposite direction, their triumph fluting the cold February wind. One of the riders hesitated and looked round. She thought it was Rhodri, but through the distorting blur of tears could not be sure, and neither did she really care.

'Christ, but I really thought he was going to die on us!' Davydd ap Tewdr laughed with the jubilation of desperate relief. 'If we'd left it until dawn tomorrow, it would have been too late. He'll not last out the night.'

Rhodri swallowed the bile clogging his throat and said nothing. He was remembering the sunken, blue-tinged flesh and hearing the old man's dragging fight for breath.

'You didn't have to do it this way,' he said when he had control of himself.

The wide shoulders twitched irritably within the encasing half-hauberk. 'Not developing a conscience are we Rhod?' he scoffed. 'Would you rather have swung from a gibbet on Candlemas eve?'

179

'It wouldn't have come to that. It was only a ruse to get you to come. De Lacey wanted to treat with you.'

'A lure hmmm?' Davydd ap Tewdr chuckled sour amusement into his moustache. 'Well, de Lacey got more than he bargained for, didn't he?'

'And sweet Christ so might we. Do you know how much outrage this will cause? We'll have every marcher lord between Hereford and Chester down on us for this!'

Davydd reined to a halt and slewed to glare at the dark stripling beside him. 'You dare to lecture me, whelp!' he roared, and fetched Rhodri a buffet that reeled him in the saddle. 'You dare to preach at me like a belly-aching priest, when it was your idiocy that brought about this whole predicament. Christ on the cross, I should have left you to rot on a *saeson* gibbet!'

The blow had opened Rhodri's cut lip, and dark blood dripped off the end of his chin and soaked into his mount's coarse winter fell. 'I'm not ungrateful,' he muttered thickly, 'I just thought that you could have gone about it in a different way. There's enough bad blood already. We killed Lady Heulwen's first husband, and now you've as good as murdered her grandfather.'

Davydd let drop the reins he had picked up and stared hard at Rhodri. 'What do you mean, her first husband?'

'Ralph le Chevalier, don't you remember?'

'Le Chevalier? She's *his* widow?' He leaned on his pommel and stared, and suddenly surprise gave way to laughter. 'God, she ought to be eternally grateful to us that she's rid of him. I wish I'd known!'

Rhodri studied his brother, a new maturity stripping the scales of childhood from his eyes. Davydd was only aware of the ground directly beneath his feet, without a thought for the looming horizon. It had been his own shortcoming until his wounding and imprisonment had taught him a different, wary discretion. He twisted his injured lip. 'Why couldn't you have made peace with de Lacey? All right, he's a Norman and out for his own gain, but he's no glutton. He'd have listened to reason, and he's the Earl of Ravenstow's own son-in-law now.'

Davydd spluttered at the notion. 'I'd as soon invite a pack of wolves to kennel among my flocks!'

'You probably just have. Miles le Gallois is respected both sides of the border. His son's an earl and wed to the English King's own daughter, and he has Welsh connections on the distaff side with half the nobility of Gwynedd and Powys!' And this time Rhodri jerked his mount sideways, avoiding the intended blow.

'A wolf in sheep's clothing!' Davydd roared, thoroughly beside himself, spittle flecking his moustache. 'And fostered at my own hearth. You've gone soft, turned into a Norman lick-arse!' He dug his heels into his pony's flanks, and cursing, swept on ahead, leaving Rhodri to blink after him, unexpected tears stinging his eyes.

Had he turned into a 'Norman lick-arse'? He thought back over that jousting episode this afternoon, the superior, good-humoured amusement quickly becoming rage as the pet animal rounded on its captors with a snarl. The calculating falcon-amber eyes of Adam de Lacey and his deceptively smiling mouth. Davydd did not know what he was facing.

Rhodri thought of the old man, Miles le Gallois: Miles ap Heulwen uerch Owain of the line of Hwyel Dda. There was Welsh blood there, as good as or better than his own. He had grown fond of the old man during the months of his confinement, perhaps more than was wise. Miles had been perceptive and tolerant, compassionate without pitying, for he understood Welsh ways having been born to them himself, and despite the plentiful opportunity had never mocked or belittled Rhodri. He deserved better than he had received. Rhodri wiped at his eyes and swore because he was moved to grief for a man by tradition his enemy. Then he touched his cut lip, and glowering at his brother's broad back, kicked the horse and cantered to join him.

It was late afternoon when Adam and his men came upon the

remains of the Welsh raid. The jingle of their harness, the snorting of their mounts and the creak of men shifting uneasily in their saddles broke the silence of the grave, sending small animals scuttling for cover and birds winging with calls of alarm.

One of Adam's Angevins leaped down from his destrier and examined a soldier's sprawled corpse. His leather hauberk had been stripped and there was a pale band of skin upon one of his fingers where a ring had very recently existed. Stony-faced, Adam nudged Lyard forward through the wet grass. There were no weapons beside the bodies. Swords, axes, lances, shields, all had been taken, including the harness from the dead horses.

'The bastards,' Sweyn muttered at Adam's shoulder. 'I wish I had been leading this escort.'

'Be thankful you were not,' Adam said shortly, and dismounted to prowl across the desecration to the overturned cart. Miles' destrier was there, pale belly curving towards a rain-heavy sky. Adam stepped over its outstretched neck, the open mouth with stained yellow teeth, the blood-streaked eye socket, and squatted beside the stripped body of Gervase de Cadenet. He did not try to press the eyelids shut, for he could see that the body was well into the stiffening stage. A wild, dark rage against the perpetrators of this outrage filled him. He made the sign of the cross over the young knight and murmured a short prayer in a soft, monotone voice, then beckoned to Austin and another knight to bring a pack pony.

They loaded the bodies onto the animals they had brought and draped them with blankets, then moved slowly back up the march, and as the sky started to darken towards dusk, swung away from the border in the direction of Thorneyford.

'I will write to Earl Guyon as soon as we reach Thorneyford,' Adam said to Sweyn as they splashed through a shallow, swiftly running stream. His mouth tightened bleakly. 'God knows how he will take this news.'

'Lord Miles ain't strong enough to bear rough treatment,'

Sweyn said. 'I saw the way you helped him on the stairs the other night. He's beginning to fail quickly now.'

Adam pulled a face. 'Was I as obvious as all that? I thought I did it with subtlety.'

'You did, my lord, but it is not your way to put your arm across a man's shoulders in conversation, even when you are fond of him and have the right.'

'Now I know why Aubrey calls you my watchdog!' A momentary rueful humour glinted across Adam's grim expression.

'And you can't teach an old dog new tricks,' Sweyn retorted with the fierceness that masked deep affection. 'I've had my eye on you since you were a puling swaddled babe!'

'And I haven't changed, don't tell me,' he rolled Sweyn a sarcastic look and slapped the reins across Lyard's neck, increasing the pace.

They cut across the woodland using the carriers' well-worn track, and with the dusk hard upon them reached the common grazing land that Thorneyford shared with a neighbouring village, and there encountered the Welsh, riding out of the damp twilight mist in the direction of the border.

A mutual moment of shock held both groups immobilized, and then Adam issued several sharp commands to his own men, delegated Austin and an older knight to take care of the burdened pack ponies, and grouped the rest into a tight phalanx of iron and solid horseflesh. His lance swung smoothly to the horizontal.

The Welsh saw what was happening and tried to break and run, but got no further than the first splintering before the fury of the Norman charge engulfed them. Adam had marked his man as Lyard galloped down upon the Welsh, marked the place to strike as clearly as he always marked the four nailheads on the quintain shield.

Davydd ap Tewdr's bodyguard was carried from the saddle by the impact of the honed battle lance and died as he hit the ground. Adam pivoted Lyard with his knees, left the lance embedded in his victim's body, and drawing his sword, engaged the man on his right. Behind him, swearing, Sweyn hacked and manoeuvred to stay with him.

Adam's opponent had no shield, and the grating shriek of steel on steel as the Welshman parried, shuddered Adam's bones and set his teeth on edge. The second blow shattered the inferior Welsh steel, leaving the man naught but a short, jagged dagger for defence. Adam swept it aside and concluded the matter, moving on like a reaper in a field of red wheat.

The shield that was butted forward in protection by his next adversary was a Norman one, raided from Miles' escort, good and solid, but its new owner wore no armour, only an ill-fitting helm to guard his skull. In the split second before Adam struck him down to hell, he recognized the horrified young face partially concealed behind the helmet's broad nasal, and with an explosive oath changed his grip on the hilt, and with a rapid flick of the wrist sent Rhodri's blade spinning from his hand.

'In the name of Christ's ten fingers, what are you doing here?' Adam roared, saw the dark eyes widen, heard Sweyn's choked warning, instinctively crouched behind his shield and commanded Lyard sideways. The blow came in hard from the left, clipping the top of his shield and jarring his left arm to the bone as he strove to hold against it. He brought his right arm over in a solid retaliation and had the satisfaction of hearing his enemy grunt with pain, but the retort was fast and determined, and the short Welsh blade ripped open the blue velvet surcoat and splayed a diagonal line through the rivets of Adam's mail.

He pricked Lyard with his spurs and the destrier reared up against the Welshman's mount, forehooves slashing, teeth bared. Adam swung his sword back-handed from shoulder height. Trained from infancy, there was so much power behind his blow that it took the Welshman's head clean off. It hit the ground and bounced beneath Lyard's dancing hooves like a pig's bladder football. The body, jetting blood, remained upright in the saddle and hung there for a seeming eternity, until twitching, it toppled slowly sideways. The Welsh pony, cut by the sorrel's flailing hooves and frightened by the blood-reeked press of battle, took the bit between its teeth and bolted for a gap on the right. The body flopped over; one foot was entangled in the stirrup-leather and the neck trailed the ground, smearing long strings of blood.

Breathing rapidly, Adam looked around. The Welsh were in retreat now, fleeing for the safety of the forest. 'Where's the lad?' he demanded sharply of Sweyn.

'He ran for the woods, my lord. And the others with him.'

Adam pursed his lips in the direction of the trees. Behind them, the sky was as grey as steel.

'If the lad's loose, and they were coming from Thorneyford ...' Sweyn began.

'Then the exchange must have already taken place,' Adam finished, a knowledge that had been with him since the first impact of the charge. His chest expanded on a deep breath sucked through his teeth. 'They didn't waste much time, did they?'

'Do we go after them, my lord?'

'What ... No, Sweyn. They'll split up the moment they hit the forest and it is their own ground. We'd be picked off one by one that way. Anyone hurt? Go and find out, will you?'

'What about the Welsh?' asked Aubrey. 'The bodies, I mean. What shall we do with them?'

Adam glanced down. The head of his last victim returned his look balefully from its muddy bier, the blood still crawling from severed flesh and sinew. 'Leave them. They'll be claimed when all is quiet.' He wiped his sword on his thigh and sheathed it, looked up and said sharply to the man who had come to ask instructions of Aubrey, 'What are you staring at?'

'My lord, that is Davydd ap Tewdr, I would swear an oath on it. I saw him at a fairing in Shrewsbury last year, and quite close to. I was going into an alehouse as he was coming out with some of his people ... He was laughing.' His eyes flickered with unwilling fascination over the hanging jaw, the stained

185

teeth exposed in the eternal grin of death to threaten the living with their own, inevitable fate. The soldier shuddered and crossed himself.

Adam gestured the man away and grimaced at Aubrey. 'I was wondering to Heulwen how it would be without ap Tewdr breathing down my neck and Rhodri in his place. I shouldn't have tempted the Gods, should I? No gain without a ritual sacrifice. Go on, muster the men. There are still three miles ahead of us and it's nearly dark.'

On first sight of her husband, Heulwen almost fainted, for as he stepped into the torchlit hall, the brownish-red colour of drying blood almost obliterated the rich blue of his torn surcoat. His face too was liberally spattered in the areas where it had not been protected by helmet and ventail.

'Holy Christ!' she cried, and stopped short of running into his arms, her expression one of sheer horror. 'Adam, what happened? How badly are you hurt?'

He followed her eyes down. 'It's not mine, love,' he reassured. 'It's Davydd ap Tewdr's. I cut off his head.' His voice was matter-of-fact, as if he was discussing a mundane, every-day occurrence. He kissed her awkwardly. 'They told me at the gatehouse that Miles is here. Where is he?'

'I had him carried up to our bedchamber. He's very weak – barely conscious. He took a fall and I fear that perhaps a piece of broken rib has pierced his lung.'

'Yes, we found his horse.' His mouth tightened as he remembered the scene they had come upon. He decided not to tell Heulwen, and plucking at his surcoat grimaced and said, 'Do you think you could organize a bathtub? I took the full flood of ap Tewdr's lifeblood.'

'Yes, of course.' She snapped her fingers at a waiting maid and issued a brisk command.

Adam took a cup of wine that was given to him and drinking it thirstily, made for the stairs.

*

'Lord Miles, can you hear me? It is Adam. Davydd ap Tewdr is dead. We met his warband coming away from here and there was a battle. Rhodri took to the woods with the survivors and I let him go ... Lord Miles?'

Miles struggled up through a floating, weightless darkness towards a burden of light and pain. There was a hand gripping his own, and the voice, although low-pitched, was anxious, almost pleading.

'It's no use!' he heard his granddaughter say on a soft sob. 'No use Adam, he's too far gone. Elswith, run and fetch Father Thomas.'

Miles forced his leaden lids to open. The candles burning on the coffer were a yellow blur; everything was a blur. His granddaughter's hair merged with the candle flame, and link-mail silvered his vision with shifting discs of light.

'Adam?' he breathed weakly, vaguely puzzled until he remembered. A faint smile. 'Don't go chasing your tail lest you catch it. My will lies in the dower chest at Ashdyke ... Guyon knows.'

'I am going to write to him this very night. He should be here within the next few days.'

Miles moved his head from right to left on the pillow. 'It doesn't matter. I'd rather die without a host of weeping relatives around my bed. Guyon knows that too ... No great tragedy for me, I'm glad to go ... I've stopped fighting it ... '

'Grandpa, no!' Heulwen let out the words with an involuntary cry, then pressed the back of her hand across her mouth.

'Child, it is a blessing. You have your life before you .... Do not grieve for me. I have lived mine to the full and beyond.' He closed his eyes again, and seemed to sink down into the bed as if only his shell remained. His hand relaxed in Adam's.

'Adam?' Heulwen's voice was thin with fear. She clutched his mail-clad arm. 'He's not ...?'

'No, not yet.' Adam removed his hand from the dead-leaf texture of the old man's. The aftermath of hard battle was in his bones, making him feel as limp as a wrung clout. 'But it won't be long, certainly before your father can get here. You have to accept it – he wants to die. Let him go.' He took hold of her shoulders, kissed her forehead and became aware again as she stood resisting in his embrace, of the state he was in. 'Where have you lodged us for the nonce, Heulwen? I'm reeking in blood, and in no fit state to comfort my wife or let her comfort me.'

Heulwen stood a little back from him, dragged from her grief by his words to the realization that there were still things to be done; that she had a husband who was entitled to her attention and her ministrations.

'The wall room that was Rhodri's.'

Adam paused at the door to let the priest enter and spoke to him for a moment before continuing on his way. 'Well, Rhodri certainly doesn't need it any more,' he said, the glint of an edge to his tone, then stopped again as he caught sight of his squire whispering to one of the younger maids, his hand in the act of curving around her waist. 'Austin, go and fetch me parchment, ink and quills, and bring them to the wall chamber!' he snapped. 'You girl, about your duties!'

She blushed, and bobbing a curtsy fled, the empty leather bath pail banging against her skirts. Adam shook his head. 'That boy!' he muttered beneath his breath, but with more irritation than anger, and shoved aside the curtain to enter their temporary bedchamber. Another maid finished emptying her pail into the tub and flitted from the room. The water steamed, vapour laden with the scent of bay and rosemary.

'Adam, I had to ransom him, I had no other choice,' Heulwen said, beginning now to feel nervous as he reached to the heavy German buckle of his swordbelt. 'FitzSimon wanted me to send to you first, but I was too frightened for my grandfather.' She rubbed her hands together, watching him. 'I was very curt with him, and I think I wounded his pride.'

'You're good at that.' He flicked her a look from beneath his brows. 'You find the sore spots in a man's soul and prick them sometimes until they run with blood.' And then, thoughtfully, 'I know all about your behaviour towards my designated constable. He was waiting in the gatehouse for me to ride in, and as full of righteous indignation as a blown-up Christmas bladder. I heard him out, and then I deflated him to a manageable size.' He clinked the swordbelt across the coffer.

Unable to discover from his tone whether he was annoyed at her or at FitzSimon, she said, 'For my sake?'

His smile was slight and sour. 'Not entirely. FitzSimon hides his inadequacy in arrogance and the belief that he's always right. He's a good soldier when directed, but he doesn't enjoy surprises such as women who snatch his authority and make ransom deals with Welsh brigands.'

'Adam, there was no other way. By the time I had sent for you ...'

'Did I say that I wholeheartedly agreed with him? You might have handled him with more tact, although I doubt that's in your nature, but in the matter of the commands you gave you were right. My own would have been the same. No harm done, except that Rhodri is loose sooner than I expected, and I still don't know him well enough to be sure which way he'll jump next.' He pulled off the rent surcoat, tossed it to one side, and waited for her to help him off with his hauberk.

Half a day since she had aided him to don it. Now the gleaming, pristine steel links were spotted with mud and splotches of blood where it had saturated through the surcoat. There was also on his left side a line of splayed, warped rivets, showing how close he had come to being riven himself. Heulwen stared at the discarded, ruined surcoat and suddenly her hands were icy, unable to take the hauberk's weight so that it slithered to the rushes at her feet. She swallowed, fighting nausea.

Adam had turned his back on her and was removing his gambeson and shirt. When he rounded and sat down on the bed, she stared sickly at the comet-shaped bruise empurpling his ribs in the precise position of the damage to surcoat and hauberk. The livid mark was concealed from her as he bent to unwind his cross-garters, and Heulwen gazed at his bent head, her heart pounding with fear.

At Windsor, the trial-by-combat had seemed like stiff and gilded play-acting, he and Warrin just characters in some monstrous mummers' charade, real, but only half real, and herself another mummer watching it all through a dark mirror. Over the space of the past two months, the charade had receded as she lived with Adam and had begun to see unknown facets glinting behind the façades, with herself reflected in them. Now, staring at the rent in his hauberk and the bruised flesh above the new pink scar of his fight with Warrin, the dark mirror shattered and exposed her to the reality of how close to the edge of death a marcher lord lived his life.

Adam glanced up. 'Have you ...' The look on her face stopped him. She was so pale that her skin seemed translucent and he thought for a moment that she was going to faint. 'Heulwen?' He dropped his cross-garters and stood up, but before he could reach her, she had reached him. One arm went hard around his neck, clinging, and she fastened her mouth on his, not just offering, but wildly demanding. He tasted tear-salt, felt her shudders, and her other hand was stroking him intimately, kindling a blaze. He broke away from the kiss with a gasp like a drowning man and clamped his hand upon her working one, holding her away before his control snapped and he took her to the bed and used her in the way she was demanding.

'No Heulwen, not this time,' he said, his voice soft but raw. 'I'll not deny that I want you, but not like this in a way I'll regret afterwards. If you want to rage against your grandfather's dying, do it some other way. Go and kick the wall, or slaughter a pig, ride a horse into the ground, but do not bring it into our bed. God knows that's a haunted enough place as it is.'

Heulwen shook her head, eyes brimful. 'You don't understand, Adam. It's not my grandfather I fear to lose, it's ...'

There was a discreet cough outside and hard upon it, Austin came into the chamber, sheets of parchment tucked under his arm, quills and an ink-horn in his hands, and behind him a maid bearing food and wine.

Adam set Heulwen gently to one side. 'Thank you, Austin. Put them down over there, then leave us.'

While the squire did his bidding and the maid set down her tray, Adam removed his braies and chausses and set about the matter of a perfunctory bath.

Austin bowed and left; the maid was dismissed. Heulwen lifted the flagon to pour Adam a cup of spiced wine. Her hand shook on the engraved handle.

Presently, Adam put down the sponge, set the soap dish out of reach and said with sudden, quiet decision, 'Heulwen, go to my chest and bring me the casket you'll find at the bottom.'

She handed him the goblet and giving him a curious look, went to do as he asked. The casket was beneath his summer cloak and lighter linen tunics – a small, but exquisitely executed box made of cedarwood overlaid with enamelled copperwork depicting the signs of the zodiac – not a masculine possession at all.

'It belonged to my mother so I believe,' Adam said, watching her circumspectly from beneath his lids. 'Brought back from the east with a host of tall tales by one of her brothers. I meant to give it to you some time ago, but it slipped my mind until now. The jewels inside are yours. They were my mother's own personal ones, not bound to be passed on with the estate titles.' He gave a deprecatory shrug. 'There isn't much. Apparently her first husband saw no reason to deck a woman in gauds when he could better use the money elsewhere, and my own father – well you know all about my own father.'

Heulwen sat down on the bed and after one glance at her husband, raised the lid of the casket. A modest collection gleamed at her from the interior. Two pairs of earrings in the Byzantine style, probably gifts from that same brother, a girdle of enamelled bronze links, and a purse with a clasp worked in cloisonné to hang from it. There was an Irish torc bracelet of woven gold, a plain silver cloak clasp, and some dainty gilded

191

shoe buckles. She thanked him warily, wondering why he had chosen to give these things to her now: a sop to her pride? A comfit to an upset child?

Adam left the tub, dried himself and donned his bedrobe, then sat down beside her. 'You haven't opened the drawer at the bottom,' he said, nodding to the copperwork panelling the base of the casket. She narrowed her eyes to look closer and saw that what she had thought were merely decorative knobs were there for a purpose, and when she gently pulled them, a drawer slid easily out. She made a small sound of surprise, and picked up the brooch that lay within.

'Your grandfather said that I was to give it to you when I deemed the time right,' Adam said, studying Heulwen pensively.

She stared at the piece. 'Grandpa gave you this? The wolf brooch?' Her eyes lifted to meet his.

'On that first night we returned from Windsor, with a warning to beware of futility, which we haven't heeded very well have we?' He gave a small, wry shrug.

'He set great store by this,' she murmured, and traced the figure of the wolf with a gentle forefinger.

'And by you.' He touched her braid. 'Are you going to sit in vigil with him tonight?'

'Yes,' she said through a tear-constricted throat.

'Then wear it for him.' He leaned round to kiss her, but did not linger, and crossed the room to the onerous duty of parchment and quill. She listened to him setting out the materials, heard the wine splash into a cup and the soft sound of tearing bread. The brooch took on warmth from her hand and the carnelian eyes seemed to flicker with a life of their own in the candlelight. She thought of Ralph. Light, charming, irresponsible Ralph, who would have long since bolted for the safety of another woman's arms rather than face such an emotionally charged passage as this. Then she thought of Warrin, who would have comforted her with a superficial show of concern and then expected her to rally. Behind her a

192

quill snapped and Adam cursed through a mouthful of bread; more wine trickled into the cup.

He had withdrawn himself a discreet distance, giving her space to think and recuperate, there if she needed him, but not intruding. She looked round to him where he was laboriously toiling on the letter to her father. Already there were ink stains on his fingers and when he rubbed his hand over his face in perplexed thought, he left black streaks upon forehead and cheekbone and nose. A wild tenderness stirred within her, as different to her feelings for Ralph as a caterpillar was to a butterfly: an awakening, an acceptance of wings. She rose and, going behind him, put her arms around his neck and rubbed her cheek against his. 'Adam, thank you,' she said softly.

Her words were greeted not with a smile or an acknowledgement, but with an oath as the second quill split, splattering ink everywhere. He hurled it down in disgust and in so doing, sent the ink-horn flying. A spreading puddle of ink rapidly obliterated the few words he had struggled onto the parchment. Several profanities rent the air and caused Heulwen to gape in astonished curiosity, for she had thought to be aware of every last soldier's curse this side of Jerusalem until now. Concealing a giggle at the sheer impossibility of the most lurid, she scrambled for one of the bath towels and used a corner to blot up the ink. It was too late, the parchment was ruined. She bit her lip and looked at him. 'Shall I do it? I know that you and quills have a mutual enmity.'

'Would you?' A look of abject relief crossed his face as he relinquished the hastily snatched-up clean parchment sheets into her hands. 'I didn't want to burden you more ...'

The feeling increased, soaring aloft, unfettered. She smiled up at him and he caught his breath at the expression in her eyes, dazzled by it. 'I was going to say earlier, before we were interrupted, that it was not my grandfather I was afraid of losing – it was you.' She slipped her hand inside his bedrobe and traced the livid bruise above the scar. 'And if our bed has been haunted by Ralph's ghost, I do not believe it is haunted any more.' She rested her palm lightly on his flesh, but went no further. The next move had to come from him. 'Ralph used to mouth words of undying love to me at the same time as he was mounting another woman. Empty words – anyone can say them. Actions speak the louder.'

Adam's eyes were stinging. He swallowed hard, and knowing that his voice would not serve him, set his arm around her waist and bent his mouth to hers. The first kiss was long and gentle, as was the second. The third was deeper and its impetus carried them towards the bed, but without undue haste, for this time there was no wish on Heulwen's part to force the pace, or on Adam's to possess what he could not have.

He left her mouth to investigate the hitherto unknown delight of her eyelids, her earlobes and the soft, tender hollow where her collarbones joined. He unwound her braids and played with her hair, a cool, streaming river of fire, drew off her overgown and turned her around to unfasten the lacings of her tight-fitting undertunic, discovering the white nape of her neck where it gleamed between a parting in the rich copper-gold strands. Heulwen gasped at that, her throat arching.

Adam swallowed again, this time against a different primal emotion, and sought to distract his mind. He concentrated on the lacings, which were difficult enough to make him swear beneath his breath, but when they were undone and the tunic removed, there was only her short shift and the light shining through it, outlining the contours of her body. She turned in his arms and put her own around his neck, and those contours were fitted intimately against his own, two halves of a puzzle becoming a whole.

For a moment he almost yielded to the surging greatness of his need. He thought about tilting at the quintain. If you went at it too soon, all the power was wasted and you ended flat on your back on the tilt yard floor. It was all a matter of balance and timing – of controlling your lance. That thought, so irreverently appropriate, made him shake with silent laughter and the tension eased. An image of the tilt yard in his mind, he took her to the bed.

A soft cry was drawn from her as his fingertips strayed lazily to investigate the swell of her breast, caressing inwards to tease her nipples into budding erection. He made a necklace of butterfly kisses around the base of her throat, then another one a little lower, and a third dipping into the valley between her breasts. He nuzzled sideways, and the wet heat of his tongue upon her nipple made her writhe and clutch at him. He kissed his way back to her throat and fastened his lips upon the pulse that beat there in time with his own, like the hoofbeats of a galloping horse swirling in the dust at the end of a tilting ground.

Heulwen arched and rubbed herself against the swollen heat of his shaft. Adam groaned and closed his eyes, envisaging the discipline of the tilt yard. Not too soon, not too soon. Her body opened to his like air streamlining a driven lance. He felt the pressure of her fingertips, the fluid undulation of her hips, the sleek, stroking pressure of the flesh enclosing him, and each thrust drove him nearer to the red centre of the quintain.

Heulwen was tossing her head from side to side. A strand of her hair caught in his mouth, and the distraction of removing it slowed him down. He heard her inarticulate murmur of complaint, felt her strive against him, fingernails digging deep and sharp into his shoulders and back, and gasping he resumed his movements, all sensation centred with exquisite inevitability within his loins. Heulwen, thrashing frantically beneath him, suddenly stopped. Her eyes flew open, locked on his, and behind her kiss-dammed lips, he heard the wild cry in her throat as she rose against him and he let go, his spine arching as the lance struck the heart of the quintain and shattered and shattered and shattered.

When he regained his own senses, it was to feel Heulwen's lips on his shoulder, imprinting it with small kisses. Sweat was glueing their bodies together and he could feel the places where she had scratched him twinge. She made a contented purring sound and wriggled upon the still firm length of his shaft.

'That was wonderful,' she murmured breathlessly, and slanted him a rich green-blue glance, replete and provocative at one and the same time. Adam kissed the tilted tip of her nose and nibbled her lips, loth to relinquish the moment's triumph and tenderness for what lay beyond. 'Only wonderful?' he teased, finding it enjoyable now to touch her body without having the urgency of desire to contend against.

'I would not want your head to swell out of all proportion to the rest of you,' she retorted.

'I wasn't thinking of my head,' he gave back promptly, laughter in his voice, then yelped and was out of her and off her quicker than a pick-pocket at a fair as she dug her sharp fingernails into his buttocks. He looked at her reproachfully. 'Vixen,' he complained, but marred his protest with a grin, and then a kiss. She responded. Her hands slid down over his shoulders, tangled in the sparse golden hair on his chest, and it was with a sigh of genuine regret that she broke away. 'This is not getting your letter written is it?' She looked round for her shift.

'You had better use the tub before you go to your grand-father,' he said, still grinning, eyes raking her from head to toe. 'I may not be any use at writing letters, but I seem to have written my love all over you.'

Heulwen followed his gaze down. Breasts and belly, ribs and thighs were haphazardly smeared and streaked with ink transferred by sweat from his fingertips. She giggled mis-chievously at him. 'Knowing your talent with a quill, I suppose this is the only love letter I shall ever receive. It seems a pity to wash it away.'

He slapped her rump. 'Baggage!' he declared. 'And it's not a love letter.' He stretched out his arm for his half-finished wine.

'No? What is it then?'

'A receipt for dues paid.'

She made her eyes round and wide. 'But Adam,' she cooed,

'I thought you kept that kind of account with a tally stick?'

He choked. Laughing, she ruffled his hair and went past him to the cooling tub.

Silent, keeping vigil by candlelight, Heulwen sat at her grandfather's bedside, holding his hand, and watched his last moments slip away. The letter to her father had been written and despatched and the dead victims of the Welsh raid had been composed, their bodies now waiting in the chapel for the dying to join them.

She glanced across to Adam. He was sitting on a stool, his back propped against the wall, his head nodding as he dozed. She had said that he should sleep, but he had refused, insisting on keeping this vigil with her; but as the hours passed in silence, so had the strength of his will to remain awake.

The hand beneath hers stirred, and the eyelids strove like moths beating at a window to reach light.

'Grandpa?' She leaned over him.

Her voice, soft but frightened, woke Adam. He jerked upright with a start, saw her leaning over the bed, and was quickly on his feet, cursing himself for having fallen asleep. He went quickly to her, expecting to see a corpse; instead he looked down into lucid, knowing eyes. The faintest suggestion of a smile was upon Miles' livid lips.

'The brooch,' he mouthed, for there was no strength in his breath to make a sound. His eyes were upon the gleaming circle pinned to Heulwen's gown. Almost imperceptibly, he nodded approval.

Adam set his hand on Heulwen's shoulder. 'The brooch,' he confirmed. 'I can't promise not to go chasing my own tail, but I'll try.'

Miles made a sound that might have been a chuckle but was never completed, as his heart shuddered and stopped beating and the last breath sighed into silence.

'Grandpa?' Heulwen said again.

Adam leaned in front of her and gently, reverently, used

197

forefinger and thumb to close the half-open eyes which in their youth had been the same glorious colour as Heulwen's, and in death were swallowed to sightless black. 'He's gone,' he said gently, and making the sign of the cross stood back. Then he looked at Heulwen, and silently drew her into his arms. She pressed her face into his breast and clung to him, but only for a moment; wet-eyed but composed, she released him and looked up into his face. 'I'm all right, Adam.'

'Are you sure?' He brushed away her tears on the edge of his thumb.

She nodded and gave him a watery but genuine smile. 'I can accept it now. It was my own fear that would not let him go.' She paused and drew a deep, steadying breath. 'I will do whatever needs to be done. This is women's work now. I'd rather you sent in Elswith and Gifu to me and went to bed. I'll join you when I've finished.'

He studied her intently, then gave a brief nod, recognizing her need to be alone with her thoughts upon which the maids would not intrude, but his own continued presence might. 'Don't be too long,' was all he said as he headed for the curtain, 'the living need you too.'

A SCOWL BLACKENING HIS brow, mouth set in a thin line concealing hard-clenched teeth, Adam strode across Milnham's moon-washed bailey, oblivious of his destination, only knowing that if he had stayed in the great hall for one moment more he would have committed the act of murder on at least one and probably more of the gathered funeral guests. *Guests*, hah! They were more like a flock of kites descending to eat, drink, mouth empty regrets and platitudes, and declaim fulsome eulogies that were naught but expended hot air!

Slowing his pace, he breathed out hard. No, that was an injustice born out of his own foul temper. Most had attended out of genuine respect and affection for Miles and it was only men like Ranulf de Gernons, who had never really known him, who came out of curiosity and a malicious desire to make mischief, being entitled by their high marcher rank to a place at the crowded trestles. De Gernons was heir to the vast earldom of Chester whose borders blended into Ravenstow's, and could hardly be turned away.

A fire was burning in the ward; guards stamped beside it while they warmed their hands and talked about the torchlit feasting within. Cold began to seep through Adam's velvet tunic and embroidered linen shirt. He wished he had stopped to pick up his cloak, but there had been no time for rational thought, only the need to escape before he leaped at de Gernons and violated the strict laws of hospitality. He paused by the welcome heat of the flames. Illuminated in firelight, the soldiers acknowledged and withdrew a little, their faces impassively curious. He held out his hands, rubbed them together, blew on them and shivered.

'Here,' rumbled John's rich deep voice, 'you forgot this.'

Adam turned and took the cloak held out to him. 'Thank you.' He looked guardedly at his brother-by-marriage.

John's eyes were as dark and bloomy as grapes and his brows were drawn heavily together above them. 'Pay no heed to Lord Ranulf, he does it apurpose. Papa's just given him the bladed edge of his tongue and Lord Gloucester backed him to the hilt. I don't think he'll open his mouth again – at least not this side of the curtain wall.' He gave a cynical shrug.

Adam swung the cloak across his shoulders and fumbled with the pin. John's frown remained; he rubbed one finger over the bald, slightly prickly skin of his tonsure.

'You don't believe what he said, do you?' he asked sharply. 'Oh come on Adam, he was winding you up like a rope on a mangonel just to watch you let fly. Everyone knows that my grandfather's death wasn't your fault. You couldn't have prevented it.'

'Yes I could,' Adam said woodenly. 'I could have hung Rhodri ap Tewdr higher than the man in the moon long before it happened. I could have left him in the road to die on that first encounter. I could have given Miles a larger escort or made him take a different road home.'

'Hindsight is a wondrous thing,' John said with more than a hint of his mother's impatient asperity, 'and de Gernons certainly knows how to make of it a weapon. If you had left Rhodri ap Tewdr lying in the road, Heulwen would now be Lady de Mortimer, wedded to her own husband's murderer.'

Adam's head jerked up.

'Yes,' said John, nodding emphatically. 'Think about it. God's will is oftimes strange.'

Adam snorted and looked away into the flames. Greedy tongues of fire wrapped around the wood and scorched his face.

'Are you going to go after the boy?'

Adam sighed and shook his head. 'If it was left up to me, no. Davydd ap Tewdr's dead and Miles wouldn't have wanted it. He liked the lad, had high hopes for him. I think your father understands that. He's got Welsh blood himself. It is men like de Gernons who worry me. They have the scent of war in their nostrils and they're doing their utmost to flush it into the open.'

John lowered his arm. 'De Gernons might be trailing the scent of war with our Welsh, but that is as far as he will get. When Papa stands his ground, there's no moving him.'

'I hope not,' Adam said softly, 'because I think de Gernons is testing our strength for the times to come. If I were your father, I'd look to strengthen Caermoel and Oxley against future assault, and I don't mean from the Welsh.'

John gave a bark of startled laughter. 'Don't be ridiculous, Adam! De Gernons might not be everyone's view of a *preux chevalier*, but he's hardly going to start a war with his neighbours!'

'Not in the present situation, no,' Adam conceded. 'But what if the King died tomorrow?'

'All the barons have sworn for Mathilda,' John said, but the laughter left his face.

'And how many would hold to their oath – de Gernons? de Briquessart? Bigod? de Mandeville? Your own Lord Leicester? You tell me. With William le Clito to look to and his father still alive, not to mention the claim of the Blois clan, Christ, Henry's dominions would explode into war like so many barrels of hot pitch!'

John crossed himself and shivered with more than just the damp cold of the February evening. 'Then I must pray wholeheartedly for the King's continued good health,' he said, and looked round with something akin to relief as Renard emerged from the forebuilding ushering their youngest brother before him together with a half-grown brindle-and-white hound.

Renard was laughing so hard that his face was suffused and tears were streaming down his cheeks. 'Sorry,' he spluttered. 'I know it's no occasion for mirth, but Will's dog just did to

201

Ranulf de Gernons what we're all desperate to do but dare not!'

'He bit him?' guessed John, beginning to grin with an unholy delight.

Renard shook his head and sleeved his eyes. 'No!' he gasped, 'pissed up his leg! It was Will who bit him when de Gernons went for his dagger. I haled dog and boy out by their scruffs before anything worse developed and left Papa to deal with it. Christ Jesu, you should have been in there!'

'He was going to stick a knife in Brith!' William snivelled indignantly, his own tears those of anger and distress as he squatted beside the dog, his protective small arms around its shaggy shoulders. The hound whined, and swiped a pink tongue sympathetically over the boy's wet face.

Renard tousled William's profuse black curls. 'Don't worry, fonkin, no one's going to harm you or Brith. Mama might scold your manners and Papa might be annoyed because it's dishonourable to bite your enemy, but I doubt anything worse will come of it. Perhaps Papa might even give you that sword you've been craving for the past year and a half!'

William's face brightened and his eyes sparkled. 'Really?'

Renard winked. 'Just wait and see ...' He held out his slender, graceful hand. 'Come then. I'm supposed to be marching you off to bed in disgrace.'

'I'm hungry,' William protested, looking pathetic.

Renard flashed a white grin. 'So am I, being as I left half my dinner behind in there. I daresay we can find some honey cakes in the kitchen on our way – better fare at least than Ranulf de Gernons' leg!'

Adam burst out laughing and waved him away.

'Nothing to do with that little butter-haired kitchen girl?' John asked with a faint, knowing smile.

'Well, yes,' Renard retorted, looking seriously innocent, 'you should sample her honey cakes.'

Adam and John watched the youth, the boy and the dog cross the ward and go down the steps into one of the auxiliary kitchen buildings. John's shoulders shook with laughter. He folded his arms within his cassock and said, the smile still on his lips, eyes a trifle pensive, 'The new lord of Milnham-on-Wye and Ashdyke by the tenets of his grandfather's will, and only just seven years old.'

Adam fiddled with a loose piece of fur on the lining of his cloak. 'I can understand it not going to Renard,' he said slowly. 'He stands to inherit an entire earldom so he's not in any need of these estates, and you being a priest aren't likely to continue the line by legitimate means, so you're debarred.'

John snorted, but inclined his head.

'But what about Harry? He's the third son. Why did Miles pass him over in favour of William?

'Harry gets Oxley when he reaches his majority,' John explained, unperturbed. 'Like Ashdyke, it came into the family through my English grandmother Christen. It isn't a large holding, but enough to keep body and soul together. Apparently Grandpa gave it to my father when he was knighted, and Papa intends doing the same for Harry. If Ashdyke and Milnham-on-Wye had gone to him too, there'd have been nothing left for Will except a sword, hauberk and horse. Besides, Grandpa always had a special place in his affections for Will – and for Heulwen too.'

Adam tugged the fur loose and scattered it from his fingers. 'A man worries about breeding up sons to follow him, and when he has them, he worries about how he is going to furnish their helms,' he said, with a pained smile.

John darted him a quick look: in ten years of marriage to Ralph, Heulwen had quickened only the once and miscarried early, and although these were still early days, she had shown no signs of breeding with Adam. He was unsure of Adam's attitude to the likelihood of her barrenness and decided that now was not the best moment to probe lest he make a mis-judgement and say the wrong thing.

A baron, crossing the ward to one of the storesheds that had been cleaned out and provided with braziers and mattresses to accommodate the guests who overspilled the capacity of the main keep, nodded a frosty goodnight to the two men standing at the fire. Adam stared wide-eyed after Hugh de Mortimer. He had ridden in at the last moment to attend Miles' funeral, ignoring the surreptitious nudges and speculative stares of his fellow barons and mourners. The atmosphere at first had been strained to say the least, but gradually it had eased. De Mortimer had not once mentioned his son or alluded to the painful events at Windsor, and an attempt by de Gernons to bring them into the conversation had been squelched aborning by Guyon. De Mortimer had pointedly avoided Heulwen and Adam, but had been at pains to extend the olive branch to the Earl and Countess.

'He's still after a blood bond with the earldom,' John said, from the side of his mouth, 'Hugh wants Renard for his youngest daughter, Eleanor, and he's willing to let sleeping scandals and feuds lie in order to get him.' John grinned wryly at the look on Adam's face. 'It's not as stupid as it seems. Renard is a future earl, blood-related to the throne, and every marcher lord with a daughter between the cradle and thirty years old is looking at him with the words son-in-law shining in their eyes.'

'God's life,' Adam muttered, shaking his head. 'How old's the girl?'

'Just coming up to six. She's from his second marriage, obviously.'

'What does Renard say?'

John chuckled. 'You know my brother. He just smiles and says that practice makes perfect, and hasn't he got a lot of time?'

'And your father?'

'Keeping his head down. Ren's right, there is plenty of time yet and at least a dozen interested parties. Papa will let Renard do the initial winnowing and make a decision from there. Mind you,' he reflected, 'a match with the de Mortimer girl would heal the rift caused by you and Heulwen, and the dower lands he's offering would be very useful; and the girl herself is a real heart-melter. Mama fell for Eleanor straightaway when she saw her at a wedding last year – a willowy little thing with hair blacker than Renard's own and eyes like turning leaves.'

'Perhaps because she has no daughter of her own,' Adam suggested. 'I know she brought up Heulwen, but she was still very young herself then, and Heulwen married at fifteen. It must be lonely for her sometimes, particularly now that William is growing up.'

John looked startled. 'Mama lonely?' The thought had never occurred to him, for she always seemed so composed and brisk and capable. 'I suppose so,' he said dubiously, 'but even if the betrothal does take place, Eleanor won't come to Ravenstow until she's at least ten, and there'll not be a wedding for another two years if not much longer. Anyway ...'

'Anyway,' interrupted Heulwen, 'Ranulf de Gernons is snoring drunk across his trencher because Mama's been giving him raw ginevra, and everyone's going to bed, including me. Adam, are you coming?'

She was wearing a very fetching green silk bliaut that shimmered like the surface of a lake, and her braids in the firelight were a warm, rich red, catching on the curve of her breasts and reaching to the bronze and enamel girdle encircling her hips.

'How could I refuse an offer like that?' he murmured, slipping an arm around her waist and drawing her sidelong hip to hip against him.

Heulwen elbowed him in the ribs. 'Your mind is a treadmill,' she remonstrated, but smiled, knowing that he but teased her. There was barely any standing space in the small keep, let alone the room for privacy to indulge that kind of need.

'And who could blame me?' Adam answered equably, not in the least set down, and he planted a kiss on her raised eyebrow.

John smiled. 'Three's a crowd,' he said, and bid them goodnight.

'Is de Gernons really asleep in his dinner?' Adam asked, as arm in arm they went back towards the keep.

'He was, but Mama got two of the servants to stretch him out on the floor and put a sheepskin over him – and a bowl beside him for when he wakes up.' Her eyes glinted at the memory and then hardened. 'If it had been left to me, he'd have spent the night blanketless in the midden.'

'Now Heulwen, you can't do that to the future Earl of Chester,' he admonished gravely.

She made a rude sound down her nose. 'Couldn't I? It is where he belongs, rooting with his trotters. He has the manners of a pig; not only that but he looks like one. If this was Martinmas, I'd be salting him down for the winter by now.'

Adam snorted with contained laughter. His mood lightened and his head came up. 'Belike he'd go rancid on you,' he said, and took a deep breath of the dank, river-smelling night air.

'Very likely,' she agreed, and then, 'by the by, Earl Robert of Gloucester said that he wanted a word with you, but that it could wait until tomorrow.'

'What about? Did he say?'

'No, but from the way he spoke to me it is not something that he wants to air in public.' She slipped him a look along her shoulder, but his face was bland, no expression on it to reveal what he was thinking. 'Have you any ideas?'

Adam shook his head. 'Not an inkling, unless it is something to do with Ralph. The King was going to investigate the matter. Perhaps Robert has news.'

Heulwen shivered. 'I don't think I want to know.'

Adam squeezed her waist. 'It might be nothing of that, love. No point in conjuring ghosts out of thin air.'

'No,' she said, and leaned against him.

They went into the keep, where Ranulf de Gernons was snoring stertorously in the straw near the door. Adam was very tempted to tread on him, but discretion won out at the last moment. 'I wish that I was a dog or a small boy,' he murmured, as he stepped delicately over de Gernons' scuffed, ceiling-pointed toes. 'There's so much more leeway for lack of manners.'

Heulwen's upper lip curled with disgust. 'Why not just be a pig,' she said, with soft intensity.

CHAPTER 18

Rhaeadr Cyfnos cascaded like a white mare's tail over the green, fern-edged rocks and foamed into a basin four hundred feet below, where the water became as dark as polished onyx before it trickled in crystal rills over the lip of the basin and into the stream beneath. Adam drew rein at the head of the falls and stared, half-hypnotized by the roar of the water and its wild beauty. His skin was damp, his hair and garments cobwebbed by dewy droplets. Lyard bent his neck to snatch at the grass, which even this early in the season was a lush green. The bit-chains jinked, while the stallion's teeth tore rhythmically at the grass. Munching, he raised his head and looked round, ears curiously pricked, nostrils flaring to catch the new scent. He uttered a greeting nicker.

Adam laid one hand on the crupper and turned. Robert of Gloucester, astride Heulwen's rangy dark bay, was picking his way carefully along the narrow track and then down over the shallow leap of rock to join him. The two knights with him hung back to speak with Austin and Sweyn so that he reached Adam alone. The earl looked briefly at the tumbling water then away. He had an aversion to heights: looking over battlements was a necessity to which he had schooled himself, but staring at waterfalls for pleasure was a different matter entirely.

'Spectacular,' he said dutifully, and backed his stallion from the spray.

'There are better ones in Wales,' Adam said, to the contrary exhilarated by the wild, foaming power of the water.

Gloucester smiled sourly, 'I'll take your word for it.'

Adam laughed. The Earl of Gloucester was wearing a rather

fine, elaborate hunting cap adorned with bright male pheasant feathers. Hats were Gloucester's weakness, worn and cherished to compensate himself for the loss of his hair. He nodded at the other destrier. 'Is the horse all right?'

'Excellent.' He slapped the elegant bay neck. 'Maud tried him out while we were at Windsor – he suited her very well. I might make of him a betrothal gift.'

Beyond the black damp tree trunks a watery sun was trying to break through the clouds. Adam squinted up, then looked along the foxfur collar of his cloak to his companion. 'Is that a means of introducing what you wanted to talk about?'

Gloucester eyed him cagily. 'In a way, I suppose.'

Adam laughed. 'I can just see the Empress astride a destrier, she likes to have firm control of the male.' And then, almost on a challenge, 'What sort of way?'

Gloucester tugged gently at an overlooked short stalk of straw knotted in his stallion's mane. 'The King wants you to take letters of enquiry to the father of the prospective bridegroom.' The words bore a slightly pompous ring, as though he had been rehearsing them.

Adam watched the pheasant feathers in the Earl's cap begin to droop in the fine water vapour from the falls. The news was not unexpected, but even so, he felt queasy. 'What makes you think that I am the man to be the King's herald in this matter?'

'You know how to keep a close mouth. You've done this kind of work before, know its dangers and pitfalls, and it would not be politic to send a man of any higher degree and notice at this delicate early stage.'

Adam shook his head. 'I have the Welsh to deal with, my lord, and I am an English baron. I witnessed the King's oath to us all that he would not seek a foreign husband for his daughter, and Geoffrey of Anjou is not only foreign, he's Angevin, an enemy.'

Gloucester blinked rapidly. 'How did you . . . ?'

'I overheard the King and the Bishop of Salisbury talking about it last autumn.'

'And you said nothing to anyone?'

'They were only discussing the possibilities at the time, and as you say, I know how to keep a close mouth.' He turned his head towards the falls.

'Geoffrey of Anjou is an excellent choice.'

'Is he?' Adam felt the cold beginning to seep beneath his cloak, chilling him. 'Convince me.'

'He's young and strong ...'

'He is fifteen years old,' Adam scathingly interrupted.

'With his life before him,' Robert argued, 'and likely to be a sight more potent than her last husband who apparently had, er, difficulties.'

'You surprise me,' Adam said sarcastically. 'She would shrivel any snake to the size of a worm with that way she has of looking.'

Robert's face reddened. 'I'll thank you to keep a civil tongue in your head when you speak of my sister.'

Adam gave him a look and gathered the reins. 'Why? She never extended that courtesy to me.' He clicked his tongue to the horse.

Gloucester caught at his bridle. 'Wait, my lord, at least allow me to finish what I have to say. It avails us nothing if we each ride away in anger.'

Lyard started to jib and half-rear. The Earl took his hand off the bridle. Adam checked the stallion and in so doing, mastered his own anger. Robert of Gloucester had always had a blind, soft spot for Mathilda, and Adam liked the Earl who, despite his royal blood and high status, still managed to be as genuine and honest as a plain rye loaf. He slapped Lyard's neck, and said, 'You are right, it avails us nothing. I'm sorry.'

Earl Robert removed his hat and looked dismally at the dripping feathers. 'I leap to her defence because no-one else ever does,' he said wearily. 'Like you, everyone sees a bad-tempered bitch who needs a whip taking to her hide to teach her humility, but that's just a façade. If you knew her as I did, you would be more charitable.'

Adam raised a sceptical eyebrow but forbore in the interests of peace to comment.

The Earl sighed, cast him a doubtful look from beneath water-beaded brows and said, 'Geoffrey of Anjou is far more than a champing young stallion bought to prove his worth at stud. I grant you that he's tall and handsome to look upon, but he's also well-educated, and certainly no political innocent. His father has taught him well and he has the makings of a fine warrior and general. If we make Geoffrey Maud's consort, then Fulke, as his father, won't be as eager to stir up the mud using William le Clito as his stick.'

'Ah,' said Adam, beginning to understand. Henry's obsession. 'It has to do with le Clito again.'

'It has to do with a very dangerous thorn in our side,' the Earl refuted a trifle sharply. 'Pluck out the root from which it draws sustenance, and it will wither and die.'

'You are gambling for very high stakes.' Adam leaned to adjust his stirrup. 'If you succeed and your father can hold the reins until he has grandsons old enough, then it will be a gamble well repaid. If it fails ...' He straightened and looked bleakly at the cascading water without finishing the sentence.

'It won't fail,' Gloucester said with the forceful conviction of his own belief. 'Can I give my father your yeasay that you'll go herald in payment of your forty days' service this year?'

'I'll think about it,' Adam said, his voice flat.

'When will you let me know?'

'When I'm ready.'

'But I need – my lady.' The Earl inclined his head to Heulwen as she guided her grey mare carefully down to join them.

'Lord Robert.' She slackened the reins to let Gemini crop at the grass and looked at the Earl. 'Mama wants a word with you ... something about getting Harry to learn English. She thinks it will stand him in good stead when Papa gives him Oxley, and she also wants you to write down the name of that stone carver from Bristol whom you mentioned yesterday.'

The Earl smiled at her, but in a distant way, his mind

211

obviously not on such day-to-day trivia. He looked hard at Adam. 'I need to know soon,' he said, and set his cap back on his head at a rakish angle. 'Is de Gernons still at the keep?' he asked Heulwen.

Her lip curled. 'Just preparing to leave. His temper's about as vile as the headache he's nursing; I shouldn't go near him.'

'I won't. I think I'll take the long way back. Sorcerer needs a good workout, anyway.'

They watched him leave. The hoofbeats and the voices of his escort faded through the trees. The falls roared. Adam's face felt stiff. He slid his fingers along the reins and applied gentle pressure.

'Trouble?' Heulwen followed him back to where Austin and Sweyn were waiting.

He turned his mouth down at the corners. 'Only to my conscience. I have known this has been coming for a long time. I should have been better prepared, but I'm not.'

Lyard's hindlegs slithered on mud, but he lunged powerfully with forequarters and neck and recovered. The woods enclosed them, smelling of damp and fungus. Dormant bramble bushes snagged at their cloaks as they rode through the forest in silence. Heulwen let the reins hang slack, for Gemini was placidly following the stallion's lead. She stared anxiously at Adam's back, knowing that she could not force him to tell her what was on his mind. Persuade perhaps, with bedchamber wiles, but he would recognize them for such and how he had been used, and something would die. Her own experience with Ralph had taught her that.

The trees thinned and they came suddenly upon a clearing and the mossed-over remains of a once-proud building, now reduced to chunks of tumbled stone. Some white edges only just beginning to rethread with green gave evidence of pieces having been recently cut.

Adam dismounted and tethered Lyard to a young tree. A weasel leaped over his boot and streaked away through the damp grass. The sunlight broke through the clouds and trees

212

to stroke weak fingers over the ruins. Heulwen jumped down from the mare and tied her beside the destrier.

'Why have we stopped?' She shivered slightly and stooped under a low hanging branch before it could snag in her braid. The twigs stretched like fingers. She felt as if hidden eyes were watching her every movement.

Adam caught her hand in his. 'Whimsy,' he smiled. 'I used to come here sometimes as a boy when we visited Milnham-on-Wye with your father.'

'You never brought me!' she said half-indignantly, for in childhood she had thought to share every secret and experience of Adam's – the still clear backwater of the Wye so wonderful for summer swimming, the haunted well at the farmstead where the Welsh had raided, the rock upon Caermoel ridge with its strange carvings.

He tightened his fingers around hers and raised them briefly to his lips. 'It was in the days when you did nothing but dream about Ralph and scheme how to get him,' he said with a rancourless shrug, and drew her around an outcrop of masonry and between some broken stumps of rock. 'I wasn't good company myself, then. I think it's Roman. Look, you can see where they've taken pieces recently for that new section of curtain wall.' He rubbed his hand over a jagged white edge, then wiped away the smear on his cloak.

Heulwen gnawed her lip. 'Was I really so heedless?'

He shrugged again, his eyelids lowered, trying for lightness and not quite succeeding. 'You had other matters on your mind, and I had long been a piece of familiar household furniture taken for granted – your foster-brother.'

'Oh, Adam!' A lump obscured her throat and she felt her eyes begin to sting.

'Everyone blamed my moods on my growing body, not on jealous sulks – and this was an excellent place to come and sulk alone, opportunity permitting.' Abruptly he tugged at her hand. 'Come.'

He led her onwards until they came to a short avenue

213

overgrown with brambles, straggling grass and tree saplings. Out of the tangle grew jagged slender pillars of grooved, weathered stone, and at the end of the avenue, its colours as brilliant as the day it had been abandoned, was a section of tessellated mosaic floor depicting a hunting scene. Fragments here and there were missing or displaced by tree roots, and there were chunks of stone from what had once been a roof marring one edge, but the overall effect was still magnificent.

'There's another one over there,' Adam nodded his head. 'Leda and the swan I think, but it's more broken than this one.'

Heulwen picked her way among the ruins to look. He followed her. A spring of icy water bubbled up near their feet and meandered away in the rough direction of *Rhaeadr Cyfnos*. Rooks cried somewhere above the dark trees. Behind them the horses snorted and champed. Adam returned to Lyard and, unslinging the wineskin from around the cantle, brought it to Heulwen where she now sat on a block of lichened stone, swinging her legs and regarding the hunting mosaic.

'Drink?' He unstoppered the skin and held it up to her. Companionably they shared the wine and contemplated the ruins.

'I wonder who lived here?' Heulwen mused.

Adam wiped his mouth. 'I don't know. Some of the stones have inscriptions, but they're either too weathered to read or parts of them are missing. I had thought to make a copy of the hunting mosaic at Thorneyford in the plesaunce. What do you think?'

Heulwen nodded firm approval and swallowed her mouthful of the rich, tart wine. 'And the herb beds fanning out from it.'

Adam pursed his lips and cocked her a quick, amber glance. 'I thought I'd change some of the animals though – wolves and vixens instead of boar, perhaps a leopard or two being as they are your father's device, and most certainly some horses.'

'A sorrel with cream mane and tail,' she smiled.

He raised one eyebrow. 'In pursuit of the vixens?'

She laughed and swiped at him. He ducked and dragged her

down off the stone and into his arms. Cold, tasting of wine, their lips met and through the laughter, desire rippled suddenly like a bright thread decorating a garment.

'I think you should also include a priapus,' she murmured against his mouth, taking shameless advantage of his body's rapid response.

'Only if there are nymphs in it too!' he retorted. 'Stop that you hoyden, Austin might not bat an eyelid, but Sweyn's somewhat more set in his ways. You'll shock him for certain!'

She glanced over his shoulder. 'They can't see us from here,' she murmured, and kissed him, her tongue flickering as delicately as a serpent's. His hand strayed down to the curve of her buttocks and squeezed her against him. Despite his protest, he even began to wonder hazily where they could lie, or failing that if it would be possible standing up, for there was no great discrepancy in their heights. The novelty of that thought increased the heat and dimension of his need, and his breath caught and shortened as Heulwen tightened and relaxed against the hard bulge at his thigh. What had started out as a jest was swiftly becoming a desire-driven imperative.

His hand went down to the sensitive place between her thighs and she gasped. 'Heulwen, let me . . .' he began thickly, but the jingle of harness and the noise of horses thrusting through the trees made him look up and then stop what he was doing and swing her hard around, so that she was shielded by his body.

'Adam, what's the matter, why are you . . . ?'

Behind them a sword cleared its scabbard. 'Sweyn, put up,' said Adam without taking his eyes off the men who were moving through the trees and surrounding them. The sword grated back into its sheath, but the old warrior moved closer to Adam, as did the squire.

Rhodri ap Tewdr drew rein and sat his dark stallion in contemplation of the small group before him. Behind, his men shifted restlessly.

'Welcome to the tryst.' Adam inclined his head and performed a half-mocking bow. 'May I enquire what you are doing so far from home?'

'A matter of unfinished business.' Rhodri levelled the lance he was carrying and directed it at Adam's breast.

Heulwen stiffened, her thoughts flying to Thorneyford's tilt yard and the moment when the Welsh prince had almost ridden Adam down. She took an involuntary step forwards, and her husband pushed her back. 'Such as?' he said, and as before stood his ground, matching Rhodri look for look.

The latter held the moment for as long as he could before eventually tossing the lance to the soldier beside him. Adam breathed out, cold sweat slicking his palms. Rhodri smiled as he saw the tell-tale trail of vapour coil the air and dismounting, tied his horse to a sturdy beech sapling.

'I want a truce,' he announced. 'There has been too much blood spilled already and I don't want to see this summer's harvest go up in flames – mine or yours.'

'I'm in full agreement with that,' Adam said, steadying the euphoria of relief into a careful neutrality. He reached for the wineskin on the stone and handed it to Rhodri. 'If you cease raiding over the dyke and making a nuisance of yourself among my father-in-law's tenants, I'll try to persuade him and the rest of the funeral guests that exterminating you is not the next best thing to going on crusade.'

'I am sorry about Lord Miles.' Rhodri drank from the skin and gave it back. 'Believe me I am. I learned respect and fondness for him during the time that I was your prisoner. If I could undo the manner of his dying I would. Davydd went too far.'

'And paid for it,' Adam said, the faintest hint of satisfaction tinting the grimness of his tone.

Dull colour suffused Rhodri's skin. His cloak brooch flashed as he took a deep breath. 'Yes, he paid for it,' he said, his voice over-controlled. 'But our raiding began as revenge, we were provoked. Our grazing lands are being ruined by Ravenstow's tenants, and yours too on the southern side. Only last autumn one of your villages cleared an assart on our side of the border, and on le Chevalier's former lands the boundary stones have been moved. I know they have. I came down that way to be here. We are only taking back what is ours!' His dark eyes burned between Adam and Heulwen, half-accusing, half-defensive.

Adam inclined his head, acknowledging Rhodri's argument. 'I will talk to my bailiffs and stewards, and I'll ride out and see for myself what liberties have been taken. Send a witness to attend on me if you want. Peace never flourishes on half-measures.' He frowned and folded his arms. 'As to your complaint with the Earl of Ravenstow, you'll need to talk to him yourself. I cannot vouchsafe for him or his tenants.'

'That is the reason I am here,' Rhodri said sombrely. 'I knew that he was bound to be here . . . and also I want to pay my respects to Lord Miles. I need you to give me safe escort to the keep.'

Adam sucked in his cheeks and looked dubiously at his wife. 'Did you say that de Gernons was leaving?'

She nodded. 'He should have gone by now.'

'Yes,' he confirmed, 'I can give you safe escort.' And then he looked at him curiously. 'How did you know I would be here?'

Rhodri slanted him a sly smile and stroked his stallion's shaggy neck. 'I knew that sooner or later you would be out from the castle to exercise your horse or hunt, that it was only a matter of keeping my eyes open and myself out of sight. I've been watching you for the past hour.' The smile deepened into an open grin.

Heulwen blushed. Colour darkened Adam's face but it was not for the reason first imagined.

'How much did you hear?' he asked quietly.

Rhodri looked round at his men, lounged against his mount's shoulder, and deliberately misunderstood the question. 'Enough to know how much you were enjoying yourselves,' he guffawed, his gaze flickering over Heulwen with ribald appreciation.

'You know what I mean.'

Rhodri opened his palms. 'Not a great deal. The roar of the falls unfortunately concealed most of what you and that other Norman were saying. Still, I suppose from the look on your face that if I were to bellow the news abroad, you'd cancel my safe escort.'

'You know the strength of my sword arm.'

Rhodri's face was unreadable. The smirk, however, had gone. The prince untied his horse and flung himself nimbly into the saddle. 'You Normans,' he said contemptuously. 'Always conspiring in corners against each other.' He looked round at his war band. '*Fe fynn y gwir ei le eh?*'

Adam's colour remained high. *The truth will out*: he knew enough Welsh to understand that simple proverb. He was aware of Heulwen watching him and that he could not deny Rhodri's words. 'That's rich coming from a Welshman,' he retorted, and added shortly over his shoulder, 'Austin, stop gawping like a turnip-wit and get our horses. We're returning to Milnham.'

Heulwen picked up her sewing, grimaced at it with extreme disfavour, and uttering a desperate sigh started to ply the needle through the fabric. It was a shirt for Adam, a basic, simple garment within her scope, but for her a genuine and literal labour of love since needlework of any kind was to her a form of purgatory, and it was a mark of her desperation that she tackling it beyond her daily allotted stint.

There was nothing else to do. Father Thomas, Adam's chaplain, had said that he would give her a copy of *Tristan* to read, but the howling storm outside had kept him the night at the monastery five miles away. A visiting itinerant lute-player had left them at dawn before the weather took a turn for the worse, hoping to make Ledworth by nightfall. The carrier was not due for at least another week with his budget of news and gossip, and Adam's mood was fouler than the weather that kept them closeted so close to the hearth. She darted a glance at him where he sat at a trestle near the fire, flagon and goblet close to hand. The last three days he had scarcely been sober, drinking as if to exorcize some demon. He was not drunk now, but the evening was still young, only just past dusk and the flagon full. By the time they retired it would be down to the lees.

She jabbed the needle angrily into the linen, pricked her finger and swore. He looked up at her exclamation and half-raised one eyebrow. She sucked her finger and regarded him gravely.

'Adam, why are you brooding?'

He did not deny it, but lifted the flagon and pouring the wine, took three long swallows. Then, carefully, he set the cup back down at arm's length and sighed. 'I've a decision to make and I keep trying to drown my conscience in my cup, but it keeps surfacing to preach at me, or else it mocks me from the dregs and I have to fill up and start again.'

'What sort of decision?' Without regret she put her sewing aside. 'Certainly you cannot think straight sitting in a fog of wine fumes.'

He tilted his head slightly to avoid the scorching heat that came of sitting so close to the fire. 'I've been trying not to think,' he said wryly.

'Is it about Rhodri? The Welsh?'

'Hardly.' He rubbed his forehead and winced. 'Since we all agreed a truce at Milnham and I've seen to my part of the bargain, there's been no trouble from that quarter and I don't expect any. Rhodri's got enough ado keeping his own people together without bothering mine and your father's – for the nonce at least ... Christ Jesu, Heulwen, do you have a remedy for a megrim? My head feels as though it's going to explode.'

'Your own fault,' she said without sympathy. 'What do you expect when you drink for three days solid?'

He gave her a sour glance. 'I asked for the remedy, not the cause.'

'Remedy? Leave the wine alone.' She stood up and brushed some cut ends of thread from her gown.

'If my head is aching, it is for reasons far more complex than the downing of too much Anjou,' he said tetchily.

Heulwen gave him a single look that was far more eloquent than words, and stalked away down the hall. He followed her with brooding eyes as she went, then swore and pressed the heels of his hands into his eye sockets, feeling as though a lead weight were crushing him from existence. Ralph might have thrived upon intrigue, but Adam found the conflict of loyalties almost more than he could bear. What was he supposed to do? Follow Henry's desires and have the barons all call him traitor, or tell his peers and face banishment, perhaps even death. The King had clandestine ways of dealing with men against whom he could not openly move.

Adam groaned. His responsibility was not only to himself. He had Heulwen to consider and her family – his too by foster-bond and marriage. Tell Guyon and risk being condemned by the King, or not tell him and be slighted. Somewhere, amid the wine fumes, the shadow of his long dead father mocked his honour with brimstone laughter.

'Here,' said Heulwen, bending over him to hand him a cup of some cloudy substance that smelled revolting and tasted on the first, tentative sip even worse.

'Faugh!' He pulled such a face that she laughed.

'Drink it,' she commanded, and then added in a barbed tone, 'pretend it's wine.'

Adam glared at her, but held his peace and gulped the concoction down, then shuddering, plonked the cup upon the trestle. 'Torturer,' he complained, and struggled not to retch.

From behind her back, Heulwen brought forth a small comfit dish. 'Sugared plums,' she said, her eyes sparkling. 'Do you remember? It was the way Mama used to bribe us to swallow her potions when we were little?'

Adam scowled at her but was unable to maintain the expression and with a reluctant grin, took one. She put the dish on the trestle and sitting down again, picked up one of the glistening, sticky fruits herself and bit slowly into it. Adam regarded her through narrowed eyes. She returned his scrutiny and licked crystals of sugar delicately from her fingers. His crotch grew warm. 'It was sweets of another nature I had in mind,' he said softly.

Heulwen leaned over her husband, and licking forefinger and thumb pinched out the night candle. Before the light was extinguished she saw that Adam was already asleep and that the frown marks between his brows were for the nonce but vague marks of habit rather than present distress. It was one of the few positive lessons she had learned from Ralph – how to ease the tension from a man's body and leave him totally relaxed, in a state of physical, if not mental well-being. As to what was troubling his mind to the point of him drowning it in drink, only he could solve that one.

She gave a soft, irritated sigh and lay down beside him. He had ever been one to cork things up inside him, silently simmering like a barrel of pitch too close to a cauldron, giving no real indication of how volatile the mixture was until the barrel exploded.

She pressed her cheek against the warmth of his back and closing her eyes, tried to sleep. She must have succeeded, for when she opened her eyes again it was to hear the bell tolling for first mass and to find the night candle lit, with Adam watching her by its flame. Sleepily she stretched her limbs and smiled at him.

He shifted to kiss her tousled, inviting warmth, but it was a brief gesture, not a precourse to further play. 'Heulwen, if I asked you to come to Anjou with me, would you?'

'Anjou?' she repeated, eyes and wits still misty with sleep. 'Why do you want to go to Anjou?' She yawned.

He traced small circles upon the creamy skin of her upper arm and shoulder with an idle forefinger. 'I don't *want* to go to Anjou,' he qualified ruefully. 'I wished the damned place did not even exist. Henry wants me to go there as a herald by way of this year's feudal service.'

Heulwen was silent, digesting this surface information and wondering what nasty currents swifted beneath it. Three days of heavy drinking for one. She looked at his downcast golden-tipped lashes and waited for them to lift so that she could look directly into his eyes. 'Yes Adam, I'd go with you.'

'Without even knowing the kind of message I was bearing?' He moved away from her, turned on to his back and stared up into the shadows.

Thoughts of Ralph scurried through her mind. She banished them and sat up, tossing back her hair. Adam's character was totally different. To break his honour you would have to break the man. Perhaps that was the deepest, most dangerous current of all. 'Yes, without knowing,' she confirmed, and then cocked her head. 'Was Anjou the reason that the Earl of Gloucester wanted to speak to you so privately?'

Silence. 'Yes,' then more silence. Into it, he drew a slow, considering breath. 'The King is breaking a promise he made to us all, and I am to carry the message breaking it.'

'Oh Adam, no!' Heulwen breathed with indignant sympathy, and her eyes became angry as she understood his dilemma. 'Why couldn't he have sent Gloucester himself?'

Adam gave a snort of humourless amusement. 'And have everyone wondering what the King's eldest bastard was doing in Anjou? I will be considerably less conspicuous.' He turned his head on the pillow. 'I keep thinking of Ralph and Warrin and wondering if they were so wrong. Henry uses men. Time and again I've heard your father say it, time and again I've seen him do it, been used myself. Is it any wonder that I begin to feel like a whore?'

She leaned over him and smoothed at the lines that had reappeared between his brows. He stroked her in return, and then, fingers laced in her bright hair, told her the nature of the message he was to bear.

Heulwen was momentarily surprised, but hardly shocked. Henry had attempted a marriage alliance like this before, between Geoffrey of Anjou's sister and the son he had lost on the White Ship. 'As I see it,' she murmured, 'it is on Henry's conscience, not yours. He requires of you two months' service for the lands you hold. It doesn't matter what his letter says, you are only its bearer.'

'So I keep telling myself,' he said woodenly.

'And if you renounced your feudal oath which would be the only honourable alternative, you'd have to sell your sword for a living, and I warrant that Henry would still have his way in the end.'

'Principles do not put bread on your board. Is that what you are saying?'

'I am saying that there is no point in going breadless for an inevitability. If your conscience troubles you, then it is a sign that you've still got your honour. I don't think Ralph ever suffered from either, and therein lies the difference.' She assessed him through her lashes, trying to decide whether his expression meant that he had heard and was considering, or if he was just being obdurate. She folded her arms upon his chest. 'You had better tell me how long I have to pack my travelling chests, and do I bring a maid, and is Geoffrey of Anjou really as handsome as they say?'

Adam sighed and pulled her mouth down hard to his in a kiss that was as much a reprimand as it was a token of affection. 'What would I do without you?'

'Brood yourself head first into the nearest firkin of Anjou!' she retorted tartly.

It was not so far from the truth he thought, letting her go and watching her as she picked up a comb and began to work her hair into a straight skein ready for braiding. She knew exactly how to cozen him out of a bad mood, although at the present, new as it was and so long waited for, just the sight of

223

her was enough to raise his spirits and everything else. He glanced down at himself, but it was the need of his bladder rather than the need for his wife that was stirring him at the moment.

He stretched, heard the familiar sinewy crack of his shield arm and sought out the chamber pot. He was aware that the burden had lightened along with his decision to take Heulwen with him. The fact of leaving her behind had been part of the weight of his distaste for this journey he had been asked to make. Even more important had been her reaction when he told her the reason for his going. No scorn or revulsion, just a practical acceptance and words of common sense that put his fears into their true perspective: tail-chasing.

'Be sure to pack the wolf brooch,' he said over his shoulder with a wry smile.

CHAPTER 19

ANJOU,
SPRING 1127

THE COCKEREL WAS A jewelled image cast in living bronze, and looked as though he had just stepped down from a weather vane to strut in the dust. Alert topaz eyes swivelled to study his surroundings. The coral comb and wattles jiggled proudly on head and throat as he paraded the circle, his tail a light-catching cascade of green-tipped gold, legs cobbled in bronze and armed with honed, deadly spurs. Here in the city of Angers he was without rival, for all his rivals were dead.

He stretched his throat, raising a ruff of bright feathers, and crowed. Bets were laid. His owner rose from a lithe crouch, and with his hands on his exquisite gilded belt, he looked round impatiently.

'He's late,' grumbled Geoffrey Plantagenet, heir to the Duchy of Anjou. He was almost as fine to look upon as his fighting cock, being tall with ruddy golden curls and brilliant frost-grey eyes set in a face of regular, handsome features. Thread-of-gold crusted the throat and cuffs of his tunic and the dagger at his narrow hips blazed with gems; like his bird's spurs it was honed to a wicked edge.

'Have you ever known William le Clito not to be late?' snorted Robert de Blou, watching the bird which had originally been his gift to the youth at his side. 'He'd miss his own funeral, that one.'

Geoffrey grinned, displaying perfect white teeth, but his fingers tapped irritably against his belt. 'He will need to shape better than this if he wants my father's continued support against the English king.'

'My lord, he's here now!' cried another baron, pointing towards the river. Geoffrey turned his head and with a cool gaze watched the approach of William le Clito and his small entourage of mongrels – Norman malcontents, Flemings and Frenchmen, and the tall yellow-haired English knight who had been banished from his own country for the murder of a fellow baron.

'You are late,' he addressed the would-be Duke of Normandy who had recently married the French king's sister, and passed an indifferent look over the women they had brought with them. Not obviously strumpets by their appearance, but strumpets nevertheless. Le Clito might be a new husband but that was no reason for continence when a diplomatic visit to Anjou offered the chance of easy sin.

Le Clito gave Geoffrey a smile of blinding charm which, because he used it so often, had lost most of its impact. 'Sorry, our barge got held up. I'm not that late am I?' He touched the younger man with familiarity on his gilded velvet shoulder. Geoffrey stepped aside, nostrils flaring with controlled choler and regarded the bird that Warrin de Mortimer was holding under his arm – a handsome black, the feathers emerald-shot in the spring sunlight.

'You wager that sorry object can beat my Topaze?' he scoffed.

'Name your price and we shall soon see,' le Clito answered jauntily. 'Warrin, put him down.'

Someone scooped up Geoffrey's bird so that men could look at the form and condition of the black and make their wagers. The bird shook its ruffled feathers, preened, and stretched on elegant tip-toe to crow defiance.

Warrin de Mortimer leaned against the wall and rubbed his side where the thick, pink ridge of scar tissue was irritating him. He looked at the black and knew full well that Geoffrey's bird would win because Geoffrey of Anjou always won. He had never had to beg at other men's tables for his meat. His fingers paused directly over the wound: his own fault. He had underestimated de Lacey's speed, forgotten to allow for the years of experience that followed a squirehood, and for that particular error of judgement was now an outcast in the land where he had been his father's heir, reduced to the status of plain household knight in the pay of a man whose own luck was about as reliable as a whore's promise.

'Are you not wagering, *chérie*?' A woman linked her arm proprietorially through his and admired him with melting brown eyes. 'I say Lord William's bird will win – he's bigger.'

Which showed how much Heloise knew about cock-fighting, or indeed about anything. All her brains were between her legs – which had not seemed such a bad thing last night. A pity she had to open her mouth as wide as her thighs.

'No,' he said with a sulky half-shrug. 'I'm not wagering.' These days, for him, money was too important to fritter away on the fickle prowess of a fighting cock. His father haphazardly sent him funds and assurances that he would have him pardoned and reinstated in England by the time of the next Christmas feast, but neither money nor promises could be faithfully relied upon.

The girl pouted at him and turned away. He wondered if she was worth it and decided she wasn't – no woman was – and it was at that point that he looked up and across the thoroughfare spotted Heulwen.

The cocks struck together in a rattling flurry of bronze and black feathers. Beaks stabbed, spurs flashed. They danced breast to breast in mid-air and the men danced too, yelling, exhorting; and over their heads, ignoring their noise, ignoring the birds, Warrin de Mortimer stared and stared, not believing his eyes, not wanting to believe his eyes. His heart began to pound. His breath grew shaky and the hot scar pulsed against his ribs.

The birds parted, beaks agape, wings adrift in the dust, circling each other and clashing together again. Dark blood dripped into the ground. Warrin left his leman, and ignoring her querulous enquiry skirted the circle of raucous, intent spectators to step out into the open street.

Adam glanced across briefly to the cockfight, drawn by the bellows of the crowd rather than by any real interest in the sport. Nobility, he realized, for the sun flashed off jewelled tunics, belts and weapon hilts.

'Miles — my brother I mean, not Grandpa, used to own a fighting cock,' Heulwen reminisced. 'Mama never liked the sport. She used to scold him deaf the times he was home, but all the young men at court had them and he did not want to be any different.' She sighed and shook her head. 'Poor Chanticleer. He didn't even come to a glorious end. Run over by a wain in the ward while chasing one of his wives, and his corpse consigned to the pot.'

Adam snorted with suppressed laughter and hastily drew rein to allow a cart to lumber past. It was loaded with barrels of wine, the oxen drawing it a sleek, muscle-rippled red. Dust rose and puffed from beneath their shod cloven hooves, and Heulwen covered her face with her veil and coughed.

Southampton, Caen, Falaise, Mortain, Roche au Moins. Most of the time she had enjoyed the difference of scenery and customs. The land through which they had passed was gentle and pastoral, much flatter than her own Welsh hills, and dominated by its rivers, the Mayenne, the Maine, the green Indre and the majestic Loire itself. There were vineyards in abundance and great swathes of yellow broom, providing shelter for small game. There were fig trees, prickly sweet-chestnuts and elegant cedars silhouetted against a washed blue sky, and the people spoke a purer, more guttural French than the kind spoken in her native marches.

Now, at the end of their journey, she was sweat-stained, gritty and so saddle-sore that once down from her mare she thought she would never want to ride again.

'Not far now,' Adam said, as if reading her mind. 'Just over the bridge isn't it, Thierry?' They had sent half their escort on ahead to purchase and prepare them lodgings, and Thierry, one of the advance party, had been waiting for them this morning at the city gates to show them the way.

'Yes, my lord.'

Heulwen looked at the bustling wood and stone structure spanning the Maine. Beyond it and above, Count Fulke's keep thrust at the sky, his gonfanons fluttering on the battlements. 'I hope Austin has been busy,' she murmured, the thought of a feather mattress devoid of vermin pushing all other lesser considerations to one side.

Adam tilted her a smile. 'I will say this for you,' he teased gently, 'you're a better travelling companion than the last woman I had the misfortune to escort any distance.'

She regarded him through her lashes. 'I'll warrant she was not so sympathetic to your needs,' she said, and saucily poked her tongue between her teeth.

His look narrowed and smouldered. 'Not by half,' he said softly.

Colour heightened, she laughed at him, and heeled Gemini forward.

The lodging Thierry had rented belonged to a merchant absent on pilgrimage to Jerusalem, and although small – Adam nearly brained himself on the door-lintel when first entering – there was adequate stabling for the horses and a well-tended orchard garden going down to the river's edge, where it ended in a private wharf complete with rowing boat. The house also had the added benefit of being close to the castle.

Indeed, later, looking out of the unshuttered upstairs window into the street below as she combed the tangles from her damp hair, Heulwen saw a party of horsemen returning along their thoroughfare to the keep. Laughing young men with a few older nobles sprinkled among them, a seasoning of armed guards sweltering in quilted gambesons and half-hauberks, one of them clutching a tattered but victorious bronze cockerel, and for added spice there were gaily clad women of the highest rank of the oldest profession.

'Adam, come here,' she called.

'What is it?' Minus his tunic, shirtlaces dangling loose to reveal a brown expanse of chest, Adam braced his arm on the window frame and leaned behind her. Suddenly his tension was as palpable as the spring sunshine pouring in on them. 'William le Clito,' he muttered, his surprise tinged with more than a hint of displeasure.

'Who, the yellow head?'

'No, he's far too young. The dark one on the roan. I'll hazard just by looking at his clothes that the yellow head as you call him is Geoffrey of Anjou himself.'

Heulwen craned.

'What's William le Clito doing in Angers?' Adam said with a frown. His question was purely rhetorical and the answer already known: he must be seeking Count Fulke's support so that he could stir up unrest in Normandy. A pity for him that Adam came not seeking, but offering a prize beyond refusal. He touched Heulwen's shoulder. 'Come away from the shutters, love,' he murmured. 'You'll have their eyes popping out and rolling until they reach the river . . . and besides, I don't want half the court boasting to have seen the wife of King Henry's herald in her undergarments.'

'Too late for that,' she laughed, although she was aware of the warning beneath his light remark and withdrew from the window, latching the shutters. It was one thing to behave as she pleased at home, quite another when she and Adam were out to make a good impression upon the Count of Anjou.

The last man in the cavalcade rode past. Attached to his cantle by a leading rein was a fine, riderless pied stallion. In the shadow of a doorway across the street, Warrin de Mortimer stood and stared at the dwelling opposite and marked it with burning eyes.

Fulke, the son of Fulke le Rechin, Count of Anjou, was a man of middle height, middle build, and middle years. He was robust and florid with hair that would once have rivalled

Heulwen's for colour but had now faded to a softer, gingerish hue, thinning at the crown. Set above a bulbous wide-pored nose, his eyes were a bright steel-silver and they missed nothing. It was the eyes that had to be watched, not the deceptively smiling generous mouth.

Adam smiled in return and kept his responses modest as he presented Fulke with Henry's gifts of an English tapestry and a goblet, the base of which was set with sapphires and crystals. For Geoffrey there was a vellum-bound copy of Bede, tooled in gold leaf upon the cover. The young man accepted it graciously and smiled, but not as broadly as Fulke, and his own eyes, bright mirrors of his father's, were not only vigilant but cold.

Both father and son were enchanted by Heulwen. Fulke claimed the prerogative of leading her to the table and made her sit beside him on the high dais.

'You don't object do you, Sir Adam?' he said with bluff joviality to the somewhat disgruntled husband. 'It is not often that we are graced by company so fair.'

'Not at all sir,' said Adam, objecting very much. It was not that he did not trust her, but she looked so lovely in her court gown of aquamarine silk which matched her eyes, making them look more vivid than usual, and she was so accomplished at flirting, that it sent a pang through him to see her on another man's arm – a reminder of times before. His face impassive however, he took his place further along the trestle. Heulwen peeped round at him once, wrinkled her nose at him mischievously, then bent all her attention upon enslaving the Count of Anjou and the young man whom Henry intended to be his daughter's consort.

Father and son vied with each other for her notice, piling her trencher with the choicest titbits until she laughed and begged them to stop, declaring that she would burst; and through her jesting she made note of their rivalry and wondered if Adam too had seen. She glanced quickly down the board to him, but he was occupied in conversation with the prelate

231

beside him and did not catch it. She suspected that he was deliberately avoiding her out of pique, and her lips twitched with irritated amusement.

'Heulwen ....' mused a latecomer to the high table whom she recognized even before he was introduced as William le Clito. 'What does it mean?'

She dimpled him a quick smile. 'It is Welsh for sunshine, my lord. I take it from my great-grandmother Heulwen uerch Owain. She was a princess of her people.'

'I see you have pride,' said the round-faced, stocky young man, a bitter twist to his weak mouth, 'I can understand that.' The twist deepened and became malicious. 'Forgive me for asking, it is a very unusual name; surely you must be the same Heulwen to whom one of my knights, Warrin de Mortimer, was betrothed?'

Heulwen felt heat seeping into her cheeks and prickling her scalp. 'No, my lord.' She pitched her voice low for control. 'I was never betrothed to him. He was accused of conspiracy and murder and found guilty ... as surely you must be aware.' She fixed him with wide, reproachful eyes.

'Warrin de Mortimer?' the Count frowned. He had a dreadful memory for names.

'You know,' Geoffrey said, 'the big yellow-haired one that always wears more rings than he has fingers. Down there look, on your right, just sitting down.'

'Ah, yes.' Fulke stroked his beard.

Heulwen's heart began to pound, her temples throbbing to the same beat. Her vision blurred, but not enough to blot out the sight of the man taking his place at one of the lower trestles where le Clito's men were just settling to eat, nor the fact that he was watching her with steady, hostile eyes. Blue was not a hot colour, but his gaze was scorching a hole in her belly. Warrin here in Angers. Please God no, it could not be true!

William le Clito leaned lazily on the trestle. 'I took him in when he was banished from my uncle's domains. I understand, my lady, that Warrin and your husband fought a trial-by-

232

combat last Christmas feast over a somewhat cloudy issue?' He cocked a mocking eyebrow. 'I do not suppose the more lurid details carry any tinge of truth?'

Heulwen looked down at her hands, the only safe place to look. They were shaking. The food piled before her made her feel sick. 'It would be ill-bred of me to answer you in the manner you deserve, my lord,' she replied through stiff lips.

Geoffrey's silver eyes lit with appreciation. 'I like a woman with spirit,' he chuckled.

Precocious prig, she thought; he would receive his just desserts in the Empress. Ignoring him and le Clito, she looked piteously at the Count. 'My lord, please ... I would rather not dwell on this matter ... It is both painful and private ...' She did not need to feign the catch in her voice, but she dropped her head and dabbed at her eyes with the trailing sleeve of her gown.

'Come now, Lady Heulwen, do not distress yourself.' Awkwardly Fulke patted her hand and gave le Clito a sharp look. 'Lord William meant no harm, he did but tease you a little too far. I am sure he will apologize if he has offended.'

And that is precisely what William le Clito did, his words about as sincere as a holy relic bought at a fairing, and Heulwen accepted it with a comparable sincerity and forced herself to eat a morsel of the delicious herb-roasted venison. It was almost impossible to swallow, knowing that Warrin was watching her.

She looked along the board at Adam. He was eating as if there were nothing wrong, but she noticed that he made recourse several times to his cup to wash his own food down. His attention was no longer for the priest, but centred on Warrin and the brooding, thoughtful expression on his face was one that Heulwen had begun to know very well, if not yet to understand. Becoming aware of her scrutiny Adam turned, his eyes meeting hers, and his look changed, becoming a wry grimace accompanied by an infinitesimal shake of his head. Heulwen bit her lip. Fulke touched her arm and spoke to her, and she had to turn away to listen to him. It took all her fortitude and skill to smile and respond as if nothing was the matter, but even so she was aware of not quite succeeding.

The meal progressed through several courses and entertainments, chief among them a troop of Syrian dancing girls who wore veils on their faces in lieu of clothing elsewhere. The men were highly appreciative, for usually even the glimpse of a well-turned calf in public was cause for salacious remarks and the licking of lips. Tumblers tumbled; a lute-player sang two heroic lays and then one of the love songs composed by Duke William of Aquitaine, its content as explicit as the Syrian dancers' garments.

The finger-bowls were brought round again, the water infused with herbs, and fruit and nuts were served with a sweet wine. Fulke retired from the table and summoned a page to light him to his private apartments, commanding Geoffrey and Adam to attend him. He thanked Heulwen for the pleasure of her company and kissed her hand and cheek, but that it was a dismissal could not be mistaken. Women, like the entertainment, were excellent side-trappings with which to gild a feast. They beguiled away idle time, but that was as far as it went. A herald's wife did not share the herald's function.

'I will be all right,' she said, as Adam took her arm, one eye on the waiting page, the other on le Clito, who had joined a dice game near the hearth. As Fulke's guests he and his men were sleeping within the castle itself.

'Are you sure? Christ, I could well do without this particular twist of fate.' Scowling, Adam sought Warrin de Mortimer and saw him still sitting at the trestle, wine cup beside him, a red puddle slopped around the base, and upon his knee a black-haired woman with sultry, jewel-dark eyes. Her arms were around his neck, her fingers in his hair, and he had his hand on her thigh. She was whispering in his ear, but he was only half-listening, all his attention focused on Adam and Heulwen.

'Yes, I'm sure.' Heulwen suppressed a shudder and quickly kissed her husband, shutting out the sight of Warrin's accusing stare against Adam's cheek, drawing reassurance from the familiar individual scent of him.

He squeezed her waist and took her across the hall to consign her to the care of his bodyguard, saw her on her way, then returned to the impatiently waiting page. Warrin de Mortimer he pointedly ignored, but was still aware of him in the periphery of his vision, slowly unplucking the woman's embroidered bodice.

The squire poured wine, left the flagon and a plate of small marchpane confections to hand, and bowed out of the room. One of Fulke's dogs circled several times, then flopped down before the enormous hearth.

Adam gave Fulke the sealed parchment that had been his responsibility for the past several weeks and sat down at the Count's gesture on a chair that had been made comfortable by a tapestry cushion.

Fulke broke the seal, opened out the parchment in his stubby, spatulate hands and started to read. Geoffrey picked up a marchpane comfit and bit half of it decisively away. 'Interesting?' he asked through his mouthful.

Frowning, Fulke shook his head, took the document nearer to the candlelight and started to read it again. Geoffrey raised one eyebrow, but after one calculating glance ignored his father. He picked up another piece of marchpane and tossed it to the dog. It leaped and snapped and licked its jaws. 'Do you ever joust, Sir Adam?'

Adam blinked at him, taken momentarily by surprise. 'Occasionally, my lord,' he said cautiously.

'More than occasionally, I think,' Geoffrey contradicted. 'I saw your stallion in the stables earlier, and when I spoke to your squire about him, he said that you could hit a quintain shield dead centre ten times out of ten.'

Adam looked across at the Count whose lips were moving silently as he read. 'Austin tends to exaggerate, my lord.'

'There's a mêlée organized for tomorrow, le Clito's party

235

against mine. I'd be honoured if you'd take part . . . on my side of course.'

It was tantamount to an order, no matter the manner of its phrasing. Behind the neutral mask, Adam considered the young man who was obviously accustomed to having his own way and probably dangerous if he didn't get it. 'My lord, the honour is mine,' he responded gracefully. The English barons were going to love Geoffrey of Anjou, he thought wryly.

Geoffrey's charming smile widened his full lips which were already surrounded by harsh adult beard-stubble. 'Weapons à plaisance, my lord. No sharpened edges, whatever personal grudges might be awaiting revenge.'

Adam inclined his head and took a drink of his wine. 'No sharpened edges,' he repeated softly after a moment when he was sure of continued neutrality.

Fulke looked at Adam with cold, shrewd eyes. 'Do you know what is written here?'

'Yes, my lord.'

'What is it?' demanded Geoffrey. 'A bribe from King Henry to stop us getting too friendly with his favourite nephew?'

Fulke snorted. 'You might say that.' He handed the parchment across, and put both palms up to cover his mouth while he watched his son read.

'God's death!' Geoffrey choked as he reached the relevant part of the document. 'She's old enough to be my grandam!'

'She is also the Dowager Empress of Germany and King Henry's designated heir,' Fulke's voice was sharp with warning, 'and she is but five-and-twenty.'

Geoffrey's first high flush of colour had receded to a dirty white. He swallowed and reread the parchment as if willing the words to change before his eyes.

'A crown and a duchy,' Fulke said softly, watching him intently.

Adam quietly drank his wine, observing them from beneath downcast lids. They were like two stags, one in its prime, at the peak of its powers and recognizing that the only way was

236

down, and the other young, unsure, but gaining rapidly in strength and experience with the occupied peak as its goal.

'I don't want it.' Geoffrey tossed the parchment down. His throat worked.

'Think with your head, boy, not your heart. We'll not better an offer like this, not in a hundred years.'

Very much the frightened adolescent now, Geoffrey swore at his father and Fulke reached him in two strong strides to strike him back-handed across the mouth. 'Use your brains, you stupid whelp!' he snarled. 'Think of the power! The woman's only a means to an end. God's blood, once you've planted a seed in her belly, you can sport wherever the fancy takes you. Surely a few nights in Mathilda's bed is a cheap enough price to pay!'

Geoffrey wiped a thread of blood from the corner of his mouth, looked at it smeared on his knuckles, and then at his father. His chest heaved erratically and his eyes glistened with tears, but he had himself under control again. Turning away, he paced heavily to the narrow window slit and leaned his head against the wall. The dog left the hearth and padded across to nuzzle its moist nose against his thigh. After a short silence Geoffrey dragged his fur-tipped sleeve across his eyes and drew a shuddering breath. His back still turned, he said, 'You told me, Papa, that Henry of England was like a spider weaving a web to entrap all men. Why should we be lured onto its strands?'

'Is the answer not obvious? We too are spiders.' Fulke crossed the room to reach up and squeeze his tall son's shoulder with a firm, paternal hand. 'And these matters are better discussed in private.'

Adam drained his cup and stood up, neither slow nor loath to take Fulke's warning to the boy as reason for himself to depart. 'With your permission, my lords,' he said.

Fulke looked round and nodded. 'Yes, leave us.' He gave the ghost of a wry smile. 'You can see that this news has taken us both aback somewhat. You will be remaining in Angers

237

until after the mêlée? Good, attend us then, and I will have a reply for your liege lord.'

Adam made a practised obeisance. 'Yes, my lord.' He picked up the parchment from the rushes and put it carefully back down on the trestle.

Aubrey and the men of his escort other than those who had seen Heulwen home, were waiting at the stables for him. A convivial game of dice was in progress and a flask of wine and giggling kitchen girl were being passed from hand to hand.

Adam secured his cloak and strode across the ward. 'When you've finished, gentlemen,' he said in a sarcastic tone, which was redeemed by the merest glint of humour.

Thierry's teeth flashed in a white, weasel grin. He pocketed the dice. 'I was losing anyway,' he said disrespectfully and stood up. Wiry and light, he was at least two handspans smaller than his lord. He caught the girl by the arm, murmured something in her ear and slapped her buttocks to send her on her way.

Adam narrowed his eyes at the Angevin and paused, his hands on Lyard's neck, one foot in the stirrup. 'You'll lose a week's pay on top of it if you don't look sharp,' he warned.

Thierry tilted his head, unsure whether to take the words as threat or jest, and opted for caution inasmuch as he knew it. Saluting smartly he took a running jump at his bay and vaulted faultlessly into the saddle. 'Ready, my lord,' he announced, cocky as a sparrow.

Adam's mouth twitched. 'Spare such tricks for tomorrow. Young Geoffrey's got a mêlée organized, and we're fighting on the Angevin side.'

The news was greeted by cheers all round, for when not actually involved in a war, Adam's men enjoyed nothing better than practising for it. The mêlée was a dangerous game, sometimes crossing the narrow line between war and mock-war, but the hurly burly was fun and offered the chance to gain rich prizes, for a man defeated had by the rules to yield the victor his horse, hauberk and weapons, or their value in coin.

Adam listened to their eager banter and felt the excitement stir his own blood. It was his sport: he excelled at it, and the prospect of decent competition was exhilarating, or would have been had not the presence of Warrin de Mortimer buzzed like a huge black fly in the ointment.

Thierry was watching him with a tense, speculative gaze. Adam returned the look sharply and the mercenary quickly wheeled his horse into line and made himself busy with a loose piece of harness.

'A mêlée!' Heulwen exclaimed, throwing down the twin-sided ivory comb on the bed and whirling round to face him, her eyes flashing and her hair a glorious flaming swirl around her shoulders and waist. 'Have you run utterly mad?'

Adam spread his hands palms upwards. 'Warrin is no match for me on horseback,' he said defensively. 'On foot at Christmastide it was a little too close for comfort, I admit, but not astride.'

Heulwen laughed in his face. 'You do not seriously believe that Warrin will play by the rules?'

He sat down on the bed and looked at her along the embroidery-crusted shoulder of his court tunic. 'Heulwen, understand this, I *want* to fight in this mêlée.'

Adam hesitated, searching for words that were difficult to find because it was a feeling that came from the gut, not the mind. 'It is . . . oh, I don't know, bred into me, blood and bone. A sword is still a sword no matter how much you cover it in gilt.' His palms opened wider as he spoke, displaying to her the callouses of his trade and the thick white scar of an old battle wound bisecting his life line. 'Even if I didn't want to take part, it is expected of me. Henry's honour as much as mine is at stake.'

'Honour!' Heulwen choked on the word, fortunately too overwhelmed by fear and rage to add to it.

Adam's eyes narrowed and the light shivered on the gold embroidery as he took a swift breath. 'Yes, honour,' he repeated carefully, and lowered his hands to pick up the comb she had thrown down.

'Warrin doesn't know the meaning of the word!' she spat harshly.

He ran his thumb along the ivory teeth. 'Not necessarily true. He just digresses from it now and then when it's a choice between it and something he wants, and then he conveniently forgets that he ever lapsed.'

She snorted at him, not in the least mollified. 'Is that supposed to be a reassurance?'

Adam sighed. 'It was supposed to tell you that I'm not entirely naïve.' He pulled her down onto the bed beside him and gently began to draw the comb through her hair. 'Would declining to take part guarantee my life? I think not. A swift thrust from a dagger in the crowd could as easily be the manner of despatch. In a mêlée I will have Sweyn to my left, Aubrey to my right, and Thierry and Alun thereabouts; and if it has worked before a dozen times in battle, there is no reason to think it will not work on a tourney field.'

She held her head stiff against the tug of the comb and felt his palm following it down, smoothing, coaxing. Men, she thought with contempt. Willing to die for the art of showing off their prowess in the killing arts and calling it honour; fighting cocks strutting in their fine feathers. She could still see the eager gleam in Adam's eyes when he had first come to her, could hear the laughter of his men.

Adam laid his palm along her jaw and turned her face to him. She looked down but he exerted pressure, forcing her to meet his gaze. 'Look, sweetheart, I will avoid him if I can, that much I swear to you. Not because I don't want to separate his head from his neck, there's nothing I'd like more, but I cannot allow personal enmity to stand between myself and what I am here to do for Henry.' He stroked her cheek. 'It will be all right, I promise you.'

She shook her head, her eyes filling with tears. 'You stubborn, pig-headed ...'

'Tail–chaser?' he suggested with a raised brow, and bent his mouth to hers.

'In God's name Adam, do not chase it too far!' she whispered against his mouth, 'I will die if I lose you.'

CHAPTER 20

THE CHOSEN SITE for Geoffrey's mêlée was a broad green field just outside the city walls, and it was here, shortly after dawn, that the court assembled either to watch the sport, or to prepare to partake. The early March morning was mild with the promise of warm sunshine, and although furred cloaks were much in evidence, there was no real discomfort from cold. If people gathered around braziers, it was because they served as a focal point over which to discuss and anticipate the fighting to come.

Heulwen listened to the bright chatter surrounding her and was aware of an overpowering feeling of dread and isolation. She tried to smile and respond to the tide of enthusiasm, agreeing with a baron's wife that yes, the weather was fine and that the sport should be well worth watching. She bought fairing ribbons from a huckster to tie around the shaft of Adam's lance, clapped dutifully and laughed emptily at the antics of a dancing bear, and pretended to listen with attentive enjoyment to the ballad of an itinerant lute-player. Her mouth ached with the strain of forced merriment and her head with the strain of the pretence, when all she wanted to do was run away, dragging her husband with her, and not stop until she reached the haven of her own Welsh marches.

She looked for Adam across the wide expanse of virgin grass which was soon to be despoiled. He was over at Geoffrey's pavilion with the Count. She could see Austin outside keeping a half-hearted eye on Lyard, his main interest reserved for a dancing girl who was playing a tambour and flashing brown slender ankles at him. A ragamuffin child was feeding a wrinkled apple to the stallion. Austin glanced round and took scant notice as he leaned against the pole supporting the tent and folded his arms.

Adam ducked out of the tent, talking to Geoffrey of Anjou. He pointed to the helmet tucked under the young man's arm and made a comment. Geoffrey laughed and replied, and both of them paused to examine and admire Adam's powerful sorrel stallion. The child made himself scarce. Adam playfully cuffed Austin into awareness, took his leave of Geoffrey and unhitching Lyard, walked him across the field towards Heulwen.

Man and horse were all prepared for the mêlée. Adam was accoutred in his hauberk and a fine new surcoat of midnight-blue silk, stitched with a gold lozenge on the breast to match that on his shield. Lyard was also trapped out in blue and gold, and both man and horse were bursting with such exuberance that Heulwen's heart turned to ice.

Halting the stallion, hand held close to the decorated bit chains, Adam gave her a slow, measuring look that took full note of her pallor and the false curve of her lips. 'Listen,' he said gently, 'Fulke has promised to give me his written reply by tomorrow afternoon, so we'll be able to start home before the week's out, I promise.'

He was doing his best to allay her fears, she thought. A pity that he had not a hope in hell of succeeding. No point in tarnishing the shine. Instead of saying that tomorrow might be too late, she patted Lyard's glossy neck and brought out the fairing ribbons.

'I chose them to match your surcoat,' she said, and bit her lip. 'I'm sorry if I'm being a wet fish, Adam. I will make it up to you, I promise.'

He arched one brow and the corresponding mouth corner tilted up. 'I can think of several ways,' he murmured, 'and I am sure you can think of several more.'

'At least a dozen ... I wish today was already over.' She fiddled with a plaited tassel of Lyard's cream mane.

Adam ran the fairing ribbons through his fingers and looked

over his shoulder. Men were warming up with short practice charges and courtesy raps of lance on a companion's shield. Hoarse, joyful cries floated across the field. The leathery smell of harness and horses pervaded the air.

Heulwen gave him a gentle push, the most difficult thing she had ever done in her life. 'Go on, if you linger here with me you won't be ready. Just don't take too many risks.'

He hesitated, aware of her pretence, but not knowing how to reassure her any more than he already had. It was the element of danger in this kind of sport that made it so exhilarating. He took her face in his hands and set his lips upon hers. Lyard snorted and butted his muzzle into the centre of Adam's spine, jarring him forwards. Their mouths jolted apart. He turned to the horse. 'It seems I have my orders,' he laughed, and set his foot in the stirrup.

She stared up at him astride the destrier: tensile strength and agility coupled to smooth power. Try as she might, she could not prevent the misgivings that came to cloud her pride in the picture they made. Despite the increasing warmth of the spring sun, she was shivering. Brusquely she told Elswith to go and buy some hot broth from one of the hucksters, knowing in her heart of hearts that it would do nothing to melt the block of ice that was encroaching on all thought and feeling, for that was fashioned of fear.

Lyard danced on polished, pristine hooves as Adam adjusted the length of his stirrup-leather and made himself comfortable in the high saddle while Austin handed up helm, shield and the blunted jousting lance festooned with blue silk ribbons. Adam rode out onto the field and trotted Lyard over it, testing the feel of the ground and examining it for any obvious pot-holes or snags of stone that could bring a horse down in mid-charge.

On his right, Geoffrey of Anjou was cantering and turning his own destrier – a lively Spanish grey, well-sprung in the ribs but a little short of bone in Adam's estimation. Still, the lad was handling him exceptionally well, and although his constant nervous laughter revealed his excitement underneath, he seemed otherwise steady enough to acquit himself admirably.

Adam came round past Heulwen and the other women. He dipped his lance to salute her and she smiled at him, one hand leaving the bowl of broth she held to wave back. She was trying hard, he thought, his sense of joy dampening slightly. In childhood she had got them both into some dreadful scrapes, had egged him on to all kinds of folly and resultant punishment, always snapping her fingers in the face of danger. But then in childhood it had all been a game. It was frightening to realize when you grew up that the game was a reality you could not stop when it grew dark.

He slowed Lyard to a walk as they passed the assembling knights of William le Clito. Warrin was among them, leaning against the piebald stallion whose price had never been paid, arms outspread upon withers and rump, looking for all the world like a blasphemous crucifix effigy. He was talking lazily to le Clito, but broke off what he was saying to stare at Adam with a strange, sly half-smile curving his thin lips

Le Clito spoke and Warrin ceased slouching and turned his back on Adam to check and hitch the piebald's girth. Adam swung Lyard away and trotted him back to his own end of the field where his men were warming up.

Gradually, the two opposing lines of knights began to assemble. Horses snapped at each other and were reined back hard, or sent round in a circle to attempt a place in the line again. Men jostled, struggling to position their shields and lances as well as control the reins. It was disorganized chaos out of which, after much bellowing, cursing and energetic waving of arms, Geoffrey finally succeeded in bringing about a reasonable battle formation.

There were several seconds of silent, strung tension: all down the line, men fretted their destriers for the charge. Adam tucked himself down behind his shield, rested the weight of his lance upon his thigh, and stared across the expanse of field at the opposing lines. The pied horse stood out boldly among the bays and browns and chestnuts, an easy target either to attack or avoid. He glanced briefly at Heulwen. Whereas all around her people were craning on tip-toe or bending sideways to obtain a better view of the proceedings, her stance was as rigid and unnatural as one of the illuminated figures in the psalter in Ravenstow's chapel. He wanted to shout a reassurance to her, but that was impossible, and in that same moment, the cry to attack went out along the line and all his attention was swept back to the charge.

'Hah!' he cried, and slapped the reins down hard on Lyard's neck and used his spurs. The stallion lunged at the bit and spurted into a gallop. Grass tore up in great moist clods. Sun flashed on armour and blunted spear tips and gleaming, straining horse-hide. Adam singled out his man – a solid knight upon a squat dun, and guided Lyard with the pressure of his knees, his lance held loosely and his body relaxed as he counted down the strides of space.

Timing his move to the last inch of ground covered, he adjusted his aim and rising slightly in the stirrups, gripped the lance and thrust forward. The strike was true. The Norman knight's lance wavered awry. He too had been rising in the stirrups to strike, but had closed his eyes against the impact and gone a fraction too high; Adam's lance, striking true centre on his shield, sent him sailing right over the crupper to crash in a dazed heap on the muddy ground.

Adam caught the dun's bridle. The knight's squire had dismounted and was helping his dazed lord to his feet. Adam asked if he was all right, received a grudging assent, and with a curt nod of his own told the defeated man where to pay his debt, before wheeling Lyard in pursuit of another opponent.

He and a knight with a fancy bronze-decorated helm traded several sword-blows until they were separated by another group of four knights hacking desperately at each other. Adam recognized Geoffrey's grey stallion; blood was trickling from a minor wound on its near forequarter, and its nostrils were flared wide. Geoffrey was holding his own, but making no real impression on his opponent, an older thickset man who was obviously trying to wear him down. Adam gathered his reins and prepared to join and turn the balance.

'My lord, to your right!' warned Sweyn, warding his shield and sidling his bay nearer. Instead of spurring forwards, Adam pulled his right rein and turned Lyard to face a group of five young men, working as a team and obviously determined to take a prize such as the sorrel stallion for their own.

Adam grinned wolfishly, twisted the reins again, and charged Lyard at the centremost knight, leaving Sweyn and Aubrey to deal with those on his left, and Alun and Thierry with those on his right. The sorrel was sluggish to respond to his command and he had to use the jabbing reminder of spurs to bring his head up.

The two horses snapped together. Adam's opponent struck and his blade rebounded off Adam's shield. Adam's powerful backhand stroke, his most dangerous, slammed the young knight's shield inwards, clouting him in the mouth with its rim. He followed through immediately giving no respite, and the shield gave way again to a resulting howl of pain. The man groped for his reins and missed them as he tried frantically to disengage. His horse plunged, went back on its haunches, and in so doing, fouled the mount of the knight who was engaging Sweyn. The latter took immediate advantage, rising in his stirrups to belabour the opposition.

Detached from Adam by the pressure of battle, Thierry and Alun were too far away to prevent what happened next and Aubrey, although he tried, was unable to fight clear of his own encounter and come to Adam's immediate aid. 'Ware arms, my lord!' he bellowed at the full pitch of his lungs, 'in the name of Sweet Christ, ware!'

In the crowd, Heulwen screamed her husband's name and lifting her skirts began to run, until she was caught back by one of Adam's serjeants who, appalled though he was, still had the presence of mind to know that if she ran onto the field among the milling and trampling of the great war horses and the swinging weapons, she was unlikely to leave it alive. She fought him like a wild cat, but he held on grimly, begging her to stop, and at last she did so because she could not break his grip and all her strength had gone. Sobbing, tear-streaked and panting, she turned in his hold to face the field, and by that time it was all over.

Adam, his sword lifted to strike at the badly warded shield of his struggling adversary, commanded Lyard with his thighs to meet the new challenge. The sorrel pivoted and staggered badly just as Adam's raised right forearm took a vicious blow from a morning star flail. His sword became snared in the ricocheting chain and was jerked from his fingers, while some of the steel points in the weighted ball at the end of the chain caught in the mail rivets of his hauberk sleeve and the gambeson beneath, splaying iron and tearing fabric. The impetus of the blow tore him sideways and down from the saddle.

He landed hard, but extensive training made him roll as he fell, and present shield to his enemy's next assault. *Enemy*, not opponent, for the man cursing at Lyard and striking him out of the way with his shield was mounted on a foam-spattered piebald stallion. The morning star flail was certainly not a weapon of courtesy, nor was the manner of Warrin's attack: slamming in from the side while Adam was still engaged and omitting to utter the obligatory warning of challenge.

Gasping, black stars fluctuating before his eyes, Adam strove to his feet. His right arm was numb, he could not feel his fingers and his shield was about as much protection as a flimsy sheet of parchment against the man who was about to ride him down.

Cursing horribly, Sweyn fought to disengage. Aubrey had succeeded, but could see that it was futile – he was going to be too late.

With the flail swinging suggestively on its chain, gathering impetus, Warrin sent the pied stallion into a dancing rear. Adam watched death tower over him, black-and-white mane rippling against the sky, hooves like steel arcs of death, the gates to the underworld. The rear blazed to its zenith, and Warrin de Mortimer yelled his triumph.

The horse came down but twisted, crashing sideways, barged by the blood-streaked shoulder of a grey Spanish stallion. A descending forehoof clipped Adam's shield. He staggered but kept his feet, and Warrin in turn was torn down from his horse and flung on to the ground as Aubrey reached him and pricked his blade into the hollow of his throat.

Lyard was trembling and sweating, head hanging, tail limp. Moving gingerly, Adam went to examine him. The destrier's legs wove as drunkenly as those of a newborn foal. Adam's face was chalk-white with fury as he stalked back to de Mortimer.

'What have you done to my horse?' he demanded in a whispered snarl and snatched the sword from Aubrey.

'I haven't been near the poxy beast!' Warrin stared up the pattern-welded fuller of the blade and Adam stared down it, a muscle ticking in his cheek. 'Belike he took a blow on the head in the fighting!'

'Do you know why this section of a sword is called the blood gutter?' Adam's tone was almost pleasant. He began to lean on the hilt.

'Enough!' commanded Geoffrey of Anjou, dismounting to thrust Adam aside from his purpose. 'This mêlée is an affair to prove valour, not an extension of your trial-by-combat. You both shame yourselves!'

'Shame?' Adam bellowed incredulously. 'Look at the way this whoreson came at me, choosing his moment and full intending to do murder. The shame is not mine!'

'Do you know for certain that he has interfered with your stallion?' Geoffrey said coldly. His face was flushed, translucent with his own anger.

'God's blood, it's obvious!' Adam snapped. Geoffrey stared. Adam fished for control, netted a semblance, and setting his jaw returned the sword to Aubrey. 'Seek for proof and you'll find it,' he said on a quieter but still vehement note. 'I know when I have been set up like a stuffed quintain dummy.'

'What's the matter here?'

They all turned to face William le Clito who was leaning down from his champing black percheron. Sweat was runnelling his pink face, dripping into his eyes and making him squint. He wiped at them ineffectually with the edge of his gauntlet.

'A breach of honour from one of your side,' Geoffrey said. 'Best if you withdraw him and keep him confined until we can decide how serious the breach is.'

Le Clito pursed his lips. 'Personal grudges are bound to make this kind of sport more dangerous, and in the heat of the moment men tend to forget their manners,' he said with smooth complacence.

'Is this the result of impulse?' Adam gestured at Lyard. Austin had appeared and was very gently trying to coax the wobbling horse towards the edge of the field. 'Is this the kind of weapon used in courtesy?' He nudged the flail with his toe.

Le Clito took in the evidence and looked down at Warrin who was now sitting up, his helm on the grass beside him. His face was ashen, and against it a pink scar high on his cheekbone was very pronounced. 'What have you to say?' le Clito said harshly.

'I never touched the horse. I wanted to tumble de Lacey in the dust, bloody his pride as he did mine, and I took it too far.' He stared at the ground as he spoke, tone completely blank.

'Horseshit!' Adam rasped.

Geoffrey looked around. The mêlée was winding to a halt as men drifted over to listen to the altercation. 'My lord?' he said to le Clito.

The older man bit his lip, saw that he had no choice and nodded to the knight beside him. 'Etienne, escort Warrin from the field and keep him confined in my quarters until I come.'

Geoffrey nodded curtly and remounted the grey. To Adam he said in lowered, acid tones, 'Is this a sample of the kind of behaviour I can expect from your fellow barons?'

Adam made no reply which in his present mood was probably fortunate. He stared at a thick streak of mud on his surcoat, and forced his limbs to a rigid quiescence.

'I suggest you go home and get yourself and your horse tended,' Geoffrey said, and wrestled his horse around.

Adam lifted his head to watch him ride away, le Clito beside him, and became aware of the pain thundering through his arm. Warrin de Mortimer did not look at Adam as he straddled the piebald and departed from the field with le Clito's knight. The flail hung down from his saddle, catching glints from the sun. Sweyn muttered beneath his breath. Aubrey said something aloud in English, the best language for swearing. Adam said nothing at all.

'Will he be all right?' The straw crackled.

Adam turned to regard his wife in the swinging light of the Alfred lantern. She was carrying his fur-lined mantle over her arm and also the morning's abandoned picnic basket. 'I thought you were abed?'

'I was, but I couldn't sleep knowing you were down here alone. How is he?' She knelt beside him and laid a gentle hand on Lyard's stretched red-gold neck. The horse was spread out in the straw, his breathing regular but noisy, his limbs twitching now and again in strange muscular spasms.

'No real change, but if he was going to die he would have done so by now, I think.' He compressed his lips and looked at her from the corner of his eyes. 'You warned me, didn't you?'

'It is no comfort that I was right.' She took her hand from the horse's neck to lay it over his. 'When I saw you go down this afternoon ... Oh Jesu, Adam!'

He felt her shudder and, a little awkward because of his bruised arm, drew her against him and kissed her. She began to cry then, burying her face in his chest, her fingers clutching through his tunic and shirt.

Adam was somewhat taken aback by this sudden outburst of emotion. Saving an incident with one of his serjeants, who

251

now sported a badly scratched face and the beginnings of a black eye in recompense for his efforts to prevent her from hurtling herself into the midst of the mêlée, she had been as cool and remote as an icon. When he had walked off the field she had neither cast herself hysterically into his arms nor turned the termagant, but had greeted him with about as much warmth as a pane of glass. She had seen efficiently to his injuries, which consisted mainly of heavy bruising. That he had no broken ribs or fingers was a miracle, and she had said so a trifle tartly, but there had been no more reprimand than that. She had treated him with the dutiful courtesy she might yield to a stranger.

'Come, sweeting,' he said tenderly, 'it's all over now. There's no need for these tears.'

Sniffing, she drew slightly away to wipe her face on her cloak. 'Blame my stepmother,' she said, and suddenly there was an undercurrent of laughter in her tear-wobbly voice. She made herself busy finding a wine skin and two cups from the depths of the basket.

He looked at her questioningly.

'She trained me, drilled it into my head that in times of crisis the worst thing you can do is panic. When that crisis is past, then you can weep and turn into a jibbering half-wit if that is your need.' She sniffed again and handed him the wine and a piece of manchet loaf topped with a slice of roast meat.

He chuckled wryly. 'That sounds like the Countess,' he said, and took a hungry bite of food. He had not eaten since the breaking of fast that dawn, indeed had not realized until now how hungry he actually was.

'Do you know, Heulwen,' he reflected, 'I've never been so near to a blind rage as I was this morning. If Geoffrey of Anjou had not prevented me, I'd have killed Warrin there and then. Jesu God, all those high words about not jeopardizing my errand, and then I go and lean on my blade.' He shook his head, his voice wry with self-contempt, and took a swallow of the cold, sharp wine. Unnecessarily, he adjusted the blanket covering the stallion. 'Austin says that one of the city's beggar children fed Lyard a couple of wrinkled apples. He saw no harm in it, and I don't suppose I would have done either — only in hindsight. A beggar child would not feed apples to a warhorse unless paid to do it. He'd eat them himself.'

'You think that was what brought Lyard to this?'

'Assuredly. What better way of evening the odds than to have Lyard founder at the wrong moment? All Warrin had to do was watch for the coming opportunity.'

'What will happen to him?'

'Not a great deal, I suspect. For the sake of political diplomacy the whole thing will be forgotten as quickly as possible. Le Clito will go back to France with his retinue, and we'll go home to England and the ripples in the pool will drift to the bank and disappear.' He made a wry face. 'Christ's blood,' he said softly as he put the empty goblet down, 'I wish we were home now.'

She leaned her head upon his shoulder. A shiver of foreboding rippled down her spine. 'So do I,' she said in a heartfelt whisper. 'Adam, so do I.'

'How could you be such an idiot?' snapped William le Clito and glared at the man stretched out on the bed. 'All right, Adam de Lacey owes you a debt that can only be paid with his life, but what's your hurry? Surely you could have arranged something a little less obvious? It is no wonder that Mathilda reached England in safety if this is the level of your ability!'

'It was not supposed to be obvious,' Warrin said, sulkily, and folded his arms behind his head, revealing arm pits tufted with wiry blond hair. 'There was nothing wrong with the idea. It was just pure mischance that the whelp interfered at the wrong moment. If he hadn't, the world would now be rid of Adam de Lacey and no one any the wiser.'

'You think no one would notice his horse staggering about like a drunkard!' Le Clito scraped an exasperated hand through his fine, slightly thinning hair. 'You think no one would notice the hoofprints all over your victim's corpse, or not recognize that piebald you were riding? God's balls, you truly are an idiot!'

'Accidents happen in tourneys all the time. His horse was struck on the head. I could not prevent mine from trampling him. I got carried away in the heat of battle. It frequently happens, and I had a witness to corroborate my version of the truth, one of de Lacey's own men, the little Angevin with the bright red boots who likes the dice more than he should.'

Le Clito snorted contemptuously down his nose. 'Be that as it may, you are more than fortunate to be lying on that bed and not on the straw of a cell floor. I had the devil of a task persuading Count Fulke not to throw you in his oubliette. Indeed, the only thing that saved you was the fact that we're returning immediately to France.'

Warrin jerked up on his elbows. 'France?' he repeated, startled.

'You weren't there in the hall to hear it were you? A messenger came from my father-in-law. Charles of Flanders has been murdered at his prayers, and mine have been answered.' A grin split his round face. 'I've been offered the vacancy – William, by the grace of an opportune knife, the Count of Flanders. How do you fancy settling down to a Flemish fief and a broad-beamed wife with yellow plaits?'

'You have been offered Flanders?' Startlement increased, verging upon incredulity.

'By Louis of France as the overlord of the Duchy. But there are others who have also put in a claim, and that's why we have to go back straight away. There's some hard fighting ahead, but when I come through it, I'm not just going to be a thorn in my uncle Henry's side, I'm going to be an enormous barbed spear.' His teeth flashed, and the last word came out on a burst of saliva.

Warrin closed his eyes and lay back again. A fief in Flanders. A Flemish wife. Earning his bread by the sword. His eyelids tensed in pained response to the particular barbed spear in his own side. 'It is wonderful news, my lord,' he said, meaning it, but not having the enthusiasm to colour the words.

Le Clito looked at him speculatively and grunted. 'Yes, isn't it?' he said in Warrin's same tone. He picked up an orange from the dish on the low trestle and dug his fingernails into the peel. Delicate aromatic droplets sprayed into the air and their essence was carried by the draught from the window to the man on the bed. 'What I do wonder is what my Uncle Henry wants with Count Fulke. Nothing he desires the world to know, that much is certain.'

'The Count has given you no hint?'

Le Clito spat out a section of pith. 'No,' he slurped through a mouthful of fruit and juice. 'Not a word, even when delicately pressed he immediately changed the subject, so it's obviously to his advantage and not ours.' He continued to devour the orange, then suddenly paused and smiled craftily at the silent, bitter-mouthed knight on the bed. 'You could of course make amends for your behaviour today and do yourself a great benefit at the same time.'

Warrin opened wary eyes upon his benefactor as he came and sat down on the side of the bed. His hands and chin were sticky with orange juice, and there were drips of it staining his shirt. 'My lord?'

'I want you to find out why my uncle has seen fit to send a herald here to Anjou and I want you to find out before de Lacey and his wife leave for England. They're bound to have some communication with Fulke, even if it's a verbal one. I want to know what it is, and as long as I'm not implicated I don't care how you go about getting it.'

Behind the bitterness, something else uncoiled in Warrin's eyes, exultant and savage. 'Money, my lord,' he began. 'I will need ...'

'You will be given what you require, and more by way of appreciation when you bring me some proof of your success.' Le Clito rose smoothly to his feet and went to wash his hands and face in the laver. 'The details are yours to command. I trust you not to fail – this time.' He stretched for the towel and dried his hands thoroughly, the gesture almost symbolic.

'I won't,' said Warrin, and then softly on a breath that scarcely stirred the air, 'by Christ on the cross, this time I won't.'

CHAPTER 21

'HOT PIES, HOT PIES!' a vendor bawled close to Heulwen's shrinking ear. 'Fresh lily-white mussels!' another exhorted in counterpoint, a loaded basket balanced on top of her head, her wide-brimmed hat protecting her wimple from the dripping shellfish. Her wares did not smell particularly fresh to Heulwen, or perhaps it was just the fact that down here near the wharves the air was more pungent anyway, replete to surfeit with the watery aromas of a busy river and the numerous vessels plying their trade. Fishing craft in various stages of decrepitude, inshore cogs, larger sea-going merchant galleys, sleek, lupine longboats with striped sails and rows of decorated oar-holes.

Heulwen paused beside Adam to watch some sailors rolling barrels of wine onto one of the galleys. Water slapped against the stone. Rain had been in short supply that year and a green weedy line showed how far the river level had fallen, although the lowering sky and the damp warm wind suggested that this was soon to be remedied. She looked at the water, thought of the channel crossing and grimaced to remember the cold choppy sea. That she had not been sick on the first crossing was owing to the relative calm of the waves and her own iron determination not to burden her husband or put him off wanting to take her anywhere again. Adam's own travel-hardened constitution was impervious to most discomfort, and he treated those who suffered with surprise and mild impatience.

Adam set his good arm across her shoulders. His injured one had stiffened up and for the nonce he was wearing it in a sling.

'Not long now, love,' he said, as if he had caught the drift of her thoughts. 'Once I have collected Fulke's reply, we can be on our way.'

'Tomorrow dawn, then.' She wrinkled her nose, and not just at the sudden stink of hot pitch as they passed some men caulking a wallow-bellied galley.

'Too late to set out today,' he confirmed regretfully. 'I don't go to him until nones, and it's bound to be vespers at the earliest before I can get away, if not compline and full dark ... Are you hungry?'

Arm in arm they left the blended stenches of the wharves and warehouses and found a space to sit and eat spicy hot mutton pasties, bought from one of the ubiquitous street vendors and surprisingly good, washed down with a skin of the local wine. Adam had purchased several barrels to take home with them, for being bought at source, it was of a high quality at a very attractive price.

The sun was a warm white halo beyond the clouds and the warm breeze blew the market-place smells at them. Spring came earlier to Anjou than it did to England. Here the trees were preparing to blossom; in the marches the snow was still skittering in the wind. Heulwen found herself longing to put out her tongue and taste it.

Repast completed, they moved on through the seething mass of humanity. A woman, her teeth rotten stumps, tried to sell Heulwen a caged bird and was rejected with a shudder, for she had never been able to tolerate the sight of a creature in a cage. She did, however, succumb at Adam's insistence to some new hairpins and a pair of beautifully worked silver braid fillets from a haberdasher's stall, and to a vial of exotic flower oil from an Arab merchant.

Adam looked critically at the horses that were for sale. A young black Flemish mare caught his eye. She was compact and solid without being overly thickset and possessed of a bold, confident carriage. Her winter coat was coming away in handfuls, making her look patchy, but this was no detriment save to appearance and probably the reason she was still for sale. He ran his good hand down her legs and found them well formed and sound.

'Adam.' Heulwen touched his shoulder.

He turned at the warning in her voice and looked at the entourage winding its way through the market place: William le Clito with a prepossessing escort of knights in their finest array. No women this time, their presence replaced by a string of laden pack ponies, and all headed in the direction of the city gates.

'Well well,' he said, lips curving into an arid smile. 'What a pretty sight, and Warrin doing rearguard duty. It's a pity I've never been much use at left-handed knife-throwing.'

The piebald was limping from a hip strain incurred the previous day. Straight-backed, Warrin rode him competently. Beneath his helm, his square jaw jutted with determination and his left, ring-bedecked hand was clenched hard on his thigh, hinting at the violence that was so much a part of the determination.

'Popinjay,' Adam muttered, and after one hard stare, deliberately turned his back to continue his examination of the black mare.

'I will sleep easier in my bed tonight,' Heulwen said on a relieved note, and looked at her husband. Although he had affected indifference, his body was rigid and his hand movements jerky.

The group moved on. Warrin glanced once and briefly at Heulwen and Adam, his face perfectly blank. Then his blue eyes travelled beyond them to where the Angevin Thierry was whittling a piece of wood with his meat dagger, tiny slivers and shavings dropping on to his tunic, and the red boot adorning the foot that was crossed over one knee as an arm support. Thierry raised his head and returned Warrin's stare blandly. His right forefinger twitched off the knife in a gesture imperceptible to all save Warrin who was watching for it, and Thierry returned industriously to his whittling.

'He's gone,' Heulwen murmured.

'*Deo gratias,*' Adam said through his teeth, some but not all the tension leaving his body.

'What's wrong?' she asked, sensing the residue.

Adam shook his head. 'Nothing.' He twitched his shoulders. 'A knife's echo between my blade-bones, I suppose.' He spoke abruptly to the horse coper. 'How much do you want for her?'

Heulwen chewed her lip and considered him, not without a hint of exasperation. Tail-chasing again, she thought, and to no good purpose.

He bought the black mare for twelve marks, haggling the coper down from the fifteen he had first asked, and an agreement made, turned to his pensive wife. 'Can you take her home with you if I go to see the Count now?'

'Yes, of course.' She forced a smile. 'Compline, you said?'

He grimaced. 'Most probably . . . I'm sorry love, but I cannot bring you with me. I wish I could.'

Heulwen pouted and narrowed her lovely aquamarine eyes. 'You've taken a fancy to one of those Syrian dancing girls,' she accused, 'and you want me out of the way.'

'They were rather engaging,' he admitted, his face as straight as her own, but then his eye corners crinkled, marring the deception. 'But I'd rather see you do the dance of the seven veils than any houri.'

'Then I'll have to practise.' She eyed him through narrowed, sultry lids and gave a small undulation of her hips.

'Salomé,' he said, and laughing, kissed her and left for the keep.

When Adam arrived at the castle, Geoffrey of Anjou was tilting at a ring that had been set up on a quintain in the bailey, and he was making a commendable job of it. Adam joined the gaggle of spectators, among them the kitchen girl with whom Thierry had been so familiar two nights before. She blushed and giggled behind work-roughened hands. Adam ignored her to concentrate on Geoffrey's performance.

Geoffrey lifted the ring on the end of his lance and came away cleanly without encountering the sandbag. Turning the grey at the end of the tilt he saw Adam, and having handed the lance to a squire, jogged over to him. 'What do you think?' He was panting slightly, his white teeth parted in a grin that only just fell short of being smug. He knew he was good.

A rainy gust of breeze barged rudely across the ward. Adam hooked the fingers of his uninjured hand in his belt. 'Not bad, my lord,' he nodded in reply, 'you check yourself slightly before you go for the strike. It would be better if you could maintain the pace.'

Geoffrey's smile diminished slightly. He favoured Adam with a glittering look. 'I'll bear it in mind,' he said, and then gestured at Adam's slung arm. 'How do you fare?'

'It is sore, my lord, but no lasting damage, I think.'

Geoffrey dismounted gracefully. His riding boots were of the finest tooled buckskin and embossed with gilded leopards. 'And your horse?'

'He's got his legs back and took a handful of oats from my hand this morning, but he's still a trifle subdued. A splitting skull, I hazard.' His lips tightened. 'God knows the kind of potion he was given.'

Geoffrey snapped his fingers at a groom, and as the grey was led away drew Adam across the bailey in the direction of the hall. 'We found the lad who gave him those apples,' he said, watching Adam through eyes that were half-shut against the downcoming rain and something else.

Adam checked. 'Did you? What did he say?'

'Nothing. They took him dead from the river this morning and by the looks of him he'd been all night in the water. He must have slipped on one of the wharves. It's easily done. We've had three drownings already, this year.' He spoke without inflection.

'I see,' Adam said softly.

'I thought that you would.'

They went into the hall. Smoke from a badly tended hearth

stung his eyes and caught in his throat. He coughed and blinked rapidly. 'Where does it all end?' he demanded of the rafters.

'William le Clito told me all about your quarrel with de Mortimer.' Geoffrey balanced on alternate legs as he removed his spurs.

'How generous of him.' Adam's lip curled.

'Not at all. He was explaining why we shouldn't clap the whoreson in irons and leave him to moulder in a cell. Said the man had a right to be aggrieved by what you had done.'

Adam's expression became intractable. He said nothing.

'Is it true?' Geoffrey asked, persisting where an angel would have feared to tread. Between his thick golden lashes, his eyes were very bright.

'That he was responsible for Ralph le Chevalier's murder? That he was involved with le Clito in plotting against the Empress? Yes, both counts are true.'

'And the other?'

Adam gave Geoffrey a hard, sidelong look that told the youth he was walking a very dangerous edge, then he transferred it to the banners above the dais and said quietly, 'When he discovered myself and Heulwen together, King Henry had already vouchsafed her hand in marriage to me.'

Geoffrey's mouth twitched; with difficulty, Adam suppressed the urge to hit it and see its supercilious curve dissolve into blood.

'But snatched from beneath his nose.' Geoffrey's smile deepened as they mounted the stairs to the private rooms above. 'Was that the reason you did not kill him?'

Adam's anger, caught in mid-stream by surprise, submerged into thoughtfulness. He disliked Geoffrey of Anjou, but then he was not particularly fond of King Henry, and the latter's ability to rule had never been in dispute. Geoffrey, it appeared, read men as easily as he read the vellum-bound copies of the romances which were currently so popular. 'One of them,' he answered, rubbing the back of his neck.

Geoffrey paused on the stairs and glanced over his shoulder 'Is Mathilda really as beautiful as they say?'

Adam struggled to keep pace with the fluctuating levels of Geoffrey's mind: mirror-bright shallows, tepid mid-waters and opaque, cold depths. 'She is handsome,' he heard himself respond. 'Red-brown hair and milk-white skin.' *A mouth to make your loins ache and when she opens it, the venom to shrivel them.*

'And a temper?'

Adam smiled faintly. 'A royal temper, my lord, but then you said yourself that you liked spirit in a woman.'

Geoffrey continued on up the stairs. 'A mare too spirited to permit a man in the saddle is a waste of time . . . is she?'

There was a hint of satisfaction in Adam's tone as he said, 'You called her old enough to be your grandam, but the difference in age is a double-edged blade. She is hardly going to run with enthusiasm into the arms of a boy barely out of tail clouts. Believe me, you will have to catch and saddle her before you can even think of mounting.'

Geoffrey threw him a hard stare that eventually dissolved into a snort of reluctant laughter. 'I thought you were supposed to be a diplomat?'

'I am, my lord. I did not say that the Empress was unrideable. When she is not being haughty and impossible, she makes interesting company, but you will need curb and spur and God's own patience to deal with her.'

'Ummm,' Geoffrey said non-committally, 'and your barons?'

'They will hope that you get a son on her and the sooner the better – those of them that do not will hope that you fall off and get trampled in the act.'

The neutrality became another smothered ripple of amusement. 'So that the child can grow to manhood before Henry dies and your barons change their fickle minds?'

'You have nailed the shoe to the hoof, my lord.'

'The mare's hoof,' Geoffrey compounded with a mischievous twinkle as he swept aside the fine Arras curtain and led the way into his father's rooms. 'You have heard I suppose that le Clito's gone to claim his own destiny?' He took a snuffed candle from the holder on the trestle and kindled it from another wavering in a wall bracket.

'Yes, my lord.'

Geoffrey eyed him thoughtfully now, the mockery flown. 'William le Clito's going to be too busy to look to England for no small time. Flanders is a bubbling stew of trouble, and it's going to take all the housewifely skills he does not possess to simmer it down.' He returned the candle to its holder. 'Mind you, your King is not going to like this promotion one small bit. He has a better claim himself through his mother. She was Count Baldwin's daughter, and le Clito is a generation removed.'

'Flanders depends on English wool,' Adam murmured, 'so therefore Flanders depends on King Henry's goodwill.' He pushed his hair back from his brow. 'I'm glad I'm not William le Clito.'

'We are all pawns.' Geoffrey shrugged and picked up a sealed package from the trestle, turned it over in his hands, deliberating, then gave it to Adam. 'Here, you might as well take it. It is my father's reply to your King.'

Adam lowered his hand from his hair to accept the document. 'Does the Count not wish to give it to me himself?' he asked doubtfully.

Geoffrey gave him a twisted smile. 'It's more appropriate coming from the sacrificial pawn, don't you think?'

Adam frowned.

Geoffrey forced a laugh. 'Don't worry, it's not treason. My father should be here any time now. He's busy with an envoy from the Holy Kingdom of Jerusalem and a couple of papal messengers – arranging another appointment with destiny.' He sprawled gracefully on a chair and considered the slightly scuffed toes of his exquisite gilded boots. 'Have some wine, and tell me more about my delectable future bride.'

CHAPTER 22

'I'LL LEAVE THE fur-trimmed overgown out, shall I m'lady?' Elswith held up the said garment for her mistress's inspection. 'You don't want to catch cold on the road tomorrow, especially now it's raining so hard.'

Heulwen considered the gown of blue Bruges wool, the hanging sleeves edged with marten fur, then glanced towards the sound of the rain on the shutters. The candles had long been lit and outside a wet, blue dusk was settling. 'No Elswith, pack it with the others,' she said. 'Last time I travelled in that it was raining and it got so waterlogged that I nearly drowned. I've never been so uncomfortable in all my life.'

'But my lady, what will you wear instead?'

Heulwen turned to a pile of garments on the bed. 'These,' she said with a smile that quickly became a splutter of laughter as she saw the maid's horror.

'By the Virgin, m'lady, you cannot!' Elswith squeaked.

Heulwen tossed her head. 'Why ever not?'

''Tis ungodly, m'lady, not decent!'

'But a sight more comfortable and practical. Come, unlace me, I want to try them on.'

Close to tears, the maid baulked. Heulwen first cajoled sweetly, then snappingly commanded, and under pain of a whipping, Elswith was finally coerced into helping her mistress, but not without continuing verbal protest.

'What will Lord Adam say?' she moaned as Heulwen discarded her gown and undertunic in favour of a pair of Adam's braies and chausses and one of his tunics. She was tall for a woman, but not as tall as Adam or as broad, but her breasts

265

took up some of the slack and a firmly buckled belt dealt with the rest.

'Lord Adam?' She sat down on the bed and neatly tied the cross-garters, her eyes dancing with mischief. 'I don't know what he will say, Elswith. I think that his eyes might pop out of his head, but then it's useful to keep a surprise or two up your sleeve!' She laughed at her own weak joke and lay back on the bed, her arms folded behind her head, one knee bent sideways.

Elswith made a shocked sound and Heulwen giggled again. 'Do you know,' she observed, 'men have by far the fatter end of the wedge. Could you imagine me lying like this in a skirt ... or like this?'

'My lady!'

Heulwen's giggles became open, helpless gales of laughter. Her face suffused and tears poured down her cheeks, but at last she took pity on her maid's suffering, rolled over, and sat up on the edge of the bed. 'It's true though!' she defended, wiping her eyes. 'Men's clothes are a deal more practical to wear.'

'My lady, tomorrow ...' Elswith's eyes bulged with dread, 'you're not really going to ...' She could not bring herself to say it.

'Yes, I am!' Heulwen said forcefully, and folded her arms. 'I'll be wearing my cloak over everything and a wimple and pilgrim's hat to cover my braids. Don't be such a goose. If you ...' She stopped and stared at the door as it shook to the violent thumping of an agitated fist.

'My lady!' Thierry cried, voice urgent. 'Come quickly, it is Lyard. He's down and threshing in the straw and I fear he's dying!'

Heulwen shot to her feet, all her merriment flown. 'Jesu no!' she exclaimed and grabbed for her cloak. 'All right, Thierry, I'm coming!' She fumbled about, found and donned her shoes and struggled to tie on her pattens.

'My lady, you cannot go out dressed like that!' Elswith held out an imploring hand which Heulwen pushed impatiently

266

aside. Her eyes flashed, anger making their colour vivid.

'God's blood, if I'd known you were going to be so prim and purse-mouthed for a trifle, I'd never have brought you to attend me!' She tossed her braids over her shoulders and stood up, adding coldly as she went to the door, 'I expect you to have finished packing that trunk by the time I return, including that fur-trimmed gown!'

Elswith's chin wobbled; she bit her lip and looked at the floor. Heulwen unbarred the door to the wet, windy night. Water was dripping from the brim of Thierry's hat which was dipped low, concealing his eyes in shadow. The rushlight made dark spangles of the raindrops on his cloak and caught the quick glint of his teeth as he spoke.

'Quickly mistress, I beg you!' He took hold of her arm and drawing her out of the room, began to help her down the stairs. He did not appear to have noticed her strange attire but she felt him trembling and his face, caught for an instant in the full light before Elswith barred the door, was a tight-fleshed battle-mask. Her anxiety increased as she prepared herself for a gruesome sight. Having come to know Thierry in their weeks of travel, she had found his nature to be quick and fox-sly, with a propensity for women and dice and a devil-may-care attitude to life that left very little room for trembling distress over the death of a horse.

'What has happened to him? When did it start?' She shook her arm free as they reached the foot of the stairs. Her wooden pattens squelched and stuck in the mud and an unswept mulch of horse droppings, loudly sucking free as she moved.

'About half a candle-notch since, mistress. His legs just suddenly buckled and down he went ... I do think he ought to be put out of his pain, but I need yours or Lord Adam's yeasay.'

Heulwen looked up at the opaque dark sky in supplication and received a face full of rain.

'Perhaps I should send to the keep?' Thierry said doubtfully and took her arm again.

'I'm all right,' she reassured him. 'I'm not about to faint or take a fit of the vapours.' But his grip tightened pincer-like and his teeth flashed again, white and decidedly vulpine before he hooked one leg neatly behind hers and brought her down bruisingly hard on a pile of wet straw sweepings outside the stable door.

Heulwen screeched and struggled, but Thierry, fifteen years the trained mercenary, adept at brawling and totally undisturbed by any feelings of moral nicety concerning her womanhood, efficiently set about immobilizing her thrashing limbs and trussing them as though she were a shot deer he was preparing to carry home from the forest. She did, however, succeed in biting him, clamping her teeth into the fleshy part of his hand between the base of his little finger and wrist. His skin punctured and she tasted his blood. He gave a smothered exclamation of pain and pressed the arch of his free hand across her windpipe, until choking, she was forced to let go.

He wadded a piece of rag brought for the purpose into her mouth and bound it tightly with a length of cross-garter, then sat back on his haunches to study her and regain his breath. Blood was still trickling down his hand. He staunched the wound on a fold of his cloak. 'Vixen,' he panted, but without too much rancour, and his smile flashed briefly when he took his eyes from her face to admire the rest of his handiwork and realized that the reason she had given him such a hard time was that she was wearing men's garments instead of two layers of heavy, encumbering skirts.

'I always did wonder which of you wore the chausses!' he chuckled maliciously. 'Now I know.'

Heulwen writhed, frantic with anger and the stirrings of a fear that existed on a far more conscious level than that of pure instinct. She was trussed like a fly caught in a web, but somehow she did not believe that Thierry was the spider. His appetite was not of that kind.

He stooped over her now, grinning cheerfully at her ineffectual struggles, and laying one hand on the belt at her waist, hauled her up and over his shoulder in true huntsman's style, setting off with her across the path and down through the dark, rain-sodden orchard.

His gait was slightly uneven, for Heulwen, despite being slim, was no light weight. Hanging upside down, her breath foreshortened by his shoulder butting into her mid-section, by her bruised throat and the clogging wad of fabric in her mouth, she felt consciousness recede to a dark, striving undulation. Her wet braids slapped across her cheek. Momentarily her eyes flickered upon tree trunks darker than the sky, and a crack of rushlight from a loosely fitting upstairs shutter in the house they were leaving behind.

Unbalanced by her weight, Thierry staggered and bumped against one of the trees. A deluge of fat, cold droplets struck the exposed nape of Heulwen's neck, arousing her with a jerk from the edge of oblivion. Thierry cursed good-naturedly. She wondered hazily what he was receiving to make all this worthwhile. Adam paid all his immediate retinue twelve pence daily, thirteen when they were on active duty such as now. Good wages, but a man like Thierry had his eyes set upon a sudden sunburst of gold rather than a steady trickle of daily silver – probably the reason he gambled. In many ways he was like Ralph.

He lurched again, almost missing his footing on a moss-covered step, and then they were down at the river's edge. Heulwen heard the water lapping on stone and saw a wheeling, glittering darkness of solid water and rain-slashed sky as he swung her down off his shoulder and dumped her on the slick stone slabs of the merchant's small private wharf.

'Don't do anything stupid,' he warned. 'If you roll, you'll go into the river and I'm not going swimming in the murk to fish you out.' He stepped over her, executing a neat leap as she tried to trip him up. 'Tut tut,' he said, wagging his forefinger and shaking his head, 'you ought to know better than that, *ma poupelet.*'

She glared at him and uselessly fought her gag, jerking her body as he picked her up again and with an effort heaved her into the merchant's flat-bottomed fishing boat, where she lay at his feet wriggling like a new-caught salmon. The small craft see-sawed precariously as Thierry cast off the mooring rope and sat down on the bench. Water puddled the planks on which Heulwen lay and the wood bore the ingrained stink of fish and stale river-weed.

'It's hardly a royal barge, my lady,' Thierry mocked as he positioned the oars and began sculling out into the current, 'but I can promise you a royal welcome when we get to where we are going.' And then he laughed, a high-spirited, nervous sound like the whinney of a horse.

The journey downriver was a nightmare. The boat was leaky and every now and then Thierry had to cease rowing and bale out the water with a large leather tankard. The wind-chopped river kept slopping over the sides, drenching her, for while Thierry was quite capable of rowing, he was by no means an expert.

Frozen to the marrow by shock and exposure, Heulwen shivered violently at Thierry's feet while her fear crystallized and took human shape. Warrin had obviously not left Angers this morning with le Clito and his retinue. It had been a ruse. Somehow and somewhere he was still here and she was being taken to him. This thought paralysed her mind as surely as Thierry's efficient binding had paralysed her limbs: bound and at Warrin's mercy, and no one aware of her predicament. Water slapped over the boat's bows again and Thierry had to ship oars and bale. Heulwen closed her eyes and prayed to drown. Her brother Miles had drowned. They said that it was an easy death, but perhaps that was just to comfort the living.

Thierry started rowing again. After a little while, he started to sing softly — a soldier's ditty that Heulwen knew although she was not supposed to. She had been ten years old when caught singing *The Coney Catcher's Ferret* for a dare during the mass. Her stepmother had marched her to the laundry by the scruff and there scrubbed out her mouth with disgusting tallow soap, the near apoplectic priest as a witness and Adam and

Miles, who had put her up to it, hovering in the background, terrified that she might tell. Public penance done, she was taken in disgrace to the bower where Judith had given her a dish of sugared comfits to take away the taste of the soap, and then, lips twitching, had asked her if she knew all the words because she had never been able to discover the entire version herself!

The memory scalded her eyes. Tears oozed from between her lids, grew cold and seeped sideways into her soaked braids. She wondered how her resourceful stepmother would deal with this situation. Her shoulders shook. She thought of Adam and her throat wrenched, making the ache there unbearable.

'Feeling sorry for yourself?' Thierry broke off singing to ask. 'Aye, well I hazard you've got cause. It's a pity for you I don't have a conscience. Rather see gold than a woman's gratitude any day.' He winked at her, tilted the brim of his hat against the sweep of the rain, and continued to row in time to the words of his song:

> *'I kissed her once, I kissed her twice*
> *I kissed her full times three*
> *I let her feel my ferret bold*
> *As she sat on my knee*

> *And when I popped him in her ho ...'*

The boat bumped and grated against a larger bulk, and he stopped singing to guide the fishing boat alongside the complacent fat-bellied side of a small Angers cog that was anchored at one of the main wharves close on one of the wine warehouses.

'Hola!' A pale moon-face appeared at the side and stared down at them. 'What's your business?'

'Promised cargo for Lord Warrin de Mortimer!' Thierry called back. 'Delivered on payment of agreed sum, of course.' And removing his hat, he performed a brief, sarcastic flourish.

The face withdrew. There was a short pause, the sound of

voices, a thumping, dragging noise, and then the face was back and a rope ladder was tossed over the side.

'I'll wait here for my money,' Thierry announced, narrow-eyed and watchful. 'It's a mortal long way to fall, especially with a cut throat.'

There was a pause. Thierry folded his arms and sat down. The face disappeared again. More muttering, a raised impatient voice, and then two faces materialized and stared.

'Christ on the cross!' Thierry's good-nature began to show a little ragged at the edges. 'Is this going to take all night? Perhaps I'll just row away and barter my goods somewhere else, eh?'

'All right, I'm coming down,' the second man said, and lifted himself over the ship's side to take purchase of the swaying ropeladder. He paused on the final rung, judged carefully and stepped into the small boat, but he still caused it to wobble violently from side to side. Thierry fought to balance it and prevent it from capsizing.

'Careful, my lord,' he said on a rising note, 'you'll have us all in the water and I've no mind for a swim.'

'When I want your opinion, I'll let you know,' growled Warrin de Mortimer and transferred his interest to the bottom of the boat and its bedraggled occupant. Heulwen turned her head aside and tightened her closed lids. 'Why is she wearing men's clothing?' he demanded suspiciously.

Thierry shrugged. 'How should I know? It hasn't been the kind of journey for pleasant chit-chat. Ask her yourself. Perhaps her and my lord her husband like to play games.'

Warrin's eyes snapped up again, his anger burning bright and dangerously. 'Don't go too far,' he snarled.

'Pay me what we agreed and I'll leave you in peace,' Thierry suggested reasonably, and held out his hand.

Warrin fished beneath his cloak and brought out a leather pursing, ridged and bulging and promisingly musical. His lip curling with scorn, he handed it over, fastidiously ensuring that their fingers did not touch.

Thierry noticed this with a scornful amusement of his own. 'Mind if I count it?' he grinned, not caring if de Mortimer did or not, and tugging on the drawstring poured the coins out into his palm. 'Jesu, but for a man exiled you're mortally rich,' he observed. 'Or you were ... I congratulate you, it's all here.' Thierry trickled the coins back into the purse, the smile on his mouth pure acid, for he was fully aware that were it not for the precariousness of this tiny fishing boat, de Mortimer would long since have leaped on him with dagger drawn.

Warrin swallowed hard on his anger and bent carefully to lift Heulwen from the bottom of the boat. The craft tipped and reeled. Heulwen kept her eyes closed but could not feign unconsciousness, for when he laid hold of her his fingers bruised and her body contracted from the pain.

Thierry reseated himself and started bailing the boat out again as Warrin manoeuvred himself and his burden carefully onto the ropeladder. 'What about her husband?' he asked curiously as he worked. 'He is bound to scour the whole city for her.'

'He won't find her,' Warrin said, pausing on the ladder to gain his breath. 'Not until I'm ready, and by then he'll be glad to die.'

'I shouldn't be too sure of that,' Thierry said. 'A word of advice: don't think you've won until you're standing over his body.'

Warrin's knuckles whitened on the ladder-rung. He pressed his forehead against it. 'Get you gone,' he said through his teeth, 'now, while you still have the chance.'

'There speaks a man of decision,' Thierry grinned, not in the least set down, and performing a mocking salute at Warrin's turned back, took up the oars.

On the wharfside a drunk staggered, singing on his way, and a woman called to him. Warrin puffed a hard breath through his cheeks and completed the journey up the ladder, and stepping over the vessel's side took his burden to an aftward's awning — a somewhat flimsy affair of oiled canvas and wooden struts, where he threw her down on a leaky straw mattress at the far side.

For a moment he stood panting, his heartbeat thundering in his ears, almost blinding him. Heulwen lay inanimately where she had fallen, face pressed in the straw, waiting and wanting to die.

'You can stop pretending,' Warrin said between breaths. 'I know that you are aware.'

The canvas billowed in the wind. She heard the scrape of his feet on the planking as he moved and with difficulty turned to stare at him. He stared back, and chest still heaving, slowly drew the dagger from the tooled sheath at his belt.

'Wondering what I'm going to do with this?' he mused, flipping it end over end like a juggler. 'Well, soothly, so am I.' And then his cheeks creased into the mockery of a grin as he squatted down beside her.

Heulwen flinched, her eyes showing a rim of white all around the variegated iris.

'There's no cause to be afraid,' Warrin mocked softly. 'If you're a good girl, I am sure we can come to a bloodless agreement.' And setting to work, he cut the cords that bound her ankles.

Heulwen stared at his rain-darkened pale hair which was just beginning to thin at the crown, and wondered with a horrible queasy feeling if this was an appetizer to whet his hunger for rape. However, after he had freed her legs, he cut the ropes at her wrists and then released her mouth from the foul gag. She watched the rings sparkle on his fingers as he worked and found herself fixing on them with unnatural concentration, for she did not dare to look at his face and see what was written there.

He frowned at her as she lay as still as a young deer in the underbrush, unsure of what to do with his prize now that it was wholly in his possession. Her chin was trembling, not with distress, but with cold, and her flesh was a pinched, bluish-white.

He thought of her in de Lacey's arms last Christmastide –

her hair a lustrous copper swirl, skin flushed with the glow of aftermath and eyes a brilliant, drowning blue-green – and he contrasted the memory with the shivering, half-dead draggle lying at his mercy now.

'Sit up!' he commanded harshly, disturbed by the ambivalence of his own thoughts.

When she did not move, he seized her by the wrists and dragged her up. Heulwen screamed in agony, for his fingers dug savagely into the weals left by Thierry's expert binding.

'I said sit up!' he snarled, covering his uncertainty with anger just as he had always done.

Her hair, heavy with water, had begun to untwist from its braids, and hung about her face in thick, wet strands. She bent her head, breathing in shuddering gasps and keeled sideways towards welcome unconsciousness. He slapped her across the face. Her head snapped back at the blow and her eyes opened, but they were glazed, barely focusing, and in the next moment she flopped limply forward against him.

Warrin swore and shook her to see if she was feigning, but she jerked back and forth in his grip like a child's rag mammet.

'Bitch,' he said between his teeth, but with more irritation than malevolence, and laying her back down on the straw he studied her, darkly scowling. He had sufficient experience of cold season battle campaigns to know the signs and what would happen if he just left her, and he did not want her dead ... at least not yet.

Methodically, quickly, he stripped away her soaked garments and then, starting with her dripping hair, began to rub her vigorously with the coarse woollen blanket from the pallet. Her flesh was goose-pimpled and ice-cold to the touch, but under the rapid friction it began to warm and turn a scrubbed red.

Her breasts were full and firm, tipped by taut pink nipples and they undulated against the linen as he worked. Lower down at the juncture of her thighs, a red-gold triangle drew his eyes and for a moment his imagination ran throbbing riot as he thought of it tangling in a lover's knot with his own flaxen bush. He quelled himself sharply. De Lacey's father had been the one to pleasure himself in futtering corpses; such a desire had never been the core of his own need.

Heulwen moaned and stirred; her eyelids fluttered and her limbs moved jerkily. He dragged the pallet into the middle of the room, close to the brazier, and wrapped her in his own fur-lined cloak before fetching from his belongings a flask of aqua vitae and a small, braided glass cup.

One of his men-at-arms poked his head through the opening and he harshly snarled at him to get out. When he tried to pour the aqua vitae from flask to cup he discovered that his hands were shaking. He set the cup down abruptly and turned round to Heulwen. Her eyes were open now, heavy-lidded, watching him with awareness and apprehension.

'Is this in the cause of revenge?' she asked weakly.

'Revenge?' He knelt down beside her and drew her towards him to tip the contents of the cup down her throat. He felt her tense and try to resist him, applied pressure to the back of her neck and felt a small flicker of triumph as she was forced to yield and choking, swallow it. 'It's more than revenge, sweetheart,' he said with sombre joy, 'much more.'

'What, then?'

He refilled the cup, his hand steady now. 'Drink,' he commanded.

'I can't ... I don't want to.'

'Shall I force it down your gullet?' he threatened softly.

Heulwen looked at him, saw that there was no way out except to comply and shuddering, gulped the stuff down in two fast swallows. It hit her stomach and exploded into her blood. She gasped for breath. Tears stung her eyes.

He adjusted his cloak around her shoulders and drifted his hand casually down the midline of her body within the folds as he arranged it. His palm brushed the crest of her nipple, paused, travelled lower. Heulwen writhed away with another choking gasp. A peculiar wry smile twisted his lips. 'You might be a whore, but you're still a beautiful one,' he said huskily, his mouth descending to within an inch of hers.

'Why did you murder Ralph?' she asked into the slight wine scent of his breath.

His head reared back at that. 'I didn't,' he said.

'As near as makes no difference.'

Warrin made a small, defensive gesture. 'He was playing a double game: selling information to us and then selling us back to Henry. I put a stop to it before he went too far. I had to.'

'And you are not playing a double game?'

Warrin shook his head vehemently. 'It is my father who owes his allegiance to King Henry and then to the Empress. I have given my oath to neither of them, so how can I be forsworn? William le Clito has more right to England and Normandy than that sulky bitch will ever have. He is the eldest son of the eldest son.'

'I see,' she said in a small, distant voice.

'No you don't, you never have!' Goaded by her tone, he pushed her down on the straw with her arms braced either side of her head. 'You promised yourself to me, played the whore behind my back, and now you dare to talk of double games!'

'You murdered Ralph and your honour to get me!' she retorted. 'I counted that promise null and void.'

The distance receded. He saw her eyes begin to flash with anger, felt the resistance of her body and his own flamed hard in response. 'Come on Heulwen,' he muttered, his voice and loins congesting, 'kiss me ... Kiss me like you kiss de Lacey.' His mouth descended, hot and avid.

All her senses rebelled, but were whipped into line by the common one, aided by an instinct for survival. If she fought him, he would beat her. She could see the wildness in his eyes, as if he were more than half-hoping for her to do just that, and beaten or maimed, there was far less chance of escape than if she offered no resistance. And so she parted her lips to the violent demand of his and responded with all the superficial expertise taught to her by Ralph, using it as a shield.

What followed was unpleasant and painful, but not beyond the limit of her endurance. She understood a part of what drove him and was therefore prepared to permit him his petty victory. Without love or even a seasoning of lust, the act for her was meaningless. She closed her eyes and ignored the exultant sound he made as he thrust into her – a dunghill cock treading a rival's hen to mark his ownership.

She wondered if it would have been like this had she married him. Probably. Instead she had married Adam. The thought of her husband darted across her mind like a flare of lightning and made her gasp aloud in anguish. Warrin, conceited, took a different meaning from the sound entirely. He panted something obscene in her ear, his hips grinding powerfully back and forth. Heulwen bit her lip and stifled a cry behind her tongue. It could not last forever she told herself, not at this level of fury.

His mouth crushed down on hers, his fingers twisting in her damp hair, gripping convulsively as his whole body stiffened and shuddered in the throes of climax. She stared over his shoulder at the brazier's glow, the heat blurring her eyes as he collapsed on top of her.

After a while, when his breathing had eased and his senses risen above the purely basic level, he withdrew himself and lay down beside her, drawing the fur-lined cloak up and around them both. One hand reached out to idly fondle her breast. Heulwen folded her lips in upon each other and pressed them hard together, clutching at the dry straw lining the floor so that she would not strike him away.

'I've been waiting a long time for this,' he said lazily, and with obvious self-satisfaction. 'Don't tell me that it wasn't good for you too.'

'Where would be the point?' Heulwen said in a tired voice. 'I doubt you'd listen.'

'And still she bares her teeth,' he smiled, his fingers still caressing. 'Tell me then vixen, how much do you hate me?'

She drew a sharp breath to spit at him that words could not

describe the depth of her revulsion, but looking into his face she caught the fleeting glimpse of another expression behind the gloating mockery – a child peeping out from behind a wall to survey the ruins of an unthinking prank that had gone monstrously wrong.

'I don't hate you, Warrin,' she said instead, wearily. 'God help us both, I pity you.'

The fleeting glimpse vanished, masked and then obliterated by a swift narrowing of his brilliant blue eyes. He hit her open-handed across the face – not enough to really hurt, but sufficient to give due warning of what was to come if she dared too far. 'Careful,' he said gently. 'De Lacey might be soft enough to let you insult him, but don't expect it of me.'

Heulwen met his gaze then quickly looked away before he should see her loathing. Warrin smiled and stretched with languorous satisfaction. 'Do you want some wine?'

She tossed her head and willed herself to smile. 'Why not?'

He sauntered over to the flagon and splashed wine into the cup. 'There's only one,' he said, raising it to her. 'Never mind, we can share it like a pair of lovers.'

She sat up, the cloak tucked around her breasts, and reached out sidelong for Warrin's discarded shirt and tunic.

He looked at her sharply. 'What are you doing?'

'I'm cold,' she protested, 'and these are warm and dry.' She flashed him a look full of wide innocence. 'Surely you don't believe I'd be so foolish as to try and run?'

He grunted. 'I don't know. That Welsh blood of yours is too fickle to be trusted.' He took a gulp of the wine and returned, but despite his words he did not prevent her from pulling on the garments, amused by the novelty. When she reached for his chausses, however, he rubbed his index finger gently along her naked inner thigh. 'What are you doing here in Angers?' he murmured.

So this was it. If her submission to him had been the heart of the matter, then this was the cold blade of reason. Her lashes swept down. 'Adam wanted me with him,' she said in a subdued voice.

Warrin had not missed the slight hesitation. He splayed his hand on the soft, tender skin and dug in his fingers. 'Not just half the truth Heulwen, all of it,' he said, 'and do not plead innocence because I won't believe you.'

She swallowed. 'Adam had messages from King Henry to Count Fulke. I do not know what was written, I swear it.' Which was the literal, if not the perfect truth.

'Try harder.' Warrin's mouth tightened into a thin, cruel line. 'As you value your life Heulwen, try harder.'

'What more do you want me to say? How can I tell you what I do not know?' She made her voice sound tearfully puzzled. It was not difficult.

Warrin stared into her eyes. They were like her father's in all but their colour and she had that same ability to widen them into spacious innocence, shielding her true thoughts.

'You're lying.' he said savagely and his hand left her thigh and snaked to her throat.

'I'm not, I'm not!' she choked, flailing against him, panicking as his grip tightened on her windpipe.

'My lord!' cried one of his men-at-arms, poking his head through the canvas flap. 'There are soldiers searching the wharves upriver and their lights are coming down towards us.'

Warrin swore and shoved Heulwen down on the straw. 'How far away?' he demanded, and wrapping his cloak around his nakedness, went quickly outside to see for himself.

Heulwen dragged air down her abused throat into her starving lungs. It still felt as though his fingers were squeezing the life from her. When she was able to move, she rolled over and scrambled to her feet. The flask of aqua vitae lay on its side nearby. She picked it up, pulled out the stopper with clumsy, shaking fingers and choked down a mouthful, her eyes on the tent flap. Outside she could hear Warrin talking to his men, his voice quick and agitated.

He ducked back into the shelter and she took an involuntary

280

backstep, the neck of the flask gripped tight in her hand.

'I'll give that whoreson husband of yours his due, he's fast,' Warrin growled with more than a hint of irritation, 'but not fast enough. By the time he arrives, there'll be nothing to find except his own death. Do you want to watch?' His arm reached out. 'Come here.'

She shook her head and moved sideways. He came after her, moving with the heavy graceful purpose of a hunting lion. 'There is nowhere to go,' he said. 'Do not make me lose my temper.'

Heulwen circled around the brazier. He followed and made a sudden lunge. She swooped from his reach so that his finger-tips just grazed the ends of her hair, and she flung the contents of the flask into the brazier.

A blinding, white pyramid of flame whooshed upwards and Warrin reeled back, his eyebrows singeing, forearms crossed to shield his face. Heulwen kicked over the brazier and ran for her life. Warrin roared a warning to the men without and sprang after her.

The flames licked experimentally at the straw, nibbling deli-cately at first, beginning to chew and then greedily devour.

A soldier made a grab for Heulwen and caught her right wrist. She used her left one to snatch his dagger from its sheath and slash at him. He howled and let her go, the arch of his hand gashed to the bone. Breath sobbing in her lungs, she dashed for the side of the vessel.

Warrin seized her as she reached the ladder and spun her round, his hand reaching for the dagger, his eyes on its deadly flash. He did not see the sudden, violent jerk of her knee until it was too late, and doubled up retching as she caught him straight in the soft base of his testicles. She wrenched herself free, scrambled and jumped.

The black, cold water closed over her head and rushed into the fibres of her makeshift garments, weighting her down. She lost the dagger. Blind and deaf, encapsulated, she kicked for the surface and broke it gasping, trod water, sank a little, and choked on a gulped mouthful of the river. Through water-blurred eyes she saw the outline of the wharf and struck clumsily out towards it. Her clothes hampered her. The water was cold and leached her strength, as did sheer terror as she heard a splash behind her and realized that Warrin was coming after her.

He was a strong swimmer, she knew it only too well. Ravenstow overlooked the Dee, a large, commercial and dangerous river and her father had insisted that his children and his squires learn the art. In childhood, she had been taught beside Adam and her brothers in the backwater shallows ... and so had Warrin.

She floundered frantically towards the wharf which never seemed to come any closer, although it could only have been a matter of a few short yards. She swallowed water again. The back of her throat stung as the river washed into her nose. Her fingertips grazed weedy stone and her knees jarred into it. She was beyond feeling pain, knew only relief as she started to drag herself onto the rain-washed dockside.

A hand fumbled at her ankle. She screamed and kicked hard. The hand lost its grip and with the strength of panic she pushed her body to its limit. Stars flowered before her eyes, maiming her vision, but she reached the entirety of solid ground, got her feet beneath her, and began to run towards the distant, bobbing torchlight. Her legs felt as though they were made of wet rope. Her head was ringing like a deserted hall, high-vaulted, cold and dark.

Warrin came after her. He was frighteningly fast and he still had breath to spare for curses as he ran to catch her. She heard his footsteps right behind, and then he was level with her. She twisted away, but he twisted too, caught her arm and spun her off her feet, a knife flashing in his other hand.

Heulwen saw the blade descending and screamed out all the breath that remained in her body before the world darkened beyond darkness.

CHAPTER 23

URSING THE RAIN and hoping that it would have emptied its worst and moved on by dawn, Adam squelched into the house and hung his dripping cloak on a clothing pole near the fire. The men-at-arms were organizing to bed down for the night, but the rush dips were still kindled against his return and a trestle stood close to the hearth upon which a platter of cold meat and fruit and a pitcher of wine were laid out.

Adam glanced and then ignored the repast. The fare at Fulke's table had been rich and spicy and the wine potent. Although not drunk, he was not entirely sober and had no wish to begin the morrow's journey with a blinding headache and churning gut.

He left Sweyn and Austin peeling off their sodden garments and went back out into the downpour and up the outer stairs to the floor above. Elswith opened the door to his knock. 'My lady, thank the Virg ... Oh it's you, Lord Adam!' The maid wrung her hands together and looked at him with a mingling of relief and consternation.

Adam removed his sling, and picking up a towel from beside the small laver began to rub his hair dry. 'Where's your mistress?' He looked round the room. The travelling chests were packed, all save one small one of oxhide for their personal effects, and the room was tidy, almost as bare as a monk's cell.

'Lady Heulwen went down to the stables more than a candle notch since with Sir Thierry. He begged her to come quickly, said that Lyard was dying!'

Adam's hands stopped. 'What?'

Elswith burst into tears. 'Oh, my lord, she was cross with me, ordered me to stay here and finish packing ... I said it wasn't decent, but she wouldn't heed me. I didn't mean to be insolent, truly I didn't!'

Adam stared at the maid, thoroughly bewildered. 'What wasn't decent? What are you babbling about?' He threw the towel down.

'My lady was japing. She tried on some of your clothes and said that she was going to travel in them tomorrow – I begged her not to – and then Sir Thierry came and she went with him without even bothering to change.' She buried her face in her palms and shook her head from side to side.

'To the stables?'

Elswith peered at him through her fingers and gave a loud, mucus-laden sniff. 'Yes, my lord, but it has been a long time now ... I was wondering whether to go down, but I did not want her shouting at me again.'

Adam began to feel cold, and it was nothing to do with his wet clothing. 'Elswith, stop snivelling and go and tell Sweyn and Aubrey not to unarm,' he said with quiet intensity, and went back out into the rain.

Lyard raised his head from the manger, and munching noisily, stared at Adam with alert liquid eyes. His cream tail swished softly against his hocks and he pricked his ears. In the next stall, the new black mare was dozing slack-hipped, and beside her Heulwen's dappled mare was asleep. Except for contented, normal horsey sounds there was silence. Adam stared round, his eyes feeling too large for their sockets, ears strained to the limit of his hearing. Nothing. The cold sensation in the pit of his belly crystallized into a solid lump of fear.

He turned to the groom who had emerged from a empty stall in the stable's far reaches, knuckling his eyes and yawning. A woman's voice complained, calling him back, and he gave Adam a sheepish grin. 'Thought I'd get an early night ready for tomorrow, my lord,' he said to Adam's set features.

'Have Lady Heulwen or Sir Thierry been here tonight?' he demanded curtly.

'No, my lord.' The man scratched his head, examined his forefinger, then cracked the louse on it between his nails. 'Not since your mare was settled in. Is there some trouble?'

Adam ignored the query. 'Has Lyard been all right?'

'Yes m'lord.' The groom gave him a gappy grin. 'Dancing on all fours he were when we brung the mare in. I reckon as she'll come into season 'afore long.'

'Saddle him up.'

'Now, my lord?' The man's eyes opened wide and not without a little dismay.

'No, in three years' time!' Adam snarled. 'Of course I mean now you idiot! And you can do the same for Sweyn's and Sir Aubrey's. And be quick about it. You don't get paid for doing nothing!'

The man's face became as blank as a dunce's slate. He louted and scuttled off to find harness. Adam returned to the hall.

Thierry's cousin Alun was all numb astonishment. 'Thierry? Take Lady Heulwen?' He shook his head emphatically. 'I know he has some mad fits and starts, but he would not do such a thing, I know he wouldn't!'

'And you have no idea of his whereabouts?' Adam said. Outwardly his control was excellent, but standing beside him, Sweyn was aware of the vein pulsing rapidly in his throat and the hand that held onto the door jamb was not casual, but bone-white with directed pressure.

'My lord, if I did, I swear I would tell you, if only to prove his innocence.' He shifted his feet and cleared his throat nervously. 'Perhaps Lady Heulwen had an errand and he went to escort her?'

'Then why did he need to use the pretence of a sick horse to lure her from the room?' Adam retorted.

'Perhaps it was just an excuse for the maid to hear.'

Adam's hand flashed down to his sword hilt, then stopped. Carefully, breathing hard, he transferred his grip to his belt and squeezed the leather as though it were a man's throat.

Alun, features ashen, eyes bright and ferret-black said: 'Thierry has a girl at the keep, a kitchen wench called Sylvie. Probably he's with her, she's given him a very warm welcome. I know there has been a mistake.'

'So do I,' Adam said grimly. 'Sweyn, Austin, come with me. Aubrey, take the men and search the street.'

'Yes, my lord.'

Adam collected a brand and set off for the back of the dwelling.

'It's Warrin de Mortimer isn't it?' grated Sweyn, pacing beside him.

Adam did not answer, but Sweyn received his reply in the rapid increase of Adam's stride as though he were propelling himself away from the very thought. Passing the stables, Adam slowed his pace to wait on his bodyguard and said, 'You've had more command of Thierry than I. What do you think of him? Alun's biased.'

Sweyn grunted and gave Adam a sideways look. 'You've seen him fight, my lord.'

'He's damned fast in a tight corner,' Austin contributed.

'Usually of his own making,' Sweyn growled. 'Got no moral backbone. He wenches, he drinks and he gambles. Christ's balls, how he gambles! And then he gets into a fight.' The old warrior cleared his throat and spat. 'Alun's the steadier one, covers up for him when he can. If you recall, when you took them on it was Alun who did most of the talking.'

'Is he covering up for him?' The question was half-rhetorical. They reached the edge of the garden. The rain pattered and dripped. Beyond the orchard, unseen but heard, the river lapped at the wharving.

'No, I'd say not,' Sweyn said to his master's silence, 'but probably he will try to find him and warn him what's afoot.'

'Send one of the men to follow his movements and make sure Alun's given the chance to break away. Austin, take the message back to Aubrey.'

Hunching into the collar of his cloak, the youth saluted and left. Adam paused and leaned against one of the trees and said quietly to the older man, 'Sweyn, if I stopped to think what might be happening to her, you'd be dealing with a madman. Forgive me if I seem cold. It is the only way.'

Sweyn hesitated and then set his huge hand on Adam's soaking shoulder and gripped it. 'We'd all go mad if we stopped to think, lad,' he said gruffly.

Adam acknowledged Sweyn's attempt at comfort with a stiff nod, and holding the torch aloft, started off again. His right foot came down on something small and hard that made him catch his breath and swear. He thought it was a broken twig, but the torchlight reflected off a shiny surface instead of the matt darkness of bark. Sweyn stooped and picked up a small metal object and gave it silently to Adam.

It was an engraved silver braid fillet, one of a pair that Heulwen had bought that morning in the market, and Adam recognized it immediately since he had made the final choice for her. 'It is Heulwen's,' he said hoarsely to Sweyn. 'She would not have come down here in this rain unless she had solid reason – or was forced.'

'The river . . . ' Sweyn began, but Adam had already moved off in that direction at a brisk pace.

The merchant's wharf was deserted. Adam rested his hand on the weed-slippery mooring post and stared out across the dark water at dark nothing. The torch hissed and sputtered and the wind wavered streamers of heat back into his face. 'The boat isn't here,' he said over his shoulder to Sweyn. 'There was one moored here when we took these lodgings, and it's gone. It would be the safest means of abduction; no guards to pass.'

'What now? He could have taken her anywhere.'

'We alert the Count and turn Angers inside out,' Adam said, tight-lipped.

'Where do you want me to start?'

The smell of the river was very strong. Adam's nostrils clenched. 'Try the wharves and warehouses along the water-

287

front; start on this bank and work your way across to the other – I'll join you as soon as I've seen the Count – try the drinking dens too. It may be that we can run Thierry to ground. He can't get out of the city until the gates open.'

'What about by boat?'

'The chain is down across the river until dawn.'

'My lord ...'

Adam turned. Sweyn closed his mouth. 'Nothing,' he muttered into his beard and trudged back towards the house. Adam stared down at the small silver fillet in his hand, then closed his knuckles over it and clenched them so hard that he distorted the shape of the ornament. Then he set off after Sweyn.

Thierry took a cheek-bulging mouthful of wine, swilled it round his mouth, swallowed and sighed with enjoyment. Then he picked up the waiting dice, blew on them and threw. They landed in his favour. Grinning from ear to ear, he scooped up his winnings amid the groans of his fellow gamblers.

He had been here longer than he should, he knew that, but outside it was still pouring down, and he was winning hand over fist. He promised himself that as soon as he started to lose he would leave. A girl who was filling up jugs of wine kept smiling at him. She had sparkling eyes and dimples. He winked at her and wondered if he could spend the rest of the night comfortably bedded down in the hay store with her breasts for a pillow. It was just as he was about to call her over and explore the possibility that his cousin strode into the room wearing an expression as black as the weather.

'Alun!' Thierry croaked instead, and strove to his feet, staggered, and planted his legs wide apart to hold his balance. 'What the devil are you doing here?'

'Fuck the devil!' Alun spat, grabbing a handful of his cousin's tunic and dragging him face to face. 'What kind of stew have you been stirring your fingers in? Where's Lady Heulwen?'

'I don't know what you're talking about!' Thierry tried to push him off, but without success. 'Let go of me. You're mad!'

'Maa, am I? What's this then?' Alun had felt the bulge beneath Thierry's tunic and snatched out the bag of silver from its nestling place against Thierry's breast. 'Winnings from dice?' He flung the silver down on the table. Men turned and looked. 'Christ Jesu, you're in dead trouble, soon be just dead ... Come on!' He dragged at his cousin's arm.

Thierry belched. 'Stop panicking,' he said, slightly belligerent with drink. 'I was as cosy as a clam in a shell here until you came bursting in.'

'Idiot, if you don't ...' Alun stopped. 'Christ's balls,' he muttered under his breath, and stared at Aubrey who was blocking the doorway.

'You tripe-witted dolt, you've led them straight to me, haven't you!' Thierry howled, and went for his sword. Aubrey moved equally fast, but was tripped by Alun.

'Run, Thierry!' he cried.

Aubrey found his feet. 'Keep out of this!' he snarled, and plunged out of the drinking den in pursuit of his quarry.

Water spurted from beneath his boots as he ran. He tripped over a startled cat, almost falling again. The cat yowled. He cursed, narrowed his eyes, and licked water from his scrubby moustache, and after a listening pause, ran down the narrow black throat of an alleyway running parallel to the waterfront. Before him, faintly, he could hear lurching footsteps. Thierry's, he hoped, and his stomach knotted at the thought that he might only be pursuing a worthless ragged drunk.

The footsteps ceased. Aubrey stopped, pulse thundering, heart threatening to burst as he drew his breath shallowly, the better not to be heard. Further up the alley a shutter was flung open and someone peered out amidst a dim splash of candle light. He saw a rope of dark hair hanging down.

'Who's there?'

Silence. Aubrey flattened himself against the wall and side-stepped softly along it, gently drawing his dagger.

'Come away,' commanded a querulous, sleepy voice from the depths of the room, 'it's only cats.'

The shutter banged shut. Aubrey shot out of the shadows, grabbed the man hiding in the darkness of the recessed doorway, and laid the blade at his throat. 'Where is Lady Heulwen?' he hissed.

Thierry's larynx moved convulsively against the knife. A shudder ran through his body and his weight started to sag against Aubrey. 'The *Alisande*,' he croaked.

'Louder, whoreson, I can't hear you.'

Thierry laughed. The sound became a bubbling choke and Aubrey realized that it was not rain on his hands but the heat of blood, and that the man he held was badly, if not mortally wounded.

'Waiting for me outside,' Thierry gargled, 'tried to run ... Too much drink. Can't always throw to win ... She's on the *Alisande* ...' The last word was an indistinguishable choke that faded to nothing.

'Listen, you poxy Angev ...' Thierry's head lolled, and Aubrey realized that he was holding a literal dead weight. A terse, soft oath issued from his lips. His scalp prickled. He was in a pitch-dark alleyway with a freshly stabbed man and most probably his murderer. He backed up against the door, every sense straining; silence, but that did not mean it was safe.

His alertness gave him a split second's warning; enough time to sense the direction of attack and to thrust Thierry's body towards the dark shape that came at him: his attacker. He heard a grunt of surprise, saw the faint gleam of light along the edge of a knife, and ran sideways out of the doorway which was protecting his back but giving him no room to manoeuvre. He thrust his poniard into his belt and drew his sword in a rasping shiver of metal.

His attacker leaped and struck. Aubrey felt the dagger-tip prick through his mail, but the hauberk was of the finest triple-linked type and the rings held off the force of the knife. He tried to swing the sword, but a gauntleted fist crashed into the side of his face, making him reel, and the long dagger flashed again, striking not for his body this time, but for his throat.

Aubrey got his arm up in time, and again the hauberk saved him from certain death, but he was stunned, his vision and reflexes impaired. Light blossomed, contracting his pupils; he had a momentary impaired glimpse of the face of his assailant, staring upwards at the shutters above which once more had been flung open, and recognized him for one of Warrin's men.

'Drunkards, go and brawl in someone else's doorway!' shrieked the woman with the dark braid, and accompanied her abuse with the well-aimed contents of a chamber pot. The other man involuntarily recoiled. Aubrey reversed his sword and buffeted the hilt up beneath the other's ribs with as much force as he could muster. He heard the air retch out of him, saw him double up, and was feverishly upon him, fingers winding in the rain- and urine-soaked hair to jerk back the head and expose to the sword a pale expanse of throat. Above him, the woman screamed more abuse and banged the shutters closed again.

More footfalls splashed in the darkness coming at a soft run, and voices echoed. Breathing hard through his mouth, Aubrey stared towards them. Torchlight flared against the slick alley walls; horses' hooves rang on stone; were muted by mud. It looked like a scene from hell.

He gave a great gasp of relief and the wildness went out of his face as he recognized first the sorrel and then, half-concealed behind a pitch-soaked brand, his lord. Sweyn and Austin were with him and half a dozen serjeants on foot. 'She's been taken to a ship or a boat by the name of *Alisande*,' Aubrey said on a sobbing gulp for air. 'If we can make this whoreson sing, he'll tell us precisely where.' And then, eyes flickering sideways to one of the men on foot who was crouching over the form in the doorway, 'it's no use Alun, he's dead for his sins. One gamble too many.'

'I know where the *Alisande* is moored, I saw her today,' Adam said in a voice whose very quietness betrayed how close to the edge of reason he actually was. 'Aubrey, deal with this. You can have the footsoldiers.' Backing Lyard up, a difficult

291

feat in the narrow alley, he turned him and spurred towards the wharves at a speed that would have been considered reckless in the light of day, and was pure insanity in the middle of a black, rainy night. Sweyn spat an obscenity and struggled after him, Austin not far behind.

Aubrey closed his eyes for a moment. There was blood running from a deep cut on his cheekbone. He wiped at it with the back of his hand, looked at the dark smear, then lifted his weight from his semi-conscious assailant.

'Bring him,' he said tersely to one of the gawping foot-soldiers, and rammed his sword back into his sheath before he gave in to temptation and used it.

Lyard skidded on a patch of mud and almost lost his hind legs. Adam's fingers clenched convulsively on the reins. He bit his tongue. The cantle rammed his spine and made him gasp. He lost a stirrup and had to fumble with his foot to find it. Bubbling pitch from the torch oozed onto his hand and burned – solid pain – practical considerations. The stallion was sweating and trembling. He patted the satin sorrel neck and murmured soothingly, and in so doing brought himself once more under control.

It was several hours since the search had first begun, and as building after building had been scoured and found empty, black imaginings and the self-indulgent guilt of 'if only' had clawed at the bulwarks of his sanity, undermining them, threatening them with collapse. And then one of Aubrey's men had come running to find him with the news that Thierry was found and being hunted down. Desperate hope, desperate prayer, desperate bargains with God. If onlys.

'Good lad,' he said softly to the horse, drew on the reins and urged him forward again. Sweyn and Austin joined him, and they rode at a jog trot towards a group of moored merchant cogs. Austin, whose eyes were as sharp with youth as a falcon's, rose in his stirrups and pointed. 'God's bones, look, one of them's on fire!'

Adam followed Austin's finger towards the deck of a merchant cog that was cheerfully ablaze. Fanned by the wind, they could hear the roar of the flames and the cries of men who were frantically bucketing them out. 'It's the *Alisande*!' Adam said with a surety born of the gut, not the mind.

As they watched, momentarily frozen with shock, a figure half-rolled, half-dragged itself out of the river onto the wharf, thrashed blindly to its feet and started towards them at a stumbling run, a woman, for the streaming hair was as long as the tunic it wore. Adam stared, and the disbelief gave way to a heart-stopping jolt as he recognized his wife, and saw behind her Warrin de Mortimer in hard pursuit and drawing a knife from his belt.

'Hah!' Adam cried to Lyard, and once again risked spurring him, but this time he was in cold, sure command of every faculty. The stallion's hooves struck blue-white sparks from the cobbles. Adam drove him straight at his enemy.

Warrin, as preoccupied with Heulwen as a spider with a new-caught fly, did not realize what was happening until it was far too late. Kneeling over her, the knife at her throat, he glanced up as the sound of hoofbeats became louder than a mere subconscious noise.

Adam did not think twice. It had gone beyond that kind of reason. He drove the burning brand, lance-fashion, straight into Warrin's shocked, upturned face. Warrin screamed and reared up and back, the knife clattering to the ground. His shrieks rent the air like those of a hare at the end of a hunt. He went to his knees, arms over his face, fell, and rolled over and over in mindless agony.

Adam dismounted, dropped the torch into a puddle where it sputtered and smoked out. With the same calm, deliberate purpose that had carried him through thus far, he followed Warrin's contortions, drew his sword, and silenced him by setting the blade to his windpipe and leaning on it until the pressure pierced skin, cartilege and bone, grating finally on wet cobbles. After he had watched him die, Adam jerked the blade free, wiped it meticulously on Warrin's sodden shirt, and without looking back, sheathed it and went to Heulwen.

Round-eyed, Austin gaped. Sweyn, of a more practical mind, dismounted. 'Come on lad,' he jerked his head at the ground, 'help me throw this fish back whence it came. We can't leave him in the middle of the street.'

Adam knelt down beside his wife. 'Heulwen?' he said tentatively and examined her quickly for signs of injury. His mouth tightened as he saw the blue and red fingerprint bruises lacing her throat. Lower down on her thigh there were marks too. He swallowed bile and lifted her up against him, and knew that he would never be able to see Warrin's death as a confessable sin.

'Sweyn, get me a blanket,' he said over his shoulder.

Heulwen's throat moved. Her eyelids shuddered and half-opened. She felt a strong arm supporting her head and another gently around her shoulder-blades, but then Warrin had been gentle and violent by turns, and she remembered that he had been about to kill her. She stiffened and struggled.

'Lie still love, you're safe,' she heard Adam's voice say, easy and calm and familiar.

'Adam?' She drew back slightly to look into his face to make sure that it was not her imagination playing tricks. Surrounding torchlight flared, marking out golden-hazel eyes and thick, bronze-brown hair. She touched his face and bewildered, looked around. 'Where's Warrin?'

His hand tightened across her back. 'Dead,' he said with a certain taut satisfaction.

'Dead?'

'Dead,' he repeated, dropping the word like a weighted body into the river, and taking the blanket Sweyn had managed to find, wrapped her in it and then in his own fur-lined cloak.

Heulwen closed her eyes, feeling sick and weary unto death. 'He wanted to know why we were in Angers,' she said in a faint voice as he mounted Lyard and she was handed into the saddle before him. 'I didn't tell him.' Her teeth were chattering. She turned her face into his tunic and clung tightly to him like

294

a child beset by a nightmare. Adam kissed the top of her head and blinked hard, then pressed Lyard to a gentle walk.

People were crowding onto the dockside to investigate the commotion and give what aid they could to the burning cog. The fire was almost out. In her mind's eye, Heulwen saw herself throwing the aqua vitae on the fire, and shuddering, leaned her cheek against the cold, wet velvet of Adam's tunic. Her fingers tightened in the fabric until they cramped as she strove not to see the other things. Adam's voice was gentle, trembling slightly, and although she took comfort from it, it seemed to be coming from the other end of a vast, echoing hall, and it was the memory of Warrin that seemed the more real.

CHAPTER 24

THORNEYFORD, SUMMER 1127

A DAM CURLED HIS fingers around his belt and contemplated the mosaic that the two craftsmen were so painstakingly working on. It was a copy of the ruined Roman one in the forest beyond *Rhaeadr Cyfnos* with a few adaptations of his own, and when finished, it would transform Thorneyford's plesaunce from a merely functional herb garden into a delightful place to sit on warm summer evenings.

He moved back now to the old turf seat and studied the mosaic from a different angle. The colours were autumnal — cream and bronze, russet, gold and brown. His attention wandered towards his wife where she was discussing the siting of the new mint and sage beds with the gardener and whether they had room for another patch of stavesacre to combat the current epidemic of lice.

Busy, he thought with a twist of his mouth. In the two months since their return from Anjou she had not stopped. She was not just busy but frantic, and she would not talk to him — at least not beyond any trivial, bright, meaningless chatter masking God knew what. He could not get close enough to find out.

He watched the sunlight burnish her braids, the tilt of her head as she listened to what the gardener was saying and the gesture of her arm as she pointed to the soil-bed at their feet. Superficially there was no difference, but it was like skimming the surface froth off a tankard of beer and never reaching the drink itself.

She had not spoken of her time as Warrin's prisoner on board the *Alisande* – not one word, but he had been able to deduce much from her actions. In the early days she had just about lived in a bathtub and scrubbed herself raw, and it did not take a great alacrity of mind to realize that Warrin had done more than just question her. Once he had asked her outright, but she had pretended not to hear him, her brightness so brittle that its broken edges had cut him to the quick.

He had opted for time and gentleness to bring her round, but they seemed to be having the opposite effect. Heulwen retreated further into her shell with each day that passed, and nothing that he said or did seemed able to draw her forth. The nights were difficult too. It was not that she rejected him: on the contrary, she frequently demanded more of him than he was capable, and with such desperation that there was no real pleasure in it for either of them.

He looked at the wolves that made up the centrepiece of the mosaic. Black wolves chasing their tails surrounded by a ring of red vixens. The men were working on the huntsmen now. The gardener had gone. Adam rose and strolled casually across the pleasaunce to join his wife. She was pressing her hand to her stomach and her naturally pale complexion was the unhealthy shade of whey.

'Heulwen?' He put an anxious arm around her. 'What's wrong?'

'Nothing.' She gave him that vapid, closed look that he was learning to hate, and smiled brightly. 'It's those salted herrings we bought last month. They've been disagreeing with me. Cuthbrit says the mint should go here and the tansy over there, but I don't know. There's more sun ...'

He tightened his hold, silencing her. 'Heulwen, for God's love, I cannot bear any more of this hoodman blind!' he said on a pleading note. 'We need to talk about Angers. When I look at you, I feel as though I'm looking across the Styx at a being from the underworld.'

'Angers?' She drew a deep breath, let it out again shakily

and looked around the plesaunce, which was taking graceful shape from the silver of Henry's gratitude for Angers. A King's price. Cheap. She felt hysterical laughter rising in her throat, and then the nausea. 'It is with me every waking moment without having to talk about it as well,' she said through stiff lips. 'I, I don't feel well. I'm going to lie down.' She pushed herself out of his concerned embrace and ran from him.

Adam stared vacantly down at the prepared herb bed. He wondered if he ought to go after her, but the thought daunted him. He was still wary of rejection even when he knew it was not personally intended. He chose the coward's way, and deferring the confrontation went to tell Austin to saddle up Lyard.

He took the men out on a wide-sweeping patrol. After a few miles he paused in a village to speak to the reeve and accept a cup of new ale from the beaming, flustered ale-wife, and then rode on. The open spaces and the silken gait of the stallion eased him. He drew rein on the crest of Thorneyford Dyke, looked across to Wales, and inhaled deeply of the sweet spring air.

He found himself wishing that Miles was still alive. He could have confided in him. Guyon had lost Heulwen's own mother to rape and butchery, and Heulwen's situation was too close for him to broach it. Countess Judith would offer him abrasive advice in her usual forthright manner, and just now, that thought was unpalatable. All that Miles had left them was the Wolf brooch – a light in darkness, but a light did not show you which path to take, only illuminated the way you chose.

He shook the reins and paced Lyard along the top of the Dyke, examining its state of repair. Not that he expected to clash with the Welsh this year, thank Christ for small mercies. It was rumoured that Rhodri ap Tewdr was getting married to the daughter of another local Welsh lord; he wondered how true the rumours were and if it would alter the delicate balance along the borders. It was a way of occupying his mind with thoughts of policy, because to think of Heulwen hurt too much.

He moved down the Dyke to visit a fortified manor held by one of his vassals and sat down to meat with the man while they discussed the need to put more of the forest under plough, and declining his invitation to hunt, set out for home.

It was a little before vespers when he rode into the bailey, and although the slanting sun was still warm and golden, he felt the hairs prickle erect on his spine at the atmosphere as he dismounted.

He started to ask his groom what was wrong, decided that he would rather not know in so public a place, and hurried towards the hall. There was no sign of Heulwen or Elswith. His steward, Brien, was busy at a trestle with talley sticks and an exchequer cloth, an inky quill between his fingers, but when he saw Adam he rose and came quickly to him.

'Lady Heulwen was taken ill while you were out, my lord.' He looked anxiously at Adam. 'We did not know where you had taken the patrol, so we put her to bed and my wife took it upon herself to fetch Dame Agatha from the village.'

The information hit Adam like a well-aimed rock. Dame Agatha in her capacity of local wise woman and experienced midwife was a frequent visitor among the keep's women. Adam had known her literally since his own birth. White-faced, he pushed past his anxious steward and took the tower stairs two at a time.

Dame Agatha was just emerging from the outer chamber, the comfortable folds of her face marred by a slightly bewildered frown as she dried her hands on a clean square of linen. Like the rest of her they were pink, plump, and capable. 'Lord Adam,' she said deferentially, but blocked his way, forcing him to stop his headlong stride towards the bedchamber.

'Where's my wife? What's happened?' He stared at the drawn curtain behind her.

'Calm yourself, my lord, 'tis naught too serious.' Her French was mangled by a heavy English accent and hard to understand.

He had to concentrate and it brought him off the simmer. He breathed out once, hard, and held himself to patience. 'She is sleeping now, I have given her a posset. What she needs is plenty of rest with her feet well raised. The bleeding has stopped, but she will need to be very careful.'

'Bleeding?' Adam said stupidly, clutched by the horrified thought that Heulwen had perhaps attempted her own life while he was gone. 'What do you mean?'

Dame Agatha gave him a curious look, then her face softened into comfortable folds. It was not the first time she had come up against this kind of stunned disbelief. Men might profess themselves the stronger sex, but they were naught but frightened ignorants when it came to this particular arena. She patted his arm solicitously. 'It sometimes happens. With rest I do believe she will settle down. Leastways she hasn't lost the babe. A few spots of blood, no more.'

'Babe?' Adam reeled. 'What babe?'

Dame Agatha sucked a sharp breath between the gap in her upper front teeth, and stared at him in dismayed surprise. 'Forgive me, my lord. I did not realize she had not told you – perhaps waiting to be sure, eh?'

'You're telling me that my wife is with child?' he asked unsteadily.

She regarded him pensively. Beneath the first gold of early summer he had no colour, and had he been one of the women, she would have burned some feathers beneath his nose and dosed him with valerian in wine. 'Somewhere between two and three months along,' she nodded. 'Sometimes bleeding happens at this time. It is my opinion we'll see a healthy babe this side of the Christmas feast.'

Adam stared at her blankly. *Somewhere between two and three months along.* Christ's sweet wounds, no!

'My lord, are you all right? Shall I get . . . ?'

He looked down at the thick-fleshed, sympathetic hand on his sleeve and forced himself to be rational. 'Yes, I am all right,' he said stiltedly. 'Just taken by surprise, that is all.' He withdrew his arm. 'Thank you for coming.' He fumbled in his scrip, found a silver penny and pressed it into her hand.

Dame Agatha folded her several chins into her chest and looked puzzled. There was the same checked, wild tension about him that there had been in Lady Heulwen, as if this pregnancy was a disaster instead of a boundless joy. It took some people that way, usually those who already had a dozen offspring to feed and no hope of nourishing a thirteenth beyond the breast. A man in Lord Adam's position was normally delighted at the prospect of an heir, his wife too, at having proved her ability to conceive.

She lowered her eyes from the disturbing expression in his and fixed them on the coin before she folded her knuckles over it. 'I'll come back in the morning, sooner if you need me,' she murmured, made her obeisance and left.

Adam eyed the thick curtain. He did not need to master his feelings, for just now he did not have any. He was numb. At last, he forced his limbs to move and on leaden feet went into the bedchamber. Elswith was there, folding up some strips of absorbent linen. She darted him a quick, frightened look and her industry increased.

'Did you know?' he said curtly.

Elswith blushed and fumbled. 'My lady said nought to me,' she answered defensively. 'I suspected a month since, but it weren't my place to speak ...'

Adam went to the bed. Heulwen was sleeping deeply, her breathing natural and even as if nothing had ever troubled her life before. Still numb, disbelieving, he wondered what he was going to say to her when the effects of the posset wore off and she woke up. He sat down on the stool beside the bed and mechanically unpinned his light summer mantle. 'Elswith, go below and tell them not to wait the dinner hour for me. You can bring some bread and pottage up later.'

He watched her curtsy and leave, then leaned his chin on his laced fingers and stared at Heulwen.

*

Heulwen opened her eyes and gazed vaguely around the bed-chamber. Her feet were propped up on a swaddled brick and the blankets were tucked up to her chin. The light in the room was dim and grey: morning or evening she could not tell, nor understand what she was doing in bed. And then her stomach churned queasily as it had done for the past several weeks, causing her to remember, and turning her head in discomfort on the pillow she looked straight into Adam's eyes. It was as if he had struck her and she flinched away with a small cry like a wounded animal.

Adam flinched too, then with a soft oath leaned quickly over the bed and gathered her to him. 'Heulwen, don't.'

Tears filled her eyes and overflowed. Through them she saw that Adam wept too. He swore again, dashed his sleeve across his face and left her to fetch the flask of aqua vitae. Heulwen watched him tremble a measure into a cup, watched as the fine russet hairs upon his wrist became in her mind's eye blond and wiry. The smell of the drink was evocative and more than her stomach could bear, and in a sudden, violent movement, she lunged from the bed, scrabbled for the chamber pot and was violently sick.

Adam flung down the cup and flask and hastened to her, but he was floundering in quicksand, did not know what to do. 'Shall I send Elswith for Dame Agatha?' he said anxiously.

Heulwen shook her head. Her face was clammy with cold sweat, her colour horrible. 'It's not because of that,' she panted weakly, 'it's the aqua vitae ... Warrin forced me to drink it before he ...' She broke off, retching uncontrollably.

'Christ Jesu!' Adam held her shuddering body, bracing her up until the spasms had ceased, and spent, she leaned wearily against him.

'I set fire to the ship with it too,' she gulped. 'I threw the flask on the brazier when I saw my chance ...'

'Hush, love.' He squeezed her shoulders, kissed her bright hair.

'You asked me about Angers ...'

'It doesn't matter, don't distress yourself.'

She heard the hint of panic in his voice and wondered if it was for her or for himself. 'But it does matter,' she insisted. 'I've been trying to deny it ever happened, but I can't now, can I?' She laid her palm against her belly; it was still flat, an illusion. Haltingly, pausing for respite when the narrative became too painful, she told him everything.

Listening, Adam was scalded by pity and love and a rage too still and deep for physical motion to express. It held him immobile, his cry of anguish jailed inside his head. When she finished, there was an absolute, frightening silence.

'I do not expect you to acknowledge the child,' she whispered when he said nothing, just sat staring at the tapestry on the far wall as though it were of vital importance.

Slowly he dragged his eyes from it and focused them on her. 'It could as easily be mine as Warrin's,' he said flatly. 'We lay together several times in Angers – and beyond.' He grimaced, remembering.

'Yes.' Heulwen turned her head aside. 'It is the not knowing that tears at me. Dame Agatha says I must not ride a horse or run up and down stairs if I want to keep this child. All I need do is disobey her instructions and I'll miscarry.'

'No!' he said with involuntary force, clenching his knuckles. Then taking hold of himself said on a calmer note, but without any lessening of intensity, 'No, Heulwen. Mine or Warrin's, the child at least is innocent. What would have happened to me if your father had deemed me accountable for my father's sins? If you deliberately lose this babe, you exchange one burden for another much heavier to bear.' He dug his fingers through his hair and gave a short, bitter laugh. 'God, I'm sorry, I sound like a priest!'

'You have the right,' she said and her lips curved into the travesty of a smile, 'and the right of it too. I could no more ride a horse over rough ground or dash about the keep like a maid at Martinmas than I could commit murder with a knife. A life is a life – it is just seeing a way out and knowing I

303

cannot take it – oh Adam!' She clutched at him in misery and frustration.

He held her, tried to gentle her, but was too unsettled himself to succeed. 'All those years with Ralph you were barren,' he murmured against her hair, 'and now this. God in heaven, we pay for what we want, don't we?'

Heulwen dropped her head against him. 'I was barren of my own choosing,' she said, her voice so low that he had to strain to hear it.

'What do you mean?' He held her away so that he could look into her face.

Heulwen met his gaze and then slid hers away. 'In the early months of my marriage to Ralph I quickened and miscarried. I was in my third month like now, but I lost so much blood that Judith said another child too soon would like as not kill me. She knows as much lore as any herb wife.' She hesitated and looked at him again quickly. 'If I did not conceive, it was by the artifice of sponges soaked in vinegar and daily portions of gromwell in wine.'

Adam gaped at her. He stood on the threshold of a room that very few men were permitted to enter and suddenly he did not want to be numbered among the privileged. 'If Ralph had known . . .' he began uncertainly.

'He would have beaten me witless. I don't think Judith ever told my father. Safest not to, and besides, it doesn't always work, or else my brother William would not be here.'

Adam bit his lip and struggled to set reason over his instinctive masculine reaction. 'Did you . . . I mean, have you ever . . . ?'

'Practised that deceit on you?' she finished starkly for him. 'No, Adam. That was an easy choice to make – or so I thought.' She laid her hand upon her stomach, and a sob caught suddenly in her throat. 'Jesu, I wish I had done that night . . .'

'Heulwen, no . . .'

There was a discreet cough outside the curtain and Elswith came in with a wooden platter of bread and a dish of pottage.

Behind her a younger maid carried a fresh pitcher of wine and some new candles.

Adam subsided. The two women hesitated, obviously discomfited by his presence. A woman's domain; he was desecrating the shrine. He tightened his lips, looked at Heulwen, saw that she was shivering and picking her up, tucked her back into bed.

Elswith removed the chamber pot. 'Still sick?' she muttered to him, looking worried.

Adam shook his head and indicated the flask. 'It was the smell of the aqua vitae.'

'My sister was like that with cheese,' volunteered the other maid, and subsided with a blush as Elswith threw her a look.

'Adam, don't go!' Heulwen implored in a frightened voice as he moved away and the women closed around her.

'I'm not,' he half-turned to reassure her, 'but it might be as well if I eat over here where it won't disturb your stomach any more.'

She lay back against the pillows and stared at the candle flame, flickering as the new life flickered within her body, and watched her husband by its light, feeling so wretched that she would have been glad to die.

CHAPTER 25

WALES,
DECEMBER 1127

'TRY THIS,' SAID Renard, handing a pasty to Adam, who took it and sniffed suspiciously.

'Leeks again. Jesu I'm starting to feel like one.' He took a bite and discovered himself not proved wrong. There was curd cheese in it too and a lethal dose of sage.

'When in Wales,' Renard reminded him with a grin and held out his cup so that it could be replenished with mead. 'You must admit, this is excellent.'

'Until it kicks you in the skull tomorrow morning,' Adam qualified wryly. 'That girl over there keeps looking at you.'

'I know. Do you think she's available, or would I be offending the laws of hospitality if I tried to find out? I'm supposed to be on my best behaviour. No fondling forbidden fruit to test how ripe it is.' His eyes sparkled with self-mockery. He would never be handsome in the classical sense like his father. The maturing features were plain in repose, but when animated by laughter or intense emotion, his looks were striking enough to make people – especially women – turn and look twice. The rich crimson velvet trimmed with gold suited him, and the broad wolfskin collar of his cloak reflected his quartz-grey eyes.

Renard was here in Wales at the hall of Rhodri ap Tewdr, representing his father at Rhodri's wedding to a neighbouring Welsh lord's daughter. The truce had to be seen to be functioning, the reason that Adam himself was present. Were it not for the political necessity of attending, he would have remained at Thorneyford with Heulwen. She was very near her time now – 'as huge as a beached whale', she had said ruefully to him on the morning that he left. Judith was with her to attend the lying-in, and Dame Agatha. She would have the best possible care, but Adam was anxious.

From somewhere during the past six months, he had found the fortitude to stand against the storm, but sometimes in the stillness of the night, listening to Heulwen toss and moan, or holding her while she wept, he would stare up into the darkness and find himself filled with fear. She thought him strong, was leaning upon that strength, drawing from it, and it frightened him. If the child was born with blonde hair and blue eyes – which was possible even without Warrin's paternity, then he did not know if he would have strength enough – and if he broke – he took a jerky gulp of his mead, spilled some down the front of his tunic and swore.

'It's not me who's going to have the kicked skull in the morning,' Renard remonstrated with a swift white grin.

Adam scowled at him. 'Just because you have to curb your tongue with the Welsh, do not think you can let it run riot with me!' he snapped.

Renard sucked in his cheeks and gave Adam a speculative look, wondering whether to make a remark about the latter's short temper and link it to Heulwen's imminent motherhood, but decided against it. The Welsh would revel in an open brawl between their Norman guests. 'Sorry Adam,' he said, making his tone genuinely apologetic.

Adam rubbed the back of his neck. 'No, it's me who should be sorry, lad. Pay no heed. I'm not fit company just now.'

Renard cradled his mead. 'Heulwen's as strong as an ox. I know you'll think I'm just saying it to comfort you, but it's true and I should know, some of the slaps I've had.' He smiled at Adam and was rewarded by a token stretching of the lips in response.

'Change the subject or shut up,' Adam said in a level voice, his attention directed at the energetic footsteps of the dancers stamping around the fire.

Renard shrugged. 'All right then. I'm getting betrothed at Whitsun to the de Mortimer child, God help me. Papa and Sir Hugh are discussing dower details and the like.'

Adam bit the inside of his mouth. Renard was not to know that the very mention of the de Mortimer name was like a burning brand in his side. 'Congratulations,' he managed to murmur after another swallow of mead.

'No need to say it like that!' Renard laughed. 'The chit's worth having. Now that Warrin's dead, she's Sir Hugh's sole heir, and there's some prime grazing land and flocks to be acquired.' He looked swiftly through his lashes at the Welsh girl, then back to consider Adam's reticence. 'Warrin's death hit Sir Hugh hard, you know. He was hoping to have him pardoned.'

'Was he?' Adam strove for indifference, but the words for all the flatness of his tone were vicious.

'A street brawl in Angers. Not the more glorious exit to hell is it?'

Adam's flatness became a rough snarl. 'He got less than he deserved!'

'Is that what happened? Did he really get into a drunken fight on the dockside with some sailors and end up in the water?'

A muscle bunched in Adam's jaw. 'How should I know?' he snapped. 'If that is the official version given to his father then that must be the truth.'

Renard dropped his lids. 'I just thought that with you being in Angers at the same time ...'

Adam shot out his hand and grabbed Renard's shoulder with bruising force. Mead tilted and spilled. 'Well keep your thoughts to yourself!' he hissed, putting emphasis on each word.

His face was close, the firelight reflecting burning in his eyes. Renard held him look for look, but felt his innards dissolve.

308

He was reminded of a wolf. Adam made a disparaging sound and thrusting Renard aside, jerked to his feet and stalked away from him.

Renard smoothed the mark of fingerprints from the crushed fur on his shoulder and deliberated whether to go after him or not. Did he owe Adam an apology? He pursed his lips and decided that he didn't. It was Adam's reaction that was at fault, not the imprudence of his own tongue. He narrowed his eyes thoughtfully.

The Welsh girl was smiling at him. She lifted a pitcher and came to replenish his cup. He watched the flow of her body within the simple linen gown and decided that whatever was troubling Adam, he was best left alone until he was cool enough to handle.

It was cold outside the hall, a crisp frost drifting upon the twilit air. Adam watched the vapour steam from his breath and his urine. Laughter floated out to him and singing, and the warm greasy smell of roasting mutton. He finished and went slowly back within the hall and leaned his shoulder against a supporting pillar to watch the roistering. He not only felt like an outsider, he knew that he was one. Renard was thoroughly occupied now in cozening the Welsh girl to sit down beside him. Adam thought about making amends and decided that keeping his distance was probably the best way.

'He's on a promise there!' grinned Rhodri ap Tewdr, using the English vernacular.

Adam turned to the young Welsh leader who had come to stand at his side. Rhodri was flushed with mead, although only to the point of merriment, but then he had a vested interest in remaining sober tonight. 'Seldom a time when he's not,' Adam snorted. 'Do you mind? I don't want some enraged husband or father leaping on him and starting up the war again.'

Rhodri guffawed. 'There's only one kind of war I want to wage on my wedding night, and it's certainly not with you Normans. No, there's no objection. Branwen's husband threw her out a year ago when he caught her in the bushes with a wool merchant. I tell you, the path to her nether door is so well trodden that I'm amazed there's any grass left growing round it – not that I have any personal knowledge.'

'Of course not,' Adam agreed gravely.

'*Duw*, she'll wring him dry!' Rhodri chortled, and half-turned as another dance started up and people shouted and beckoned to him. 'I'm sorry your wife couldn't attend, but for a good reason eh? I'll pray for her safe delivery and wish you a fine son. I only hope my own bride's as quick to vouchsafe me an heir!' He slapped Adam's arm and shouting, ran to join his bride in the centre of the dancers, thus sparing Adam the need to make a reply, which was just as well.

The girl had her hand on Renard's lower thigh and was leaning forward, affording him a perfect view down the front of her gown. Adam found a pitcher of mead and went off to find oblivion.

Heulwen caught her breath and screwing her eyes shut, braced herself against the wall and gripped it, panting. The pain tightened and squeezed until she was aware of very little else. Her belly beneath her shift was a huge, taut mound, a monstrosity of which she longed to be rid, and which at the same time she feared to lose.

'Come on lass, don't tighten yourself up,' scolded Dame Agatha, taking her arm. 'It only makes it worse. Scream if you want. There's only me and the Countess to hear. That's it, gently now.'

Heulwen gasped with relief as the pain released her. 'I wish I was somewhere else.'

Judith straightened from putting a hot brick in the bed and looked round, rueful humour glinting in her hazel eyes. 'When I was having Miles, I didn't scream once,' she said roundly.

Dame Agatha raised a sceptical brow. 'You had an easy birth then, m'lady?'

'No. I was a day and a half in labour and I swore the vilest soldier's curses through every single minute of it. Guy said that it was a good thing for the sake of my mortal soul that the others were quick into the world.'

The midwife chuckled delightedly. 'Best way. Nowt like a good bit o' swearing to help matters along ... Is that another one lass? Come on, breathe through it now, slowly ... good, good.'

Heulwen subsided, gasping. It was no use saying that she could not go on; she had no choice, but the niggling pre-dawn pains had increased their intensity down the hours until now, near noon, they were rapidly becoming unbearable.

Judith went to the brazier and set about making her a posset containing beaten egg to keep up her strength, and powdered raspberry leaf to aid and ease the pains. 'It's best that Adam is away at Rhodri's wedding,' she said practically as she worked. 'He'd only be wearing a hole in the floor and getting underfoot. Men usually do, especially with a first one.'

Heulwen burst into tears and Judith turned and stared at her, quite unable to understand the change that this pregnancy had wrought upon her bright and lively stepdaughter. Yes, the carrying was a burden towards the end, and the labour less than pleasant, but Judith had expected Heulwen to weather it with a shrug and a smile, impatient to have the child in her arms, and instead she was acting like a martyr in the act of being martyred.

Dame Agatha crooned and soothed. At a loss, Judith made Heulwen drink the posset and went below to see how the keep was faring in the hands of the steward's wife. Emerging from the turret entrance into the hall, she was just in time to witness the arrival of Adam and Renard home from Wales, and raised her eyes heavenwards in a silent plea for patience.

Outside, the fine sleet known as mizzle was falling and as she drew nearer the men, her nostrils were accosted by the pungent stink of wet wool. She forced a smile of welcome onto her lips.

'Where's Heulwen?' Adam demanded with a complete lack of courtesy. 'Is she ... ?'

'Her time is here,' Judith said calmly. 'All is going as it should. Dame Agatha is in attendance, but my guess is dusk at least before you'll meet your heir.' She took his cloak and stood on tip-toe to kiss his cheek — a rare gesture of affection, for she was not by nature demonstrative.

'Can I see her?'

Judith in her time had scandalized the rules of convention, but she was more than taken aback by his request. Men simply did not go near a birthing chamber until well after the event. It was forbidden, a mystery, and jealously preserved that way. 'Adam ...' she began, trying to phrase the refusal kindly, but something in his expression stopped her before the words were spoken. She sensed that he was asking her yeasay, but did not really care whether she gave it or not. It was his keep and she could not prevent him.

'Look, she is in some pain. If it is going to overset you, then you had best wait without.'

Adam nodded curtly. 'I'll manage,' he said.

Judith gave the ghost of a smile. 'I suppose you were there at the sowing,' she said, and did not understand why he gave her such a peculiar look.

Renard, ignored by his mother aside from an abstracted peck on the cheek, approached the hearth, blowing on his cold hands, and crouched down to the heat.

Dame Agatha was horrified to see a man enter the birthing chamber and would have driven Adam out again immediately, her sleeves rolled up, had not Judith dragged her forcibly to one side and begun whispering to her urgently.

'Adam!' Heulwen gave a great gasp, and ran into his arms and clung to him. He took her face between his hands, fingers laced in her loose hair, and kissed her wet eyes, her cheeks, her lips, tasting the salt of sweat and tears. The swell of the imminent baby intruded between them.

'I can't stay, sweetheart, but I'm here,' he said with a catch in his voice. 'Judith says that all is going well?'

She heard the nervous uncertainty in his voice, saw him

glance towards the two women in the corner of the room and nodded. 'So I'm told, but it's no consolation.'

She rubbed her face on his cloak, and realized that it was damp and cold. 'Is it snowing?'

'Sleet.'

'How did your wedding feast fare?'

He snorted. 'The same as all wedding feasts. I've got a splitting headache for my indulgences and Renard's got some rare bite marks that I hope his mother never sees!'

Heulwen actually laughed through her tears and hugged him. Her burden was suddenly lighter. 'Oh Adam, what would I ...' She broke off and cried out, clutching him not with affection now but desperation as the contraction gathered with savage speed and crashed over her, and for a moment he lost her completely to the primordial sweeping pain. He bit his lip, utterly helpless as she clawed at him.

'They're coming closer and harder,' muttered Dame Agatha to Judith, not in the least convinced by Judith's plea for clemency on Adam's behalf. 'He shouldn't be in here now. 'Tisn't decent!'

The pain receded. Heulwen pressed her forehead against him, panting.

'I think,' Adam said against her ear, 'that any man who objects to vinegar-soaked sponges should be made to spend some time in the birthing chamber.'

'Wrong!' she managed to jest shakily. 'He should be made to bear the baby himself.'

'I would take your place if I could.'

'And I'd let you ... OH!' And she grasped him again with a cry she could not stifle that rose with the peak of the contraction towards a scream.

'Heulwen!'

Dame Agatha was not to be thwarted any longer and thrust herself forward between them, taking Adam's place. 'My lord, you must leave!' she said urgently, her voice far from cosy.

313

'There is naught you can do here except get in our way! We will send word out as often as you need it.'

Judith, seeing the anguish on his face, took his arm and drew him firmly to the door. 'Adam, please!' she implored. 'You have overstepped the bounds far enough already.'

The contraction was easing. Heulwen slumped with relief and raised her head to look with slightly glazed eyes beyond Dame Agatha's bulk to her distraught husband. 'I'll be all right, Adam,' she said, her voice breathless but level.

'Are you sure?' He turned, resisting Judith's pull.

Heulwen nodded and clenched her jaw, trying to hold off another surge as it gathered like an incoming wave. It was impossible and she dissolved into the cramping pure agony. Dame Agatha soothed and held her, massaging her back. 'Come on lass, let's have you walking again, round to the flagon, that's it, good girl.'

Judith dragged Adam forcibly out of the room. 'You've gone green,' she observed in her usual tart manner, 'and the last thing I need on my hands just now is a sick or fainting grown man.'

'Judith, is she really all right? You're not just saying it as a sop to keep me comforted?'

Her features softened from their exasperation. 'No, I'm not just saying it. Heulwen's a healthy mare and the pains are coming good and strong, just as they should. Now, get out from under my feet. Find yourself something to do. I promise you'll be the first to know any news!'

'My lord, you have a son,' Dame Agatha said, placing a blanketed, bawling bundle in his arms, her expression slightly censorious, for she had not yet forgiven him for trespassing on forbidden territory.

He looked down into the baby's furious red face. A tiny fist had found its way out of the blanket and was being waved irately beneath his nose.

'A healthy pair o' lungs and no mistake,' the midwife added

with satisfaction as Renard came to peer over Adam's shoulders at his new nephew.

'He looks as though he's been boiled,' he commented unfavourably, then gave Adam's shoulder a bruising thump. 'I don't suppose you want to celebrate in Welsh mead?'

Adam took no notice. 'Heulwen, is she all right?'

Dame Agatha saw the fear in his face and relented, her mouth softening into its customary plump smile. 'Your lady is exhausted and somewhat bruised, the child was big and strong, but she's taken no lasting harm.' Her smile deepened. 'Do not for Jesu's sake tell her what my own husband told me after our first – that the next one would be much easier, not unless you want a piss-pot emptying over your head!' She stood aside and gestured towards the stairs like a sentinel indicating the throne room to a menial.

Heulwen slowly lifted her lids and rested heavy eyes on her husband and the bad-tempered bundle he was holding so awkwardly in his arms.

'I'm sorry it isn't a girl,' she whispered, and the easy tears of exhaustion filled her eyes. 'It would not have mattered so much then would it?'

Adam glanced quickly towards Judith, but she was busy in the far corner of the room, well out of hearing range.

'As long as you are safe it does not matter at all,' he said, and meant it. 'I don't think I've ever been so afraid, not even on a battle eve, as I have been these last few hours.' He leaned down and kissed her, then with a grimace carefully placed the baby in her arms. 'He sounds like a set of Hibernian pipes. Do you suppose he's hungry?'

Heulwen slipped down the shoulder of her bedgown and dubiously offered the baby her breast. He screeched, bumping his face against her until quite by accident he found the security of her nipple and covered it with a desperate gulp. As if by magic the wails ceased, replaced by small, gratified snufflings.

'Thank heaven for that,' Judith said tartly, giving Heulwen a cup full of some herbal smelling potion. 'Bugloss to promote the flow of milk. It looks as if you have a glutton on your hands. I haven't heard such a noise since Renard was born, and he still hasn't learned to be quiet. I'll go and fetch you something to eat. You'll need to keep up your strength, either that or get a wet nurse.'

It was an excuse to leave them alone for a time. Heulwen knew that she would be quite unable to eat whatever was brought. She touched the baby's hair. It was soft and dark. His eyes were closed now, the lids lined with brownish-gold lashes. The waving arm was still, fingers fanned on her breast as he sucked. She felt his vulnerability and it tugged at her heart as much as the doubts.

At the exact moment of his birth, when he had slipped from her body, she had only been able to think of the rape. Now, alongside that memory, others warmed her. Herself and Adam and some ink stains that wrote their own story; a dish of sugared plums; a stable in Angers and the straw prickling her naked thighs as the bedstraw had done while she laboured.

She looked from her son to her husband. Adam said that it did not matter, but he had been quick to put the baby into her arms. It could be a natural male response to something so feeble and tiny. She could not tell from his face and she could not ask him.

'How would you have him named?' she asked into his silence.

Adam watched the busily working small jaws, drawing life and comfort from her. His son or a changeling, the child was still Heulwen's, and as he had said, an innocent. He played with a strand of her hair. They had unbraided it, following the superstition that twists and knots of any kind could impede the smooth passage of a child into the world. 'There is only one possible name,' he murmured. 'He has to be Miles.'

Heulwen's throat closed on a sob. Her body jerked as she tried to control herself, and the baby, losing his grip on security, bawled his indignation, rooted frantically until he found it again, and settled, sucking at double-speed. 'Yes,' she managed huskily, 'he has to be Miles.'

Dame Agatha came back into the room with a large wooden bowl of warm water and some aired, warm swaddling, Judith behind her. 'They are waiting below for you to present the child, Adam,' Judith said.

'All right.' He sighed and scraped one hand through his hair, knowing his duty, but not particularly enthusiastic to go and perform it. It was an old ritual, going back to pagan times when a sickly or deformed baby was rejected by the clan and put out upon the nearest bare hillside to die. A healthy male child by contrast was presented, accepted, and everyone got roaring drunk. The church might frown on the custom even though it had lost its former barbarity, but everyone else expected it of right.

'When he's finished,' he added, nodding at the still suckling infant. 'If I take him now, he'll need no presenting other than his own.' He squeezed Heulwen's hand and smiled, but the gesture did not quite reach his eyes, which were troubled.

CHAPTER 26

RAVENSTOW,
SUMMER 1128

ELEANOR DE MORTIMER, seven years old, stretched out her arm and considered with pensive pride the enamelled gold betrothal ring shining on the fourth finger of her dainty right hand. It was where Renard would one day place her proper wedding ring when she was a woman and old enough to be married to him. As of now they were only betrothed – pledged to each other as in the tales of the romances that her nurse sometimes read to her. He had given her another ring too, to be worn when her finger grew, but too big now. It was upon a silk cord around her neck for today, but her father said that she must put it away in her coffer when they went home.

All the grown-ups were still eating and drinking in the hall and talking about another wedding. Someone called Mathilda had got married to someone called Geoffrey, and there seemed to be some kind of disagreement about whether they should have got married at all. She had become restless, then bored, and used the need of the garderobe as her excuse to leave the high dais and climb the stairs to the apartments above. Then, although knowing that she should return the moment she had emptied her bladder, curiosity had overcome caution and she had begun to explore this stout border keep that would one day be her home.

One of the rooms contained a sewing bench and two looms. A dog was asleep in a pool of sunshine near the window, but it raised its head and barked when it sensed her presence.

Nervous of it, she hurried out and came to a small wall chamber which she knew was reserved for herself and her nurse tonight. It smelled musty and dried lavender was posied everywhere to combat the odour of the stone.

A short turn up another spiralling set of stairs brought her to the Earl and Countess' chamber that one day, too distant for her child's mind to contemplate, she would share with Renard, a Countess in her own right.

An expensive Saracen gazing glass was propped up against the wall and she stopped short with a small gasp that was half awe, half delight. She had heard of such objects of course, even seen a poor imitation of one at a fairing, but this was smoothly polished, so bright that she could see every tiny detail without the least distortion.

It showed her a child with hip-length, blue-black hair, wavy and strong, a crown of fresh flowers pinned grimly in place and still defying the pins. It showed her wide-set golden-green eyes, a milky skin, a smile made gappy by missing teeth, and a mischievous expression emphasized by a small, snubbed nose.

She pirouetted before the mirror, admiring her green linen undergown and scarlet silk bliaut with its girdle of gold silk and a real gold clasp. Her father had smiled sadly at her fine attire as he twitched a fold straight before the ceremony, and said in a voice rough with emotion, 'Child, you look just like your mother.'

She had never known her mother, her father's second French wife and much younger than he, for she had died of a miscarriage not long after recovering from Eleanor's own birth, her body not strong enough to fight. Papa was often sad, more so these days since the news of Warrin's death.

Eleanor wrinkled her nose at the mirror. She had never really liked her much older half-brother. He would bring her presents, expect her to enthuse over them, and then ignore her. Papa had ignored her too when Warrin was at home, telling her to go and play or find her nurse.

A sudden sound made her gasp and whirl round guiltily

from the mirror, and for the first time she noticed a woman sitting in a high-backed chair nursing a baby. Eleanor recognized Renard's half-sister, for even in the shadows where she sat, her hair was as bright as flame.

'Don't worry, I won't eat you,' said Heulwen with a smile, and lifting the baby from her breast, covered herself.

Eleanor tip-toed to the chair and unable to resist, put a curious finger on the golden-brown spiky fuzz crowning the baby's head. 'What's his name?' she asked.

'Miles, for his great-grandfather.'

'Oh.'

Heulwen studied the child. She was impishly appealing and bore no resemblance whatsoever to her late brother, lest it be a suggestion of stubbornness about the small, round chin. 'Do you want to hold him?'

Eleanor's whole face lit up. 'Can I really?'

For answer, Heulwen took and placed her son in Eleanor's arms, showing her how to hold him, not that he needed as much support now. He was able to sit on his own, and turned his head frequently to take note of what went on around him.

'I'm going to have lots of babies when I'm married to Renard,' Eleanor confided seriously. 'How many teeth has he got?'

'Two.' Heulwen put her palm across her mouth to conceal her amusement lest it hurt the child's feelings.

Eleanor sighed. 'I wish I had brothers and sisters. Warrin was lots older than me, and he never played with me.'

Heulwen stiffened at the mention of the name. The smile left her expression. 'Never mind,' she heard herself sympathizing. 'You have a whole family by betrothal now. William's your age, and Henry's only a little older.'

Eleanor nodded and gave Heulwen a beaming smile, then looked down at Miles who was studying her out of round, curious eyes. 'I like babies. Are you going to have any more soon?'

Heulwen coughed. 'That lies in God's hands,' she managed

to strangle out, and sensing a change in the light, looked beyond the absorbed little girl and saw, with a clenching of her stomach, that Eleanor's father stood in the doorway.

'There you are!' he grated at Eleanor. 'What do you mean, running away from your own betrothal feast. Do you know how bad-mannered that is?'

Eleanor caught her lower lip in her teeth. 'I wasn't, Papa,' she said in a small, forlorn voice. 'I just went to the garderobe and, and ...'

' ... and then came to watch me feed Miles,' Heulwen rescued quickly with a brief, reassuring smile at Eleanor. 'It is my fault for keeping her.'

Sir Hugh grunted and looked from his daughter who was biting her lip, eyes liquid with distress, to the copper-haired woman now lifting the baby back into her own arms. The infant almost dislocated its neck as it swivelled to stare at him.

'She still should not have run off,' he said, and then cleared his throat and added with abrupt gruffness, 'what you did to my son was wrong, but I accept that he too compromised his honour in more ways than one. For the success of this betrothal, I'm prepared to let the past lie. I've spoken to your husband already and he says ...'

'And he says that he'll do his best,' Adam said, following Sir Hugh into the room, and going to Heulwen, kissed her cheek. She stood up, Miles struggling in her arms, met Adam's eloquent look and although she felt cold, managed a half-smile at the older man.

'The servants are setting out the trestles in the plesaunce for the afternoon. Are you coming down? You can put Miles on a fleece among the women.'

Sir Hugh stared at the two of them together, the swaddled infant held between them. There was a bitter taste at the back of his mouth as he thought that given different circumstances, that baby could have been his own grandson. Eleanor ran to him, the garland askew on her unruly raven curls. He set his arm around her narrow shoulders, squeezed them hard, and turned to the doorway. On reaching it he paused and looked round. 'You have a fine son,' he said heavily. 'I congratulate you. May he bring you more joy than mine did to me.' Then he left with Eleanor.

There was a taut silence, broken by Miles, who gurgled and held out hopeful arms to Adam. After a hesitation, Adam took him from Heulwen and walked to the unshuttered window to look down on the somnolent, sun-steeped bailey. Ranulf de Gernons was being dragged across it by a huge black alaunt, choking against its leash. 'It's a pity de Gernons had to spoil the gathering,' he remarked desultorily.

Heulwen murmured something and pretended to tidy away the baby's things from the bed. Surreptitiously she looked over at the window. Adam was holding Miles gently now in a relaxed pose, and the baby had stilled, eyes agog on the dust motes drifting in a band of sunlight. He leaned to try and grab them and his hair took on a red-gold tint as it was touched by the sun.

Heulwen swallowed a painful lump in her throat. She was never quite sure how Adam felt about Miles. While carrying him in her womb, she had been afraid of rejecting him, but after the first difficult moments her doubts disintegrated. He was helpless, dependent on her. The feel of him at her breast filled her with love and a pang too powerful to be understood. Adam did not have that closeness of the body to bind him to a child perhaps not of his siring, and frequently it fretted at her for she could not, dare not, search beneath Adam's outwardly calm exterior to see what lay beneath. He had acknowledged Miles as his heir, but sometimes she feared that it was only for her sake, and the child's; doing what was right rather than what he personally desired.

Her thoughts panicked her. Quickly she asked, 'Has Papa said anything to you about the Empress's marriage?'

Adam turned from the window and came back into the room. 'No, Guyon's been avoiding me, biting down on words he'd like to utter but knows he can't without risk of a rift. I

322

suppose we'll come to it soon enough – a discussion I mean, not a rift.' He went towards the door. Heulwen followed him, pausing in front of the mirror to smooth the folds of her gown and adjust her circlet and veil. Adam stopped beside her. Miles reached out a chubby hand and patted the glass, laughing at himself.

'He looks like you,' she said softly. 'Adam, he's yours, I know he is.'

Miles' hand shivered and distorted the reflection. For a moment Adam stood silently, watching the baby and the man and the woman; one joyfully innocent, and two balanced on a knife-edge. 'Do you think it would make any difference whatever I saw in' the mirror?'

Heulwen swallowed. His tone was gentle, but it frightened her. 'It might,' she said, her mouth dry, and saw his jaw tighten and his eyes narrow the way she had seen them do on a tilting ground. 'Adam ... '

'Don't say anything else,' he said, still gentle, and replacing Miles in her arms, walked out on her.

Heulwen put her head down, and eyes stinging, nuzzled her son's fuzzy hair. All unwittingly she had just offended Adam's honour, and she would only dig herself into a deeper pit if she went after him and tried to explain. She knew that look of his by now.

Sniffing, she wiped her eyes on the turned-back hanging sleeve of her gown, balanced Miles on her hip, and went slowly downstairs.

The plesaunce smelled of grass and the spicy, slightly peppery scent of gilley flowers. Bees throbbed among the blossoms. Carp-scales winked lazily as the great fish cruised the surface of the stewpond in search of May flies. The sky was a glorious, soft blue, the sun hot, but tempered by light ripples of breeze.

Sidelong from beneath his brows, Adam watched Heulwen join the other women and put Miles down on his tummy upon a thick sheepskin. He was chewing on a ball made of strips of soft coloured leather, and the women were cooing over him and making a fuss. As if drawn by a magnet, Eleanor left her father's side to crouch beside him.

Two servants carried some trestles past on which to lay out the food and drink. Adam met Heulwen's gaze across and between them and turned sharply away. It did not make any difference, or so he had told himself a thousand times over; and a thousand times over the doubt crept in, and she had seen it. He was more angry at himself than her.

Ranulf de Gernons was showing off his dog. Slab-muscled and glossy, it lunged on the leash and snarled savagely at Brith, young William's own pet bratch.

'Owning the biggest horse, the biggest dog and the biggest mouth does not necessarily command you the respect for which you had hoped,' Guyon said wryly from the side of his mouth as he joined Adam against the rose bushes that climbed the wall, a cup of wine in his hands.

'It also makes you the biggest fool if you can't control them,' Adam qualified. 'Why's he here in the first place? Surely you did not invite him by choice?'

Guyon snorted rudely. 'I didn't invite him at all. He's on his way up to Chester and sought lodging and hospitality on the way. That it happened to be the eve of Renard's betrothal was unfortunate.' He gave Adam a look. 'The seeking of hospitality was not I think his main motive.'

'No?'

'His father wants to know what we are going to do about this illegal marriage between Mathilda and Geoffrey of Anjou, and Ranulf's gone bloodhound for him.'

'Illegal?'

'Oh don't play me for a fool!' Guyon snapped irritably. 'You know what I mean. Eighteen months ago at Windsor we were guaranteed a say in the choosing of Mathilda's husband, a say which has been utterly ignored. As usual, Henry has quietly connived behind our backs to get his own way.'

Adam felt his face begin to burn. 'So what are you going to

do? Get it annulled out of pique and start a war? And who will you put in Geoffrey's place? Ranulf de Gernons perchance?' His voice was harsh. He shut his mouth.

Guyon took a slug of the wine and arched one brow at Adam. 'I am not an inexperienced hound to run yelping after a false scent. If the truth were known, I'd prefer not to run with either pack. You knew about this marriage, didn't you?'

Adam breathed out and scraped his hair back from his forehead. 'I'm sorry,' he said with self-exasperation. 'I should not have spoken like that, but Heulwen and I have just had a disagreement, and I'm still on the edge of my temper. Yes, I did know, and for the sake of my honour which God knows is frequently a millstone around my neck, I could not tell you.'

Guyon grimaced. He knew all about King Henry and the knots he tied in men's honour. 'And is Geoffrey of Anjou likely to be a millstone too?'

'He has the ability to control his wife and all of us if given the chance. For good or bad, I don't know. By God's will, he'll breed sons upon Mathilda who will be of an age to succeed their grandfather when his time comes.'

'It has caused a great deal of ill-feeling,' Guyon said, and finished his wine. 'Henry might have solved his problems across the Channel, particularly now that William le Clito's done the honourable thing and got himself killed in Flanders, but I'm not so sure about England. Many of us are far too insular for our own good.' He watched Renard and Harry and a group of laughing young men head towards the tilt yard. Harry's voice sounded like a creaking gate; it was on the verge of breaking. Suddenly he felt old.

Adam had turned to watch them. Guyon laid one hand on his shoulder. 'If you have quarrelled with my daughter, I should go and set matters to rights now. If you disappear with my sons you'll only make it worse for yourself later.' His expression was one of wry experience.

'Easier said than done.'

Guyon grinned and pushed him. 'Go on ...' And then,

while Adam still hesitated, reluctant, 'The babe's shaping well. He has eyes like Heulwen's mother, but he looks like you. Wolves breed true, as my wife's maid was always saying darkly of you when she rocked your cradle.'

Adam gave him a sharp look and then laughed between his teeth. 'Oh God!' he snorted. 'I don't need force-feeding, but I'm certainly having it rammed down my throat today.'

Guyon gazed at him, puzzled. 'What?'

'Nothing.' Adam shook his head and still smiling, took a step towards the women.

De Gernons lost his grip on the black hound's leash and with a snarl, the dog tore away from his hands and bounded across the plesaunce to leap among the women and attack William's dog. The two animals rolled together, snarling and snapping. Eleanor screamed and ran to her father, hiding her face against his tunic. Shouting, William tried to reach for Brith's collar and recoiled with a high-pitched cry, a dripping red slash bisecting his knuckles. De Gernons bellowed the alaunt to heel and went completely unobeyed.

Heulwen, who had been talking to Judith at one of the trestles, cried out and picking up her skirts started towards her son, who was lying in direct line of the biting, frantic hounds, about to be rolled upon or worse, for de Gernons' alaunt was in a state of frenzy, foaming at the lips which, black and moist, were curled back to reveal its snagged, savage, yellow-white teeth.

The women screamed. Miles wailed. William's young hound, lighter of build and gentler of nature, was striving to disengage, blood-drenched and yelping. Adam, running, grabbed Miles out of harm's way as the massive alaunt, victorious but still full of mad rage, snarled and launched himself at the nearest thing that moved.

Unable to defend himself because he held the baby, Adam went down beneath the massive forepaws. He smelled the dog's rank breath, saw the white-rimmed eyes and froth-spattered jaws, and tried to roll and avoid the savage array of teeth.

326

Something splashed over him. He tasted wine and realized that someone had emptied a flagon over the dog to try and drive it off him. Heulwen screamed and screamed again. Then above him there was a solid, vibrating thud, a crunching sound, and a dreadful, deathly howl that faded into silence. The dog's weight slumped, and was then dragged off him. He breathed again, and rolling over, slowly sat up. Miles screeched in his arms, a trifle rumpled and red with indignation, but otherwise unscathed.

To one side the dog lay in a puddle of blood, a honed jousting lance pinning it to the soft turf of the plesaunce through its stoved-in ribs. Heulwen threw down the empty wine-pitcher she held and dropped to her knees beside Adam, sobbing with reaction and relief. Behind her, face bleached, eyes as dark as flint, Renard was facing a sputtering, furious Ranulf de Gernons.

'You, you have killed my dog!' he howled with the dis-believing fury of a spoiled child who has had a favourite toy confiscated.

'Have I?' Renard's voice came through lips that appeared to be almost too stiff to part. 'What a shame, and before he'd finished performing for us too.'

De Gernons' jaw worked. 'Do you know how much he was worth?'

'Oh yes,' Renard disparaged. 'The length of a jousting lance at least.' And turning his back on the enraged heir to Chester's wide domains, he gestured to two gawping, frightened servants. 'Get rid of this. Throw it on the midden.'

Too breathless to speak and prevented from physically attacking de Gernons by the baby he still clutched, Adam stood up, his tunic splattered red with wine and blood, and made a look serve in lieu. Guyon stepped quickly between his son and son-by-marriage and the 'guest' before a situation too volatile to be contained developed. The laws of hospitality might be inconvenient, but they were also sacred. 'Only a fool brings a beast like that among company,' he said, each word soft but distinct with scorn. 'It is too much to expect your apology, I know, but that you should try to turn the blame around astounds me beyond contempt!'

De Gernons looked around the circle of accusing, hostile eyes, at hands that hovered above dagger grips, leashed by custom but straining to whiplash free. He hawked and spat, and without another word pushed past Guyon, roughly nudging his shoulder, did the same to Renard, and stalked out. They heard him yelling for his horse to be brought.

'Like dog, like owner,' Renard muttered.

Guyon grimaced. 'We have just made a powerful enemy, and one who will harbour a grudge beyond all reason.'

'Who wants him for a friend?' Judith said acidly as she bathed in wine the slash on her youngest son's hand. William tugged away from her, anxious to see to his wounded dog.

'That depends on how matters develop at Court,' Guyon said bleakly. 'Adam, are you all right?'

'Bruised,' he said with a brief nod and watched the servants dragging the alaunt's body away. 'Thank Christ it's nothing more serious. I thought I wasn't going to reach Miles in time.' He kissed his son's cheek and hugged him close for an instant before handing him, fretting, to Heulwen. A mutual look passed over the baby's head, but there was no opportunity for the nonce to explore it further.

One of the women handed Adam a cup of double-strength wine.

Guyon shook his head. 'He didn't find out what he wanted to know.'

'I think,' Adam contradicted over the rim of his cup, 'that he found out more than he bargained for – and so did we.'

The night was as still as a prayer. Heulwen's gilded shoes whispered softly over the grass of the deserted plesaunce. In the pond a fish plopped ponderously. Moths blundered among the flowers. A bat was outlined briefly against the green-streaked sky. She looked down at her hand linked in Adam's as they stopped beside the pond. The water near their feet boiled as a frog dived in panic. Behind the wall, heady with the delicate perfume of roses, the keep towered, luminous and white. Faint sounds from the guard drifted from the ward.

Adam pulled her against his side and squeezed her waist, lightly palming the curve of her hip. 'You were right this afternoon,' he said, staring out over the dark, glassy surface of the water. 'Sometimes I have found it very difficult indeed.'

'Adam . . . ' She half-turned, meaning to say that she did not need an explanation, but he took the hand she meant to lay against his mouth and held it prisoner.

'I suppose I should thank de Gernons,' he continued wryly. 'Until I thought that hell-hound of his was going to kill Miles, I never truly realized what he meant to me.'

'He is yours, Adam.' She laid her hand on his sleeve. 'I wasn't just saying it this afternoon.'

His smile was ghostly, like the last of the light. 'Well, that's a welcome blessing along the way, but it won't alter the depth of my feeling for him – enrich it, perhaps.' He dipped his head and kissed her. She responded, arms tightly around his neck. Her gown was loose so that she could slide it down from her shoulders and feed Miles without having to get undressed. He slid it down now. 'Lie with me?' he said between seeking kisses.

Surprised, she looked up at him. His eyes were as dark as the glitter of the pond beside them. 'Here? Now?'

He was unpinning her cloak and his and spreading them on the summer-scented grass. 'Can you think of a better place? The keep's crowded.'

Her breathing caught. A delightful warmth pierced her, contracting her loins. She went down into his arms.

The horizon was dark and the moon had risen, a fat white crescent silvering sky and land. Adam stretched lazily, and sitting up, reached for his shirt.

Heulwen sighed and extended a languorous forefinger to run it down the knobbled ridge of his spine, smiling to feel him quiver. 'I suppose,' she said regretfully, 'that Miles will be roaring to be fed, and Elswith will come seeking me before he rouses the whole keep.'

Adam laughed at the thought of the maid's face should she seek them here and see them like this.

Heulwen sat up beside him, her unbraided hair tumbling down, and pressed her lips to his shoulder. 'Adam, can we go home tomorrow?' She helped him tug his shirt down.

'I don't see why not.' He turned his head to kiss her, and continued dressing. 'Any particular reason?'

'Not really.' She began shrugging into her own clothes. 'I'd like to see our own plesaunce finished before the summer's end.' There was a sudden hint of mischievous laughter in her voice.

'It would be more convenient than visiting Ravenstow every time,' he agreed, and gave her rump a familiar slap as she stood up.

She nudged him with her foot in retaliation, then sobered. 'I want to dedicate a chapel too, for my grandfather's soul ... if you are willing?'

Adam stood up and said quietly, 'How could I not be willing? We owe him more than we can ever repay. Of course you can have a chapel.'

'Thank you, Adam.' She kissed him warmly.

He donned his cloak and then swung hers around her shoulders. The moonlight caught the wolf brooch into a brilliant, white glitter.

'No more tail-chasing?' she said as he fastened it.

'No more tail-chasing,' he agreed, and smiling, turned with her towards the keep.